MARTA
PERRY

SOUND
OF
FEAR

HQN™

ISBN-13: 978-0-373-80369-9

Sound of Fear

Copyright © 2017 by Martha P. Johnson

Recycling programs for this product may not exist in your area.

For questions and comments about the quality of this book, please contact us at CustomerService@Harlequin.com.

www.HQNBooks.com

Printed in U.S.A.

Dear Reader,

I'm so excited to introduce you to the second book in my Echo Falls series. I had such a good time visiting Echo Falls again for a new adventure, and I hope you enjoy it, as well.

Welcome to Echo Falls, Pennsylvania. This small, isolated Amish and English community seems like a haven of peace and security. But dark secrets lurk here, as elsewhere, and events are coming that will crash through the serene, pastoral landscape. All the strength and compassion the community can muster will be necessary as never before to meet these challenges.

Echo Falls is based on several small towns north of us here in central Pennsylvania, and I hope I've captured their charm in my writing. Most of my story ideas begin with a place, and this series of stories is no exception. The falls themselves are based on the falls at Ricketts Glen State Park, and I've actually climbed those trails and felt the spray in my face.

Please let me know if you enjoy my story. You can reach me via my website, www.martaperry.com, on my Facebook page, www.Facebook.com/martaperrybooks, and via email at marta@martaperry.com. I'd be happy to reply and to send you a signed bookmark and my brochure of Pennsylvania Dutch recipes.

All the best,

Marta Perry

This story is dedicated to my husband, Brian, with much love.

Every man must live with the man he makes of himself.
—Amish proverb

CHAPTER ONE

AMANDA CURTISS HAD hoped that going back to work would distract her from the grief that threatened to drown her. It didn't work. Every person at the veterinary practice felt they had to commiserate with her on her loss.

"So very, very sorry about your mother's death. So shocking to have one of Boston's most noted artists taken away by a random street crime." Alicia Farber's prominent blue eyes, so like those of her pampered Pekingese, welled with tears. "Pookie is sorry, too. Aren't you, Pookie?"

Pookie's expression exhibited its usual disdain for lesser beings. The sight of Amanda's white lab coat always brought out the worst in him, and he bared his teeth.

"Let's just see what's going on with Pookie, shall we?" Amanda lifted the small dog to the exam table with gentle hands, careful to stay out of the way of his needle-sharp teeth.

"He's been barely eating a bite of his food." Alicia hovered anxiously. "I just knew you'd want to see him. Tell me the worst. I can take it."

To do her justice, Alicia was genuinely apprehensive. They all were—all the owners of the pampered pets that came through the doors of one of Boston's

most successful veterinary services. Amanda's job, one
of the lowest rungs of the ladder, was to reassure the
owners while treating their pets. And to refrain from
pointing out that both pets and owners would benefit
from more exercise and less rich food. No one took
that kind of advice well.

By the time Amanda was ushering Alicia and her
pet out of the exam room, her head was throbbing and
her throat was tight, as it had been since the police
officers had come to the door with their grim news.

Gracie, the receptionist, caught her as she passed.
"Dr. Curtiss, there's someone here to see you." Lowering her voice, she added, "He said it was personal business, so I put him in an empty exam room. Number 4."

"Thanks, Gracie." Brushing any stray Peke hairs
from her lab coat, Amanda headed for the exam room,
her stomach clenching. *Personal business* had taken
on an ominous meaning lately, since it invariably had
to do with her mother's death.

But when she opened the door, her face relaxed into
a smile. Robert McKinley was not only her mother's
attorney but a longtime family friend, as well… *Uncle*
Robert until she'd felt she was too old for the term.

"Robert. I didn't expect you…" She stopped, her
brain catching up with her tongue. Robert wouldn't
come to her workplace on anything routine. "What's
wrong?"

"Why should anything be wrong?" He kissed her
cheek, and she smelled the faint aroma of musk that always advertised his presence. "Are you sure you should
have come back to work so soon? It wasn't necessary."

Maybe not financially, but it was for her mental

health. "I'd rather be busy. I need something to occupy my mind."

"If you're sure." He didn't sound convinced, and Amanda read the uneasiness behind his warmth.

"You wouldn't come here unless something had happened. Out with it." Amanda fought to keep her voice steady. "Whatever it is, it can't be worse than what's already happened."

Nothing could be worse than losing her mother in such a brutal way...never again to see her forehead wrinkle in absorption over a new painting, never to feel the warmth of her hug, never to hear the laughter in her voice...

Robert frowned, taking a step away. "I know." His voice wasn't entirely steady, either. He'd adored Juliet in his own staid way. "It may be nothing, but one of the detectives dropped by with the coroner's report. It had raised some questions in his mind."

"Questions?" Her mind shied away from imagining a coroner's report.

"Perhaps I'm making too much of this. You might already know." He shook his head slightly, as if to clear it. "The autopsy confirmed something that seemed... odd." He held up a hand to silence her when she would have burst out with a demand to hear it, whatever it was. "It seems that Juliet Curtiss, your mother, never had a child."

Amanda froze, staring at him. The words were in English, all right, but they didn't make any sense. "What do you mean? Of course she had a child. I'm standing right here."

"Juliet never bore a child," he repeated. "There isn't any doubt, Amanda. I read the report for myself, and then I called the coroner for confirmation. Juliet never gave birth."

Her sluggish wits started to work. "You mean I'm adopted? But why on earth wouldn't she have told me?"

Robert shrugged, seeming relieved that the worst of his news-breaking was over. "I believe specialists do recommend that the child be told, but it could be that Juliet couldn't bear the idea that your feelings about her would change if you knew she wasn't your biological mother."

At some level she wanted to laugh at that, because it was so ridiculous to think of Juliet in those terms. But if she started to laugh, she wasn't sure she'd be able to control her emotions.

"Be serious, Robert. Juliet wasn't a clinging mama. That wasn't the sort of relationship we had."

Amanda paused to consider what she'd just said. She and her mother had certainly been close, but Juliet didn't dote. It hadn't been in her nature. True, Amanda had lived at home since her practice and her life had fallen apart in Pennsylvania, but they'd lived very independent lives. Juliet had her work, and Amanda had hers.

"You never thought..." Robert began, stepping delicately in what no doubt seemed like a minefield to him.

"Never," she said flatly.

"You see the problem," he said, frowning again. She thought he held back impatience when she looked at him blankly. "Legally," he explained, "your mother... Juliet...must have adopted you prior to the time I met her. You'd have been about eight, I think, when she bought the brownstone. That was the first bit of business I did for her."

Obviously Robert expected her to concentrate on the problem. She tried to rein in her wandering thoughts. *Focus*, she ordered herself. "Yes, I'd have been eight when we moved uptown. She'd had her first really successful show, and our lives changed."

Not that she'd minded the life they'd had before that. The tiny apartment in one of Boston's many ethnic neighborhoods had been home. But Juliet had wanted more…for herself, but certainly for her daughter.

"If you don't remember any other life, Juliet must have adopted you when you were quite small." Robert wore his worried look. "There surely are papers to that effect somewhere."

"Aren't all her legal documents at your office? She always said she didn't have the talent or the energy to deal with things like that. Her work…"

"She *was* an artist, of course. But that's no excuse for not having your affairs in order." That was as close as Amanda had ever heard him come to sounding critical of Juliet. "You can see the quandary that leaves us in now. We must establish your legal position in regard to your mother's estate."

"But she had a will. You showed it to me, remember?"

"At my insistence, she did." He sounded grim. "It leaves everything she possessed at the time of her death to her daughter, Amanda Elizabeth Curtiss."

"Well, then…"

"Come, Amanda. Concentrate. You've always been the practical one. If you're not her biological daughter, the language becomes ambiguous."

"You mean our home might not be mine?" That possibility did penetrate the fog in which she groped.

The brownstone was home. It might be lonely without Juliet, but every inch of it was filled with memories.

"If someone contested the will on the grounds that you are not Juliet's daughter, that might well happen." Robert clasped her hands in a firm grip.

"Someone must be aware of the circumstances. What about her brother, George? They'd been estranged for a long time, but he did come to the funeral. Surely he'd know..." *Know where I came from.* She finished the sentence in her mind.

This was crazy. It was like spinning on ice in an out-of-control car. Every anchor she reached for slid from her grasp.

"George Curtiss is the last person I'd confide in at this point. Don't you see, Amanda? He can't know there's any question, or you can be sure he'd have brought it up." Robert's frown deepened. "There were good reasons for the breach between him and your mother. If half of what she said about him is true, he'd be contesting the will in an instant if he even suspected."

"Then what should I do? How can we find out?" If her uncle didn't know...but he wasn't her uncle, it seemed, any more than Juliet had been her mother.

"First of all, it's essential that we find any documents relating to you. You'd better have a good search throughout the house for papers. You must have a birth certificate, at least. We may want to hire a firm of private investigators to look into it. And whatever you do, don't talk about this to anyone but me."

She blinked at that. "But my closest friends..."

"Not your friends, not anyone. Not until we have a better handle on your identity than we do now."

Her identity. Amanda had always known who she was and where she belonged. Now it seemed she didn't know at all. Who was she?

AMANDA WALKED THE four blocks home, glad to be outside even in the chill dampness of the mid-October afternoon. The wind was strong enough to wipe away some of the fog from her thoughts.

But that didn't help much. It served only to expose how much she didn't know. She'd always been able to talk to her mother about everything. Amanda couldn't begin to come up with an answer for her silence on this crucial subject. *Why didn't you tell me?*

She rounded the corner and the brownstone came into view—a three-story building sandwiched between two taller ones, looking squat in comparison. Someone was just coming down the three stairs from the glossy black door.

In another step Amanda had identified him. Bertram Berkley, Juliet's agent. She wondered, as she always did, if that could possibly be his real name, or if he'd taken it to fit his persona—the sleek, successful artists' representative whose sponsorship, according to him, ensured entrée to people of influence in Boston's art world.

He spotted her and swooped down on her, kissing her ceremoniously on each cheek. "Amanda, my dear. You poor child. I just came by to see how you are. You surely haven't been out already." He made it sound as if she'd breached some unwritten rule of mourning.

"I went back to work today." Bertram's extravagant manner always made her feel even more intensely grounded than she already was. "I have a job, remember?"

"Surely they didn't expect you to be back a scant two weeks after your mother's tragic demise." He linked arms with her and marched her up the steps to the door. Obviously he intended to come in.

She detached her arm. "I wanted to go back, but I have to admit, I'm wiped out. I appreciate your stopping by."

His face stiffened for an instant before his dark eyes grew mournful. "Won't you let me take you out to dinner?" He turned persuasive. "We can have a nice long talk."

"Not tonight. Another time." She put her key in the lock and heard the usual answering bark from Barney, her yellow Lab, greeting her.

"But I wanted to talk to you. We really must plan a show of your mother's work, just as quickly as possible." His voice became urgent. "A tribute show, you see. I've already looked into arrangements, and there's considerable enthusiasm for it. A retrospective, including all her work, even the private pieces you have that aren't for sale. If I could just take a quick look at what's here…"

"Not tonight," she repeated, putting a bit more emphasis on the words. Maybe she was being unfair, but she suspected that his eagerness stemmed at least in part from a desire to cash in on the publicity that had surrounded Juliet's death. "We'll talk soon," she added, then slipped inside and closed the door before he could come up with an argument.

For a moment she just stood, leaning back against the door, relief sweeping over her. Home. It felt like a refuge at the moment. As long as she didn't let her mind stray to the possibility that it might not be hers.

Barney was pressing up against her, whining for her attention. She ruffled his ears. If only she could talk this over with someone. Her friend Kara would be ideal—she knew how to listen without trying to solve your problems for you. But Robert had said to tell no one.

No sense in paying an attorney if you don't take his advice. Her mother had said that when she'd been brought, reluctantly, to making out a will. Had she realized the will could be contested? Obviously not, or she'd have told Robert the truth.

In a crazy way, that was reassuring. It seemed to show that Juliet hadn't conceived of anyone thinking Amanda wasn't her child. Not that Amanda doubted her love, even in the face of the news that had turned her world upside down.

Barney nudged her hand impatiently, then let out a single bark. He trotted a few steps away and then looked back at her, whining.

Supper? But he was headed for the den, not the kitchen. She frowned when he barked again. "All right, Barney. Enough. What's so important?"

He trotted toward the den and again looked back at her. Obviously she was expected to follow him. She obeyed, knowing he wouldn't quit. "Whatever is wrong with…"

She stopped in the doorway, staring, shivering a little when chill air reached her. The window that overlooked the tiny garden behind the house was broken. Shards of glass lay on the Oriental carpet. Fear kept her immobile for another instant.

She should run, get out, call the police…but clearly the intruder was gone. Barney looked at the broken window with an air of triumph, his tail waving as if he announced that he'd vanquished the invader. He'd hardly react that way if someone were still in the house.

"Good dog, good boy." She patted her knee, drawing him back to her. The glass could give him a nasty cut on the paw. He came, rubbing his nose against her palm. "Good Barney," she said again, holding him by the collar.

Calling the police was the obvious next step, but a quick glance told her there'd be little they could do. It didn't look as if the thief had been in here long enough to take anything. The only sign of disturbance besides the broken window was the painting that lay facedown on the rug, its frame broken.

Amanda had to restrain herself from rushing to pick it up. Juliet had done that painting the summer Amanda went to camp for the first time, when she was ten. A realistic-looking view of a waterfall, it was very different from her usual work. But Juliet had been attached to it, and it had hung over the fireplace in the den since that summer. If it was damaged—

She'd have to wait until the police arrived to see. She backed out of the room, dragging Barney, who clearly wanted to remain at the scene of his triumph. Amanda closed the door, ignoring the way he whined at the crack, and pulled out her cell phone.

The police first. Assured they'd be there soon, Amanda leaned against the wall, discovering that her knees were weak. Silly, but normal, she supposed.

Clutching the cell phone in one hand and Barney's collar in the other, Amanda went through the rest of the downstairs. Nothing was disturbed. The thief hadn't gotten far before Barney caught up with him. Thank goodness he apparently hadn't had a weapon.

Shaken by what might have happened, Amanda sank down on the rug and put her arms around the dog. If she'd lost him, too...

It seemed an eternity until the doorbell rang. She peered out the side window. Reassured by the sight of the uniforms, she opened the door.

Much ado about nothing, she told herself a half hour later, when she closed the door behind them again. One of them had been obliging enough to help her tape cardboard in place over the broken panes and sweep up the broken glass while the other filled out a report.

Their attitude said she'd been lucky. Nothing missing and only minor damage that her insurance would most likely cover. With a parting admonition to use the alarm system at all times, they'd gone.

"So that's it," she told Barney. "Let's see how bad the damage was to the painting."

He woofed as if he understood and followed her back to the den. Amanda shivered a little when she paused inside the door. This room, at least, wouldn't feel like a refuge again for a time. While Barney nosed around the broken frame, Amanda lifted the painting gingerly. She turned it over and let out a sigh of relief. The only damage was to the frame.

Odd, that the thief had gone straight to the painting. A burglar would probably look for expensive electronics, rather than a painting. Unless he'd thought it hid a safe. Or perhaps the thief knew whose house this was and had some idea of the value of a Juliet Curtiss painting.

Amanda smoothed the canvas out flat, trying to look at it as if for the first time, but it had become so much a part of the surroundings that it was impossible. The falls were very realistic, as was the dark water at the base and the jagged rocks that interrupted the water's flow. A little shiver went through her. She'd always found the tone of the picture rather ominous. Her mother must have loved it, since it had pride of place in the room where they usually spent the evenings. But there had been times when she'd regarded it broodingly, her face set, maybe dissatisfied with her own work.

Amanda started to put the painting on the side table until she could arrange to have it reframed, but something on the back caught her eye. Along the bottom, in her mother's impeccable printing, ran a tiny line of text, so tiny she had to carry the painting to the lamp to make it out.

In memoriam. M, April, 1989. Echo Falls. Too young to die.

It was the date that jolted Amanda: 1989. She'd been born on February 10, 1989. If that date, at least, was true.

Amanda sank into the desk chair, studying the face of the painting, then turning it again to read the words on the back. It was too much of a coincidence. Or was she thinking that only because of the shocks she'd had?

No. She couldn't buy that. It had to mean something. She had no idea where Echo Falls might be, or who M had been. But she intended to find out.

If she were punctual, the new client should be showing up in the next few minutes. Theodore Alter, Trey to his friends, straightened his tie and prepared for the novelty of a new client. New clients had been thin on the ground for the firm of Alter and Glassman since the scandal broke involving the former head of the law practice. He wanted to make sure this one didn't slip through his fingers.

Unfortunately, he had no idea what Ms. Amanda Curtiss of Boston wanted with an attorney in tiny Echo Falls, Pennsylvania. The contact had been made by someone he'd met at a conference last year. He and Robert McKinley had sat and talked one evening, exchanged business cards and parted, sure they'd never see each other again. Until his call came out of the blue.

McKinley had been downright evasive on the phone when he'd set up this appointment. It was the sort of approach Trey might have instinctively refused back in the day when they'd had more business than they could handle. Not now. He could only hope this Amanda Curtiss wasn't a nutcase.

The intercom buzzed, and he stood as the door opened. "Ms. Curtiss, Mr. Alter," Evelyn Lincoln, their office manager, murmured.

She closed the door discreetly, and Trey had a moment to assess the woman who came toward him. Slim, average height, with blond hair pulled back in a tie at her nape and intensely blue eyes that were looking him over, as well. And perhaps a bit disapprovingly. He had a quick impression of expensive casual clothes and an assured manner before they were shaking hands and murmuring conventional greetings.

"I see you brought a friend to our meeting." Trey nodded to the yellow Lab that followed at the woman's heels.

"I didn't want to leave him in the car. Your receptionist said it would be okay if I brought him inside. I hope you don't dislike dogs." She sounded as if that would end this meeting in a hurry.

"Not at all." He held out the back of his hand to the animal. "I hope he likes attorneys."

"Barney's quite indiscriminately affectionate." The tight control she'd been exercising over her expression became evident only when her face relaxed in a smile as she looked at the animal. The dog proved the truth of her words by licking Trey's hand with enthusiasm.

She took the chair Trey had indicated, and the dog sat obediently next to her. "Thank you for seeing me on such short notice." The reserve had returned.

"No problem," he said easily. "Tell me what I can do to help you. Robert McKinley didn't say much, just that you needed an attorney here in town."

"Yes." She frowned, studying him so seriously that he began to wonder if he had something on his face.

When she didn't continue, he raised an eyebrow. "I'm not what you were looking for?"

A flicker of annoyance crossed her face. "I expected you to be older."

"Sorry I can't oblige." If that sounded flippant, too bad. The woman's attitude didn't bode well for their relationship.

But her lips twitched, and she looked human again. "Sorry. I just assumed a friend of Robert's would be around his age. And this is…rather complicated. I'm not sure you can help me."

"We'll never know unless you tell me what it's about, will we?"

Amanda Curtiss was actually quite attractive when

she relaxed her guard for a moment, with those mobile lips and long, slim legs. Not that he ought to be noticing anything of the kind about a client. Oddly enough, there was something vaguely familiar in the oval face and regular features, but he couldn't place it.

"No." She paused, as if not sure how to begin. "This situation arose when my mother died a few weeks ago."

"I'm sorry for your loss." Maybe that explained the air she had of holding a tight guard on her emotions.

Amanda nodded, accepting the words of condolence. She'd probably heard them often recently. She couldn't be more than about thirty herself, so her mother had apparently died young.

"She had been caught in the cross fire of what the police thought was gang violence. In the course of the postmortem, it was determined that she'd never given birth to a child." She met his gaze briefly and then looked away. "Robert and I assumed I was adopted, but we couldn't find adoption papers anywhere. He's started a search through court records, but without knowing where or when, it seems impossible to trace."

Trey tried to imagine himself in that situation and ran up against a blank wall. He couldn't even begin to think what it must be like. His family roots went deep here in Echo Falls, where everyone knew everything going back several generations. "But you must have a birth certificate."

"I have a baptismal certificate from a church outside Boston that appears genuine, but that's when I was three. What we thought was a birth certificate was actually a hospital form, not a state-registered certificate. And no such birth actually occurred at that hospital on that date."

Trey frowned, caught up in the story in spite of himself. "Your mother must have been very determined to wipe out traces of who you really were. If she were desperate to have a child…"

"No. If you're thinking she took me because she was mentally unbalanced…well, you never knew my mother. That's not something she would do."

He'd reserve judgment on that one. Children weren't always the best judge of what their parents would do. Come to think of it, that worked the other way around, too.

"So you've run into a lot of blind alleys. But what brought you to Echo Falls?"

She hesitated, and for a moment he actually thought she was going to call the whole thing off, say goodbye, send me a bill and walk away. But instead she took something from her bag and handed it to him.

"Do you recognize that?"

It was a photograph of what seemed to be a painting.

The subject was familiar to him. "That's Echo Falls." He studied it closely. "But I've never seen that painting of the falls."

"My mother painted it. She was Juliet Curtiss. I don't know if you're familiar…"

"Yes, of course. I read the account of her death somewhere." That shed a bit more light on things. Juliet Curtiss most likely had a considerable estate to leave her heir, which was now in doubt. On the other hand, if the woman thought the painting would lead her to answers about her parentage…

"This is a photo of the words on the back of the painting. I enlarged it to make it more readable."

He read the short line of printing, struggling to

make sense of it. "It sounds as if your mother did the painting as a tribute to a friend, but that doesn't mean there's a connection to you."

"It's a memorial, so it's logical to assume that the date on it was the date when this person died."

He nodded. "M. I'm with you, but..."

"The date is two months after I was born." She seemed to think that made everything clear. It didn't.

"Even so," he began.

"You think I'm imagining a connection that isn't there." Her face flamed with sudden anger.

"I think you're building a great deal on a slim chance. If I thought I could help you..."

"Never mind." She held out her hand for the photos. "Robert suggested I see you rather than a private investigator, both because he trusts you and because as a local attorney, you're more likely to know what to search for. Maybe I'll do better looking into the situation on my own."

Annoyed, he held the photos out of reach. "Hold on. I didn't say I wouldn't try. I just don't know that I can come up with the answers you want."

"I want the truth." Her tone was uncompromising.

"Good. So do I. Now we have common ground, at least. May I hold on to these?"

"Why?" She shot the word at him.

"Well, mainly because I was four years old in 1989. I'd like to show them to someone who might remember something from that year."

She frowned. "I assume you have a copier in the office. Suppose you keep a copy."

Trey nodded. "We can do that on the way out. Now, where are you staying?"

"At a motel down near Williamsport. It was the closest place I could find that would allow dogs."

"Let me have your cell number, then. I'll call you if I find anything." He hesitated, but it ought to be said. "In the meantime, it probably would be best if you didn't start investigating this in Echo Falls yourself."

"Why not?" She was instantly defensive.

"It's a small town. And like most small towns, people don't like outsiders poking around asking questions." He could see by her expression that she didn't understand. Obviously she'd never lived in a place like Echo Falls.

"I'll think about what you said." She stood, and the dog lumbered to his feet, his nap interrupted. She handed Trey a card with the number he'd requested. It also identified her as Dr. Amanda Curtiss, DVM. A vet. He'd never have guessed that, but it seemed to explain that air of competence.

Trey rounded the desk to join her. "Meaning you'll follow your own instincts?"

That seemed to break through her guard for an instant, and she smiled. "I suppose so."

"Tell me something." He opened the door for her. "Did Robert McKinley approve of this investigation of yours?"

"Probably not. But I told him, and I'll tell you." There was a fierce quality to her determination that he hadn't seen before. "I intend to know the truth. I'm going to find out who I am, no matter who stands in the way."

He tried for a noncommittal expression. "That's your right." He wished he could say it was wise, but he couldn't. For no reason that he could put his finger on, he had the feeling that Amanda Curtiss's quest could land her in a big bunch of trouble. And him with her, if he let himself be sucked in.

CHAPTER TWO

WHEN AMANDA REACHED the sidewalk a few minutes later she paused, considering. That appointment hadn't gone as badly as it might have, she supposed. She'd almost become accustomed to the series of disturbing events that had turned her life upside down, right up until she'd tried to verbalize them to a stranger. If the story sounded off-the-wall to her, she could imagine how it had sounded to that attorney.

To do him justice, Alter hadn't escorted her politely to the door and suggested she consult a mental health professional. Maybe he was a bit too staid and reserved, despite his age, for such an act.

Barney pressed against her leg as if to ask why they were standing irresolute on the sidewalk. "Walk, Barney?"

A wave of the tail answered her. Barney was too well trained to give his usual ecstatic bark in public, but there was no denying a walk would suit him fine. And it made a good excuse to have a look at the place that had seemed to hold such significance to her mother.

To Juliet Curtiss, she corrected, starting down the sidewalk away from the law office. Was she ever going to get used to the idea that she wasn't Juliet's biological daughter?

Juliet had seen her as a daughter. Hadn't she said so plainly in her will? That was the important thing, Robert had told her over and over in the past two weeks. He'd been distressed by what he saw as Amanda's obsession with finding out who she was and where she'd come from.

And as her attorney, he'd been firmly opposed to her leaving Boston at all. "Stay in residence at the brownstone" had been his repeated refrain. That way, if Juliet's brother did get a hint of any irregularity, he'd have much more difficulty in getting her out.

Amanda couldn't do it. She couldn't live her life cautious and afraid. It would have been a betrayal of the way Juliet had raised her. Juliet Curtiss had taken her own course all her life, and she'd taught Amanda to do the same.

Robert had been sympathetic, but he hadn't understood. As for the attorney he'd sent her to…well, Alter didn't understand, either. He clearly wanted her to do nothing except, possibly, go away.

Had he been right about the people here and their attitude toward outsiders? So far as she could tell, Echo Falls inhabitants appeared friendly. Instead of the usual eyes averted posture of a busy city, most people she passed here gave her a pleasant smile or a nod.

The main street of Echo Falls was lined on either side by small shops and offices. A gift shop, a bank, a bookstore…she checked them off as she passed. Ahead of her was the town square, with a small plot of grass, a fountain and a memorial to someone or other. The redbrick buildings around it looked solidly turn of the century. Another bank anchored one corner, while the town hall and the public library accounted for two more. The last was occupied by the local newspaper.

A library and a newspaper office were two of the first places she'd thought to check for information. It was tempting to go in now, but Barney probably wouldn't be welcome, and her stomach informed her it was long past lunchtime.

With a longing glance at the library, Amanda turned back the way she'd come. Noticing a bakery-café across the street, she put Barney in the car, cracked the window a couple of inches and headed in search of lunch.

Several people were coming out of Beiler's Café as she reached it. Judging by the quiet interior, she must have missed the lunch rush, if there was such a thing in a town this size.

The pleasant-faced woman behind the counter waved her to a table. "Wilkom. Will you have coffee?"

"Yes, please." The fact that the woman was Amish surprised her. She'd grown accustomed to seeing the Amish when she'd done her veterinary training in Pennsylvania, but somehow she hadn't expected to find an Amish settlement this far north in the state.

A steaming mug appeared first, followed quickly by a menu. "Lunch, or maybe a cruller to go with the coffee?" The woman's smile widened. "I'm Esther... Esther Beiler. And you are a visitor, ain't so?"

Amanda relaxed, whatever tension she'd held on to evaporating at the woman's friendliness. "That's right. I haven't been to this part of Pennsylvania before. You have such a pretty downtown area." True enough, and it occurred to her that she should seize the opportunity to chat when offered.

"Ach, it's not so bad," Esther acknowledged. "I

think the valley is at its best in the fall, when the ridges have so much color. It's already close to the peak, I think. We get a fair number of tourists coming through on weekends."

Nodding, Amanda scanned the menu. "What do you recommend?"

"Chicken potpie is most popular. I have homemade vegetable beef soup, too, and it's not so bad."

Deciding that "not so bad" was high praise, Amanda opted for the vegetable beef soup. As the woman headed back toward the kitchen, Amanda noticed tourist brochures on a rack inside the door. She picked up one to look at while waiting. Her preliminary research had told her that the actual falls for which the community was named was a couple of miles away. She was eyeing a sketch map in the brochure doubtfully when Esther returned with the soup and a basket of rolls that smelled fresh from the oven.

"You're interested in the falls, yah?" Esther seemed to have no inhibitions about looking over Amanda's shoulder.

"I'd like to see them, yes." She couldn't expect that looking at the falls would tell her anything about why her mother had painted them, but somehow she had to see for herself. "But this map…"

"That's for pretty, not for finding your way." Esther dismissed the tourist brochure. "Best if you have someone take you there the first time. It's not an easy walk."

"Walk?"

"Yah. You can park not too far away, but you'll need to walk through the woods." Esther gestured toward the street. "I saw you coming out of the law office. Trey could take you. Or was it Jason Glassman you came to see?"

The firm was Alter and Glassman. Obviously news spread fast here. "Trey?" she questioned.

"Theodore James Alter." Esther's smile widened. "His father and grandfather had the same name, so everyone calls him Trey."

Amanda stowed that information away. Obviously Alter was well-known here. Whether that would help her or not, she didn't know.

"I had some business with the office. I don't know Mr. Alter socially." And the idea of having him along when she went to the falls didn't appeal. "I saw a painting of the falls once," she added. If Esther knew everything that went on in town, she might have been aware of Juliet's visit, although there didn't seem much chance she'd remember it after all these years.

"A painting. Think of that, now. I've seen lots of photographs of the falls, but never a painting." She shrugged. "Funny, that is, but people have kind of odd feelings about the falls."

"Odd?" Amanda had her own reasons for mixed emotions about the falls, but...

"Lots of superstitions, you know." Esther seemed vaguely uneasy. "I don't put much stock in those old stories myself."

"What kind of old stories?" She asked the question around a spoonful of vegetable soup, rich with tender beef chunks.

Esther frowned, brushing her palms down the front of her white apron. "Ach, old Indian tales and the like." She hesitated. "There's one that says you should never climb up the trail by the falls alone. Seems if you do..."

The pause might have been for effect, but Amanda suspected the woman's hesitation was genuine enough. "Yes?"

"They say if you do, you'll hear something following you. Coming after you. All you can hear is the rushing water and the footsteps behind you."

Esther's rosy face had lost some of its color. She wasn't putting this on to entertain the tourist. Suddenly she flicked her apron, as if shaking something off it.

"Ach, that's all nonsense, probably made up to keep kids away. I don't believe a word of it."

Amanda didn't, either, of course. She was far too sensible to be frightened by ghost stories.

But the words lingered in her mind like a cobweb clinging to her fingers, impossible to shake away.

"SO HOW DID the appointment with the new client go?" Jason Glassman, Trey's law partner, tossed some mail on Trey's desk. "Anything there?"

Trey shrugged. "Doubtful." He and Jason had spent plenty of hours trying to rebuild the firm in the past few months, and he didn't think Amanda Curtiss's wild-goose chase was going to help them.

"Don't tell me your big-shot Boston friend sent you someone who doesn't have a case."

"Worse." He frowned. "At least, I think it's worse. It's either going to be time wasted on nothing at all, or it's going to be something…"

"What?"

"I'm not sure." He couldn't rid himself of the feeling that if there was any substance to Amanda's story, it would lead to a messy situation that wouldn't do the firm or himself any good.

Jason was waiting patiently for an answer, something that showed how much he'd changed since he'd arrived in Echo Falls last spring. Then, *patience* hadn't been part of his vocabulary. Credit his recent engagement for that, Trey supposed.

"It's too soon to say whether there's anything to it or not. I'll let you know once…" The sentence trailed off as he glanced out the window. There, on the opposite side of the street, was Amanda Curtiss, apparently having a heart-to-heart with Esther Beiler in front of the coffee shop.

If Amanda was looking for town gossip, she'd somehow landed right in the spot where the latest news was shared, embellished and passed on. Even as he watched, Esther pointed at the ridge, clearly showing Amanda the location of the falls.

"I'll catch you up on it later," he said, and hurried for the door.

Trey dodged an older model pickup coming down the street at a snail's pace and reached the sidewalk to find Esther Beiler beaming at him.

"Ach, Trey, you're chust in time. I was telling your friend that she'd best have you go with her up to the falls, ain't so?"

His friend? He'd have to let that go with Esther's curious gaze fixed on him. "Sure thing. I'd be glad to take her."

He turned to Amanda, trying to keep a smile on his face. "If you're ready, I'll walk back to the car with you. We'll set up a time to go."

Amanda evaded his glance. Thanking Esther, she stepped off the curb. But any plans she might have to avoid talking to him were foiled as she had to pause for an Amish buggy to roll slowly past.

Trey raised his hand to Eli Miller and his oldest boy, probably headed to the hardware store, and then touched Amanda's elbow to guide her across the street as if she were his elderly grandmother.

She glared at him, shaking her arm free. "I can walk across the street on my own, thank you. And there's no need to take me to the falls. Esther gave me very good directions."

"I'll bet." His lips quirked. "I've heard Esther's idea of directions. 'Go down the Pauley Road until you come to where Stoltzfus's barn used to be before they built the new one…'"

Amanda preserved the glare for another second before her lips curved in a smile that showed a dimple at the upper corner. "They were something like that, I have to say. But really, there's no need for me to take you away from your work. Just tell me something I can put into the GPS."

"I doubt if there is an address it would recognize." Besides, keeping an eye on Amanda Curtiss seemed like a good idea, if not a full-time job. "Tell you what. I'll meet you tomorrow and take you up there. Okay?"

"Why not now?" Her eyebrows lifted.

"First, because you're not dressed for a hike." He nodded toward her suede boots and light wool slacks. "And neither am I. Second, because that will give me a chance to look for some of the answers you want."

She studied him, as if wondering whether he was stalling. "You think you'll be able to find something that quickly?"

"If there was a death that was somehow connected

to the falls in 1989, I'm sure my dad would know about it. And he can be trusted not to spread your story all over town."

"That's really worrying you, isn't it? I don't see why."

They'd reached the car by then, and he put a hand on the door when she would have opened it. In an instant the dog had sprung to the window, baring a formidable set of teeth.

"Nice to know you're so well-protected," he commented, moving his hand away from the glass. "This is a small town."

"You said that before," she pointed out. "I still don't see why anyone would be interested in why I'm here."

"You don't know a town like this. Esther will be talking about you to the next person who comes into the café. Not maliciously, you understand. Just sharing. And that person will mention you to someone else."

Amanda's firm jaw set stubbornly. "I'm not hiding anything."

"Then you're not thinking it through." He resisted the urge to raise his voice and glanced around, but no one was within earshot. "From what you told me, you obviously think there's a good chance your birth mother was connected with Echo Falls. People here are old-fashioned. Do you think they'll welcome someone stirring up what might have been an old scandal? Or sharing their private family secrets with the world?"

Her clear blue eyes seemed to darken. "You think I'm an illegitimate child no one will want to claim."

"That's not what I think. I think you're building too much on something that probably has no relationship to your parentage. I get it, really. It must have been an enormous shock to be faced with that news so soon after your mother's death."

For a moment he thought she'd argue with him. Then she seemed to swallow whatever it was she'd almost said. "You're sure you'll be able to find out something by tomorrow?"

"If there's anything to find, I will. If my father doesn't know, someone else will, but I'm betting he'd remember anything that dramatic." He tried to read her expression and found it impossible. "So, what do you say? I'll meet you at the office tomorrow at ten, and I'll bring the insect repellent. You wear something you can walk in the woods in. Okay?"

She hesitated for so long he thought she was going to turn him down. Finally, she nodded. "Okay." Her expression softened. "Look, I know I'm not going to find anything there. I just... I need to see the place."

"I get it." To his surprise, he actually did. It was a connection to the woman she'd always thought was her mother. "In the meantime, could you refrain from going around town asking questions?"

"I'll consider it." A smile took the sting from the words. "Until tomorrow, then. And thanks..." She hesitated. "Trey."

"You see?" He kept his voice light. "Esther knows all and tells all."

He opened the door for her, and at a word, the dog lay down in the back seat.

"I'll see you at ten, then."

She closed the door, and Trey stood where he was to watch her drive down the street. Not toward the highway and her motel, he noticed. That was too much to hope for.

He'd warned her. That was all he could do. Whatever waves she made now were unavoidable.

BY THE TIME he left the office for the day, Trey had
stopped trying to dismiss Amanda Curtiss and her
troubles from his mind. He couldn't do it. His mother
would say he was conscientious, like his father, but he
knew better. It was apprehension, caused by the sense
that Amanda was going to cause problems for anyone
who became involved in her hunt for answers.

Stubborn, that was the word for her—just like a lot
of the hardheaded Pennsylvania Dutch he'd grown up
with. Once they'd made up their minds, a person might
as well save his breath and prepare either to get out of
the way or to pick up the pieces.

He'd headed automatically for his own place, but a
sudden impulse made him turn at the corner of Oak
Street and make for his parents' house instead. He had
to pick his father's brain on the subject of Amanda's
search, so he might as well do it now.

A few minutes later he pulled into the driveway at
the comfortable old Queen Anne house where he'd
grown up. In his mind's eye, he could still see a bicycle
leaning against the mammoth oak tree that Dad threatened periodically to have cut down before it fell on
the house. And a skateboard abandoned on the porch
steps, providing the material for a fatherly lecture on
the proper care of one's belongings.

When he got out, the October sun slanted through
the branches of the oak tree, picking out bronze and
gold in the leaves. The lawn could use a raking, but
Dad was forbidden to do that sort of thing since his
heart attack in the spring. Trey would have to take

the initiative and either do the fall cleanup himself or hire someone.

Scuffing through the leaves that had already fallen, he headed for the side door that led into the kitchen. "Mom? Dad? You home?" Since the car was in the garage and the door unlocked, that was a safe assumption.

"Trey!" His mother looked as delighted as if she hadn't seen him in three months instead of three days. "How nice. You'll stay for supper."

He grinned, giving her a quick hug. "Now, how did you know that was on my mind?" Nothing pleased his mother more than having her cooking appreciated.

"You don't eat enough, cooking for yourself," she chided.

"Where's Dad?" he interrupted, before she could tell him he ought to get married so he'd have someone to take care of him. There was never any use telling her that none of the women he dated cared any more for cooking than he did.

"In the study. You go and chat with him while I add a few more potatoes to the pot. Go on. Pork chops tonight, and luckily I got extra."

She always had extra, of course. Dad claimed she'd never gotten past the years when as often as not Trey would bring a friend or two home for supper at the last minute.

Dad put his newspaper aside when Trey entered the round room that took up the first floor of the typically Victorian turret. Upstairs, this area was a sunroom off the master bedroom, and here it was his father's domain. The golden oak desk still sat in front of a bank of windows, although it wasn't littered with a slew of papers as it had been during his father's working years.

"About time you were coming by," he said. "Your mother convince you to stay for supper?"

Trey grinned. "You should know I never take much convincing." Concern lurked behind the smile as he pulled up a rocking chair next to his father's recliner. Dad was still looking too pale, too drawn, since the scare he'd put them through a few months ago.

His father seemed to see past Trey's casual manner. "Something on your mind?"

"As a matter of fact, something has come up I'd like your advice on." Maybe it would do his father good to be involved in the business of the firm he'd spent his life building. "I had a new client come in today—a woman who was referred by a Boston attorney I met a couple of years ago. She had a rather odd story to tell."

"I'm retired, remember?" But he was leaning forward, obviously interested.

Trey reached in his pocket, pulled out a couple of ones and put them on the lamp table. "There. Consider yourself a consultant."

"Right. So what am I consulting on? You can surely handle whatever it is."

"My memories don't go back far enough to be helpful, and I figure yours do. And you won't go blabbing it around town."

"Thanks for the compliment. So tell me." In spite of the sarcastic words, he looked pleased.

But as the story unfolded, Trey saw his father's expression change. He seemed to freeze up as he looked into the past, as if he'd seen something he'd rather not look at.

Trey faltered to a stop. His mother had been on a campaign to keep anything worrisome away from Dad, and he seemed to have tripped right into it.

His father leaned back in the chair, his mouth tight. It took a few minutes for him to speak. "If I were you, I'd tell the woman you can't help her."

"That was my first instinct," Trey admitted. "But she struck me as the kind of person who doesn't give up easily. If I don't help her, she'll go around town asking questions on her own. It seemed to me…"

Dad waved a hand tiredly. "No, you're right. That would be worse." He mused for another moment. "If you're looking for a death in 1989 that is related to the falls, there's only one I can think of that fits. Elizabeth Winthrop's granddaughter was found dead at the base of the falls sometime in the spring."

"Winthrop," Trey repeated. It was like saying "Rockefeller" by Echo Falls standards. The Winthrop family had established the town, lumbered the surrounding hillsides, built up a thriving business that still provided employment to half the town.

"Exactly." Dad's eyes met his. "The story was hushed up, of course. If people knew, they were generally sensible enough not to talk about it, but word got around, of course."

"So what was it? Suicide?" That was the first thought that came to mind. Elizabeth Winthrop was an elderly autocrat who would find it unthinkable that such a thing could touch her family.

"It was ruled accidental, of course. Still, not even the Winthrops could eliminate all the speculation, especially since Melanie Winthrop had left town suddenly some months earlier. She'd have been about seventeen at the time, I suppose."

"Pregnant or an addict?" Those were the obvious answers.

"Pregnant," his father said reluctantly. "She was sent off to have the baby and put it up for adoption."

"So that may be Amanda Curtiss's answer. There must be records…"

"It's not as simple as that. Melanie didn't go through with the plans. She disappeared, and as far as I know, she wasn't seen or heard from until the day she was found lying on the rocks at Echo Falls."

He leaned back in the chair, breathing as if he'd been running, his face gray. Alarmed, Trey clasped his wrist. "Dad…"

"Now that's enough talk." Trey hadn't realized his mother was standing at the doorway until she hurried to his father. "Ted, you know you shouldn't tire yourself that way." She picked up a glass of water and held it to his lips.

"I'm sorry." Guilt had a stranglehold on Trey's throat. "I shouldn't have kept him talking so long."

"Nonsense." His father pushed the glass away fretfully. "Don't fuss, Claire. I'm fine."

"Supper will be ready in five minutes. Trey, you can set the table." She shooed Trey out of the room ahead of her.

"I didn't mean…" he began, but his mother shook her head.

"You couldn't have known it would affect him that much." She didn't bother to deny she'd been listening. "But he wouldn't want you to keep it from him."

"I don't get it. Why should it upset him that much?

It's not as if you were close friends with the Winthrops."

"Your father was the family's attorney in those days." His mother stirred gravy vigorously with an air of not knowing what she was doing. "They fell out over this business of Melanie's pregnancy. He thought they were making a mistake to handle it that way, disregarding the girl's wishes. That was the last thing he did for them, and I remember that his partner was furious that he gave up such a lucrative client. But when it comes to principles, your father is a stubborn man."

Trey wasn't sure what to say. "I didn't know he'd ever represented them."

His mother handed him a pot of mashed potatoes. "Put that in a bowl." She gave him a half smile. "I'm sure your father never regretted losing them." She hesitated. "I'd like to tell you to drop the whole thing, but I know better. You're just as stubborn and principled as your father. You're going to help this woman, aren't you?"

He paused, but there really was only one answer. "Yes. I guess I am."

CHAPTER THREE

AMANDA WASN'T QUITE sure how she'd let Trey Alter talk her into changing the plans she'd made. She had no particular reason to trust him. Just because Robert had recommended him, that didn't mean she should let him dictate what she did.

But after telling herself all that, here she was, getting into Trey's car in front of his office the next day.

"Somehow I thought this was the kind of car you'd have." She snapped her seat belt.

Trey sent her a startled glance. "What's wrong with my car?"

"Nothing. Nice, conservative sedan, tan, sedate— just the thing for a family lawyer to drive."

Instead of taking offense, he grinned. "Stodgy, in other words. If it'll make you feel any better about me, I also own a beat-up, four-wheel drive pickup. Red."

"With a gun rack behind the seat?" she inquired.

"You bet. Now you don't know whether I'm a good ole boy or a stuffy lawyer."

She couldn't deny that he'd intrigued her. "So which is it?"

"Both. Or neither, depending on your point of view."

"Sorry. I guess I shouldn't succumb to stereotypes."

He shrugged. "No problem. We all do it sometimes."

"Yes."

People had thought that because Juliet was an artist, she couldn't possibly have been a typical soccer mom. Maybe she wasn't, but she'd been there for every single event in Amanda's life, including being a room mother and chaperoning school trips.

They hadn't gone more than a mile out of town, and she hadn't managed to ask him what, if anything, he'd found out, when he turned off the main road onto a farm lane.

The car hit a pothole, and he winced. "Sorry. Guess I should have made you ride in the pickup. The milk tankers really tear up this road."

Amanda glanced across a cornfield, stalks yellow and ready for cutting, to a tidy white farmhouse. "No power lines," she commented. "I assume it's Amish?"

He nodded. "How did a Boston vet become able to identify an Amish farm at a glance?"

"My graduate degree is from the University of Pennsylvania. A lot of their large animal work is carried out in the Lancaster County area. And I had a practice there for a time."

"So you know enough not to gawk when you see a bonnet, or try to take a photograph of an Amish person?"

"At least that much," she said gravely. "Look, shall we stop evading the point and get to it? Did you find out anything?"

"I'm not sure how much…" The car hit a rut, and he broke off abruptly. "How about I concentrate on getting us there without ruining my shocks? Then I'll tell you what I've been able to find out so far."

"Fair enough." She gripped the armrest. "Are the falls on private land?"

"No, but this is the shortest access to the bottom of the falls, and Eli never minds folks driving up his lane as long as they don't make a mess. You can take a township road to the state lands, but it's out of the way."

She subsided, letting him concentrate on the road, if she could dignify it by calling it that. She had been so taken up with her own problems the previous day that she hadn't really noticed him. Now she had time for a closer look.

Not bad. Nice, even features in a strong face, brown hair with just a hint of bronze when the light hit it, a pair of level brows and a strong, stubborn jaw. He was in is early thirties, and she wondered what he found to do for fun in a town like Echo Falls.

Of course, he could be married with a couple of kids, but she didn't think so. She hadn't seen any family photos or childish artwork in his office, and he didn't wear a ring.

Not that it mattered in the least what his marital status was, she assured herself.

"There are a few hunting cabins out that way." He waved a hand toward a road that cut off around the curve of the hillside. "When the state took over the falls, they didn't buy up much of the surrounding land. Probably thinking the less accessible it was, the better."

He reached a slightly wider place in the road and pulled to the side, turning off the ignition. Ahead of them, the road seemed to peter out to a mere track. "We'll park here and go the rest of the way on foot. You don't mind a walk in the woods, do you?"

"No, and Barney will enjoy it." She got out and opened the back door for Barney to jump down from the seat. He stood for a moment, nose raised to the unfamiliar scents.

"This way."

Trey slung on a small backpack and gestured to a path. No sign. As he'd said, the state didn't care to make it easy for tourists.

They headed along a path that slanted slightly upward. Barney, happy to be released, scampered along, dodging from one side of the trail to the other to explore.

Trey eyed him. "He's not going to run off chasing a deer, is he?"

"I won't say he wouldn't be tempted, but he's well trained." She smiled. "Although he was actually a dropout from a service dog organization I'm involved with."

"What did he do? Flunk his final?" Trey gave her a quizzical look.

"Not exactly. He could master the techniques, all right, but he didn't have that extra edge of concentration and empathy that's needed for a service dog. So he came home with me, and we're both happy."

"Your mother was a dog person, then?"

"Let's say she and Barney tolerated each other. He's a good watchdog, though. Did I tell you about the burglar he thwarted?"

"No." He frowned. "Was this recently?"

"Within the last couple of weeks." It seemed longer, given all that had happened since then. "The police seemed to think it was just a random act."

He must have caught the hesitation in her voice. "You didn't agree?"

"Whoever he was, he came in through the window in the den. There were some expensive electronics there, but the only thing disturbed was the painting of Echo Falls. I found that odd." She shrugged. "He may have been interrupted by Barney before he could get any farther, but still, it was strange that he'd go for the painting first."

Trey, slightly ahead of her on the trail, glanced back to study her face. "Could it have been someone who knew the value of a Juliet Curtiss painting? Maybe the artwork was the goal all along."

"Possibly. That was my first thought, but it seems strange that someone as sophisticated as an art thief wouldn't have taken the elementary precaution of finding out that there was a guard dog. It looked as if he went back out the window faster than he'd come in."

Trey looked at Barney with what seemed increased respect. "A good thing Barney was on the job. So the painting was the only thing disturbed. Damaged?"

"No, but the frame was broken. That's how I found the inscription on it." She could hear her own voice flatten at the reminder of why she was here. This wasn't just a pleasant walk in the woods with an attractive guy. "The wording had been placed so that no one would have noticed it unless the painting was out of the frame."

"Right." He seemed to recognize that it was time to talk. The path widened out, the ground becoming more level, and they were able to walk side by side. "Like I said I would, I spoke to my father. He was able to identify a death that is likely the one your mother memorialized. A young woman named Melanie Winthrop."

"M," Amanda said, her heart pumping a little faster. "Who was she? How did she die?"

Trey frowned, giving her the impression that he was reluctant to talk about it. "You have to understand first that the Winthrop family is a big deal in Echo Falls. Owners of the mill, town founders, with a finger in just about every pie there is here."

"Bad things hit rich families, too," she said, impatient to get on with it. She was on the point of possibly learning the truth about her mother, and he wanted to chat about town history. Didn't he understand that her stomach was roiling with emotions even she couldn't sort out?

"True enough," he said. "But that wasn't quite my point. The matriarch, Elizabeth Winthrop...well, to hear people tell it, she rules the family. Has done for years. Melanie would have been the daughter of her only son, who died in a plane crash along with his wife, leaving Melanie to be raised by her grandmother, her aunt and uncle."

She wasn't particularly interested in all this family detail, not now. "How did Melanie die?"

"According to my dad, she had left town abruptly some months before her death." Trey seemed to be choosing his words. "Apparently she was pregnant, only seventeen."

Pregnant. The odds were growing that this girl had been her mother. "They kicked her out?" Anger cut through Amanda.

"No, nothing like that. They sent her away to have the baby and give it up for adoption. Then she was supposed to come home and pretend it hadn't happened."

That didn't seem much better to Amanda. "That's... barbaric."

"Old-fashioned. Conservative. Proud. That's the Winthrop family. Or Elizabeth, anyway."

"I'm surprised Melanie ever wanted to see them again." *Focus. Don't think of her as your mother, not yet, or you won't be thinking straight.*

Trey took her arm as she climbed over a tree trunk on the path. "Maybe she didn't. According to my dad, she didn't go through with their plans for her. She disappeared, and nothing more was heard of her until her body was found at the base of the falls."

For several minutes, Amanda had been aware of a faint roaring noise, growing louder as they walked. Now they stepped into a cleared area as the path ended at a stream. And above them loomed the falls.

For a moment Amanda couldn't speak. She'd lived with the painting for years, and she'd seen numerous photos since she'd identified the location. But nothing had prepared her for the overpowering force of the water rushing down the steep face of rock.

"She fell from up there?" She finally found her voice. "It must be close to a hundred feet."

"Ninety-some," he said. "I don't think they know how high up she was when she fell. It wouldn't have needed to be all the way to the top to be fatal."

The story Esther had told her, that if you climbed up the trail by the falls alone, you'd hear something following you, coming after you, slid into Amanda's mind like a snake. She chased it out again. The trail was a faint, almost impassable-looking line winding up along the right side of the rushing water.

Amanda gave herself a mental shake. There had been nothing eerie about what happened to the girl. Just tragic.

"What was she doing here, of all places? If she came back, it must have been to see her family, wasn't it?"

"Apparently not," Trey said. He was staring at the falls, too. "At least they claim to have heard nothing from her. I haven't had a chance to talk with the police chief yet, but I will. Still, I'm not sure how forthcoming he's going to be."

Amanda registered his words without really taking them in. She felt drawn nearer the base of the falls, her eyes on the jagged rocks. The girl who might have been her mother died there.

She tried the words out, but they seemed meaningless. Juliet was still the person she pictured as her mother, and Juliet had died in a spate of meaningless gunfire on a city street.

"Are you okay?" Trey clasped her arm, his hand warm even through the sleeve of her shirt and the sweater she wore.

"Yes." She clipped off the word. "Can you actually get to the top from here? It looks impossible."

"It's actually not that bad." He pointed to the small opening between two boulders. "Look, there's a path that winds up through the rocks. Once you get started, it's pretty easy to follow, but the rocks are slippery, especially when it's windy and the spray is carried onto the path."

"I see." The safe thing would be to stand back and feel…whatever it was she'd thought she'd feel when she came here. But she felt compelled to see what it was like to climb up.

Would Juliet have climbed to the top when she was here? Maybe not—the painting had been done from the bottom. But the unknown Melanie might have.

Amanda clambered over the intervening rocks and took the first few steps up before Trey reached her.

"Hey, wait a second." He caught her arm. "Always take a buddy with you when you climb. That's what our scoutmaster told us."

"I won't go far. I just want to see…" That quickly, she hit a wet patch on the rock, and her foot slid.

Trey grabbed her in an instant, holding her steady against his solid body. "Take it easy. You don't want to add to the accident count."

She tilted her head back so she could see his face and nearly lost track of what she was going to say. He was so close she could see the small scar at the corner of his eyebrow, close enough to smell the faint, clean scent of him.

"I couldn't kill myself falling from here," she said, annoyed with herself for sounding breathless.

"No, but you could easily break an ankle on the rocks." He looked away, as if he found their closeness uncomfortable.

She had to ask the question that had filled her mind. "Was it really an accident? How could they know if no one saw it?"

"You mean it might have been suicide?" His eyes narrowed, considering. "I don't know how the police came to that decision. The police chief may have some ideas about it, if he's willing to talk to me."

"If I ask him…" she began.

"He'd freeze you out at the first implication that the police hadn't done their job properly, especially where the Winthrop family is concerned."

She suddenly needed to distance herself from him. She stepped down, then down again, well aware of his steadying hand on her arm. When they reached the bottom, Barney stopped running back and forth in agitation and nuzzled her hand. She patted him and then turned to face Trey as he jumped lightly down the last step.

"Are you saying the Winthrop family owns the police force as well as everything else in this town?"

"No." Trey's face darkened, and he seemed to make an effort to speak evenly. "I mean that a man in the chief's position isn't going to speak to an outsider about a police case to begin with. And if there was any question about whether Melanie's death was accident or suicide, the kindest thing would be to opt for accident and spare the family that added pain."

She thought of the seventeen-year-old, sent away at what had probably been the most difficult time of her life. "Maybe they deserved it."

"That wouldn't be for the police to judge. Or you either, for that matter, at least not without knowing more than you do now."

She had a sneaking suspicion he was right about that, but she wasn't about to admit it. Trey Alter had too self-satisfied an opinion of himself already.

"If the police chief won't talk to me, what makes you think he'll talk to you?" She recognized an edge to her voice. He probably heard it as well, but he didn't react.

"Well, for one thing, he's known me all my life. And for another, I'm an officer of the court, which gives me some status with him." Trey took a few steps past her. "Let's get away from the falls so we can hear ourselves think."

Amanda had almost become used to the roar, the

way they said people who lived in Niagara Falls no longer heard the sound. But she had been straining to speak above it, so she nodded, following him back away from the rocks.

"Is there anything else you want to see here?" Trey didn't sound impatient, she'd give him that, but he might well want to get back to work.

"I'd like to find my mother's vantage point of the falls, if I can." She felt herself getting defensive. "And no, I don't think it's going to tell me anything after all these years. I'd just like to see it."

He nodded as if it was perfectly reasonable. If he'd been annoyed with her, he had himself well under control. "Sure thing. It shouldn't be hard to find. Did you bring the photo with you?"

Amanda retrieved it from the pocket where she'd stowed it for safety. Drat the man—why did he never react the way she expected?

Holding the photo, Trey paced slowly along the bank of the stream, looking up repeatedly to compare the view to the image. On the opposite side of the rushing stream, the thick growth of rhododendrons made an impenetrable barrier. The painting had to have been done from this side.

Trey reached a point at which a slight curve in the streambed had left a little spit of sand and gravel. He stopped, making the comparison again.

"Got it. I thought it might have been about here. Take a look."

Amanda stepped out onto the sandy spot and looked from the photo to the falls. "You're right. What made you think it might be here?"

He shrugged. "I've tried to get a good photo of the

falls a few times. This is the only vantage point that lets you get in both the top and the bottom."

Amanda stood where she was for a moment. She could so easily imagine Juliet on this spot, the legs of the easel shoved into the sand, a brush behind her ear and another in her hand, brooding over the canvas as she so often did.

As for the other person Juliet might have been imagining in the scene…to Amanda's disappointment she could see nothing at all. Didn't they say that blood called to blood? If so, either hers was deaf or she was on the wrong track entirely.

Then it hit her. "This whole thing started because the autopsy on my mother—on Juliet Curtiss—showed she'd never had a child. So wouldn't the postmortem have shown, at least, whether Melanie Winthrop had carried a child to term? If so…"

Trey seized on the fragment of provable fact. "I'm no expert, but I'd think it would. *If* they bothered to do a full autopsy in a case of accident. But if they did, the results should be in the coroner's records, and I ought to be able to access those."

"So, you're going to check the coroner's records." She surveyed him. "You're going to talk to the police chief. What am I going to do?"

She could swear there was a twinkle in Trey's eyes. "I suppose it's too much to hope you'll go back to your motel and wait for answers. Or better yet, back to Boston."

"You sound like Robert McKinley," she said sourly. "I can't do nothing."

"I suppose not." He sounded regretful. "What about the newspaper accounts from the time? I don't know how much they'd have reported, but it might give you a fuller picture of the events."

"That was going to be my first stop before you sidetracked me. I suppose the newspaper has the files? I've already checked online, but the archives of the paper don't go back that far."

Trey bent to ruffle Barney's ears absentmindedly. "They haven't been in a rush to digitize them. There's not that much call for old copies. The historical society has some, but they wouldn't have digitized anything that recent."

"There must be some way of finding them."

He nodded. "The library has all the back issues on microfiche. It'll turn you cross-eyed searching, as I know from experience, but you should be able to find what you want there."

"Good." Something she could do, at least. "I'll work on that this afternoon and check back with you. I just wish I could find a place to stay in town. That drive back and forth to the motel is getting old already."

Trey frowned, looking down at Barney. "I just might be able to find a place that wouldn't mind a well-trained dog around." He grinned. "Even if he did flunk out of service dog school."

The tension involved in being on this spot slid away as she smiled in return. "Where? Lead me to it."

"There's an Amish farm near here that takes farm-stay guests in the summer. They recently added a cottage, complete with gas heating and lighting. They don't normally take guests this time of year, but they might be persuaded to accommodate a friend of mine."

"Is that how everything around here operates?" She

couldn't help but ask the question. "Based on the good old boys' network?"

He shrugged. "You might be able to ignore your neighbors in the city, but not in a place like Echo Falls. If you're done here, we can check it out now."

Her spirits lifted. "Great. Thanks, Trey." Impulsively she put out her hand.

He took it in both of his, and in that instant the mood changed abruptly. A not-so-lighthearted connection grabbed her, skittering along her nerves from their clasped hands. Their gazes caught, arrested as the attraction ricocheted between them.

The moment seemed to last forever. Then Trey dropped her hand as if he'd seized something hot. His breathing came as fast as if he'd been running, and hers was about as bad.

Well. That was unexpected. *Unwelcome*, she added defiantly. She didn't have room for complications right now, so this had to stop before it started. Didn't it?

BY THE TIME they'd gotten back to the car, Trey had given himself the lecture of the day—namely, don't get involved. Relationships were difficult no matter where you lived, but in a small town, they could lead too easily to disaster, as he knew from experience.

Like the situation with Marcie Hampton last year, the then-new teacher at the high school. They'd gone out three times...count 'em, three...and the town had had them all but married.

Worse, Marcie had been infected by the assumptions, thinking their relationship more serious than it was. It had led to a messy breakup that he was determined not to repeat. Since then, he'd been considerably more circumspect.

Trey darted a sidelong glance at Amanda as they reached the main road. She seemed as reluctant to recognize that blast of attraction between them as he was. That should make it easier to keep their relationship strictly business.

He glanced in the rearview mirror to find that Barney was watching him with what seemed like skepticism in his eyes.

"Is the farm with the cottage far from town?" Amanda broke the silence between them.

"Not far. About three miles. Amos and Sarah Burkhalter took over his parents' dairy farm a few years ago, and they added the farm-stay business to make a little extra in the summer. Sarah and the kids handle most of it. With eight kids between five and nineteen, the extra income is welcome."

"Eight." She shook her head. "I know the Amish have big families, but I'm still amazed at how well they manage. I have friends with one or two who can't seem to keep up."

"Everybody works on the farm. It keeps them busy and out of trouble, for the most part."

"I'm sure that boggles the minds of their English farm-stay visitors. I remember the first time I saw a barefoot Amish boy chasing a gigantic Holstein into the barn for me to examine. I wanted to run to the rescue, but luckily I had better sense."

He frowned, remembering her business card. "I thought your practice was with small animals."

"Yes." Amanda clipped off the word, and he saw her hands clench. After a moment, she went on. "I was originally a partner in a large animal practice in Lancaster County. But it…didn't work out." Trey had a sense of something suppressed. "So I went back to Boston."

Her lips closed firmly. Obviously time for another subject of conversation. Luckily, they were coming up on the Burkhalter place.

"Here it is, on the right." He nodded to where twin silos and a windmill loomed over a cluster of white frame buildings. "Like I said, the Burkhalters don't usually take guests this time of the year, but I'll sound them out."

"Fine." She looked back at Barney. "We'll be on our best behavior, right, Barney?"

The dog whined in response to his name, and his muzzle poked between the seats as he attempted to lick Amanda's face. They both chuckled, and the tension between them seemed to disappear.

When Trey pulled up at the back door of the farmhouse, Sarah was already coming outside with a welcoming wave, her youngest hurrying to keep up. When little Mary Elizabeth saw that Trey wasn't alone, she took up a hiding place behind her mamm's skirts.

"Trey, wilkom. We weren't looking to see you today." Sarah must be around forty, he knew, but she had a rosy, youthful face, and her brown hair didn't yet show any signs of gray. She smiled at Amanda. "You've brought company. Komm, the coffee is hot and there's apple pie."

"Whoa, slow down." He grinned at Mary Elizabeth, for whom he had a soft spot. "Sarah, this is Amanda Curtiss. She's visiting Echo Falls for a while. Amanda, Sarah Burkhalter. And that pretty girl is Mary Elizabeth."

"Sarah, it's nice to meet you." Amanda didn't attempt to shake hands, probably knowing that might make Sarah uncomfortable. She knelt and smiled at the little girl. "I'm Amanda. Would you like to meet my friend?" She pointed to Barney, looking out the car window at them.

When Mary Elizabeth nodded, Amanda opened the door, and Barney leaped out lightly. At a command, he sat at her side, ears cocked, head on one side as he looked at the child. She edged out from behind her mother and petted him tentatively.

While the two of them were getting acquainted, Trey explained Amanda's predicament. "I thought you might want to rent out the cottage to her."

Sarah's question showed in her face as she looked from Amanda to the dog.

"Barney is well trained," Amanda said quickly. "I can promise he won't go off chasing the stock. I'd be grateful for the chance to stay here, if you agree."

"Amanda's a vet," Trey added helpfully. "She worked in Lancaster County for some time."

Sarah's expression relaxed. "Guess you know your way around a farm, then. Komm, we'll look at the cottage."

By the time they'd looked around the simple two-bedroom cottage, Sarah and Amanda were chatting like old friends, and he was confident that this one aspect of her problem was solved. As for the rest…well, he didn't feel so hopeful. If she was Melanie's daughter, it would have to be proved, and he didn't know what Elizabeth Winthrop's reaction would be to the prospect of an illegitimate great-granddaughter showing up.

His uncomfortable line of thought was interrupted

by the arrival of Amos, Sarah's husband. Sarah filled him in with a quick rattle of Pennsylvania Dutch, at the end of which he nodded.

"Wilkom, Amanda. We're glad to have you here." He gave a quick glance at his wife. "Is there any apple pie left, by chance?"

"Only because I hid half a pie from you and the boys," she said. "Komm along to the house, all of you. We'll have a little snack, yah?"

The women went ahead, and Amos fell into step with Trey. He gave him a nudge with his elbow strong enough to make him stagger. "So you finally found a woman willing to look twice at you. Looks to me like you picked a fine one."

"Business," Trey said quickly. "She's here on business."

"Tell that to someone who hasn't known you most of your life," Amos said, his face splitting in a grin. "I saw the way you looked at her. You're caught at last, ain't so?"

"No such thing," he said firmly. "I'm doing some legal work for her, that's all."

"If you say so," Amos said, but Trey knew he wasn't buying it.

Just the kind of talk he didn't want to get around. And if he knew Sarah, she was thinking exactly the same thing as her husband. Maybe this hadn't been such a good idea after all.

CHAPTER FOUR

AMANDA HAD INTENDED to spend the afternoon at the library, but since Sarah said she could move in right away, Amanda headed back to the motel to check out and pack. By late afternoon, she'd settled in the cottage and was busy familiarizing herself with the workings of the gaslights and heating.

Barney, after giving the cottage a thorough going-over, had apparently decided to lay claim to the hearth rug in front of the fireplace. He circled a couple of times, sighed and lay down, resting his head on his paws.

"I'm glad you approve," she told him. "Since I'm not sure how long we'll be here."

She glanced at her watch, realizing that it was too late for even a cursory survey of the library's files. That would have to wait until tomorrow. In the meantime, she could make an opportunity to talk to Sarah. From what Trey had said, they'd lived here for ages. Sarah might remember something of the accident to Melanie Winthrop, even if it were just what Amanda had already heard.

Pausing at the window, Amanda looked down the lane that led to the farmhouse. A stand of evergreens surrounded the cottage, cutting off her view of most of the farm buildings and giving the cottage an air of privacy.

Trey's mention of her work in Lancaster County had probably sealed the deal, influencing Sarah to accept her. The Amish here were most likely one of the many daughter settlements from the Lancaster County Amish. She was annoyed that just the unexpected mention of that time had the power to make her stomach clench. Had he wondered why she'd been so terse about it?

Probably not. Trey barely knew her, even though they had been forced into a situation of some intimacy. He certainly didn't know about the disaster that had sent her scurrying back to Boston and her mother.

Juliet had never been in favor of her going into practice with Rick. *Better not to mix work and relationships*, she'd said, carefully avoiding any hint of censure of Rick O'Neill's character.

Juliet had been right, but she'd never so much as breathed an *I told you so* when Amanda came home, her relationship broken and her practice at an end. She'd dried Amanda's tears, insisted Rick wasn't good enough for her daughter and helped her find a new job.

It had been over a year. Rick should be a forgotten footnote in her life by now. Still, did anyone ever really get over the realization that their loved one was busily cheating all those times he'd been supposedly called out on a job?

Her cell phone rang before she could get too far along the road of beating herself up for being so wrong about him. The sight of Robert McKinley's number yanked her attention back to her current problems, and she answered quickly.

"Robert? How are you? Is there any news?" At least she'd managed to ask how he was before barreling into her own concerns.

"I'm just a little worried about you," he replied. "Are you all right?"

"Fine." She felt instantly guilty. "I'm sorry, I should have called you. I saw the attorney you recommended, and he's being helpful."

"You mean there's actually something in this...suspicion of yours?"

She suspected that he'd deleted the word *harebrained* from his question. "It seems like a good possibility that my mother was a young woman who lived here. Nothing is certain yet," she added quickly. "Please don't worry. I'm being cautious about it."

"I have to admit that I didn't think this trip would be useful, but this will be good news if it pans out. Just don't forget that the crucial question is whether or not Juliet legally adopted you."

Crucial from his perspective. Robert would always see things from the legal point of view. He wanted to take care of her as her mother would have, she supposed.

"I haven't forgotten, but it's worth exploring this lead if it turns out the woman was my mother. It will give you a place to look. Has your records search turned up anything?"

"Not yet, but it still may. When are you coming home?" There was an urgency in his voice that hadn't been there before.

"I don't know. Not until I'm satisfied one way or the other with what I've learned here. Why?"

Robert hesitated for so long that she thought he wasn't going to answer. Finally he spoke.

"I hate to bring this up, but unfortunately your uncle—well, Juliet's brother—has been nosing around. Maybe I'm wrong that he didn't suspect anything about your parentage. This must mean that he has some idea Juliet's will isn't entirely straightforward."

GOOD OLD GEORGE. Juliet had had no illusions about her brother's character, and she'd apparently been right.

"I wish you'd come back here." Robert sounded fretful. "I'd be happier if you were actually in residence at the house. Possession does count, you know."

"I understand. But I'd rather be searching for the truth of my parentage than sitting there in Boston waiting for the roof to cave in. Isn't knowing the truth more important?"

"I suppose," he admitted. "I just hope you're not opening up something that will hurt and disappoint you."

Poor Robert. She couldn't let him take care of her any more than Juliet had ever been willing to. "Thanks, Robert. It makes me feel better to know I have you in my corner. You're a sweetheart."

"Yes, well..." He became flustered, as he always did when touched by emotion. "Just take care of yourself. And give me your address, so I know where to find you."

After she'd given him the information he wanted and been soothed to the best of her ability, Amanda stood for a moment at the window, phone in hand. She glimpsed movement and spotted Sarah approaching up the path, carrying a basket on her arm.

Amanda opened the door even before Sarah reached it. Here was her chance to speak to Sarah privately, and she hadn't had to go looking for it. That seemed to bode well for her goal.

"Sarah, hi. Come in."

"I don't want to disturb you. Are you getting settled in all right?" Sarah's cheeks were like two red apples when she smiled.

"I'm all set. Thanks again, so much. The cottage is perfect. As you can see, Barney is making himself right at home."

Stepping inside, Sarah glanced at Barney, who was sitting up, looking, Amanda hoped, like a perfect gentleman. "It's gut you have him. I'd hate to think of you alone here."

Amanda shook her head. "I wouldn't be lonely, but he is good company." Sarah probably couldn't understand that, living in a house with so many family members crammed in.

"Well, here is some streusel coffee cake, just in case you get hungry before you have a chance to get groceries in. And milk. Just to tide you over."

"That's so nice of you." Amanda took the basket and set it on the kitchen table. The coffee cake looked so delicious she was tempted to have a piece immediately.

"Ach, it's nothing." Sarah waved a hand to dismiss her kind gesture. "I'm sure you have things to do. Trey said you have business in town."

Something about that sentence made it into a question. It seemed Sarah was as curious about her as she was about what Sarah might know.

"I'm here looking into some questions that came up after my mother's recent death. There seemed to be a...a connection to Echo Falls." How could she find out anything and still be as careful as Trey and Robert seemed to want?

"Ach, I'm so sorry for your loss." Sarah's face clouded, and she reached out and touched Amanda's hand lightly in sympathy. "It's hard to lose your mother."

Amanda nodded, her throat tightening. "Yes."

"So you said something about Echo Falls? Was your mother from here?" Sarah leaned against the table as if prepared to stay and talk for a while.

"Not exactly." She hesitated, trying to think how to ask the questions she wanted without getting into an explanation she didn't want to give. "But I think she may have been friends with someone who grew up here."

"Yah?" Sarah looked puzzled but interested.

"You might have known her. She died in an accident at the falls. Her name was Melanie Winthrop."

For an instant Sarah's face seemed to freeze. Then, before Amanda could say anything, she'd turned away and headed for the door.

"I... I'd forgotten something I must do. I'm sorry. I can't help you." She left without waiting for a goodbye.

Amanda stood at the door and watched her go— fleeing, almost, as if from something she didn't want to face. Slowly she closed the door.

Well. Amanda blew out a long breath. If that was the sort of reception she'd get whenever she mentioned the name Melanie Winthrop in this town, she wasn't likely to find out anything.

LEAVING THE LIBRARY behind the next day, Amanda walked toward the café. She'd agreed to meet Trey there for lunch to share the fruits of their efforts. When she'd suggested that they didn't need to have lunch together to do that, he'd countered with the fact that they'd have lunch in any event, so they may as well eat while they talked.

She hadn't found an argument to that, at least not without coming out and admitting that she was trying to prevent a repeat of the feelings she'd experienced the previous day at the falls.

Trey, however, seemed friendly in a businesslike way, and his manner reassured her. Once Esther waved them to a table in the corner, he looked around as if something were missing.

"No guard dog today?"

Amanda shook her head. "I thought he'd better stay at the cottage. Somehow I didn't think he'd be welcome at the library."

"No, I don't think so. Mrs. Gifford runs a tight ship. She used to make us kids empty our pockets before we went back to the stacks, just to be sure no sticky candy was going to get on her books."

She had to smile. "I did think her rather intimidating. To say nothing of curious. She seemed to find a lot of reasons to walk behind me while I was scanning the microfiche."

"That's unfortunate, but it's about what I expected. It won't be possible to keep your mission a secret very long."

Trey seemed to take that more seriously than she did. Maybe it was a sign of his mixed loyalties. Or possibly being overly cautious was part of the attorney's job description.

"I never thought keeping it quiet was a viable option. If I'm going to find answers, people will have to know what the questions are." A spurt of annoyance went through her. "What's wrong with that?"

"Isn't it obvious?" His eyebrows lifted, giving his face a momentary look of caricature. "The Winthrop family might well take offense at a stranger bringing up the painful past." He held up a hand when she would have spoken. "Okay, let's not go over the same ground again, especially when Esther is heading this way."

Maybe he was right. She tried to focus on the menu, but ended up ordering the chicken potpie because Esther seemed to expect it. Meanwhile she wrestled with the unpalatable fact that if she made enemies of these people to start with, they were hardly likely to be cooperative.

Once Esther had gone, Trey glanced around the café, and he was apparently satisfied that the other customers were focused on their own meals and conversations. "How did you make out with the newspaper accounts?"

Amanda shrugged off her irritation. "Slim, very slim. Pictures of the falls, an account of the difficulty the volunteers had in bringing her out, a sketchy account of her being spotted by a hiker. And a carefully worded obituary a day later." She toyed with her spoon. "It allowed me to visualize Melanie a little better, but it was short on helpful facts. I ran across a photo of her," she said, setting it on the table. "She looked very young, very naive. She was barely eighteen when she died." That was inexpressibly sad. Amanda glanced at Trey, to find him studying her face. "What? Do you see a resemblance?"

"Not in coloring, so much, but maybe in your features. What do you think?"

"I don't know." She'd wanted some confirmation one way or the other in the photo, but she didn't see it. Certainly no one had ever said she looked like Juliet, and now she knew why. "For an instant I thought she looked familiar, but then it passed. Anyway, a black-and-white newspaper photo hardly gives an idea of how someone looks."

"True enough. Did the newspaper say anything about where Melanie had been? Or mention her leaving town at all?"

Amanda shook her head. "It said she'd recently returned from a visit to friends in New York. I suppose that was what the family told the reporter."

"And he'd be unlikely to print anything else, even though the town had been whispering about Melanie's departure for months."

"But what was the point, if people already guessed the truth?" She let her exasperation spill over. "What's the use of trying to manipulate the news, then?"

"Darned if I know, but obviously it was important to the Winthrop family. Pride, I suppose. Things were a little different then in terms of what was acceptable."

"I guess. It's difficult to envision how much society has changed in the last thirty years or so." But this wasn't getting them anywhere. "What about you?"

"I didn't have much more luck with the records..."

He cut the words short when Esther arrived with their meals. Beaming, she slid steaming bowls in front of each of them and added a basket of rolls. "There now. You get that inside you, and you'll have plenty of energy for whatever you have to do today."

"It smells delicious," Amanda said. And it looked that way, too.

Esther picked up her tray, gratified. "I hear you're staying with the Burkhalter family."

She blinked. "How did you hear about that already? I just moved in yesterday afternoon."

"Ach, you haven't run into the Amish grapevine yet, ain't so? We don't need telephones for word to spread fast. You'll be happy there, I know. Sarah will take gut care of you."

"She's already brought me a streusel coffee cake, just to be sure I wouldn't go hungry," Amanda said. Somehow she doubted that any more gifts would be forthcoming, not if Sarah's abrupt departure at the mention of Melanie Winthrop meant anything about her future behavior.

"Ach, that's Sarah all right." Someone hailed Esther, and she moved off, unhurried.

Trey buttered a roll, watching her. "You looked a little funny when she mentioned Sarah. There's nothing wrong, is there?"

She wasn't sure she liked the fact that he could read her expressions so easily. "Something happened that was rather odd. Sarah and I were having a nice conversation, and she asked about what brought me to Echo Falls. I didn't tell her the whole story, but when I mentioned Melanie Winthrop she just…froze. I don't know how else to put it. Her whole manner changed. She said she had to do something and rushed away. I didn't know what to make of it."

Trey's forehead furrowed. "That is strange. I'm surprised she even knew about Melanie's disappearance. She wouldn't have been much more than in her early teens, I'd guess."

Shrugging, Amanda scooped up a fragrant spoonful of the chicken broth and noodles. "Teenagers seem to know everything. I don't suppose it was any different then."

"Could be." But he still looked troubled. "It's odd, all the same. I can't even guess what would make Sarah act that way. What did you say to her?"

Was he imagining that she'd given Sarah the third degree?

"I told you. I'd barely gotten Melanie Winthrop's name out before she reacted. I didn't have time to ask her anything."

He shook his head, frowning a little. "There has to be a reason, but I'd guess she wouldn't tell me, even if I asked."

"I'll cross her off my list of possible sources of information," she said. "How did you make out?"

"The court records showed little or nothing. There was an inquest, of course, but it was more a form than anything serious. It brought back the verdict of accidental death and expressed sympathy for the family."

So they'd been quick to sweep Melanie's death under the rug, in other words. "What about the postmortem?"

"There wasn't one." Trey's voice flattened, as if in disapproval. "The family was opposed to having it carried out, and according to the coroner, the cause of death was fairly obvious. Head injuries, as you might expect. Reading between the lines, I'd say the decision makers saw no point in going farther. An unfortunate accident or maybe a despairing suicide. They picked *accident*, issued a few warnings about the dangers of the falls trail and dropped it."

She pounced on his words. "So you think they didn't pursue it as they should have."

"I didn't say that." Frustration edged his voice. "Don't put your own spin on my words. If I'd been in that position, I might have done the same. It can't be easy to make that sort of decision when you know the people involved."

Obviously arguing the point wouldn't get her anywhere. "Sorry. What did the police chief say when you talked to him?"

"He wanted to know why I was asking, of course." He rested his spoon on the side of his empty bowl. Somehow he'd managed to scoop up a whole bowlful of potpie while they were talking. "As I predicted, he wasn't exactly eager to talk about a local scandal just to satisfy your curiosity, so I had to tell him why you're interested. Carmichaels won't gossip, at least."

She must have made an impatient movement, because he frowned before he went on.

"He didn't have much to say beyond what I'd already found in the records. He did confirm that the family agreed they hadn't heard anything from Melanie and didn't know she'd come back."

"That was strange, wasn't it? I mean, why would she return if not to be reconciled to her family? If she'd had the baby, she might have realized how difficult it was and wanted to have their help."

"I agree, that seems logical, but if they all said that she didn't approach them, I don't see how you can prove otherwise after all this time. It's a dead end." He made a gesture of finality.

She was beginning to think it delighted him to present obstacles. "Maybe I can't prove anything, but I have the right to ask questions. This is my life we're talking about and you—how do I know you're not trying to protect the Winthrops?"

Trey's face hardened. "You don't. You'll have to take me on trust. Or not. Look, what are you really after? To find your birth mother? If it was Melanie, you may never be able to prove it."

"It's not that simple." She couldn't keep the annoyance she felt from showing in her voice. "This isn't just a sentimental journey. I have to find proof, if it exists, that Juliet actually adopted me. Otherwise…"

"Otherwise I suppose you might stand to lose your inheritance from her." He was quick, she'd say that for him. "You must want that inheritance pretty badly to go to these lengths."

"Is that your considered objective opinion?" She put some frost in her voice, which wasn't all that easy when anger was like a fire on her nerves. She stood, grabbing her bag.

"Where are you going?" He got up, glancing around and lowering his voice. "Don't make a scene."

That infuriated her for a reason he couldn't understand and probably wouldn't appreciate if he did. "I'm going to see the police chief for myself." Her bag strap hooked over the chair, and she yanked it free.

Trey tossed some money on the table and grabbed her arm. "Not without me, you're not. He already knows you're my client, so don't even think about it."

She glared at him for a moment and then jerked a short nod. Like it or not, she seemed to be stuck with him.

THEY'D GOTTEN HALFWAY to the police station before Trey realized how ridiculous they must look, striding along without speaking or even glancing at each other.

"Sorry," he said. "I shouldn't have said that about your inheritance. Didn't her will make her wishes clear?"

Her expression tightened, if anything. "It says that she left everything to me, by name, but then it says, 'my daughter.' Robert's afraid..."

"Right, I see. That could conceivably leave it up to the interpretation of the judge if someone brought suit. Would anyone?"

"Robert says that Juliet's brother, George, has been asking questions. He must have some doubts."

Tricky. What might seem clear to a layperson could become anything but if it went to court. "Okay. Naturally you want to prove that you were Juliet Curtiss's daughter."

"I suppose..." She still didn't look at him, but she shook her head. "If you're asking me why this search is so important to me, I don't know how to answer. At first, my only goal was to find the proof of my adoption. Now that I have an idea of who my mother might have been..." She pressed her lips together as if in need of control. "I do know you can't imagine what it's like to have everything you've believed about yourself suddenly in question. Not until you experience it."

For an instant she looked lost, and Trey winced. He didn't want to be the one who caused that feeling.

"Sorry," he said again. He tried to think objectively about her situation. "Was there ever a time that you suspected the truth? Or questioned your mother?"

"Not really." Amanda seemed to look into the past. "Juliet always made me feel so secure. Even when someone kidded me about not inheriting her looks or her artistic talent, she laughed it off. I looked like my father, she said, and everyone had unique talents." She slanted a sideways look at him. "But I suppose you always wanted to be an attorney, like your dad."

"And my grandfather," he added, relieved that the ice had melted between them. "I don't know that I ever considered any other option. I was born to go into the family firm."

And it had nearly faltered on his watch. He could never forget how close they'd come. And how close they still were, for that matter.

"No siblings to take your place?" she asked.

"One sister. Shelley flirted with the idea of law school, but then a guy came along, and she decided she didn't want to spend that many more years in school."

"Married?"

"Yes, she's married and lives about an hour's drive from here. Three kids, so at least my mother's stopped expecting me to produce grandchildren for her."

"That must be a relief." Her lips curved, showing her dimple.

"It is," he said with emphasis. There was also the matter of his father's health to keep Mom occupied, so she'd stopped worrying about Trey's single status. Not that that would stop her from putting in her two cents' worth if he so much as went to a movie with a female.

"Here we are." He nodded at the mellowed brick building that had been the police station for a hundred years. Its classic lines were a bit distorted by the one-story, three-bay garage with its metal roof, providing space for emergency vehicles.

He considered asking her to exercise a little discretion with Chief Carmichaels, but feared doing so would have the opposite effect. At least she was in a better mood than when they'd left the café.

Chief Mike Carmichaels was in and willing, albeit reluctantly, to see them. Once they were seated in the chief's minuscule office, Carmichaels leaned back in his creaking desk chair and surveyed Amanda with a speculative look on his square, honest face.

"So you claim you might be the Winthrop girl's child, I hear from Trey."

Amanda perched on the edge of her chair, looking wired enough to dart from it at any instant. "I'm not making any claims, Chief Carmichaels. I just want to know the truth. It came as such a shock to learn that I wasn't who I thought. There must have been some relationship between my mother—between Juliet Curtiss—and Melanie Winthrop. I'd have been two months old when Melanie died. You can see why I might wonder if that's the answer to who I am."

Mike's expression softened, and Trey saw he'd been moved by Amanda's words. So maybe it hadn't been a mistake for her to talk to him.

Carmichaels cleared his throat. "I get that. Trouble is, I don't see any way of proving it one way or another—not unless someone from the family agreed to DNA testing."

Amanda slid back on the chair, sending Trey a look that might have contained a little triumph. "That would be the only definitive answer to my parentage, but I'd want to feel more sure of the facts myself before I'd even ask them to do that. So I hoped you might help me."

"How?" The chief's gray eyes became guarded. He might be sympathetic to Amanda, but he wouldn't be eager to alienate Elizabeth Winthrop.

She hadn't mentioned the need to find out whether or not she'd been legally adopted, but Carmichaels didn't need to know the importance of determining that. He couldn't know anything.

"Just tell me anything you remember about what happened when Melanie died. For instance, were you able to find out when Melanie had arrived back in town?"

He seemed to look at that question from every angle before deciding to answer it. "No, we weren't. That was odd. We couldn't even find out how. She hadn't come on the bus, and there was no abandoned car that might have belonged to her."

So the police had been more thorough than Trey had thought. Mike would have been a patrolman then, and Clifford Barnes the chief. Too bad Clifford wasn't around any longer to answer any questions.

"Strange," Trey said while Amanda seemed to digest the chief's words, sifting them for anything useful. "It almost sounds as if someone drove her to town and dropped her off. But if so, you'd expect them to come forward when she died."

Carmichaels moved as if he'd suddenly found his chair uncomfortable. "Unless she'd been hitchhiking and was dropped off by a stranger. That was what Chief Barnes decided must have happened."

"You didn't agree?" Amanda was onto the doubt in his voice in an instant.

But he stiffened. "It wasn't my business to disagree with the chief." He shrugged. "Besides, I wasn't in on any of the decision-making. Too high up for me at that stage."

To forestall Amanda making another remark about toadying to the powerful, Trey broke in with a question. "What about the person who found her? I never did hear who that was."

"An Amish kid from one of the nearby farms, it was. Course there weren't any cell phones then, even if he'd been allowed to have one. Way he told it, she was partly in the water at the base of the falls. He pulled her out."

"She was dead already?" Trey asked.

Carmichaels nodded, his face grave. "As I recall, he realized pretty quick it was too late, but he ran all the way to the nearest place with a phone. You can imagine how long it was until we actually got on scene." The chief fell silent, staring down at the green blotter on his desk as if he saw again that tragic image. "The chief and I got there first, but the rescue crew wasn't far behind. I could hear them crashing through the woods with their gear while we were standing there looking down at her, all broken…"

He stopped abruptly, probably realizing he might be talking to Melanie's daughter.

Amanda drew a shaky breath. She was probably trying to think what else to ask. "Do you know his name? The boy who found her, I mean."

"Let me think a minute. It was one of the Miller kids, I believe, but I don't remember which one." He shook his head. "It'll come to me. I'll let you know when I think of it."

"Why wasn't there a postmortem?" Obviously that was still bothering Amanda.

"Like I say, that wasn't my decision. Besides, it was obvious what caused her death." His face tightened. "If you'd seen her…well, I wouldn't wish that on anyone. That's a long way down, and nothing but rocks and water at the bottom."

That shook Amanda visibly. He suspected she was finding it impossible to hold on to the detachment she'd had initially. It was probably coming home to her just what kind of Pandora's box she was opening with her search.

The silence that fell was his cue to get her out before she had a chance to push too hard with Chief Carmichaels. He stood, holding out his hand.

"Thanks, Chief. It was good of you to answer my client's questions."

He shrugged it off. "No problem. After all these years, I'd think it's impossible to find out much of anything, but I can understand why Ms. Curtiss wants to know."

Amanda stood, managing a smile. "Thank you. If I have any other questions, I hope I can come to you."

Carmichaels's expression stiffened, but he nodded. He went to the door and opened it, obviously just as glad to see them out.

A wave of sympathy swept over Trey as he walked beside Amanda out of the office. Amanda was still grieving the loss of the woman who had always been her mother. Now she had the challenge of mourning a birth mother, as well. How did anyone cope with that load of trouble?

CHAPTER FIVE

DARKNESS SEEMED TO fall earlier here than in the city. Especially when she was alone in the cottage with just Barney for company. Amanda knew that was an illusion, caused by the lack of ambient light in the surroundings, but it was isolating.

She crumpled the paper in front of her and tossed it in the direction of the trash can. And then got up to throw it into the can when it landed on the floor.

Barney, who'd been lying on the rug he'd appropriated as his own, raised his head and looked at her.

"I know, I know. I'd better give it up for a bad job."

She'd been trying to compose a letter to Elizabeth Winthrop, explaining the situation and asking for an interview, but she couldn't find the right words. One draft had sounded pleading, another vaguely threatening. Neither was the impression she wanted to make on the woman who might be her great-grandmother.

There had been a photo of Elizabeth accompanying one of the newspaper articles—obviously a staged head shot. Even in that, the lined face had portrayed both grimness and determination. A woman with a face like that wasn't likely to be guided by emotion.

At least Amanda's research had given her a clearer picture of the Winthrop family. Melanie had been the daughter of Elizabeth's only son. He and his wife had been killed in a plane crash when Melanie was only a few months old, leaving Elizabeth to raise their child.

Elizabeth had a daughter as well, Betty Ann, who was much younger than her brother. An afterthought? An accident? Who could say?

Betty Ann was married to Donald Shay. From what Amanda had been able to glean, Shay ran the mill and managed the various properties owned by the family.

Aunt Betty. Uncle Donald. No, she didn't imagine she'd ever be on those terms with them. Especially when she couldn't compose a simple letter stating her case. All of this searching and interviewing was frustrating, when a DNA test could give the answer.

And it still wouldn't tell her whether Juliet had legally adopted her. If Robert's investigators weren't able to find anything one way or the other, what then? Did she have any rights at all? She and Robert hadn't discussed the worst-case scenario, and maybe they should have. Juliet had referred to Amanda as her daughter in her will. She'd think that would count for something with a judge, assuming it went that far.

She could ask Trey, she supposed. Always assuming he wasn't fed up with her and her problems. She'd lost her temper with him earlier. Or maybe it was fairer to say that they'd both been exasperated with each other, but he'd been the first to extend an olive branch.

Barney raised his head again, but this time he wasn't looking at her. He stared for a long moment at the front window of the cottage, as if looking for something out there in the dark.

"What is it, boy?" She went to the window and peered out, but could see nothing. The darkness was complete except for the rectangle of yellow light that lay across the porch from the window. "There's nothing."

Barney whined a little in apparent disagreement. He got up, padding softly from one window to the next. A little frisson of alarm slid down her spine.

"Come on, Barney. Are you trying to unnerve me?" She forced herself to turn away from the windows and took hold of his collar.

Barney gave a sudden, sharp bark, followed by a volley of barking and a lunge at the window. She swung around, and her heart jumped into her throat. Something—a face—pressed against the window, distorted by the glass.

Then the person withdrew a few inches and raised a hand in a wave. Amanda had a hysterical desire to laugh. It wasn't a monster or an enemy pressing against the glass. It was Bertram Berkley, her mother's agent. What was he doing here? She couldn't imagine anything that would take him away from the city.

She went to the door, clutching Barney's collar while she reassured him. Unlocking the door, she swung it open.

"Bertram! What are you doing here? You startled me. I didn't hear your car."

"Are you mad?" He hustled inside as if eager for shelter against the dark. "Drive my car up the rutted lane? Never. I left it down by the farmhouse. That road is bad enough." He shuddered elaborately, overacting as always.

"Come now, it's not that terrible. I've been bringing my SUV in and out with no problems." She closed the door, realizing that he hadn't answered her question about why he was here.

"Forgive me, dear, but your SUV is not a mint condition BMW."

"Then you should have rented something more sensible to come here. And what are you doing here, anyway? If you'd called…"

"If I'd called, you'd have told me to stay in Boston." He seated himself in the most comfortable chair and adjusted the crease in his trousers. "The famous Bertram Berkley charm doesn't come across as well on the telephone."

Amused in spite of herself, Amanda smiled as she sat down across from him. After a suspicious sniff at Bertram's shoes, Barney returned to his hearth rug. Silence fell, almost oppressive. Bertram had brought a different atmosphere with him, but she couldn't say it was an improvement.

She studied him, trying to figure out what he was feeling, but as always, she had a sense that his face reflected a carefully cultivated facade. "What's so important that you chased me all the way up here on a workday to talk about? If this is about putting on a show again…"

"It's Friday, dear," he said gently. "I'm taking the weekend off. How better to enjoy it than a nice trip into the Pennsylvania mountains?"

"I should think a nice trip into New York City would be more to your taste." He was right; it was Friday. She'd lost track of the days since she'd been here. Echo Falls seemed to exist in a world of its own.

"True." He sighed elaborately. "But I'm endlessly self-sacrificing when it comes to my work."

"I'm afraid you're wasting your time. I'm really

not at a place where I want to talk about my mother's painting yet. It's too soon."

"My dear girl, it's not too soon at all. The time to do a tribute to Juliet Curtiss is now, while she's still in the public mind."

"You mean you want to capitalize on her death." She should have realized Bertram wouldn't give up so easily. Her mother had been able to shut him down when he got carried away, but Amanda had yet to develop that gift.

"Not capitalize." He shook his head, his expressive face drawing down into lines of sorrow, either at Juliet's death or at Amanda's failure to recognize his opinion. "A tribute, I said. We must remind the public of what has been so needlessly lost. A gifted artist, cut off in her prime by this horrific plague of gun violence—it's a comment on our time."

Amanda rubbed her forehead. "I can see some sense in what you're saying, and I know you mean well. But I really can't focus on that now. We'll plan it together once I get past the shock, all right?"

She thought he looked as if he'd like to tell her she'd had three whole weeks to recover, but maybe she was wrong.

"That will be too late." He leaned forward, intent. "Don't you see? The market for Juliet Curtiss's work is at an all-time high right now. We can't let this slip away. You're losing money with every week that passes."

He meant sales. She supposed he knew what he was talking about, but... Then reality hit her like a hammer blow. Did she even have the right to sell Juliet's paintings? A pit seemed to open in front of her, warning of all the possible missteps she could be taking.

That was another unarguable reason why she couldn't agree with Bertram about the show he wanted. And it was one she didn't dare tell him. She didn't have any illusions about Bertram, any more than her mother had had.

Bertram's good at what he does or I wouldn't let him near my work. But his moral sense is nonexistent.

"Here." Bertram pulled a folder from the leather portfolio he'd carried in with him, thrusting it toward her. "I have all the details worked out. You'll see. It will be perfect, and you don't have to do a thing."

She took the folder because it was easier than arguing. She'd need to have legal advice before she sold even one of her mother's paintings, but she couldn't tell him that.

"I'll look it over, I promise. I'll let you know what I think. But it's still going to have to wait awhile. Maybe next month."

Maybe by next month she'd know whether she had any rights at all in Juliet's estate, including the right to sell any of her paintings. For a moment despair swept over her. How was she going to deal with this? She didn't doubt that Juliet thought everything had been settled with her will. If only she'd confided in Robert, or even in Amanda…

But that wouldn't help her in dealing with Bertram right at the moment.

Anger had narrowed his eyes. "Next month? But I've explained all that already. Really, Amanda, you'll have to trust me in this regard. Your mother would have understood the importance of timing. Even her brother sees that..."

"Her brother? George Curtiss?" Whether he was still Uncle George was up for debate. "When did you talk to him? And why?"

Bertram seemed to realize he'd made a misstep. He stretched his hands out in a placating motion, but it was too late for that.

"Well?" She stood, giving herself the advantage of height. "Why were you discussing my business with George?"

Bertram turned sulky. "He's an interested party, isn't he? After all, he was Juliet's brother. Her closest relative. After you. Really, Amanda, I'm just trying to do my best for you."

Whether there was any suspicion or malicious intent in his words, she didn't know, but she certainly wasn't going to let herself be intimidated by him. Bertram would be doing what was best for him.

Anger stiffened her spine. "I expect discretion from you, Bertram. You shouldn't be discussing my business with anyone else, including George Curtiss. If I don't feel assured of your discretion and loyalty, I will put my mother's work into other hands. Is that clear?"

She didn't know whether she had the right to do that, either, but she suspected it would be an effective threat.

"All right, all right. I'm sorry." He rose, regaining his usual urbane smile. "I'm sure you'll be satisfied with my work. After all, your mother trusted me to handle everything. With her input, of course," he added hastily, maybe reading a rebuttal in her face. "Look, why don't you let me take you out someplace

for a glass of wine and a bite to eat? Surely this burg
has one decent restaurant that's open on Friday night."

"I've already eaten, thanks. And you'd better be on
your way to wherever you're staying tonight."

Bertram gave a speculative glance around the cottage. "If you have an extra bedroom, maybe you could
put me up."

So he could resume his argument in the morning.
She didn't think so.

"I'm afraid not," she said, blandly ignoring the guest
room. "You'll find quite a nice motel near Williamsport." She opened the door. Barney rose to his feet,
responsive to her cues, as if ready to hasten Bertram's
departure.

"But really, Amanda…" He broke off when Barney
gave a warning growl in response to his tone. "Very
well. I'll call you in the morning. At least lend me a
flashlight to get back down the excuse for a driveway."

Amanda went to the kitchen drawer where she'd
found a small flashlight. "Here you are. Don't disturb
the Burkhalters, but just leave it on their back porch.
I'll get it tomorrow."

He went out and then turned back. "Maybe we could
meet for breakfast in the morning. Just so you can give
me your reaction to the plans."

"I'm afraid I'm busy tomorrow. You may as well
get on the road without bothering to come back to
town. I'll email you once I've had a chance to look
over your plans."

He hesitated, as if thinking of making a comeback,
but Barney came and pressed against Amanda's leg, effectively filling the doorway. "Very well. Good night."
He flicked on the flashlight and marched off.

Amanda stood on the porch and watched the circle of light until it disappeared when he rounded a bend in the lane. Then the darkness closed in on her, and she shivered. Silly. But she wasn't sure when she'd last felt so alone.

NORMALLY TREY SPENT Saturday catching up on the chores he'd neglected all week in the press of work. Since he'd bought the small Craftsman bungalow on Oak, he'd learned that homeownership brought with it far more responsibilities than he'd anticipated.

Today, for instance, he should be raking and bagging leaves. But it was one of those rare, beautiful October days when the sun was warm and the world around him seemed touched by golden light. It demanded that a person get out and enjoy it, before November brought cold, rainy days and the prospect of early snow.

His fallen leaves continued to form a brown and orange carpet over the small lawn, while he headed out to the Burkhalter farm. Not necessarily to see Amanda, he assured himself. But he'd been troubled by what she'd said about Sarah, and he wanted to see for himself. He couldn't imagine Sarah being anything but friendly and welcoming.

Amanda must have misunderstood. He'd see Sarah, straighten it out, and at the same time find out if she knew who the Amish boy was who'd found Melanie's body. She was bound to know, or at least be able to find out. In fact, it had probably been one of her kinfolk. Mike had said it was one of the Miller kids, and Sarah had been a Miller before she married Amos.

Trey turned up the lane that led to the cottage, raising a hand to Amos, who was heading toward the barn. When he pulled up at the cottage, Amanda came out on the porch. He felt a wave of pleasure at the sight of her. Wearing jeans and a flannel shirt, her hair pulled back and fastened at her nape, she looked as if she belonged here.

"I wasn't expecting to see you today." She spoke as he got out of the car, coming toward him.

"I took a chance you'd be here. Thought I'd like to have a word with Sarah to see if she can identify the boy who found Melanie's body."

An expression of doubt crossed Amanda's face. "I told you she hasn't been exactly forthcoming on the subject, didn't I?"

"Yes, but sometimes the Amish can seem standoffish when they're not aware of it. Sarah has known me since I was a kid." He grinned. "In fact, she used to babysit me when she was a teenager. Let me try my luck."

Amanda shrugged, conceding, and they started down the path together. "I wondered how you came to be such close friends with the Burkhalter family. I'll have to ask Sarah what kind of kid you were."

"Obedient and well-behaved, of course," he said lightly. "My father owns some land that adjoins the Burkhalter farm. He doesn't have any use for it, so he lets Amos keep it in hay. That kind of gave me free run of the farm. I loved it out here." He looked around at the golden hillside, the fields a patchwork now of gold and brown. "I still do."

They approached the house and found Sarah hanging a row of sheets on the line. She pinned the last one in place and then turned to face them.

"Trey. I thought that might be your car I heard." She flickered a meaningful glance toward Amanda. "Amos is in the barn if you are wanting to see him."

"Actually, I'd like a word with you. We've been asking a few questions about Melanie Winthrop's accident up at the falls all those years ago. I understand it was one of the Miller boys who found her."

There was no mistaking it. Sarah's pleasant face froze, just as Amanda had said. She didn't volunteer anything.

"Was it one of your brothers?" he asked.

She shook her head at the direct question.

"Who, then?" He hated pressing her when she didn't want to answer, but her very attitude suggested she knew something that might be helpful to Amanda.

He'd never know if she would answer him directly, because she was staring past them, toward the barn. "Look at Amos! Something is wrong."

He and Amanda swung around simultaneously. Amos came running toward them. "A phone!" he shouted. "Do you have your cell phone?"

Trey yanked his out even as Amanda reached toward her pocket. "Here you go. What's up?"

But Amos was already connecting. "Is Doc Wilson there?" He paused, listening. "Yah, well, this is Amos Burkhalter. The Percheron mare is foaling, and she's in trouble. Send Doc out as fast as you reach him."

He thrust the phone back at Trey and was already hastening back to the barn. To Trey's surprise, Amanda went right along with him.

"Has she been waxing and bagging up?" He heard her ask, following after them. "Did her water break yet?"

"Yah, she's been pacing and getting up and down. For sure she's foaling but something's wrong. The foal's not moving like it should."

Amanda nodded. "There's not much time, then."

Foolish of him, but he'd forgotten for the moment that Amanda was a vet. Clearly Amos hadn't. He was confiding in her as if depending on her.

If something went wrong... Trey hurried to keep up with their pace. He didn't know much about the legalities of veterinary practice, but he sure hoped Amanda wasn't going to make herself liable in any way.

When they got inside, Trey stood blinking for a moment, letting his eyes adjust to the dimness. The big box stall on the end was the one he'd seen in use before when a horse was foaling. But this wasn't just any mare. This was one of the team of prize Percherons that Amos had invested in. He knew how much was hanging on that animal.

He caught Amanda's arm. "Shouldn't you wait for the vet? Doc Wilson is a good man. He'll come right out..."

"Amos says he's out already. He thinks it'll take him a good thirty minutes at least. That might be too late."

This was an Amanda he hadn't seen before—calm, assured, confident in her role. She gave him a smile that was probably meant to be reassuring and stepped into the stall.

He found he was holding his breath. The Percheron mare was so huge that Amanda looked like a child next to her.

"There, now, sweetheart." She ran her hand along the mare's side as she walked through the thick bedding of fresh straw. "Let's see what's wrong."

Trey didn't consider himself squeamish, but he was just as glad he didn't have a good view while Amos and Amanda held a quiet-voiced conversation at the rear of the animal. The mare was switching her tail back and forth, and it took the two of them to wrap it in a bandage.

With the tail safely confined, Amanda folded back her sleeves. Amos handed her a pair of rubber gloves, and she shoved her hands into them. Then she reached into the mare.

Surprisingly to him, the mare didn't seem to object. After a long interval, she withdrew her hand, shedding the gloves. She came to the front of the stall to sluice her hands in the bucket of sudsy water Amos had waiting there.

"Well?" He leaned his shoulder against the gate. "What do you think?"

She was frowning, regarding the mare with a concerned look. He had the feeling that she barely recognized who was speaking. "It's unusual for a mare to begin in the middle of the day, and not a good sign that we're not seeing the first foreleg yet. That should come along quickly if all is going well. I can just feel it, but it's not coming out because it's doubled back."

Amos joined them, looking at Amanda with a confidence that surprised Trey. "What do you think?"

"We can walk her around for a bit to see if the foal slips back into place. If so, the leg may unfold on its own. And maybe your vet will have arrived by then."

Amos nodded. "Walking her was my thinking, too. But not for long." Worry formed creases between his narrowed eyes. "We might have to help the foal out."

"We might, but let's not worry about that until we get there," Amanda said, giving his arm a pat.

She unlatched the stall door. "Trey, hold this clear open so it doesn't bump against her when we bring her out."

She assumed control of the situation effortlessly. He admired people who knew their business and went about it without fuss. Amanda was clearly one of those.

Remembering that she'd worked for a time with a large animal operation in Lancaster County reassured him. She'd be licensed in Pennsylvania then, he supposed, not that he knew much of anything about how that worked.

Trey held the door, grateful to keep the wooden barrier between himself and the mare. She was still restless. Even his untutored eyes could make that out. He closed the door once she was clear of it.

Then his only function was to wait while Amos and Amanda walked the mare down and back up the aisle between the stalls. The animal seemed willing enough, but her head was down and her gait slow.

Sarah came into the barn and joined him in watching the others. "I left the boys watching for the vet's car. I pray he comes soon. It would break Amos's heart to lose Daisy or the foal."

"Good thing Amanda is here," he pointed out.

"Yah," she said slowly. "I guess." She fell quiet, and he could almost hear her thoughts spinning. "Tell me," she said at last. "Why is Amanda so interested in the Winthrop girl's accident?"

"Not just the accident," he said. Obviously Amanda hadn't confided in her. "Amanda is trying to find out who her birth mother was and whether she was legally adopted. There's some indication it might have been Melanie Winthrop."

Sarah gasped, looking as if she'd just had the wind knocked out of her. "I didn't... I didn't understand." She looked at Amanda as if for the first time, her eyes wide. "That's different."

He studied her face, not understanding. It seemed there was more going on than he knew where Sarah was concerned. Or maybe more accurately, her family. He was about to question her when the mare, who'd been walking along docilely enough, head drooping, suddenly seemed to buckle at the knees.

"She's going down," Amanda said. "Try to keep her up while I check her."

Cajoling and scolding, Amos managed to keep the mare on her feet while Amanda went what seemed to Trey to be dangerously close to the mare's hindquarters.

"We've got a foreleg!" she exclaimed. "Looks like this baby has decided to arrive. Let's get her into the box stall before she lays down."

"Praise the Lord," Sarah murmured.

Once they were in, Trey watched from his spot outside the stall. The mare lay down almost as soon as they got her inside. She looked even bigger, it seemed to him, taking up much of the stall. Amanda took a few steps away, closer to him.

"If she starts to deliver on her own, we'll let her. I don't want to intervene unless I have to."

But it seemed she had spoken too soon. The mare began thrashing around. Amanda and Amos moved quickly to try to calm her. Hovering outside the stall, he couldn't hear the low-voiced conversation going on between Amos and Amanda, but he could see their concerned expressions.

He winced when he saw Amanda reaching carefully into the mare in an apparent attempt to ease the foal's passage.

Whatever she was doing, it seemed to be taking forever. His tension rose, and he found he was gripping the stall bar until the wood bit into his fingers. If something went wrong...

And then the foal came sliding out, as if the last hurdle had been passed.

"Good job." The gruff voice behind Trey startled him, and he swung to see the local vet standing there.

"Doc Wilson!" Amos looked equally surprised, while Amanda's expression was one of apprehension.

She stepped away from the mare. "Dr. Wilson, if you'd like to take over..."

"No need." He elbowed his way past Trey to enter the box stall. "Looks to me like you have everything under control. This little one was hung up, was he?" He bent for a closer look at the colt, now struggling to get his feet under him.

"The foreleg was folded back." Amanda went into some technicalities that Trey hadn't a hope of following. Doc Wilson was nodding, his normally dour old face relaxed as they checked out mother and baby together.

Finally, the three of them exited the stall. Amanda motioned him to join them, and they all backed away. "We'll leave her alone for a bit," she said softly. "She'll probably stay down for a little longer before she stands."

"But they're all right?" he asked.

"Fine." She gave him a surprised glance. "Were you worried?"

"I wouldn't want Amos to lose his pride and joy. Or for you to be involved in anything...unpleasant."

For an instant he thought she'd flare up at him, but then she grinned. "You really do see everything as an attorney, don't you?"

"Not necessarily." He held her gaze until he saw a faint flush on her cheeks.

"Looks like you've got a fine animal there, Amos." Doc Wilson spoke, drawing them back into the general conversation. "He'll be worth a pretty penny to you one day."

Amanda leaned over the bucket of fresh water Sarah had brought, sluicing it over her arms. "Sorry I took over your patient, Dr. Wilson."

The vet grunted. "Nothing I would have done any different. Went to Penn, did you?"

Amanda nodded. "I was with a large animal practice in Lancaster County for a time, but I've been working in Boston for the past year or two." She glanced at the mare and foal. "I didn't realize how much I'd missed this."

"Not easy, working in a farming area, with folks calling you in the middle of the night for a buggy horse with the colic." That comment must have been aimed at Amos, because he grinned. "It has its rewards, though." He peered at her over the tops of his glasses. "You ever decide to get back to it, I've been thinking I should take on a partner. I'm getting too old to do it all."

"I...thank you, sir." Amanda actually flushed at the implied compliment.

It was more of a compliment than she knew. Doc Wilson had high standards. He wouldn't make an offer like that lightly. For a moment Trey toyed with the idea of having Amanda in Echo Falls to stay.

Still, that wasn't likely to happen. Things were bound to get messy with the Winthrop family, one way or the other. Of course Elizabeth might be glad to have a piece of her granddaughter back, even glad enough to tolerate the resulting publicity. Or she might reject the whole thing. It was impossible to calculate which.

And Amanda would probably be glad to go back to Boston and forget about this place.

"Well, I'd better get cleaned up." Amanda looked down at her once pristine shirt and jeans.

"I'll wait," he said. He hadn't forgotten the reason he'd come.

"You bring those clothes down once you've changed, and I'll wash them with ours," Sarah said. "And Amanda…" Her face bloomed with her smile. "Denke. Thank you."

Amanda nodded and scurried off to change her clothes. He watched her go before turning back to the others.

"Seems like we could all do with coffee and shoofly pie, ain't so?" Amos turned away from the stall after another look at the new baby.

"Ach, you think it's always time for that," Sarah said. "You'll have some, ain't so, Doc?"

"Lead me to it." Doc Wilson slung his jacket over his shoulder.

As they walked toward the farmhouse, Sarah fell behind a step or two with Trey. "What we were talking about before..." She spoke hesitantly. "The person you want is my cousin, Jacob Miller."

So something had changed Sarah's mind about cooperating. Maybe it was Amanda's actions, or maybe it was the reason behind her need to know. He'd love to know which, but he probably wouldn't.

"Jacob Miller." His mind ran through the Millers he knew...a large group, since Miller was a common Amish name around the area. But he didn't come up with a Jacob.

"I don't think I know your cousin Jacob."

"No, you wouldn't." Sarah was frowning, seeming to study something he didn't see. "Jacob left here a long time ago. He's settled out in Ohio now, in one of the large Amish communities in Holmes County."

"Can you tell me how we can reach him?"

Sarah was silent for so long that he thought she wasn't going to answer. She looked at him.

"I shouldn't speak for him. You see that, don't you? It was a terrible thing, him finding the Winthrop girl like that. I'll get in touch with him and explain the situation, yah? Then if he's willing to talk to you about it, I'll let you know."

He'd like to press, but long experience of Sarah told him she wouldn't respond when she'd made up her mind that something was the right action. At least there was a chance that Jacob would be willing to talk, but it was a very long chance that he'd know something that would help.

CHAPTER SIX

THE NEXT AFTERNOON Barney gave the low bark that announced someone was approaching the cottage. A quick glance out the window showed Sarah Burkhalter. Amanda felt a flutter of anticipation. Would Sarah have been in touch with her cousin so quickly? Surely not on a Sunday. She'd seen the buggies roll out the driveway early this morning, taking them all to worship, and felt like a sluggard in comparison.

She tamped down her anticipation. When he'd told her about Sarah's admission, Trey had pointed out that the chance that the boy had anything useful to contribute was slim. After all, he'd apparently come upon the scene when Melanie was already dead. If there'd been anything else, surely the police chief would have known.

Still, it was encouraging that Trey was determined to follow any lead, no matter how slight, that might give her some answers. That kind of meticulous focus on details was essential in her own work, and she appreciated it when she found it in other people.

She opened the door before Sarah could knock and found a fragrant loaf of bread thrust in her hand. "We had this left from lunch after church, and I thought you could make use of it."

Sarah looked slightly uncomfortable, making

Amanda suspect that the bread was in the nature of a peace offering. "Thanks so much. Mmm, smells wonderful. Come in. You have time for a cup of coffee, don't you?"

"You're going somewhere, ain't so?" Sarah nodded to the bag that was already on Amanda's shoulder.

"Just into town, but that will wait." She led the way into the cottage's tiny kitchen. "It won't take a minute for the coffee."

"If you're sure." Sarah sat down at the round table, glancing around the kitchen. "Are you finding everything you need here? I'm sorry about the electricity, but most of the Englisch folks who rent the cottage are looking to live like the Amish for a week."

"They appreciate that, do they?" Amanda asked.

Sarah chuckled. "I think they leave eager to get back to their modern appliances."

"You have everything a person needs here. I confess, I was puzzled at first over keeping my phone charged up, but it's working fine to do it in the car."

"Gut, gut. Amos said maybe you'd want to charge it on the generator we have in the barn for the milk cooler, but I didn't think you'd want to leave it there. Not that anyone would bother it."

"I'll keep the possibility in mind." She poured the coffee she'd reheated and brought the mugs to the table. "Milk? Sugar?"

"Just black." Sarah took a sip of the hot coffee, as if buying time. "I wanted to tell you that I have written to my cousin. I was going to telephone and leave a message, but it seemed like I could explain it in a letter."

Amanda hid her disappointment at the prospect of

waiting for days for a response. "I understand. He'll have a chance to think it over before he responds."

"Yah." The slight frown between Sarah's eyebrows suggested that something still troubled her. She gulped down some more coffee, and Amanda thought she searched for a change of subject. "Amos said you checked on the mare and the colt first thing this morning."

"They're doing fine. He's a good, strong little guy. Being demanding about being fed already, I noticed. The mare is getting her strength back quickly." She grinned. "Horses get tired from the work of labor, just like humans do. But the little guy won't let her get too relaxed."

"Ach, that's a male for you," Sarah said, her face relaxing. "You know how thankful we are for what you did. Doc Wilson told Amos he couldn't have done it better himself, and Doc doesn't go around handing out compliments."

"That was good of him." She was unaccountably pleased.

Sarah made it sound as if the elderly vet might have been serious about his offer. Not that she'd ever be able to stay here, given the way things were unfolding, but it served as a good reminder that she hadn't been doing what she really wanted in her current job. No matter how this turned out, maybe it was time to make some changes in her life.

Sarah drained her coffee and carried her mug to the sink. "I'd best let you be on your way. I just wanted to ask you to have supper with us tomorrow night. Unless you and Trey have other plans," she added.

She opened her mouth to deny that she and Trey had

any plans beyond the job at hand, but then decided it was better to ignore the implication.

"I'll be happy to come to supper tomorrow. Thank you."

Sarah nodded briskly. If she wondered what was taking Amanda back to town on a Sunday afternoon, she didn't ask.

Just as well, wasn't it? Amanda picked up her bag and followed her out, closing the door on Barney's hopeful face. She wasn't sure where she was going, and he'd be better off in the cottage than shut in the car for the afternoon. She'd take him for a good long run later.

She didn't know herself what she hoped to accomplish in town on a Sunday, but it had occurred to her to wonder about Juliet's visit to Echo Falls. Juliet must have come here. She'd never have painted the falls from a photograph. Given what she'd written on the back of the painting, that trip had been in the nature of a pilgrimage.

Juliet had wanted to visit the place where Melanie died. That meant they had been friends at one time, didn't it? Maybe someone here remembered that visit. Maybe it had even been someone who'd known why she was here.

Amanda considered that as she turned onto the blacktop road. No, that wasn't likely, was it? There'd never been a hint that Juliet had any connection to Echo Falls other than that one visit. Still, it might be possible to find out where she'd stayed when she was here. Knowing that would help her put herself in her mother's shoes.

Telling you nothing, a voice jeered in the back of her mind.

She wasn't ready to give up, even though the chance of finding out anything about Juliet's visit was slim. Actually, there weren't many options for a place to stay. When she'd been looking for a place herself, there had been two bed-and-breakfast inns, an old-fashioned hotel that didn't look as if it had seen a customer in a generation and one tavern that let rooms that Juliet wouldn't have touched with a ten-foot pole. Neither would Amanda, for that matter.

Driving down Main Street, Amanda realized she'd left something out of her calculations. Esther's café was apparently an institution, and Esther was someone who took an interest in anyone who came through her door. She might remember something about Juliet. It couldn't have been that usual to have an artist in town to paint the falls.

Deciding to start there, Amanda took the first parking space she saw and walked to the café. A motorcycle roared by, disturbing the peace of the Sunday afternoon, and then the quiet sank in again.

Closed Sundays read the neat sign on the café door. Of course. What was wrong with her? She should have remembered that Amish-run businesses weren't open on Sundays.

Well, the inns would be open. She could try there, so the trip wouldn't be entirely wasted.

Amanda turned from the café door and came face-to-face with a young woman. Thinking she wanted to enter the café, Amanda stepped aside so that she could see the Closed Sundays sign. But the woman moved with her, so that they were still facing each other.

"I want to talk to you."

Amanda blinked. She'd never seen the woman before. "I'm afraid you've mistaken me for someone else."

"No, I haven't." The woman almost spat the words, and her pretty face was distorted with anger. "I'm Carlie Shay. Carlie *Winthrop* Shay. And you're the woman who's going around claiming to be related to my family."

Carlie. This would be the child of Betty Ann, Elizabeth's daughter. She was probably in her midtwenties, expensively dressed in designer jeans, and a sweater that had to be cashmere. Auburn hair fell to her shoulders, and her makeup was more suited to a fashion shoot than to Echo Falls. The suede high-heeled boots gave Amanda a momentary urge to ask where she'd bought them.

Focus, she told herself.

"You have it wrong." Amanda kept her tone calm with an effort. "I'm not claiming anything—just trying to find some answers. I'm sorry if that's uncomfortable for you."

"You'll be more than sorry if you try to see my grandmother with this story of yours."

Obviously, Carlie was too angry to listen to sense. Tamping down her annoyance at the woman for staging a scene on a public street, Amanda pinned a meaningless smile on her lips. Probably the best thing she could do was walk away. She turned.

Carlie grabbed her arm, her fingernails digging in. "Don't turn your back on me. You think we don't know how to deal with people like you? My father has already alerted our attorneys. You're not going to get anywhere, so you'd better leave Echo Falls before you land in real trouble."

Amanda jerked her arm free. "You can't—"

Another roar of a motorcycle filled the air. This time, the biker pulled up at the curb directly in front of them. With the black leather jacket and black helmet, he looked like a character out of the sort of film she avoided.

"You ready to go, babe?"

He spoke to Carlie, but his contemptuous gaze was fixed on Amanda.

"Just about." Thrusting her face in Amanda's, she threw the words at her. "Clear out. Or take your chances."

She spun and stalked toward the motorcycle. Shaking her hair back, she donned a helmet and climbed on behind, wrapping her arms around the biker.

With a deafening roar, they drove off, leaving Amanda staring after them, caught between anger and curiosity.

She hadn't realized anyone else was nearby until someone touched her arm lightly.

"Are you all right? You mustn't mind Carlie. She's a little overly dramatic." The woman was slim and attractive, probably in her forties, with an open, friendly smile that contrasted sharply with the look that had been on Carlie's face.

"You left out *rude*," she said lightly. "I'm sorry you had to hear that."

She shrugged. "Carlie likes an audience. My advice would be to forget it. I'm Lisa Morgan, by the way. And you are obviously Amanda Curtiss."

"Am I that well-known?" she asked ruefully.

Lisa smiled. "Echo Falls is a small town. Word spreads."

"I guess it does." Should she ask if the woman had known Melanie Winthrop, or was that likely to result in another snub? Before she could decide, Ms. Morgan was already getting out car keys and moving toward a sedan parked nearby.

"Don't let Carlie worry you," she said. "Good luck."

Left on the sidewalk, Amanda stared after her for a moment. The woman had probably acted on instinct, wanting to smooth over what had been an awkward scene to witness. But it had been kind, and she appreciated it.

She could be about the age Melanie would be now if she'd lived. Did she remember Melanie? Still, if she knew why Amanda was here, she'd probably have spoken up if she did.

Her thoughts returned to Carlie. If Melanie was actually Amanda's mother, Carlie was a cousin...well, second cousin. Melanie would have been her cousin, though she'd died before Carlie was born. Strange family dynamics, she thought, but still, maybe not that bad, since Melanie had been pregnant at seventeen.

Amanda hadn't felt any sense of kinship with Carlie during that brief encounter—which meant probably nothing at all.

"You look like you've been turned to stone." Trey had come along the sidewalk without her noticing. "What's going on?"

"Nothing. Are you following me around?"

"Innocent," he declared, displaying the Sunday paper under his arm. "Just walked down to the newsstand to pick up a paper. Did you know that was Carlie Shay you were talking to a few minutes ago?"

"Oh, yes, she made that very clear. And she was

the one doing all the talking, believe me. Basically, she threatened me with legal action if I didn't get out of town. Or worse."

His face tightened. "The family wouldn't be that dumb. It would bring on just the kind of publicity they'd hate."

"Are you concerned for them or for your client?" Did it say something about his attitude that his first thought was for the Winthrop family's reputation?

"Please," he said, his eyes crinkling. "I'm not worried about them. Just being realistic when I say that Carlie's father is too smart to allow himself a knee-jerk reaction, no matter how he feels about your presence."

She considered that statement. "If so, maybe it's time I talked with him. I could clear up any misconceptions about why I'm here. I hadn't wanted to approach them without knowing more than I do, but if they're already talking about me, that time might have come. It can't do any harm, can it?"

"Not as long as you're accompanied by your attorney and follow his guidance about what to say." His grin softened the words.

"Well, then…"

He nodded. "Okay. You're probably right." Amanda sensed a certain reservation in his manner. "I'll call him tomorrow and try to set something up, okay?"

Amanda's instinct was to do it herself, but if Donald Shay had already made up his mind that she was some kind of con artist, then like it or not, the approach would come better from someone he knew who was approaching him in a more formal manner.

"All right. We'll do it your way." But she privately

reserved the right to push if she thought Trey was soft-pedaling his approach to the man.

RELIEVED, TREY FELL into step with Amanda as she started down the street. This situation was delicate enough without having his client rocketing around town like a loose cannon.

"I noticed you were talking to Lisa Morgan," he said, keeping it casual.

Amanda nodded. "She was yet another of the many people who know why I'm here. But she was nice about it. More or less apologized for Carlie. Or at least tried to smooth over the awkwardness of a scene on a public street."

"She's that kind of person," he said easily. "Though I'm not sure even her tact would be enough where Carlie Shay is concerned."

"She said Carlie was overly dramatic." Amanda's face eased into a smile. "I'd have called her something else if my mother hadn't raised me not to use that sort of language."

"I guess." Could he ask how she'd responded to Carlie without having his head bitten off?

Maybe not at the moment. It could wait until she'd cooled down. Amanda didn't even seem to realize it, but she'd been knocked off balance by her encounter with Carlie. Her cheeks were flushed, and her blue eyes still sparked dangerously. She walked as if she'd win a prize by beating him to the corner.

She glanced at him finally. "Where are you going?"

He shrugged. "You tell me. You're the one with a plan, apparently. I'm just along for the ride. Or the race, if you prefer. Are we in a hurry?"

Amanda's smile was reluctant, and her gaze dropped. "My plan is to check out the two bed-and-breakfast places to see if anyone remembers my mother...Juliet Curtiss...staying there that summer eighteen years ago."

"That's a pretty tall order, isn't it?" he asked cautiously.

"I suppose. And you're not thinking anything I haven't already considered. Even if someone remembers her, why would they know anything about what she did here?"

He didn't speak, because those were exactly the objections he'd had in mind.

She took a few more anger-propelled steps and then slowed down, her expression easing. "It's a slim chance, I know. But I couldn't think of anything else to tackle this afternoon, and I have to do something. I'm not used to sitting around waiting for events to unfold."

"Did you ever consider a little balance in your life? You know, so much time for work, so much time for recreation, so much..."

"I didn't come to Echo Falls for relaxation. Or to enjoy myself."

"No, you want to get the answers you need and hurry back to your life in Boston." That should make him happy, but it didn't seem to. "You could, of course, go back to your job now and leave this in my hands."

"I can't." She turned to face him, and the depth of emotion in those clear blue eyes startled him. "This is one of the gaps in my mother's life that I have to fill."

"*One* of the gaps? Were there others?"

"Of course." She seemed surprised that he'd ask. "How much do any of us know about our parents?"

Her smile flickered, and the dimple appeared and then disappeared. "We're a pretty self-absorbed generation, I think. Or maybe that's natural in your twenties and thirties."

It occurred to him that he'd always taken his parents' history for granted. They'd led perfectly ordinary lives here in Echo Falls, he'd assumed, and he'd never had cause to question their past. That argued a lot of confidence on his part or maybe a lot of indifference. He didn't care for that implication.

"I really need to know more about where Juliet was at the time I came into her life," Amanda went on. "My earliest memories are of an apartment building in South Boston. Looking at it now, I guess it was a pretty bad area, but I didn't see it that way at the time. There were mostly older people in the building, and they made a pet of me, looking after me when my mother had to work."

"What was she doing then, do you know? Commercial art of some sort?" He tried to picture Amanda's early life.

"Of course not." Amanda gave a reminiscent smile. "She was a waitress, like just about every newcomer in the arts. She couldn't make a living from her painting then, but I remember her saying that one day things would be different. And they were. When I was about seven, she had a successful show, and she was on her way."

Amanda's eyes had grown misty when she looked back at the past, but he was focused on more practical matters. "Would any of the people in that apartment building have known about your appearance in your mother's life?"

"I hadn't thought of that," she admitted. "But I'm sure Robert has. And as I said, they were already elderly people. I don't know if any of them would still be around."

"Still, it's a place to check. Maybe you should mention it to him so he can put his investigators on it, if he hasn't already done so."

"I will. I want to contact Robert in any event to see if there's news." She wrinkled her nose. "Though I suspect he'd have called me with anything good."

He wasn't quite sure what to say to her. Legally speaking, he was supposed to be representing her for anything that arose in Echo Falls. McKinley was in charge of the rest. Still, he was concerned.

"I imagine McKinley told you that barring any other claimants, the terms of your mother's will would probably stand. She looked on you as a daughter, and the court wouldn't ignore that fact."

"I know. The trouble is Juliet's brother. Robert's afraid he suspects something, although if he knew for certain I wasn't Juliet's biological child, he'd be doing more than snooping."

That changed things. If the brother contested the will on those grounds, anything might happen, depending on the case he made and whether or not Amanda had been legally adopted. He frowned, wondering how likely it was that she had been. If she really was Melanie's child, he didn't see how Juliet would have pulled it off without having it become public.

"Wouldn't her brother have known, one way or the other?"

"Not likely." Amanda gave a quick shake of her head that sent her silky blond hair shimmering. "He never gave her a thought except to try to borrow money from her from time to time. She'd never have confided in him, I'm sure."

"That's a dead end, then." Amanda really was alone in the world. It wasn't surprising that she wanted to find out who her biological parents were...

That thought stopped him. Parents. "If you are Melanie's child, there had to be a man involved."

"Well, obviously." She gave him a look that suggested he wasn't too bright.

Nettled, he tried again. "You've never so much as mentioned trying to find your father. Aren't you interested in him?"

She was quiet for so long that he thought she wasn't going to answer. When she finally spoke, her tone had darkened.

"I could say that I'm following the only lead I have. That's true enough. But honestly... I've never known what it is to have a father. I guess you can't miss what you've never had."

They'd come to a stop by the fountain in the square, and the splashing water formed a soundtrack to her words.

"I can't imagine growing up without a father." He spoke before he realized the words might be hurtful to her. "But I'm sure your mother more than filled the spaces in your life. It can't have been easy for her."

"No. All the more astonishing that she did all that for someone else's child. Is that what you think?"

There went her temper flaring again. Did everyone spark it off, or was it just him? "I'd say it meant she loved you very much."

Maybe she recognized the honesty in his tone, because the flicker of anger was gone as fast as it had come. "Yes. She did. I really never felt any lack in my life." She stared at the water for a moment and then turned to face him. "That's what makes it so difficult to grasp that she never told me the truth. Why? Why didn't she tell me?"

He didn't have an answer to that any more than she did. "She must have thought it was for the best, even if you don't understand why." That was lame, but it was the only thing he could come up with.

"All the more important that I know the circumstances. What was she afraid of if I'd been told the truth? In all my life, I never saw anything that Juliet feared. She was a strong woman, and she went her own way no matter the obstacles. Why couldn't she tell me?"

"There might have been a lot of reasons." He felt helpless to assuage the pain in her eyes. For the first time, he was really seeing what this meant to Amanda, and it seemed to hurt him, too. He took both her hands in his, not caring whether anyone saw them or not. "She might have promised your birth mother that she wouldn't. Or she could have planned to tell you later on. We all tend to think there's plenty of time for the things we need to do. Hers was cut short without warning."

Amanda took a breath and released it, seeming to let go of some of the tension that had gripped her. He could feel it through their clasped hands.

"You're right, of course. Thank you. I don't know what I was imagining, but it's far more likely to be as you say. With insight like that, you must be a very good lawyer."

She smiled at him, and all he could think for a moment was how kissable those lips were. He shook off the tempting image.

"I try," he said lightly. Maybe it was just as well that she didn't know how close the firm had come to disaster on his watch. She wouldn't think so highly of him then.

AMANDA DROVE BACK to the cottage as the sun approached the ridgetop. Her stops at the two bed-and-breakfast inns had been futile. One hadn't been open eighteen years earlier. At the other, the proprietor simply stared at the suggestion that she might remember something that long ago.

Still, it hadn't been a wasted trip. She had the encounter with Carlie Shay to mull over. In fact, she probably should give Robert a call tonight and bring him up-to-date on that, as well as passing on Trey's suggestion about the inhabitants of the apartment building. She didn't have a lot of faith that it would turn something up, but she didn't want to overlook any possibilities.

And then there was Trey Alter himself. He might annoy her at least 50 percent of the time, but he had shown more empathy than she'd have expected. And that, in turn, had made her open up more than she'd ever anticipated doing.

She might live to regret it, but Amanda didn't think so. Despite Trey's reticence on some subjects and his tendency to think he was the authority on Echo Falls, she believed she could trust him. That simple conversation had moved their relationship forward in a way she hadn't expected.

The blacktop road swung in a wide curve around the side of a hill, and Amanda found that she was facing directly west, into the glare of the setting sun. Squinting, she raised her hand to shield her eyes, glad there weren't any other vehicles on the road.

She heard the roar before she saw the vehicle—a motorcycle, coming up fast behind her on the narrow road. Well, there was plenty of room. Let him pass her if he was in that much of a hurry.

Instead of passing, the motorcyclist moved in behind her as if they were the vanguard of a parade. Amanda looked in her rearview mirror again, frowning. It was impossible to make out anything about the motorcyclist except that he was male. The black jacket, helmet and reflective sunglasses made him anonymous.

Ridiculous, to let him make her uneasy. People around here probably took their motorcycles out for a Sunday ride on the back roads every week. He wasn't passing because he wasn't in a hurry. She was reminded of that unlikely friend of Carlie's, but the chance that this could be he was remote.

Amanda's instincts didn't seem to be in sync with her rationalization. Her nerves prickled, and her fingers gripped the wheel. For a moment she wished for another vehicle—anything—on the road besides her and the anonymous motorcyclist.

As if in answer, a tractor pulling a wagon filled with hay bales pulled out of a farm lane ahead of her. It began its slow progress toward her, hay bales swaying gently.

Maybe it wasn't what she'd have chosen, but at least she wasn't alone on the road with that motorcycle roaring on her bumper. He should have passed her when he could. Now he'd have to wait until the tractor went by.

But he didn't. At the last possible moment, the motorcyclist pulled out from behind her, swinging around so closely it seemed he'd clip her left fender. Between the oncoming tractor and the motorcyclist, there was suddenly no room.

Idiot. Didn't he see that he was going directly toward the tractor?

She steered onto the berm, trying to give him space to slip in ahead of her. But he was still crowding her, and she felt her wheels slide off the gravel and into the soft earth. She hit the brakes, and in an instant, the car jerked to a stop. Too late. It tilted into the ditch, flinging her hard against the seat belt.

Breathless, too shocked even to think, she scrabbled for the belt buckle. It couldn't be too bad, she told herself. The air bag hadn't deployed, so it couldn't be. She was vaguely aware of the motorcycle's roar receding into the distance. He hadn't stopped, then. Somehow she wasn't surprised.

She heard the sound of running feet, and then someone pulled open the car door, reaching out helping hands to get her out of the vehicle.

"Stupid idiot," the man muttered. "Just wish I'd gotten his plate number. I'd settle his hash if I could get hold of him. Miss? Are you okay? Miss?"

Amanda forced herself to focus, gripping the man's arm. "Yes, I think so. Just shaken a bit."

"No wonder. What that fool thought he was doing is beyond me." The speaker was the farmer who'd been driving the tractor—fortyish, sunburned, wearing jeans, a T-shirt and the inevitable ball cap. "If he'd waited two minutes, he'd have had plenty of room to pass. Instead he forces you right into the ditch."

"He'd been behind me for a mile or two. He could have passed me anytime." But he hadn't. He'd waited until his actions were virtually guaranteed to cause an accident.

She wasn't sure she wanted to think that through at the moment. At least she was in one piece. But the car...

She turned to look at the damage, her rescuer grasping her elbow as if afraid to let her move on her own. "My car. I guess I'll have to try to get a tow truck to get it out."

Her new friend climbed down into the ditch to take a closer look, pushing his cap back on his head as he bent over to inspect it. "It hit an outcrop on the side of the ditch, but it doesn't look like anything worse than a crumpled fender. It's going to need bodywork before you go very far in it."

Amanda discovered that her mind was a blank. She'd need to call for assistance, of course. But more importantly, should she call the police and report that she'd been deliberately run off the road? Somehow the thought of explaining that to Chief Carmichaels made her cringe.

She had no proof that it was intentional, any more than she had proof that Melanie Winthrop was her mother. But the two things seemed to hang together in her mind, and she wondered just how much the Winthrop family wanted to be rid of her.

CHAPTER SEVEN

AMANDA DISCOVERED SHE was hobbling around the house the next morning as if she were 107 years old. If she were a horse, she'd have prescribed liniment— too bad she didn't have any on hand.

But she had had a wonderful breakfast, carried up by Sarah and her oldest daughter, who hovered over Amanda to be sure she ate every single bite of it. It had taken quite an argument to convince them that since she hadn't been up at dawn to do the milking, she really didn't need both bacon and fried scrapple with her eggs and oatmeal. She'd ended up saying she'd reheat the scrapple for a midmorning snack if she got hungry, and they finally went back to the farmhouse.

A hot shower helped, giving her a chance to assess the wonderful collection of bruises on her rib cage, provided by the seat belt. She should just be thankful she had bruised ribs instead of having gone into the windshield.

Amanda made herself as comfortable as possible on the sofa, a quilt over her legs, a pillow cushioning her ribs and Barney draped across her feet, nursing a mug of coffee and going over the accident in detail.

Accident, her mind said scornfully. *That was no accident. It was deliberate.*

Was it? She had to think this through before she made any rash claims.

Before she got any further in her thinking, she heard a car outside. For an instant she hoped her vehicle was back already, but that wasn't reasonable. The damage to the body would take a few days at least, assuming the garage the farmer had recommended made it a priority.

Getting up with an effort, she followed Barney to the door. His tail was waving, so it had to be someone she knew. Somehow, she wasn't surprised to open the door and find Trey on the other side of it.

"How are you?" His question came before she could speak, and he came inside on a wave of concern.

"I'm fine." She moved, winced and made a face. "Well, I will be fine. How did you hear about the accident?"

"Sarah called me." He frowned, reaching out to take her arm as gently as if she were made of glass. "More to the point, why didn't you?"

"I didn't think it fell within your legal duties to a client." That was mostly true. And she hadn't wanted him to see her when she was shaken and unable to think.

"Here, sit down." Obviously, he thought she still was. He escorted her to the sofa, where the pillow and quilt gave away her position. "Now, be honest. How do you feel?"

She eased herself down, grateful for his strong hand on her arm, and leaned back gingerly. Trey set a white bag on the lamp table so he could smooth the quilt over her. Then he lifted the bag again.

"Coffee and bagels. Want some?"

"I'll take a refill on my coffee, but I'd never manage to get a bagel down after the breakfast Sarah fed me. Where on earth did you get bagels in Echo Falls?"

"I have my sources." He grinned, dispensing coffee, and settled on a chair that he pulled up close to her. "Just don't tell Esther, okay?"

Esther. For an instant something teased her mind, but then it was gone.

"What?" Trey had become adept at reading her expressions.

"I don't know. Mentioning Esther made me think of something, but it slipped away before I could grab it."

"Don't try, and it'll come back," he advised. "Come on, tell. You're obviously hurting. How bad is it?"

"Bruised ribs, from the seat belt. That's pretty much all. I'll be fine in a day or two."

"Is that a doctor's diagnosis?" He lifted his eyebrows.

"It's a veterinarian's diagnosis. Don't fuss, Trey."

He eyed her for a moment before apparently deciding she was telling him the truth. "Okay. No fussing. But all I know so far is that there was a motorcycle, Phil Shuman's tractor and hay wagon, and you in a ditch. Tell me the rest of it."

Her inclination was to minimize, but if she couldn't tell Trey the whole story, who could she tell?

"I was driving back here. It sounds as if you already know where it happened."

"I checked it out on my way here. Nothing to see now, of course, but your tire marks." He frowned. "No skid marks from the motorcycle, as far as I could see."

"No. He didn't stop, or even brake." The hand holding the coffee showed a tendency to shake, and she cradled the cup in both hands, willing it to stop. "He was following me, but he didn't try to pass until the tractor was almost on us."

Trey's frown deepened. "That's what Phil said, along with some colorful things about the motorcyclist I won't repeat. You're leaving out a few details. When did you first notice the biker?"

So he'd talked to the farmer. She might have considered that interfering a few days ago, but now she was just grateful that someone cared.

When had she first spotted the motorcycle? She tried to find a landmark. "I heard the bike before I saw it. It seemed to come from nowhere. One minute the road behind me was empty, the next I heard the noise and spotted him on my tail, coming up fast. There hadn't been anything at all behind me since I'd left town."

"He came out of a farm lane, then," Trey said. "I know that stretch of road. There isn't anything else. Then what?"

Amanda shrugged, not sure she wanted to relive those few minutes. "He stayed behind me for a good while, not even attempting to pass. Then the tractor pulled out and started toward us. All at once the biker pulled out around me, forcing me toward the berm." She couldn't help it—her voice shook just a hair at the memory of those moments.

Trey got up, stepped over Barney and sat down next to her on the sofa, putting an arm around her as comfortably as if it were a normal occurrence.

"You'd have nowhere else to go on that road, not with a tractor in the other lane." Trey seemed to be picturing it in his mind.

"No. It was either hit the motorcycle or drive into the ditch. I picked the ditch."

"Wise choice." His arm tightened just for a moment. "Phil was kicking himself for not getting the plate number."

"No need for that. He focused on helping me out of the car. And I was glad to see him, let me tell you." It was easier to talk about it now, and she seemed to be thinking more clearly. "I don't want to sound paranoid, but I don't see how it could have been an accident. The biker cut me off deliberately."

"I agree. So was it simple meanness, or something more?"

Amanda glanced at his face, a little surprised that he'd come to that conclusion so quickly. "I don't know. It could be coincidence, I guess."

"I'm not a great believer in coincidence. And besides…" He stopped at a startled breath from her. "What is it?"

"I just realized what it was that flitted through my mind earlier. When I was in front of Esther's café yesterday, where I had that little exchange with Carlie, a motorcycle pulled up. When Carlie was finished threatening me, she climbed on and they rushed off." She paused, frowning a little. "Didn't you see him? You said you saw me with Carlie."

He nodded. "I did, but then someone stopped to talk to me, and I was distracted. I did hear the bike, though."

"It doesn't necessarily mean anything." She tried to be fair. "There must be hundreds of motorcycles around here."

"Probably." Trey drew out the word, forehead wrinkling. "But I wonder. It seems to me that a short time ago Carlie Shay had a boyfriend the family disapproved of—for a lot of reasons, I suppose, but one of them was that he roared around the county on a motorcycle instead of holding down a decent job."

"You think that's who it was? Are they still together?"

"That's the rub. Supposedly, Carlie broke up with him after an ultimatum from her grandmother. Still, I'm sure it's not the first time someone in the family has lied to the old woman to get their own way."

Including her mother, if that's what Melanie was.

"Do you think Carlie would plan something like that?" She rubbed her forehead. "It's not as if I'd have been killed in that sort of accident—at least, it's not likely."

"It might have been intended to scare you away. Or she might have complained to the boyfriend, and he acted on impulse. That seems more probable to me."

Amanda considered. "This is getting uglier than I anticipated. When I came here, I thought I was doing a little simple research on adoption, important to nobody but myself."

"Things are never simple where human beings are concerned."

"Maybe that's why I do better with animals." She ruffled Barney's ears. There was more truth to that statement than she'd considered. If she'd understood people better, she might not have ended up back in Boston with a broken heart after her first attempt at a mature relationship.

"Well, I'll look into it and see what I can find out about the errant boyfriend. And I'd better get to the office and call Donald Shay about a meeting." He stood, seeming energized by having an agenda. "I'll see you for supper."

"Supper?" She looked up at him, deciding not to make the effort involved to rise.

"Supper," he said. "Sarah invited me. Assuming you feel up to it."

"I'm sure I'll be able to make it that far." Sarah, it seemed, was matchmaking.

Trey turned toward the door and then turned back. He bent over her, cradling her cheek in his hand before she guessed his intent. He kissed her...very lightly, just a tentative brushing of the lips together, but that kiss seemed to reverberate right through her.

He drew back a little, smiling. "Do me a favor. Try not to get any more damaged before I see you tonight, okay?"

"I'll try." She returned the smile, her heart lifting in a way that was entirely irrational. But good, nevertheless.

TREY WAS STILL smiling when he reached the office, but he sobered the minute he entered the door. Evelyn Lincoln, their receptionist, looked up at him with concern.

"You had a call from Donald Shay a few minutes ago. He's very eager to talk to you."

So Shay had anticipated him. Trey paused at Evelyn's desk. "Did you offer to switch him to Jason?" His partner had been in early this morning, and he'd agreed to handle anything that came up while Trey was out.

"I offered. He refused." Evelyn sounded annoyed. "He was...in quite a mood. I've never heard him so abrupt."

"Rude?" His voice sharpened. Evelyn had her own way of handling rude clients, but she shouldn't have to.

She shrugged. "On the verge. I think my reaction made him aware of how inappropriate it was. Still, you'd better call him back soon. He'll be at his office at the mill, he said."

"I'll get on it right away," he promised. Not because he appreciated taking orders from anyone, including Donald Shay, but because if he didn't, Evelyn might bear the brunt of another call from him.

He stalked into his office, relieving his temper by shutting the door more loudly than was strictly necessary. But that didn't hurt Donald Shay at all, did it? Sitting down at his desk, he looked up the number and called, tapping his blotter with a pen point in irritation. Amanda had a right to her questions. She also had a right to representation. Shay would have to understand that fact.

It took only a moment to get past the secretary and reach Shay. He'd obviously been waiting for the call.

"This Curtiss woman," he said abruptly, not bothering with conventional greetings, "is it true you're representing her?"

"That's correct." Trey leaned back in his chair, rather relishing the fact the Shay, usually suave and confident of his importance in any situation, sounded rattled.

"Given that your father represented the family for many years, it seems to me that's a conflict of interest on your part. What are you trying to do?"

Trey tapped the phone with his pen. "Did represent. Past tense. If memory serves, that representation ended over twenty-five years ago. Just about twenty-eight years, in fact." When his father tried to prevent the family from forcing Melanie into giving up her child. "As for what I'm trying to do, obviously I'm trying to serve my client as best I can."

"Serve her in what?" Shay, always so controlled, seemed to be hanging on to his temper by a thread. "Harassing my family?"

"As far as I know, Ms. Curtiss has made no attempt even to speak to your family. What harassment are you referring to?"

"You know perfectly well that everyone in town thinks she claims to be Melanie's illegitimate child. It's public knowledge. Hasn't my family suffered enough from that terrible episode? I warn both of you…"

Trey sat up straight, planting his feet as if he'd lunge out of the chair. "I have no intention of listening to threats, Shay. I intended to call you today and ask if you'd sit down with the two of us and discuss Ms. Curtiss's situation in a civil manner, but if you're not interested, we have nothing further to say."

He knew perfectly well that most business people in town would hesitate to speak to Shay that way, but he would not allow his client to be pushed around. The firm of Alter and Glassman didn't work for Winthrop Enterprises.

"Now wait, let's not be hasty." Shay drew an audible breath. "I'm afraid I rather let myself go, what with the worry over how this would affect Mrs. Winthrop."

He paused, maybe hoping for something concilia-tory from Trey, but if so, he didn't get it.

"In any event," he went on, "perhaps what you suggest is the best way of approaching the situation."

There was the sound of turning pages. "Shall we say two o'clock tomorrow afternoon at my office?"

"One moment." Trey consulted his own schedule, fairly certain that the afternoon was clear. It was. "All right. Ms. Curtiss and I will be at your office at two."

For a moment he considered adding that Amanda's main concern was learning whether she was adopted or not, rather than claiming kinship with the Winthrop family, but he let it go. Better not to give away information too readily.

"Fine." Shay's voice was crisp. He ended the call.

That was interesting. Trey leaned back in his chair. Donald Shay was more rattled than Trey would have expected. Because he had reason to think Amanda really was Elizabeth Winthrop's great-granddaughter? This promised to be an intriguing meeting.

He was tempted to call Amanda, but it could wait until he saw her at supper. He hoped she was resting at the moment, and tonight would be soon enough to discuss how they'd present the issues.

That decided, he worked steadily at a complicated will for a client who seemed to regard revising his will as a periodic chance to annoy all of his relatives. He was about ready to stop for lunch when his cell phone rang. He checked the caller—his mother.

"Hi, Mom, what's up?"

"I'm sorry to bother you at work." She sounded harried. "But I need some medication picked up for your father, and I don't want to leave him to go and get it."

"What's wrong?" His hand tightened on the phone. "Did something happen?"

"No, no, nothing like that. But he's a bit restless, eager to get on the new medication since the doctor prescribed it, and I think he should rest, but he's insisting he can go with me to the pharmacy…"

He could imagine the scene without being there. His father, normally the kindest of men, became irritable when he had to face anything he couldn't control. Like his own heart.

"I'll run by now and pick it up. Do you need anything else when I come?"

"No, that's all." He could hear his father's voice in the background. "He says to tell you there's no need to leave the office to run errands for him."

That sounded familiar, too. "Tell him I do take some time off for lunch. I'll be there as soon as I have the pills." He clicked off before his father could give his mother any further instructions. Knowing his mother, Trey was confident she'd handle him better than he could.

In less than fifteen minutes, Trey was hurrying up the walk at his parents' house, still more concerned than he wanted to admit. His father had been in good health and enjoying his retirement until the scandal about his longtime partner broke last spring. Since then his existing heart condition kept worsening, and the relaxed retirement his mother had hoped for had deteriorated into worry and doctor visits.

Trey tapped once and entered, his usual way of announcing himself. "Mom, where are you? I've brought the medication."

He found her in the kitchen, and she hurried to give him a quick kiss before seizing on the small white bag. "You wouldn't believe how determined he was to get started on this. He wouldn't take his usual pill but insisted he had to have this."

Trey rested a hand on her shoulder when she moved. "Wait a second. Tell me why the doctor changed the pills."

His mother gave him a cautious look. "Now, don't overreact. It's bad enough dealing with your father. But the doctor thought his heart sounded weaker than usual today, so he changed it. It's probably nothing," she added quickly. "You know how it is. He gets upset and…"

She stopped abruptly, as if she hadn't intended to say that.

"What upset him?" But he was afraid he knew. "If it's because of the talk going around town about Amanda Curtiss, there's nothing there to worry him. She's a perfectly nice woman who simply wants to find out whether or not the woman who raised her actually adopted her. She's not trying to cause trouble for the Winthrops."

His mother raised troubled eyes to him. "Not according to Donald Shay. He called your father this morning, and…"

A bell rang insistently. His mother seized a glass of water she had ready on the counter and the pill bottle. "I swear, I should never have let him have that bell. Come in and talk to him. Maybe you can convince him there's nothing to get upset over."

Maybe. He'd try, but a sense of failure weighed on his shoulders as he moved. What could he do? Amanda Curtiss was going to pursue her search whether he represented her or not. He'd started this job, and it wouldn't be honorable to desert her now.

There was nothing honorable about worrying his father into heart failure, either. He had an overwhelming desire to punch someone, preferably Donald Shay. How dare he call the house and worry Dad with his issues? He knew Trey's father was retired and had no part in the firm now.

Too bad that punching Shay wouldn't solve the problem. Dad had been so proud that Trey had followed his example. His belief in Trey had been absolute. Trey had repaid him by failing to see how near the firm was to disaster and now by raising havoc in the place that meant so much to his family. No matter what he did, he was going to fail someone.

SUPPER AT SARAH'S house proved to be a noisy, happy time, filled with laughter and good food. With that number of children in the house, Amanda supposed it couldn't be anything else. From the perspective of an only child, she watched the interplay between Amos and Sarah's brood with fascination. They were all so alike in looks and so different in personality.

They were clearly not in awe of Trey—he was treated as if he were an older cousin. Trey made a game of pretending not to know which one was which, not surprising in a group of blue-eyed, blond-haired youngsters who all dressed alike and had similar features.

"Now, this is Gabe, right?" He tapped one towhead on the shoulder, leading to giggles among the younger ones as the older girls cleared the table and began serving dessert and coffee.

"I'm not Gabe, I'm Ezra."

"That's funny. You're just the size Gabe was last summer."

The little boy pointed, convulsed with giggles. "That's Gabe."

Trey shook his head sadly. "What do you mean by growing so much in a few months? How I am supposed to know you? Stop it, you hear?"

Sarah leaned over Amanda's shoulder to put a generous wedge of apple crumb pie topped with ice cream in front of her. "Trey always makes them laugh. He's gut with the kinder, ain't so?"

She ought to say she didn't know him well enough to tell, but that seemed rude. "I guess he is. Your crowd really likes him."

"Ach, he's a gut man." She moved on, sparing Amanda the difficulty of framing a reply.

Certainly in this setting, Trey made an impression that was very different from the one he'd made on her that first day in his office, when she'd thought him stuffy and self-satisfied. That should be a lesson to her not to judge.

Amos claimed her attention. "Have you had a look at our colt today?"

"I stopped to see him on my way to supper. He's grown so much already. He's going to be a fine animal."

"He is, God willing. It was a chance, investing in the pair of Percherons, but he should make it worth the risk."

Amanda nodded. She hadn't considered it from a financial perspective, but it was certainly true that the pair of them would have cost a lot. She knew from her time in Lancaster County how chancy success could be for a family farm, even a dairy farm, which generally did better than others.

Sarah, finally sitting down with her pie and coffee, smiled at her. "Don't let him talk your ear off about that colt, now. He spends too much time admiring him."

"Amos and Amanda made a good pair of midwives." Trey turned his attention to the adults as the youngsters, their dessert finished, scurried off to their various chores. "Maybe Amanda ought to stick around the area."

"Doc sure could use the help," Amos said. "He's a gut man and a fine vet, but he can't get everywhere at once. It's not an easy life."

"Hey, don't scare her off." Trey polished off the last crumb of pie on his plate. He smiled at Amanda as he spoke, but then sobered quickly. "Looks to me as if you've sat about as long as your ribs will take. Want me to run you up to the cottage in the car?"

"I can walk. Moving around will do me good. But I think I will need to call it quits for the evening." Trey must have noticed that involuntary wince when she'd turned. "Sit still, Trey," she added when he rose. "I don't want to tear you away from another slice of pie."

He grinned, looking for an instant like a kid who'd been at the cookie jar. "Sarah promised me a piece to take home. Come on. If you won't let me drive you, I'll walk with you."

Sarah gazed at her with concern. "Do you want one of the girls to stay with you tonight, just in case you need help?"

"No, that's not necessary. I'm fine, just a bit stiff. The walk will help." There was a limit, she thought, to how much help she should accept from her hosts.

After the thanks and goodbyes had been repeated multiple times, they were out the back door in the gathering dusk. Trey touched her arm as they went down the porch steps, as if to ask if she needed help.

"I'm okay," she said, answering the unasked question. "That wooden chair was just starting to stick into me in the same places as the seat belt."

"I imagine. We should have carried an upholstered chair in for you." Trey settled his pace to match hers.

"And have the kids laughing at me? I think not."

He grinned. "They're too well-mannered to laugh at an Englischer."

"Never mind my sore ribs. Tell me what happened. Did you call Donald Shay?"

Trey's face darkened. "I didn't have to," he said shortly. "He called me. What's more, he called my father first and upset him."

"Your father?" No wonder Trey sounded angry. "But why? He's not involved in the firm, is he?"

"Not any longer." Trey's tone snapped with annoyance. "Shay is well aware of that fact. I suppose he thought my father would influence me to drop your case. He doesn't know either of us if he thinks that."

Amanda wasn't sure what to say in the face of his obvious ire. There was more going on than just a phone call, it seemed to her. "I'm sure someone with your father's experience would know how to handle that sort of pressure."

"He shouldn't have to." Even in the dim light, she could see the steely set of Trey's jaw. "He's not well."

"I'm sorry if your involvement with me…"

Trey shook his head with an impatient gesture. "Just let it go. I can deal with Shay. We're going to meet him at two tomorrow, so I'll pick you up about one forty.

Then I'll drive you over to pick up your car afterward, if it's ready."

"I had a call from the garage this afternoon, and it is. But I don't want to take you out of your way." And she didn't like being dependent on him, especially when he sounded so annoyed with the whole business.

He gave her a quick glance as they moved into the dimmer light under the trees that surrounded the cottage. "It's no trouble." His voice had warmed. "Sorry. I didn't mean to take my ill humor out on you."

Amanda wasn't sure how to react. It seemed plain that Trey's concern for his father was behind his attitude. Should she say something about him directly or not? Still, Trey certainly knew plenty about her own relationship with her mother.

"I didn't intend to sound flip about your father dealing with Shay on my account. I'm sorry he's not well."

"It's not your fault."

She couldn't see his face clearly in the near-darkness, but she knew how it would look from the tightness in his voice. Stern, steely, shutting her out. Clearly Trey didn't share his private life with a client.

They'd reached the small porch on the front of the cottage, and a mellow glow reached them from the light she'd left on. Barney, apparently knowing she was near, let out a soft woof of welcome.

"Good night." Amanda took a step toward the porch but stopped at his touch on her arm.

"Guess I'm supersensitive where my dad is concerned. He retired when he first experienced heart issues, figuring he was leaving the firm in good hands." He paused, and she could feel his struggle. "But then everything fell to pieces last spring. The man who'd been his partner for years killed himself after it came out that he'd murdered someone."

Amanda swallowed a gasp, not wanting to stop him.

"My father took it hard, of course. And the firm nearly went under from all the bad publicity. It almost killed Dad."

"I'm sorry," she said softly. "I guess you feel you have to protect him, especially from anything else that might impact the firm."

"Dad inherited the practice from his father. He built it up to be the most respected law firm in this part of the state. Sure, I feel responsible. Wouldn't you, if you were expected to follow in your mother's footsteps?"

She had to suppress a smile at that. "Given my total lack of artistic talent, no one ever expected that. As for what I might have inherited from my birth mother… well, I don't know enough about her to say."

Trey focused on her now, with an intentness that was like the touch of his fingers against her skin. "You never wondered about that…your artistic failings, if that's what they were?"

Amanda considered that. "I can't say I did. Maybe that means I was a pretty dumb kid."

"I'd say it means Juliet made you so secure in her love that you never had to wonder."

"Yes," she said softly. "She did."

He raised his hand to touch her face, and his fingers were warm against her skin in the cool night air. "I'm glad you have that to remember." His voice was soft; his breath moved against her cheek. The slightest turn of her face would be enough to bring their lips together.

Not giving herself time to think about it, she moved so that her lips touched his. She felt his breath catch, and then he put his arms around her and drew her close. The kiss was warm and deep and satisfying, and she drank in the scent and feel of him. At some level she remembered thinking they'd both be better off if they kept things at a professional level.

Too late for that now, and maybe it always had been.

CHAPTER EIGHT

AMANDA HEARD TREY'S car a few minutes early the next day, and she grabbed her jacket and hurried to the door. She'd thought she'd hop in the car and they'd leave, but Trey must have other plans, because he was already mounting the steps to the porch. When she opened the door he walked in, frowning and preoccupied, with barely a nod to acknowledge her.

She hadn't expected a romantic greeting, but she'd certainly thought he'd show a bit more warmth. Or maybe he was already regretting the passion that had flared between them the previous night. Chilled, she was glad that at least they'd both had sense enough to stop at a few kisses.

"I'm ready to go," she pointed out.

Her words seemed to recall him from that private abstraction. "Sorry." His face relaxed in a smile. "Let's start again. Hello, Amanda. You look beautiful today." He kissed her lightly, carefully, as if afraid of starting something.

Maybe that was for the best. They had business in hand.

"Hello, yourself. Shouldn't we be going?"

"Yes, but there's been a change of plans. I had a call from Shay while I was driving over."

"Canceling?" She was aware of a sharp disappointment, making her think she'd counted on too much from this interview.

"No, we're still on. But apparently Elizabeth got wind of what's going on and came down on her son-in-law with a demand to know why he was keeping it from her."

"That sounds like a valid question." She didn't like things being kept from her, either. Not even for her own good.

He shrugged. "He may have meant to protect her, but he should have known better. She always gets to know everything. People say that the housekeeper has orders to report on every conversation that takes place in that house. Elizabeth rules with an iron hand, it seems."

"I'm surprised they haven't rebelled." Like Melanie did, although that hadn't turned out well in the end.

"So, the bottom line is that we're to come to the house and meet the whole family. Including Elizabeth." He paused, his gaze on her face. "Are you upset?"

"No...no, I guess not. That's what I intended from the beginning, when I still had the illusion that this would be a simple matter of finding out a few facts. I just didn't expect it would be today."

Trey had a wry smile for that. "Naive, weren't you? The suddenness doesn't leave us any time to prepare, and that might have been what was in Elizabeth's mind. She may be close to ninety, but she's still as sharp as she ever was, from what I hear."

"That's a good thing to know." Amanda tried for a lightness she didn't feel. "Heredity being what it is, and assuming Melanie was my mother."

She expected Trey would at least smile at that, but

he had returned to that brooding, preoccupied look. "You're worried," she said bluntly. "Why?"

"I don't know, exactly. When you grow up in Echo Falls, you absorb the idea that the Winthrop family is untouchable. Founders of the town, prominent family, all those things that used to carry with them a certain… well, inviolability."

"Aren't you the one who is being naive now? I understand privilege, but that's carrying it too far. You'd think they were the Cabots or the Rockefellers."

"They were, to people here. The current generation has dented that idea, but it lingers in a place like this."

She tried to process that but still found it beyond her. "I thought those days were gone for good. You think that representing me will have repercussions for your firm, is that it?"

Trey shrugged. "To some extent."

Amanda turned, not wanting him to see her face. "Do you want to back out?"

"No!" He shot the word out, grasping her arms and turning her to face him. "I haven't changed my mind. I wouldn't have said as much as I did, but you asked." He lifted an eyebrow. "Are we okay?"

"We're okay," she said, smiling in return. "Let's go face the lioness in her den."

They'd reached the edge of town before she came out with the truth that lingered in the back of her mind and skittered along her nerves.

"Confession time," she said abruptly. "I'm nervous about this meeting, no matter how much rationalizing I do."

He glanced at her. "That seems natural to me."

"It doesn't to me. I mean, I don't want anything

from them except information. I don't feel as if they're my relatives, and I'm not looking for a new family. In every important way, Juliet was my family."

"We do want something from them," Trey said. "Don't forget that in the midst of your rationalizations. We want a DNA test to prove your parentage, one way or the other. And we want any information they might have about where Melanie's baby was born." He frowned. "If any. I don't expect it to be easy to gain their cooperation."

"What if they refuse? Do I have any options?"

"To force the issue, you mean?" Trey had turned onto a residential street that headed up the hillside toward the ridge above the town. He frowned, rubbing the back of his neck as if feeling the strain in his muscles. "Your only recourse would be to file suit against them to recognize you as Melanie's daughter. They'd almost have to submit to DNA testing in that case." He darted a sideways look at her. "Is that what you want to do?"

"No." That much, at least, she felt sure of. "That would imply that I wanted something from them. Besides, the publicity would do me as much harm as it would them."

"True." He turned the car between matching stone posts and up a paved driveway. "Elizabeth's first reaction to the idea of DNA testing will be negative, I'm sure. But Shay is a businessman. He'll be counting the cost of refusal, and he may be able to sway her. So don't be too disappointed if this doesn't go well."

Amanda would answer, but she was too busy gaping at the house that reared up suddenly in front of them. She knew enough to recognize it as an Italianate Vic-

torian mansion with its arched windows and distinctive
cornices. It wasn't any more elaborate than some of
the houses in her Boston neighborhood, but it certainly
was impressive here. It stood three stories, but looked
even taller because of the square tower that soared
above them as Trey parked the car, and they got out.

"Wow," she murmured.

"Exactly. The first Winthrop to make his fortune
also wanted to make a statement. This was supposedly
his idea of elegance. Or maybe the architect's idea. He
must have had a field day with a free hand to spend as
much as he wanted." Trey grimaced. "I think the family's past that policy of spending by now."

"I should hope so. I'm surprised he didn't choose
to build his mansion somewhere a little...well, bigger, at least."

Trey took her arm as they moved toward imposing
double doors that looked as if they belonged on a cathe-
dral. "He made his fortune here, from land speculation
and lumbering. From what people say, he wanted to
stay here and lord it over what he considered *his* town."

"I'm beginning to understand the Winthrops, I
think. Better to be a big fish in a small pond..."

"Exactly." Trey smiled and lifted the knocker.
"Well, here we go. Are you ready?"

"Do it," she said.

The brass knocker made a resounding thud. A moment passed before footsteps approached the door.
Amanda expected an ominous creak as the massive
door swung open, but it moved soundlessly. The man
who stood waiting was impressive in a silver-haired,
well-fed, well-groomed sort of way. His gaze flicked
over Amanda and settled on Trey.

"Ah, Trey, thank you for coming to the house instead of to the mill. Come in and introduce me."

They stepped into a tiled hallway, and Amanda realized that this part of the house was in the square tower. The ceiling of the hall was two stories up, with a glittering chandelier hanging in its center. The crystal droplets chimed softly when a faint breeze came through the door as Trey closed it.

"Amanda, this is Donald Shay. Donald, Amanda Curtiss."

Shay inclined his head with a polite smile rather than a handshake. Not warm, but polite. She got the message that this meeting was going to be conducted calmly, with no unseemly displays of emotion, at least if he had anything to say about it.

She couldn't imagine it was going to be that easy, especially if Carlie were involved, but maybe she behaved better when under her family's eyes.

"Come into the parlor, will you?" He led the way into what was obviously the front one of two parlors, typical of Victorian houses.

Three people stood waiting, and one of them Amanda already knew. Carlie Shay looked at her with the same dislike she'd displayed when they'd met in town. Would she acknowledge the fact that they'd already encountered each other, or ignore it?

"This is my wife, Betty." Shay gestured toward the older woman. Betty would be Elizabeth's daughter, sibling of Melanie's father. Amanda held out her hand automatically and then wished she hadn't.

The woman twisted her hands together for a moment as if she didn't know what to do and then managed a limp, brief handshake.

"It…it's nice to meet you, Ms. Curtiss." She glanced quickly at her husband, as if to ask if she had done it correctly.

Donald was already moving on. "These are our children, Carlie and Ethan." No mention of the fact that she'd already met Carlie, so Amanda guessed she hadn't told her family.

Amanda contented herself with a nod. She wouldn't give Carlie away, although she had no reason to spare her embarrassment. Maybe her parents wouldn't find her tirade embarrassing, if she'd only said what they were feeling.

Carlie's color was high, and she gave a reluctant nod, then tossed her head and deliberately turned away. All her movements were quick and emphatic, qualities she apparently hadn't received from her mother.

Although maybe Betty had been different as a young woman. Amanda tried to imagine the faded figure, which already seemed to be disappearing into the woodwork, as the vivid personality her daughter was. No use. She couldn't.

The son was another story entirely. Ethan must be the younger of the two. He was fair and slight. He met her gaze with a deer-in-the-headlights expression, stammered something that might have been a greeting and seemed to repeat his mother's effect of fading into the background.

An interesting mix—they appeared to be a family of positives and negatives, with the two dynamic personalities dominating the room.

"Well, shall we all sit down?" Shay didn't seem to have found anything awkward in his family's reception of her. He ushered Amanda into a chair next to his wife.

Trey, not waiting to be directed to a seat, pulled a chair up on her other side, maybe to emphasize that he represented her.

An awkward silence fell, and Amanda caught Shay giving a sidelong glance at the archway to the hall. Obviously, they were waiting for Elizabeth Winthrop to show up.

Trey moved slightly. "I had expected to meet at your office today. The change came as a surprise."

Annoyance crossed Donald Shay's urbane features for a second or two. "Yes, well, perhaps it's best this way. In view of Ms. Curtiss's claim…"

"I haven't made any claims." In this, at least, Amanda didn't think she needed anyone to speak for her.

"That's not what I've heard." Carlie sounded as if she couldn't keep silent any longer. "It's all over town that you claim to be Melanie Winthrop's daughter. If you think we're going to put up with that…"

"Carlie."

The sharp voice drew every eye to the archway. Elizabeth Winthrop…it couldn't be anyone else. She was a dominant figure even without knowing who she was. Erect, despite her age, she had one hand on the ebony head of a cane, but she didn't appear to lean on it. Her black dress, trimmed with a frill of white lace at the neck, seemed to belong to an earlier age, but there was nothing old-fashioned about the way she instantly took control of the room, sweeping it with a critical glance that made Ethan sit up straighter, silenced Carlie and brought on a new spate of hand-wringing from Betty.

Trey rose. "Mrs. Winthrop, may I introduce Amanda Curtiss."

Amanda stood, too, compelled by the force of the woman's stare. "Thank you for agreeing to see me."

Elizabeth Winthrop gave a derisive snort. "I see who I want to see, young woman. And nothing happens in this family without my agreement." She stumped forward into the room, now using the cane and accompanied by an older woman in a neat gray dress that had a suggestion of a uniform about it. This, she assumed, was the housekeeper Trey had mentioned.

Elizabeth took the upholstered chair Shay had pulled up for her, sat without looking and pushed away her daughter's attempt to put a footstool under her feet. Her gaze never left Amanda's face.

Amanda perched on the edge of her chair, ready for whatever the woman decided to throw at her. At least, she hoped she was ready.

"You're not attempting to use the Winthrop name, I take it. Wise of you."

A flicker of anger stiffened Amanda's determination. "My name is Curtiss. My adoptive mother was Juliet Curtiss, the artist." Would people out here even know the name? She wasn't in Boston anymore.

"So you say." Elizabeth may or may not have heard of her, but clearly it didn't make any difference.

"Amanda's bona fides are perfectly in order." Trey spoke before she could snap an answer. "She was raised in Boston, attended Boston College and Penn Veterinary Medicine School, and is employed by a veterinary practice in Boston."

"Then what are you doing here, poking into my granddaughter's death?" She snapped the question at Amanda, ignoring Trey.

"Not her death," Amanda said, lured off topic by the accusation, which made her sound like a ghoul. "I learned after my mother's death that Juliet was not my biological mother."

Careful, she thought. *These people don't need to know that your inheritance from Juliet might be in doubt.*

"Naturally I want to know where I came from, especially since my mother never talked about it. I found a reference in her work that seemed to link with the time of my birth, and I learned it referred to Melanie Winthrop. That's why I'm here."

That was it, in as few words as possible. At least the woman hadn't interrupted her. Or thrown them out.

"Pack of nonsense," Elizabeth muttered. "My granddaughter died close to thirty years ago. You…you…" She sputtered to a stop.

"I know." Amanda found her throat getting tight and didn't know why. After all, sad as Melanie's story had been, Amanda had no sense of relationship to her. How could she?

"Melanie died in April, 1989," Trey said, taking over smoothly. "Amanda was born in February of that same year." He opened the leather folder he carried and took something out—the photocopies of the painting and the inscription. He took them to Elizabeth. "Amanda's adoptive mother, Juliet Curtiss, was a successful artist who never, so far as I can tell, painted realistic landscapes. Except for this one."

He darted a glance toward Amanda, who nodded.

"She came here one summer and painted this view of Echo Falls…"

"That doesn't prove anything," Donald said. "The falls is a well-known beauty spot. Anyone might paint it."

"Not anyone would put this inscription on the painting." He showed Elizabeth the second photocopy. "'In memoriam. M.' And the date of your granddaughter's death."

Wisely, he didn't try to push any further. He simply let her look at the images. Donald Shay moved behind his mother-in-law, looking over her shoulder with a frown, as if at something distasteful.

Amanda studied the wrinkled face and the hooded eyes. Impossible to tell what the woman was thinking. Was she reacting at all to seeing this memorial to a child she must have loved?

After a long moment, the photocopies fluttered from her hands to the Oriental carpet.

"I don't believe it," the elderly voice rasped. "That could mean anything. It could be a fake." But her heavily veined hands trembled until she pressed them on her lap.

"It's not a fake," Amanda said. She'd never had anyone doubt her integrity this way, and she didn't like it. "That painting has hung in my mother's study from the time she painted it, the summer I was ten. It was important to her."

"There's a simple way of proving Amanda's lineage, one way or the other," Trey said. "A DNA test is simple, noninvasive, and will give us the results fairly quickly. It should tell us whether or not Amanda is related to you."

Donald Shay put his hand on his mother-in-law's shoulder in a way meant to suggest protection, but she shook it off with an irritable movement.

"This is upsetting Mrs. Winthrop to no good purpose," he said. "I don't know what this young woman expects to gain…"

"I'm not so old I can't speak for myself," Elizabeth snapped. "My granddaughter is dead. I won't relive the past for your satisfaction, Ms. Curtiss. Whatever you want to prove, you'll have to do it without our help. Good day."

Trey gave Amanda a warning glance, but it wasn't needed. She had no intention of pleading with the woman. He stooped and picked up the photocopies, and she saw Elizabeth's gaze following them as he put them back in his folder.

Then he nodded to Amanda, and she stood. "If you decide you'd like any further information, you know where to find me." He seemed to divide the words between Elizabeth and her son-in-law. "We'll say goodbye."

No one answered them, but the housekeeper, after one anxious look at her employer, showed them to the door. As they stepped out into the autumn sunshine, Amanda turned to her impulsively.

"I hope we didn't upset her too much."

The woman's stern face seemed to crack into a smile. "Bless you, it takes more than a little controversy to upset Elizabeth Winthrop. She'll be fine."

"Thanks, Helen." Trey's manner suggested that this was yet another person he'd known most of his life. "Don't let her take it out on you."

"I won't," she said, patting his arm. She stepped back, and the heavy door closed.

They walked together to the car. "Let me guess. Someone else who babysat you as a child?"

He grinned, holding the door while she slid into the seat. "Helen Lindstrom was my Sunday-school teacher when I was eight." He stood for a moment looking down at her, his smile fading. "Are you okay?"

"I don't know." That was as honest as she could be. "I keep reminding myself that this doesn't matter to me except that it's a step toward knowing who I am and learning whether Juliet adopted me. But I had an odd feeling while I was in there. Not kinship, exactly. More like…familiarity. That's as close as I can come. And, of course, it doesn't prove a thing."

That was the point, she thought as Trey rounded the car to the driver's side. This encounter hadn't proved anything one way or the other. A wave of depression slid over her without warning. Maybe that was going to be the story of this entire effort. Nothing proved, ever.

BY EVENING, AMANDA felt the need to talk to someone totally removed from Echo Falls and all its problems. A call to Boston and her friend Kara proved to be exactly what she needed. It seemed pointless to keep the story from Kara at this point, since the entire population of Echo Falls seemed to know her business, so she told her the whole story.

Kara listened with deep attention, as she always did. She had the unique gift of sharing your trouble without trying to top it with her own stories or tell you how simple it would be to solve if only you'd follow her advice.

"Wow," she said when Amanda ran out of words. "This sounds like the plot of a thriller. You know, the kind where the heroine meets a handsome guy who might or might not be the killer."

"Except that there's no murder," Amanda reminded her.

"There is a handsome guy, though, right? I could tell by your voice when you talked about him. Now, don't disappoint me by saying that attorney is married with six kids."

"No kids. And very attractive. In fact..."

"I knew it," she said triumphantly. "See, I told you your luck was going to change. Not every guy is like that idiot who dumped you."

"It's too soon to think about that," she said quickly. "Besides, I'm not going to be hanging around Echo Falls forever. I just need to find something that will help me find my adoption records. If I knew for sure that Melanie Winthrop was my birth mother, at least I'd have a lead. And if I can find out where they sent her to have her baby, that would really help."

Kara hesitated. "This means a lot to you."

"Wouldn't it to you? If I can't prove who I am, everything—my mother's work, the house I grew up in, maybe even her gifts to me—could be ripped away."

"I didn't think about it that way. You have to do something about it, and I don't blame you for not leaving it to the lawyers. But if worse comes to worst, you can always move in with me."

"What, and put up with all those out-of-work actors you keep bringing home? No way." Kara was the casting director for a show filmed in Boston, and her heart was way too soft for the job, Amanda had always thought.

"I know, I know. Listen, you stay safe. And if you need me, give a holler. You know I'll come running."

"I know. I'm okay at the moment. But thanks."

When she'd hung up, she sat for a moment in the corner of the sofa, the phone still in her hand. Barney, who'd been sleeping at her feet while she talked, got up, stretched and nuzzled her hand.

"You already had your walk," she reminded him. "Besides, it's dark out."

The phone rang in her hand, startling her. Trey. She answered.

"You must have been on the phone for the last hour," he said. "I've been trying to reach you."

"Not that long. Anyway, I was talking to a friend in Boston. Is something happening?"

"No, nothing. I just wanted to be sure you weren't worrying about what happened today. I suspect when Donald Shay has considered the options, he'll talk his mother-in-law into being a little more accommodating."

"I already told you I won't bring a suit against them."

"I know. But he doesn't."

"I had no idea you were so devious." She leaned back against a cushion, smiling.

Trey started to say something, but Amanda lost the thread as Barney sprang to his feet in a single movement. He barked, not a single welcoming woof but a volley of barking. Something thudded against the side of the cottage, sending him into a frenzy.

Amanda was on her feet with no memory of how

she'd gotten there, holding on to the cell phone as if to a lifeline.

"Amanda, what's going on?" Trey's voice was sharp and urgent.

"Barney," she said. "He hears something…someone…outside. And something just hit the side of the cottage. It sounded like a rock."

"Stay inside," he said sharply. "Don't go looking for trouble. I'm on my way."

Another one, whatever it was, hit the wall hard enough to make the calendar that hung there bounce.

"Please." She wanted to tell him to hurry, but he would obviously come as fast as he could. The door was locked and bolted. She was perfectly safe as long as she stayed inside. Something struck near the side window, sending Barney into a crescendo of barking as he launched himself toward it.

Amanda grabbed his collar, pulling him back to her. Amos was only as far away as the farmhouse, but with the trees screening the cottage, he wouldn't know anything was happening here. And if she called, the phone would ring in the outside phone shanty and then go to the answering machine.

She was on her own, but she had Barney for protection. Besides, she had no intention of going outside and making herself a target for whoever was out there.

But all the same, she hoped Trey hurried.

CHAPTER NINE

TREY TOOK THE turn into the farm lane with a squeal of brakes and a spray of gravel, his hands gripping the wheel. If Amanda had gone outside without waiting for him, he'd...well, he didn't know what he'd do. She was a strong, independent woman, but nobody should go one-on-one against an intruder unless it was the only way to survive.

Almost as soon as he turned toward the cottage, he saw the beam of a powerful flashlight. The direction of the beam turned, and he could see it was Amos. The dog wasn't barking now, so that had to be a good sign. He hit a rut that sent his head against the vehicle's roof and forced himself to slow down. Around the last stand of trees, and the cottage came in view.

The door stood open, with light pouring out across the small porch. Amanda stood outside, and she looked as if she was in one piece. Amos flicked his flashlight beam down, so it wouldn't be in Trey's eyes, and held up his hand for Trey to stop.

"Everything's okay," he said. "No need to tear up here like a crazy person."

"Isn't there?" He swung out of the car and crossed the space that separated him from Amanda. "You sure you're all right?" He scanned her face, looking for any sign of pain or distress.

"Yes, fine." He thought, in the dim light, that she looked a little embarrassed by the fuss. "Luckily Amos heard Barney barking and came to check."

Trey gave a quick glance around. "Where is Barney? And why are you outside?"

"Naturally I opened the door when I realized Amos was here. As for Barney… I'm afraid that he pulled away from me when I opened the door. Poor Amos thought he was charging at him for a second."

Amos chuckled. "Gave me a start, I can tell you. But he's a gut guard dog, that's certain sure. Took off into the woods after whatever it was."

Whatever? He glanced at Amanda, who responded with a slight shrug and a shake of her head. She didn't want to make an issue of it with Amos, and he couldn't say he blamed her.

"He's been gone too long," Amanda said abruptly, her mind obviously chasing after Barney. "We haven't heard any barking in several minutes." Taking a step away from him, she raised her voice. "Barney! Here, Barney. Here, boy!"

"Ach, he's maybe off on the trail of something else by now," Amos said easily. "He'll find his way back. They always do."

Amanda didn't look that confident. "In a strange place?"

"You've had him up in the woods most every day for a run, ain't so? He'll have picked it up."

It seemed Amos was right, because a moment later they heard something coming through the brush. Barney bounded up to Amanda, his tail waving as if with pride.

She gave him a quick hug. "Good boy, good dog. You chased him away, didn't you?"

Trey bent to ruffle Barney's ears, his eyes on Amanda. His outraged nerves had settled back to normal, but he was still worried. "Okay, so tell me exactly what happened. Did you see anything?"

"Nothing," she said. "I heard noises outside, and something hit against the wall of the cottage a couple of times. I'm not dumb enough to go out and see what's causing it."

"Could have been a coyote," Amos said. "I saw one up on the ridge one afternoon last week. They've come back, whether folks think it or not."

He was referring, Trey knew, to the perennial battle over whether or not coyotes had actually returned to the Pennsylvania woods. Some authorities scoffed at the idea, but there had been sightings.

Amanda, probably alarmed at the idea of Barney getting in a fight, was running her hands over the dog, assuring herself that he was okay.

Trey frowned. "I'm not sure why a coyote would sound like something hitting the cottage. Have you looked around the outside of the cottage?"

"Not yet." Amos seemed to pick up on his concern. "Let's have a walk around. Where did the sounds come from?" The question was directed toward Amanda.

"The side away from the farmhouse." She pointed. "They were loud, but luckily nothing hit the window, whatever it was."

With a glance at Trey, inviting him to come, Amos started around the cottage, the beam of light focused on the ground at its base. Trey followed, keyed up to a nervous edge that demanded action.

Amos kept the grass cut low around the cottage, probably to discourage any rodents who thought it might make a good winter home. They hadn't gone more than ten feet when they saw what they were after. Several large rocks lay a short distance from the wall, as if they'd bounced there after hitting the cottage.

Amos stood for a moment, staring down, and then he squatted. "They weren't here before."

"Are you sure?" Trey joined him. The largest was a baseball-size chunk, and the rocks would certainly account for the noises.

"Yah," Amos said heavily. "I mowed up here the day Amanda moved in. Wanted it nice for a visitor. I'd have seen them and moved them out of the way, that's certain sure."

Amanda came around the corner of the cottage, the dog at her heels. "Find something?"

Amos shone the light on the rocks again. "There's your answer. I'm not liking this. Sometimes there's teenagers out looking for trouble, but I wouldn't expect this. But for sure it wasn't an animal."

"No, it wasn't." Amanda reached toward Trey, handing him something that she held between her fingers. "Not unless the animals are wearing denim."

Trey took the fragment of cloth from her, holding it to the light and showing Amos. "Where was it?"

"Caught in Barney's teeth," she said.

Amos exchanged glances with him, and the older man's weathered face was lined with concern at the sight of the fabric scrap.

"At least Barney took a bite out of him." Trey tried to sound more cheerful than he felt. "Good boy."

Barney's tail waved, and he looked ridiculously as if he were grinning at Trey.

"I don't like this…somebody prowling around my land at night. Up to no good, you can count on it," Amos said. "Maybe teenagers, like I said. Or possum hunters."

"Maybe." Trey was noncommittal.

Amos shook his head. "I don't like it," he repeated. He turned to Amanda. "Maybe you'd like to sleep at the house tonight. Sarah will have a room ready for you in a minute, that's for sure."

"Thanks, but I'm not nervous. Whoever he was, he's gone now. I'll be fine."

Amos looked rueful. "Sarah will think I should have talked you into it. Sure you won't?"

Smiling, Amanda was more like herself again. "Tell Sarah I'll see her tomorrow, okay? And thanks, Amos."

"It's nothing. Nothing." He strode away, following the beam of his flashlight back down the lane.

Amanda shivered in the cool air, and Trey couldn't stop himself from touching her, running his hand down her arm. "How about inviting me in for coffee, so we can talk about this?"

"Come in for coffee," she said, clasping his hand. "Or tea. Or hot chocolate. I'm well supplied."

Walking inside hand in hand felt way too good to him. "Actually, I had enough coffee today to keep me awake for a week. Hot chocolate sounds good."

Amanda closed the door, sliding the bolt with an automatic gesture.

"I'm glad to see you're taking your safety seriously." He followed her to the small kitchen, watching as she put the kettle on and opened a box of hot chocolate packets.

"Are you kidding? I live in the city, remember? And after that break-in at home, I've been superconscious of that."

"Talk to me about that again," he said, sitting down at the small kitchen table. "The first time I was concentrating on the message on the painting. I'd like to hear exactly how it transpired."

"You're not connecting it with what happened here, are you? It was probably a random break-in." The kettle began to steam, and she poured the hot water over the cocoa in two mugs. After a momentary pause, she fetched a can of whipped cream from the refrigerator and topped each mug. "This was bad enough to warrant whipped cream, I think."

"You bet. But about the break-in at your house. You were at work when it happened?" *Concentrate on the case*, he ordered himself. *Not on how appealing Amanda looks in tights and an oversize sweatshirt with her hair loose on her shoulders.*

"That's right. Well, I don't know exactly when it did happen, but when I got home, Barney greeted me in triumph."

"Did anything else happen that day? Anyone hanging around?"

She made an exasperated sound. "The only person hanging around was Bertie."

"Bertie?" He sounded at sea because he was. "Who is Bertie?"

"My mother's agent, Bertram Berkley."

"Seriously? That's really his name?"

She grinned. "I've always assumed his real name was something considerably less artsy, like George Potts." She shook her head, the smile vanishing, and concentrated on stirring the cocoa in the heavy white mug before she sat down across from him. "The thing is…"

She paused long enough to take a sip that left her with a foamy white mustache, and he felt a nearly irresistible urge to wipe it away with his finger.

"The thing is that whatever he did for my mother, and to hear him tell it, you'd think he created her, he's been a pest since she died. He actually wormed my whereabouts out of Robert and showed up here."

"Here at the cottage?" His ears perked up at that. Someone else in the picture? "What exactly did he want?"

Amanda frowned a little. "The same thing. He thinks we should do a retrospective show of my mother's work, the sooner the better. I understand, I guess. It's his job to do the best he can to earn his fifteen percent, but I'm just not ready."

"No one can blame you for that. It's obviously too soon." He took a gulp of chocolate, rich and sweet.

She nodded. "I told him so in Boston. He was waiting for me outside the house when I came home that day. It was the first day I'd been back at work since my mother's death."

Was that important? If someone had been watching the house, they'd have waited until it was empty to strike.

"He actually wanted to come in and inventory the paintings that were in the house so he could include them. If I'd let him, he'd have been with me when I discovered the break-in."

"I take it you refused to discuss it."

"Right." She sipped at the cocoa. "*Insensitive* isn't a strong enough word for him. So he followed me here to renew his plea. He even tried to persuade me to cooperate by saying that my uncle was all for it, as if George Curtiss had anything to do with my mother's work."

"Wait a minute." He put his hand over hers. "He'd been talking to your uncle? The one you said had been sniffing around? The one Robert distrusted?"

"That's right." She rubbed her forehead as if a headache was building. "It is odd. I can't imagine how they know each other, but I told Bertie in no uncertain terms that if he discussed my business with anyone else, I'd find another agent. Do you think he had something to do with this? But how could he?"

"I don't know," he said slowly. "But I trust Robert McKinley's judgment about people. If this Berkley thought there'd be something to gain by siding with George Curtiss in any battle over the estate… Well, how would he react?"

"Juliet never had any illusions about Bertie. She said he'd sell his grandmother if the payoff was big enough." She cupped her hands around the mug, as if seeking warmth.

"I'm surprised she let him represent her if she felt that way."

"Oh, he was good at his job. And my mother always kept the reins in her own hands."

"But the bottom line is, he's someone who has a stake in what happens to you."

Amanda seemed reluctant to admit something that seemed so obvious to him. "I guess so. But if you're thinking that was him out in the woods tonight, believe me, that's impossible. Bertie in the dark woods alone? Never. Wear denim?" She touched the scrap of fabric that lay on the table. "Also never." Her gaze met his squarely. "Why are you avoiding the obvious?"

"I'm not," he protested. "But the introduction of someone I never even heard of into the tangle bears investigating. No, it's far more likely that if it wasn't, as Amos said, some possum hunter out to liven up his night or a couple of teenagers looking for early Halloween fun, then it was someone involved with the Winthrop family."

"They'd love for me go away so they can forget all about Melanie Winthrop. Still, I can't see Elizabeth or Betty or even Donald Shay lurking in the woods. The other two…"

"Yes." He considered. "Either of them would be capable of it. Carlie's ex-boyfriend certainly would be. Did he wear black denim jeans when you saw him?"

She shrugged. "Some sort of black pants. I wasn't that interested in his attire at that point."

"No, I see that. But short of catching one of them with a hole in his pants, I can't see how we'll prove it."

"That's why I didn't call the police," she said. "Well, one of the reasons. I didn't want to alarm Sarah's family or make myself look foolish for calling the police out here for what they'd think was nothing."

"They'd at least scare the intruder away." He took her hand in a firm grasp. "If you're frightened, you shouldn't hesitate to call."

"I wasn't frightened." The denial was immediate,

but then the corners of her lips curled. "Well, not much. I had Barney here, and I was locked in. And…I knew you were coming."

"As fast as I could." Their gazes locked, and her eyes seemed to darken.

"Amanda…" He wanted so much to kiss her, to hold her…

But it had better be at the door, because if they started something now, he wasn't sure he'd leave. And he had to.

He drained his mug. Taking her hand, he stood, moving toward the door with her. "I'm sure whoever did it is far away by now. Too bad Barney didn't bring back a good bite of him as well as his jeans."

"We can hope. Seriously, if Barney scented him again, I think he'd react."

He probably would. As Amos had said, Barney was a good watchdog. "Well, anyway, be careful."

"You needn't worry about that." Her voice was tart. Did she understand why he was walking away? "Would it surprise you to learn that my mother insisted I take karate lessons?"

"Just don't aim any kicks at me." He paused at the door, taking the risk of looking into her eyes. "Sounds as if she was a strong woman. And she raised a strong daughter."

Amanda pressed her lips together, her eyes misting. "I just hope I'm doing what she would want."

He touched her cheek lightly, feeling her skin warm under his hand. "As long as you're doing what you feel is right, I suspect she'd be satisfied. Call me in the morning, okay?"

"I will."

One kiss, he told himself, and claimed her lips, sliding his arms around her. Even that light caress ricocheted through him like an electric shock.

After a long moment, he drew away. Reluctantly. "Good night. Stay safe."

AMANDA CARRIED HER second cup of coffee into the living room the next morning. It was still early, but Sarah had been there and gone already, concerned for her and repeating her husband's offer that Amanda move to the farmhouse.

She'd said no, of course, preferring to be on her own, but she was touched nonetheless. If other people in town were automatically siding with the Winthrops against her, at least Sarah and Amos had no qualms about welcoming her.

That brought her thoughts right back around to Trey. She didn't consider herself very intuitive, except where animals were concerned, but she'd been able to sense Trey's mixed feelings about his part in her troubles. That hadn't stopped him from responding to her, at least. She put her fingers to her lips, smiling.

A relationship between them couldn't go anywhere, she reminded herself. Still, she couldn't help enjoying the feeling, however long it lasted. Trey had made her feel like a desirable woman again, after the emotional battering she'd taken from Rick's defection.

When Trey called, his voice had been strictly business. He'd probably been reminding himself, too, that this wouldn't work. But he had warmed when he'd suggested they have dinner tonight. To discuss the situation, he added quickly. And she'd agreed. To discuss the situation.

She was still sitting in the corner of the sofa, smiling, when the phone rang again. She didn't recognize the number, but it appeared to be local.

It was. It was Helen Lindstrom, Elizabeth Winthrop's housekeeper, of all people.

"I'm calling for Mrs. Winthrop. She'd like to see you sometime today. Will you come?"

Amanda tried to suppress a flare of hope. "Yes, of course. When?"

"This morning is best, miss. She usually sleeps in the afternoon." She paused. "And the rest of the family is out this morning."

"I see." She did see. Elizabeth wanted to talk with her without being hampered by anyone else's presence. "My attorney..." she began.

"Just you," the woman said. "That's what Mrs. Winthrop said. She wants to talk to you alone."

Not allowing herself to think about Trey's probable response, Amanda answered, "That's fine." She glanced at the clock, mentally giving herself time to change clothes and drive there. "Shall we say about ten thirty?"

"That's fine, miss. The gate will be open for you." The woman clicked off with no wasted words. Given the friendliness she'd shown the previous day, Amanda suspected she was making the call in Elizabeth Winthrop's hearing.

This was unexpected. Still, Trey had predicted Elizabeth might reconsider once she'd gotten used to the idea. She started to call Trey to tell him, but then decided against it. He might argue against her going alone, and she wanted to do this. So she'd tell him afterward.

Amanda regretted that decision only momentarily as she walked toward the massive front doors at the Winthrop house. It would be nice to have some backup. But if Elizabeth wanted to talk to her privately, that might be a positive step. She couldn't pass up that possibility.

Mrs. Lindstrom answered the door almost before Amanda's knock, as if she'd been watching for her.

"Come in, come in." She peered out, as if checking to be sure Amanda was alone. "This way. Mrs. Winthrop is in the sunroom."

Mrs. Lindstrom led the way through the foyer and a back hall, where Amanda caught a glimpse of the kitchen. She ushered Amanda into a large, glassed-in room that had obviously been built onto the back of the house. The windows looked out on flower beds, still showing some autumn color in mums and asters, and a swath of lawn dotted with large old trees.

A harsh voice called her attention to the inside of the room.

"Well, don't just stand there. Come and sit down." Mrs. Winthrop was enthroned in a padded wicker chair with a high back, and she gestured to a similar, but smaller, chair next to her.

Before Amanda could move, Mrs. Winthrop had turned on the housekeeper. "We don't need a chaperone. Go and fix the tea."

Mrs. Lindstrom didn't seem impressed by the bark. She glanced at Amanda. "Try not to let her get too excited."

Amanda nodded, but how on earth she could prevent anything the formidable old lady took it into her head to do, she didn't know.

As soon as the housekeeper had left the room, Mrs. Winthrop switched her focus to Amanda. Sitting upright, her hands clenching the top of the cane, she studied her. Looking for a resemblance, maybe?

"Well, why don't you say anything?"

Amanda blinked. "You asked me to come. I assumed that meant you had something to say to me."

She glared for a moment. "I'll say this for you. You're not afraid of me. Not like that fool daughter of mine." She paused, seeming to look past Amanda. "Melanie wasn't, either. You think that makes you Melanie's daughter?"

"No. Only a DNA test will prove or disprove that." Keeping this brief and businesslike seemed best.

"You must have at least half believed it to bother coming here."

The woman's shrewdness surprised Amanda. "Yes, I suppose I did," she said slowly. "But that may have been mostly wishful thinking."

Mrs. Winthrop nodded slowly. "I guess I can understand that. When did your mother die?"

The words still had the power to stir her grief. "A little over a month ago."

There were no meaningless expressions of sympathy from Elizabeth. "Takes longer than that," she muttered.

Amanda understood. It did indeed take longer than that just to get used to the fact, let alone accept it.

"That was our Melanie." The woman thrust a framed photograph at her, and Amanda took it in both hands.

This wasn't the stilted studio portrait that had been shown in the newspaper. The girl in this one, wearing riding pants and boots, leaned against a bay horse she'd guess was a Thoroughbred. The girl's head was tilted back, so that the fragile line of her throat showed and her light brown hair tumbled over her shoulders. The photographer had caught her laughing, and she looked very young and indescribably vulnerable.

Amanda touched the pictured face lightly, her throat tight. Suddenly she felt that sense of kinship she'd been looking for. Or was it just pity, for a young life cut short too early?

After a long moment she handed the photograph back. "She was…very lovely."

"Yes." Mrs. Winthrop put it on her lap, looking down at it. "Sweet, smart, talented. Like my son. She could have done anything, been anything. And then she had to fall for some boy and ruin her life." Her voice hardened on the last words, as if she couldn't forgive.

Some boy…possibly the father Amanda had never known. "Did you ever find out who he was?"

"No. She could keep a secret when she wanted to. Which means he was someone completely unsuitable." Her anger against the man throbbed in her voice, and her breathing seemed to rasp.

Mrs. Lindstrom arrived with a tea tray, creating a break that was probably a good thing if she didn't want Mrs. Winthrop to become upset. Maybe she'd done that deliberately, waiting for a moment when an interruption would do the most good.

The process of pouring tea, offering sugar and cream, serving what were obviously freshly baked scones, provided time for Mrs. Winthrop's color to fade to normal. Relieved, Amanda breathed easier herself. She didn't want to be accused of driving the woman into a stroke.

"She treated you well, your adoptive mother. Donald tells me your address is in a good part of Boston."

Amanda assumed that was a question. "Juliet always behaved as if I were her own daughter. We were very close."

"Not close enough for her to tell you that you were adopted."

The comment stung, and Amanda stiffened. "I don't know why she didn't tell me, but it wasn't from lack of love."

"If you were so happy, why are you bothering to find your birth mother?"

It almost sounded as if she were trying to make Amanda doubt herself. Well, it wouldn't work.

"I think anyone would want to know where they came from in a situation like this." She spoke carefully, not sure she wanted to have the Winthrop family guessing about the possibility of a legal battle over Juliet's will.

Still, she suspected Mrs. Winthrop might be more willing to cooperate if she could be convinced that all Amanda wanted was information. "For legal reasons, my attorney needs to have the adoption records to go to probate with the will. Knowing anything about where I came from could help."

Mrs. Winthrop seemed to be studying the tea in the fragile china cup she held. Finally, she looked up, her face withdrawn. "I don't see what I can tell you. Even if you were my granddaughter's child, I heard nothing from her after she left. I can't help you."

In other words, she was slamming the door on

Amanda and her annoying questions. Amanda decided to give up the pretense that this was a friendly tea party.

"You must know the location of the facility you sent her to." If her disapproval of that treatment showed in her voice, that was too bad.

There was a long silence while Mrs. Winthrop decided whether or not she was going to answer. Then she gave a short nod. "It was a perfectly reputable institution in Worcester, Massachusetts. There was nothing shoddy about it. The girls who went there had the best of care. They were able to continue their educations…"

"And then their babies were taken away and given to someone else," Amanda, tired of what she saw as rationalization, finished for her.

The woman rapped her cane on the parquet floor. "Don't you presume to lecture me, young woman. My granddaughter was only seventeen. She was no more ready to be a mother than a kitten is. I saved her from throwing her life away."

She stopped, her face working, hands gripping the cane as if she'd like to strike out at Amanda.

Well, she'd blown it, Amanda knew. The Winthrop family would never agree to the DNA testing now. When was she going to learn to use some tact?

She stood. "I'm sorry I've upset you, Mrs. Winthrop. I'll go now."

She'd reached the door before the rasping voice stopped her. "I don't regret anything I've done. Do you understand me?"

"Perfectly." Amanda reached for the door handle.

"There's no point in you expecting anything from

me, because you won't get it. But I'll consent to your DNA test. You can tell Trey Alter to set it up. Goodbye."

Instinct warned her that any comments wouldn't be welcomed. "I'll tell him. Thank you." This time she got out of the door.

CHAPTER TEN

"SORRY ABOUT THAT. I'd intended a quiet dinner so we could talk things over. I should have known that wouldn't happen at Giovanni's." Trey backed out of the restaurant parking lot that evening.

Amanda just smiled. "It's okay. The lobster ravioli was wonderful. It would have been a shame to disturb eating it with an argument."

"Were we going to argue?" He glanced at her as he turned onto Main Street.

"Argue might be too strong a word," she conceded. "But I'm sure we could have found something to disagree on. Anyway, it was nice to see how popular you are. Do you always have that many people stopping at your table when you dine out?"

"That had nothing to do with me. They all wanted to meet you. You've caused quite a stir in town."

"You're serious?" He could feel her gaze on his face and hear the incredulity in her voice.

"Very serious. Word has gotten around. I told you it would. You can sneeze at one o'clock in the library and have people offering you cold remedies in the post office fifteen minutes later. Don't ask me how it happens, because I don't know. It just does."

She shook her head. "You really do live in each other's pockets here, don't you?"

"It's not so bad. Just sometimes annoying, but it's so well-meant you can't get mad at it."

"Give me the anonymity of the city any day. I almost never see anyone I know when I'm eating out."

"Sounds boring to me." He kept the words light, but he was reminding himself that this was a short-lived interlude. Amanda would leave before long, and he'd better be sure she wouldn't take his heart with her when she went.

"Since we didn't get a chance for a private conversation in the restaurant, I still have something to tell you." She sounded just a little smug, as if she'd accomplished something he'd envy.

"What? What have you been up to?"

"I had a call from your Mrs. Lindstrom this morning. It seems Elizabeth Winthrop wanted to talk to me privately."

"You went there?"

At her nod, he felt a flicker of annoyance. "Why didn't you let me know?"

"Because I didn't have much time to get there, and I knew you'd argue about coming with me."

"I'm your attorney. I should be with you."

"Mrs. Winthrop insisted I come alone. Sorry, Trey, but she didn't include you in the invitation."

"You still shouldn't have gone alone. If we want them to think you might take legal action, it's important that you not talk to any of them alone." Didn't she understand that he had her best interests in mind?

"But it turned out fine. Although I admit, I had my doubts once or twice."

Resigned, he shook his head. Might as well talk to Amos's Percheron as a stubborn woman like Amanda.

"Maybe you'd better tell me all of it from the beginning."

"Well, as I said, she asked for me. I honestly think she's begun to believe I'm Melanie's daughter, or I don't see why she'd have said as much as she did."

He had to admit that made a certain amount of sense. He'd have expected Elizabeth to bar the doors to anyone she considered an interloper.

"Did she want any information from you?" he asked.

"She did ask a little about my adoptive mother. Almost as if she had to assure herself that I'd been well taken care of." She shrugged. "It seems to me that if she'd cared, she'd have made some attempt to find Melanie's baby long ago."

It was hardly surprising to hear a little bitterness in her voice. He found it hard to accept, too, that the family had just wiped Melanie off the map because she'd done something wrong.

"Maybe she did," he suggested. "We have no way of knowing whether she instituted a search or not."

Judging by her expression, Amanda didn't think much of that idea. "Anyway, then she went back to saying she didn't know anything that would help, insisting they'd never heard a thing about Melanie from the time she ran away from the institution they had her in until…well, until her death, I suppose."

"This institution…" he began.

"That's what I was going to tell you. She told me where it was. Worcester, Massachusetts. Not more than an hour's drive from Boston."

She had done well, not that he intended to congratulate her on acting without him. "That narrows things down a bit. She must not have gone too far, since you ended up in Boston with Juliet as your mother. You'll have to let Robert know."

"I already did," she said. "He promised to have his investigators get on it right away."

"Good." He frowned. "You know, you have to wonder how she managed to get away from that place on her own, without help, and pregnant."

He glanced across at Amanda. The last few streetlights in town lit her face momentarily, showing her frowning intensity, and then left it in darkness again.

"Maybe she didn't do it alone," she said finally. "Maybe she had help."

"From whom?" He couldn't help being skeptical, even though he was the one who'd mentioned it.

"Maybe from Juliet. Maybe they'd known each other."

"Where? I can't imagine where their lives would have crossed. Melanie hadn't even left town for college yet. And if Juliet had some connection with Echo Falls, you've been holding out on me."

Her smile flickered. "No, I haven't. But it's possible. The world is smaller than we think. And they did meet somewhere, because…well, here I am."

"So you are. Well, so some meeting between them prior to your birth might have happened. We'll have to mention that to the investigators. They're better equipped than we are to look for links like that."

"It might not be that complicated," Amanda said slowly. "What if it was someone here in Echo Falls who helped her?"

He considered. "Who? I can't imagine any of the family going against Elizabeth like that. If they did, they have more guts than I'd thought."

"It wouldn't have to be a family member. It could have been a friend. Maybe I can find out who her particular friends were."

"How? By asking Elizabeth Winthrop? I doubt she'd be interested in helping you."

Amanda seemed to pay no attention. She'd turned to him with an excited expression. "Wait a minute. How dumb we are! Who's the logical person for her to turn to?"

"The guy who got her pregnant." Trey smacked the steering wheel. "You're right. But if the family never knew who he was, I don't see how we're going to find him."

"No." That dampened her enthusiasm. "You're right. Her friends probably knew, though, if we could identify any of them."

He nodded reluctantly. He foresaw a tedious search through everyone he knew who was the right age, trying to come up with someone who remembered. "Right. I'll start looking for someone who might fit. Her close friends may have moved away from Echo Falls by now. Still, she must have confided in someone, if she was like any other teenager I've met."

"You sound discouraged," Amanda said. "This will cheer you up. Elizabeth has agreed to the DNA testing. She said for you to set it up."

"That is progress. Congrats." He reached over to grasp her hand. "How did you persuade her?"

"I honestly don't know. I'd made her mad by sounding critical of their actions in sending Melanie away. She got defensive, and I figured it was all over. And then she told me she'd do it. Can you set it up?"

"Of course. In fact, I have a friend who has a friend

who can expedite the process." This was progress. At least the DNA test would give them some solid facts, which were sadly missing in this case.

"Somehow I'm not surprised that you know someone," she said.

Trey turned onto the farm lane, grinning. "That's how things work. Sometimes I think we ought to just go back to a barter society and be done with it."

As they approached the lighted farmhouse, Trey spotted someone coming out the back door to the lane, carrying a lantern. The figure lifted it, and he saw that it was Amos, holding up his hand for them to stop.

"Something must be wrong." He could hear Amanda's tension in her voice.

"Maybe Amos just wants to tell me something," he said, lowering the window. "Hi, Amos. What's up?"

Amos didn't have his usual smile. Instead, his lean face was sober in the light from the battery lantern.

"Will you both komm in for a bit? We need to talk."

"Sure. Let me just pull over." Closing the window, he glanced at Amanda. "Any idea what this is about?"

Her face was tight. "No. Not unless they've decided they've had enough of the trouble I seem to bring with me."

He covered her hand with his. "I doubt that. But whatever it is, we'll deal with it." He was committed now, and he wouldn't back down, no matter who opposed them.

AMANDA HAD A bad feeling as she walked to the house. At some level, she must have been waiting for something to go wrong in her relationship with Sarah and Amos. After all, they didn't know her. They'd taken her in on Trey's recommendation, and they hadn't bargained for rumors, upset and prowlers.

Trey moved beside her, putting a hand at her waist as they went up the steps, reminding her of his presence.

Sarah turned from the stove as they walked into the kitchen. She, at least, was smiling, although Amanda could discern strain around her eyes. "Komm, sit. I have coffee almost ready, and there's cherry crumb pie."

Insensibly, she relaxed a little. It seemed news couldn't be too bad if it was accompanied by cherry crumb pie.

They sat at one end of the long table designed for Amos and Sarah's large family. No one said anything while Sarah was occupied with serving them, but once she was settled, there was a sense that the business of the evening was about to begin.

Amanda couldn't handle waiting any longer. "If this is about my renting the cottage…"

"Ach, no. Why would you think that?" Sarah looked honestly surprised. "No, this is about a letter I received today." She stopped, not seeming to know how to go on.

Amos cleared his throat. "You wanted to talk to the Amish lad who found the Winthrop girl when she died."

"Sarah told us it was her cousin, Jacob Miller, who'd gone out west. Sarah was going to write to him." Trey gave Sarah an encouraging smile. "I'm guessing Sarah has heard back from him. Is that right?"

"Yah." Sarah seemed to relax a little, as if that had gotten her over the difficulty of discussing it. "Jacob called and talked to me about it. He…he was shaken about the idea of Melanie's child turning up after all this time."

Amanda stared at her, processing the words. "But… why would that…" Even as she started to ask the question, she saw the obvious answer.

"When Trey asked, he referred to the person who found her as a boy," Sarah said. "But Jacob wasn't a boy. He was seventeen. A grown man. And he was in love with Melanie."

So there it was…the answer to the question that hadn't seemed so important to her while she was intent on finding her mother. If she was Melanie's child, that would mean Jacob Miller was her father.

"I see." Trey seemed to realize she was still absorbing the information. "Did you know about this at the time, Sarah?"

Sarah's forehead wrinkled. "I was just a child, but Jacob was my favorite cousin. He made a pet of me, maybe because he didn't have a little sister. I knew, vaguely, that something was going on with him. I even knew that he was meeting someone up by the falls, but I didn't understand what that meant."

Amanda's hands moved involuntarily. "He's all right with you telling us about it?"

"Yah, for sure." Sarah put her hand warmly over Amanda's. "You have to understand. He never knew what happened to the baby. Or even if it was alive. Now…he's overwhelmed that he has a daughter."

"We don't know for sure. When the tests come back…"

Sarah shook her head. "I don't need to wait for tests.

You're Jacob's child, all right. As soon as I knew why you were here, I felt it."

Amanda drew in a deep breath, trying to still her whirling thoughts. Maybe it was better to stick to the facts, such as they were, and try to put the emotions aside for now.

Trey seemed to understand that she needed time. "Did Jacob say if anyone from Melanie's family knew about him?"

"Oh, no." Sarah sounded sure of herself. "He wanted to go to them. When Melanie told him she was…was going to have a child, he wanted to go straight to her family. He wanted them to be married. He'd have taken care of her and the baby. But she wouldn't let him. She said she'd handle it herself."

"Did he hear from her after she was sent away?" Trey asked.

"No. It broke his heart, knowing she was out there someplace and not where. But then, that day in April, he found a note pushed in the door, telling him to meet her at their place."

Amanda's mind had started working again. "Where was their place?"

"At the top of the falls. If you didn't go up to the top, you wouldn't know, but there's a cave up there. You know the place, Trey?"

Trey nodded. "We always called it the Indian cave, although we didn't have the least reason for believing the Native Americans had anything to do with it."

"So they'd meet there," Sarah said, "whenever they could get away, and in her note, she told Jacob to meet her there."

"This cave…" Amanda frowned, trying to picture

the location. "Do you have to climb up beside the falls to get to it?"

If so, that could be how Melanie came to fall. For no good reason, the story Esther had told about feeling someone or something behind you when you were climbing up came into her mind.

But Sarah was already shaking her head. "Ach, no, there's an easier way in at the top. That's how Jacob went that day, cutting through the woods instead of going along the road because it was much shorter."

Sarah's gaze seemed fixed on something far away, as if she were seeing the scene as it unfolded in her cousin's voice. "He was wonderful happy to hear from her. He'd been eating his heart out with not knowing, and now, at last…"

Her voice died away.

With a look at his wife's face, Amos touched her shoulder in a soothing gesture. "You want I should tell it?"

Sarah shook her head, brushing away a tear. "I will." She took a deep breath, as if preparing herself. "Jacob said he was still in the woods, not far from the cave, when he heard Melanie's voice."

"Was she calling to him?" Amanda asked, thinking to ease her over the difficulty of telling.

"No. Jacob said it sounded like she was talking to someone."

She turned to Trey. "You know how the falls is so much louder from below than when you're above it?"

"That's true. You probably wouldn't hear someone talking if you were any distance from them at the base of the falls."

"But…" Amanda's mind seemed to be spinning. "Who could she have been talking to, if not to him?"

"I don't know. Jacob didn't know. He couldn't see her from where she was, not with the trees and brush in between them. He says that he slowed down, not sure whether to call to her or not since someone else was there."

"He'd think it might be someone from her family," Amos put in, "with her not wanting them to know about him."

"Yah. And then…" Sarah's voice shook. "Then he heard her scream."

"She fell." Amos pronounced the words with finality.

Amanda closed her eyes, trying to block out the vision of a body tumbling down the cliff face, hitting the rocks…

Trey's fingers tightened on hers. "Jacob would have run toward her when he heard the scream. Did he see anything?"

"No." Sarah wiped her face with both hands. "He said that he ran through the woods like a wild thing, shouting. But when he got within sight of the cave, there was nobody there. He went to the edge, and then he saw her."

Amos took over again. "He told Sarah that he climbed down as fast as he could, tumbling the last bit, and jumped in the water to pull her out. He carried her to the bank, but it was too late."

Amanda gave herself a mental shake. The scene had become too vivid, almost taking away her power to reason. But she had to think. There were still questions unanswered.

"I don't understand. Why didn't Chief Carmichaels tell us any of this? Why would he hide it?"

"He didn't know, did he?" Trey sounded sure of his ground.

Amos shook his head. "Jacob sat there with her. Grieving. He knew he had to do something, but what? He decided he'd have to run for the nearest telephone. Maybe the person who'd been with Melanie had already gone to call for help, but he didn't know for sure."

"By the time he got to the nearest farm that had a telephone, he'd had time to think," Sarah said. "He thought if they knew he was the father of Melanie's baby, they'd be sure he was to blame for her death. When he thought about the grief it would cause his family…well, he just decided that if they asked, he'd have to tell them, but otherwise, he'd say as little as possible."

"I'm guessing from the way Chief Carmichaels spoke of it, that never entered their minds," Trey said. "I remember hearing that one of her friends said Melanie loved the falls, and they figured she wanted to go there one last time."

Amanda blinked at that. "You mean they really thought she killed herself? But I thought it was declared an accident."

He shrugged. "In the absence of proof either way, it was kinder to call it an accident."

"But what about the other person Jacob heard? Because he kept silent, no one ever heard about that." She found herself fuming in defense of the girl who might or might not have been her mother.

Trey was probably reading her mind, because he

gripped her hand tightly in warning and flicked a glance toward Sarah. Amanda got a grip on herself. Whatever she might think, none of it was Sarah's doing.

"Maybe he did wrong by keeping silent," Sarah said with dignity. "But I understand why he did. He says I should tell you that he will come back and tell his story to anyone you say. And that he wants to see you." Her voice shook a little on the last words.

He wanted to see her. Sarah really meant that Jacob Miller was assuming Amanda was his daughter. Whatever Amanda had thought when she'd started this search, she hadn't envisioned coming face-to-face with her father, and she wasn't sure she wanted to.

She realized they were all looking at her, waiting for her to say what came next. "I… I think I'd better take some time before deciding. Is that all right?"

"Yah, of course." If anything, Sarah looked relieved. "I will tell Jacob. He'll be waiting at the phone shanty for me to call him."

"We'd better say good-night, then." Trey rose, and Amanda suspected that he felt relieved as well at her decision. Or rather, her lack of decision.

They moved toward the door. Sarah and Amos stepped out onto the porch with them into the chilly night air, Sarah pulling a shawl around her shoulders. She reached out to Amanda, an oddly tentative gesture.

"However it turns out, I am glad to know that I have a cousin in you."

Amanda felt a momentary panic. What did Sarah expect from her? She wasn't sure herself what she was feeling, and she wasn't ready to find a whole new family waiting to claim her.

Fortunately, Sarah didn't seem to expect a response.

With a soft "Good night," she walked off toward the phone shanty. To call the man who was waiting to hear what Amanda had said.

It was all too much. She should never have started this. She walked off quickly in the direction of the cottage, fumbling in her bag for the flashlight she'd taken to carrying with her.

She'd gone a mindless twenty yards before she realized that she was not alone. "You don't need to come with me," she snapped.

Trey seemed unmoved. "I think I do. We need to talk about this."

It took until they were within sight of the cottage to get herself under control. Then she had to contend with feeling foolishly embarrassed.

"Sorry. This is a lot to handle all at once."

"All the more reason that we should talk it over now. For one thing, you need to decide what you want Jacob Miller to do. Go to the police, or not?"

"I know." She unlocked the door and gave Barney the greeting he expected. "Come in."

But Trey was already in. He stood looking at her, and she couldn't decide if that was disapproval in his face or not.

"I'd offer you coffee, but I think we both have enough to keep our nerves jumping," she said, trying for a normal tone. She gestured to the sofa. "Let's sit down if we're going to talk."

"You're right about the coffee." He sat next to her, close but not touching. "We got more than we bargained for from Jacob Miller, didn't we?"

It was reassuring to hear him say "we." "I guess I never thought about actually finding either my birth mother or father. I thought only about information. Satisfaction of knowing. Not of being expected to face… Can I really refer to him as my father?"

"You don't have to, but I'd think you'd want to. It might be awkward, but…"

"Awkward isn't the word for it. I told you before that I never missed having a father. If you haven't had something, you can't miss it. I don't think I can drum up appropriate feelings for a stranger."

Trey smiled faintly at that. "I doubt that Jacob would expect anything much from you." The smile disappeared. "But Sarah…you already know Sarah. You might have shown a little more warmth at the idea that she's your cousin."

The fact that she already felt guilty about her lack of response to Sarah made her annoyed with him for pointing that out. "Juliet was enough family for me. I'm not looking for more."

Trey studied her face, his own tight with what was probably disapproval. "Maybe you ought to ask yourself why it's so important to see yourself as Juliet Curtiss's daughter."

"That's not fair," she flared. "I loved her."

But that love shouldn't keep her from loving anyone else, should it? She didn't like the question, and she tried to ignore it.

"Anyway, you're forgetting that it hit me out of the blue," she said, trying to excuse herself. "Apparently Sarah has been thinking that way for some time. She's gotten used to the idea of our being related. Maybe that's why they've been so patient in putting up with me."

"They're patient because that's who they are." He

sounded as if he were trying hard to speak evenly. "And I suspect because they like you, to say nothing of how you helped with the foal. Did you expect them to toss you out because of a prowler?"

"I guess not." He'd succeeded in making her feel small.

"Maybe we'd better get back to the facts, not feelings. If Jacob was right, and someone else was there with Melanie when she died, that means someone knows how Melanie died and deliberately kept quiet."

"I know." She rubbed her forehead, trying to think through the ramifications of going to the police with this story. "I suppose it could be someone who'd given her a ride and took fright when she fell."

He was silent for so long that she began to think he wasn't going to speak. Then his eyes met hers. "Have you considered that it might have been Juliet?"

Now it was her turn to be speechless. "I can't believe… I never thought of that. I guess I assumed that she'd have been taking care of me. If she'd been there, why would she have kept silent?"

He shrugged. "She might have been afraid the Winthrop family would take you away from her if she came out in the open. I don't know, but it's possible."

"I can't believe that. I mean, I know she kept silent about the fact that I was adopted, but that's a different kind of thing. By Jacob's account, whoever it was must have run away at once after Melanie fell in order to be out of sight by the time he got there. Whatever else Juliet might have done, she wasn't a coward, and she wasn't a person who'd turn away if someone needed her. She would have run to help, not run away."

Trey had watched her face closely, frowning a little. "I didn't know her, so I can't judge."

"There's another possibility, you know." She was reluctant to bring it up. "It could have been some member of the family."

"I thought of that," Trey said. "In a way, it's the most logical conclusion if she came back because she wanted to make peace with them."

"We don't *know* why she came back." The frustration was eating at her. "We don't know who was with her, or why. And we don't know whether her death was accident or suicide." She stopped, reluctant to give voice to the thought. "Or murder."

CHAPTER ELEVEN

TREY FOUND HE'D been staring at the same document for fifteen minutes the next morning, and he still hadn't absorbed any of it. He either he had to put everything else aside and get to work, or he had to deal with the issue that clouded his thinking and made him feel like a hamster on a wheel.

He shoved his chair back with an impatient movement and walked to the window. Main Street was quiet this morning. Across the way, Esther's helper was writing a lunch special on the chalkboard, and down the street he could see someone walking out of the bank. Otherwise all was still…a typical Echo Falls morning.

But an eruption might be coming that would shatter the peace, just as Amanda's words had shattered his. *Murder.* The worst of it was that he couldn't deny the possibility.

Possibility, not certainty. He'd tried to debunk the idea as soon as Amanda brought it up, but he didn't think he'd convinced her of anything. He'd told himself he needed to get away from her disturbing presence in order to think clearly, but that hadn't helped.

There were too many possible ways to account for Jacob Miller's story. If Amanda went to the police with the idea of murder, it would be all over town in minutes. As a scandal, there was little to beat it.

In the end, the decision wasn't up to him. Personally, he hoped Amanda would connect with Jacob Miller if he was her biological father. It would fill one of the holes in her background, at least, even if she decided not to have a relationship with him.

Warmhearted Sarah was willing to love her right now, but Amanda had backed away from that. Her explanation had been logical enough, but it made him wonder. Was it so hard for her to accept love when it was offered?

Enough poking about in Amanda's psyche, he told himself sternly. He had plenty to concern him when it came to his own feelings.

The buzz of his intercom cut short a fruitless line of thought. He pressed the button. "Yes, Evelyn?"

"Your mother is here to see…"

She didn't bother to finish, because Mom had opened his office door and sailed in. "I told Evelyn she didn't need to announce me, but she insisted." She kissed his cheek and then drew back, studying his face. "You look worried."

"I'm fine, Mom." He led her to his visitor's chair. "What's wrong?"

"Does something have to be wrong for me to drop in and see my favorite son? I'm on my way to the grocery store, so I thought I'd stop."

She was hedging, and they both knew it.

"Come on, out with it. You never come to the office in the middle of the day." Alarm struck him. "Is it Dad? What's wrong with him?"

"Now, don't overreact. It's nothing serious, I'm sure." She fidgeted with the clasp on her handbag.

"It's just that he's heard all the rumors going around town about the Winthrops and your client."

At a look from him, she held up her hands. "Not from me. But I can't stop him from going out to coffee with his friends, and you know how they sit there and talk."

He did, indeed. His father's weekly meeting had been going on for decades. He and his buddies had their own table at Esther's, where they sat for a couple of hours every Friday and solved the world's problems. He should have realized.

"I'm sorry, Mom. Probably the rumors are greatly exaggerated. Elizabeth Winthrop agreed to a DNA test, so that will settle everything. Then people will have to find something else to talk about."

He was being evasive, and he suspected she knew it. He never had been able to hide things from her.

But she didn't call him on it. Instead, she nodded, standing up. She'd made her point without telling him what to do, just like always.

"That's all I wanted to say. I know you'll do the right thing."

Sometimes he thought it would be easier if she didn't make that assumption.

"I'll stop by the house and talk to Dad about it soon. I promise."

"Good." She patted his cheek. "You know we have confidence in you."

Confidence he'd do what? he thought as she slipped away. Confidence that he'd know what was right? If so, it was misplaced, because he didn't.

What he did affected others in widening circles. His parents were affected already, and it would be worse if this thing exploded into accusations of murder. His partner was affected, he felt sure, even though Jason hadn't said anything about it to him.

Jason was newly engaged, expecting to be married soon. A man who was acquiring a wife and a ready-made son couldn't want his business put in jeopardy because of his partner's actions.

Trey had a loyalty to the firm, and all that it represented. And he had a loyalty to his client, quite aside from any personal feelings he might have for Amanda. When it came to two conflicting loyalties, how did he decide which one was the right choice?

IT WAS LATE MORNING, and Amanda still had no answer for Sarah about seeing Jacob Miller. She had to, didn't she? He had important information about Melanie's death, and now that they knew, she couldn't avoid it. But did that have to mean acknowledging him as her father?

Trey hadn't been pleased with her attitude. It wasn't any of his business. So why couldn't she ignore his opinion?

He'd implied, if he hadn't come right out and stated it, that she was too proud of her place as Juliet Curtiss's daughter. That wasn't true. She discovered she was arguing with herself.

Certainly she was proud of her mother's accomplishments, but it wasn't as if she'd lived in Juliet's shadow. She had her own life, her own career. If she didn't want to accept some stranger as her father, that was her own business. It didn't have anything to do with her feelings about herself. Did it?

A memory came drifting unbidden into her mind—

one she'd pushed down a long time ago. She'd told Trey, and she'd told herself, that she'd never doubted she was Juliet's child. But this…

She must have been about five or six at the time. They were still living in the run-down apartment house. A man had come to visit—an unwelcome visitor. Her mother's brother, she realized now, and her mother had tucked her in bed early.

She'd been wakened some time later by loud voices in the other room. Afraid to stay in bed, afraid to get up, she'd finally tiptoed to the door. Strange, how clear it was now. She could see herself, barefoot in the animal pajamas she'd loved, easing the door open a crack to the sound of a loud voice.

"…okay, if you won't help me, you won't. But don't drag in this stray kid as a reason. Where'd she come from? She's not a thing like you or anybody else in the family, and you weren't pregnant the last time I saw you. So where did you pick her up?"

His voice had been loud, but her mother's was deadly soft, with a tone that frightened her even more than the shouting.

"Get out. Don't come back if you value that miserable skin of yours."

Shaking, she'd closed the door, run back to bed, pulled the covers over her ears. Too late to block out the words. She'd known that if she called out, her mother would come, would comfort her and hold her.

But she hadn't. Why not? Was it because she was afraid it was true?

It couldn't be. She was Juliet Curtiss's daughter. Only now she knew she wasn't. If she didn't have that assurance… It was terrifying to think she'd based her entire image of herself on a lie.

She tried to dismiss the uncomfortable line of thought, but it clung like a burr clinging to a horse's mane.

Amanda quickened her pace as she walked toward the barn. She ought to be thinking of nothing more than enjoying the crisp fall weather. Not the past or the future, just now. She looked up toward the ridge as the lane came out of the patch of trees. Red and russet leaves still clung to the trees on the hillside, although one hard rainstorm would probably send them to the earth.

Stopping at the barn to check on the mare and colt had become a pleasant habit. Amos seemed happy enough to have her do it, and the kids always gave her a friendly greeting, sometimes stopping to chat for a minute or two before returning to their work. She'd seen this cheerful acceptance of shared chores in other farm families, and it struck her again how good a way it was to raise children.

The horse barn was the one place on the farm that she made a point of not taking Barney. She wasn't afraid of his behaving badly, but she'd noticed the colt was skittish around him, so she refrained. The little guy was getting used to her, cooperative about being handled, and she didn't want to mess that up.

With the younger children in school at this hour, things were fairly quiet. The older boys would have helped with the early milking and then been off to work on whatever job Amos had decided on for today. She'd heard him mention repairing fences in one of the fields.

The heavy door to the horse barn stood open, and only the mare and her foal were in the largest box stall. Amos was being cautious about turning the baby loose in the pasture, preferring to put him out only when he was close at hand. She couldn't blame him. That foal represented a big return on the money they had invested in the Percherons.

"Hello, there." She approached the stall, eager to have a look at them and pleased that they always came to the gate when they heard her voice.

But not today. To her surprise, the horses lingered at the back of the stall. She came closer, putting one hand on the top bar and holding out a carrot with the other. "Don't you want your treat today?"

The colt peered out at her from behind his mother, eyeing the carrot. Before he could move, the mare had nuzzled him back into the corner. She displayed every sign of nervousness—her back rippling, ears laid back, tail swishing.

Amanda was too good a reader of animal behavior not to take alarm. Something in the front of the stall, maybe, that they were avoiding? She bent, trying to spot anything—a snake, even a mouse, that could account for it. Nothing that she could see. Odd.

Frowning, she took a step back. The mare stamped feet the size of dinner plates, tossing her mane. Perplexed, Amanda took another step away. Even as she moved, she heard a sound from the loft over her head. She looked up in time to see a wall of hay bales plummeting toward her.

Even as they fell she plunged back, frantic to get out from under them. But it was too late. A bale caught her on the shoulder, spinning her out of control. She fell heavily, putting her arms up to shield her head as she hit the barn floor and the bales thundered down on her.

Amanda didn't know how long it was until she started to think again. Had she been unconscious? She wasn't sure. She moved cautiously, trying to see if she was still in one piece. Her arms moved, but her legs...why couldn't she move her legs?

Panicked, she tried to sit up, but she was hit by a wave of dizziness and slumped down again. Giving herself a minute to regroup, she moved her arms so she could get her elbows under her. Trying again, she was able to get up far enough to see. Hay bales, four or five of them, covered her legs. No wonder she couldn't move them.

Hooves stamped against the wooden floor. Amanda looked up to see the mare, her head stretched over the top bar, looking down at her. Yes. The mare. She'd come into the barn to check on her and the colt, but... then what happened?

A step...boots, not hooves. In an instant Amos had rushed to her, closely followed by Isaac and Thomas, his oldest boys. "What has happened? Are you hurt?"

"Can't move," she managed to say, and leaned back against her pillow of hay.

"Boys, schnell, help me get the hay bales off her. No, wait, you, Thomas, run get your mamm. Hurry!"

She ought to tell him she was okay, but it seemed too much trouble. They moved the bales off her carefully, with Amos keeping up a steady stream of recrimination aimed at his son in a mix of English and Pennsylvania Dutch. The gist of it seemed to be that the bales never should have been stacked so close to the edge of the loft.

"We didn't," Isaac said finally. "You ask Thomas. Those bales were a good two feet away from the edge."

"If they were that far back, how did they…" Amos stopped as they lifted the last bale free. He knelt beside Amanda just as Sarah came running in.

In an instant she'd joined him, bending to put her arms around Amanda and help her sit up. "Don't try to move too fast. Where does it hurt?"

She might have been speaking to one of her children, Amanda thought, and the idea made her smile. "I'm all right, I think." At least her mind was working again. "I can move everything, so no bones broken. It'll be fine."

"Ach, you could have been hurt bad. Thank the gut Lord it's not worse. Now don't you try to stand. Let the boys lift you."

Amanda wanted to say she could manage herself, but she had a feeling nobody would believe that, including herself. The two boys were quick to help her, one on either side. She stood still for a moment, grasping the top stall board. The mare put her head over and nuzzled her, blowing a warm breath at her face.

"Yes, I'm fine." Amanda stroked the mare's neck.

"Boys, you help Amanda into the house." Amos consulted his wife with a look. "Should we call for the paramedics?"

"No," Amanda said quickly. "I don't need them."

Amos didn't seem satisfied until Sarah nodded agreement. "We'll take you into the house so you can rest a bit. Then we'll see."

Amos still didn't look entirely happy, but he gestured to Isaac and Thomas. With one on either side of her, they started toward the door.

She'd protest that she could walk by herself, but her legs showed a distressing tendency to behave like rubber. Still, with their strong arms around her, she made it to the farmhouse, and by then, her legs had steadied.

Sarah hurried to put a kettle on and then wet a cloth at the sink to bathe Amanda's face. When Sarah touched her hair to push it back, Amanda winced. She put up exploratory fingers and found a small graze on her forehead.

"It's nothing," she said.

"Nothing," Sarah agreed. "But we'll wash it off and cover it, just to keep it clean."

Knowing an argument would do no good, she sat still and let Sarah minister to her, aware of Amos and the boys standing there watching.

Sarah seemed to become aware of them, too. "What are you doing, standing there gawking? Don't you have something to do?"

The crossness, Amanda thought, was an indication of just how worried she'd been. Again, Amanda had the sense that Sarah was offering her a familial affection that she wasn't ready for.

Amos, apparently in answer, jerked a nod toward the back door. At the same time, Amanda heard a spray of gravel as a car pulled up. A moment later, Trey rushed in, coming to a stop when he saw Amanda sitting there.

She eyed him, not sure she trusted the wave of happiness that swept through her at the sight of him. "What are you doing here?"

"Amos called me. I hear you were trying to catch a falling hay bale…with your head, apparently." He nodded toward the bandage Sarah was fixing in place.

"You must have broken the speed limit getting here so fast," Isaac said, grinning in what seemed to be approval.

"Maybe," he admitted. He pulled out a chair and moved it close to Amanda. "So, tell us what happened."

She shook her head and immediately regretted it. "I'm not sure of all of it. I walked down to the barn to check on the foal, like I usually do. But both the mare and the baby were huddled in the back of the stall, and she wouldn't let him come near me. I figured something had scared them, and I moved back a couple of steps, looking for whatever it was. I heard something move over my head, and next thing I knew, the whole stack of hay bales rushed toward me."

He listened in frowning silence until she paused. Then he touched her hand gently. "Are you sure you're not hurt?"

"Just some bruises and scrapes to add to what I already had." She frowned a little. "If I hadn't moved back, looking for what frightened the mare, I'd have been hit more directly. I was lucky."

"You don't look very lucky at the moment." His tone was wry. "Why wasn't Barney with you? He'd have alerted you fast enough if something was wrong."

"When I go to the horse barn in the morning, I don't take him. The colt seems skittish when he's around."

Trey's frown deepened. "So this accident happened the only place you're likely to go without him."

"What are you thinking?" Amos demanded. "That it was deliberate?"

"I could believe that faster than I'd believe you and your boys don't know how to stack hay bales so they don't fall out of the loft."

Amos was still for a moment, assessing that. Then he nodded. "Komm. Let's go look at the loft and see what we can find."

Amanda moved, thinking she'd like a look herself, but Sarah pushed her back into the chair with gentle hands.

"You're not going climbing around in the loft. You're going to sit right here and drink a cup of tea and eat something sweet. That'll make you feel better."

Trey paused in the doorway. "Sarah's right. We'll tell you if we find anything."

They went out, and the kitchen seemed empty without them. Amanda watched as Sarah brewed a pot of tea and cut a wedge of shoofly pie. She set them down in front of Amanda and added the sugar bowl and a spoon. Then she sat down across from her.

"Now, eat. I'm staying right here until you do."

To please her, Amanda took a bite of the shoofly pie, tasting the molasses sweetness of it, and then a gulp of hot tea. Sarah was right, the warmth moving down her throat did make her feel better.

"Thank you. That's just what I needed." She hesitated, but it had to be said. "I'm sorry about bringing all this trouble to your family. If I were staying somewhere else…"

"Don't you think that way." Sarah reached across to squeeze her hand. "Where else would you be? You're family. If there's trouble, we face it together."

Amanda tried to inject a bit of reality into the conversation. "But we don't know yet that I'm Melanie and Jacob's child. I can't be sure until the results of the DNA tests come back."

"I don't need any tests to know that you're Jacob's

child. I feel it." Sarah's face changed a little, as if aware that Amanda wasn't ready for her belief. "But you wait until the test comes back. You'll see that I'm right."

"It shouldn't be long until we know," Amanda said. "Trey apparently knows someone who manages the laboratory they're using, and he agreed to make it a priority." She smiled, shaking her head a little. "Trey always seems to know someone."

Sarah patted her hand again. "He does, doesn't he? It comes from living here always. And his daad's connections, too. Everyone knows the Alter family."

Amanda applied herself to eating and drinking, but it was no good. She had to talk to Sarah about Jacob.

"I know you feel sure about who I am," she said slowly. "And I understand that it means a lot to you to find out what happened to Jacob's baby. But all of this is so new to me that I…well, sometimes I think it's all a dream."

"Or a nightmare?" Sarah smiled, taking any sting from the words.

"My mother's death was a nightmare, and that's what started it all. I just wish I understood how she and Melanie got together. What led to her taking charge of me? There are so many questions I'll never have answers to."

"Ach, I'm sorry. I never thought about it that way, and I should have. It was the questions that couldn't be answered that haunted Jacob all these years."

Amanda hadn't thought of his probable reactions, and it made her feel small to think she was so obsessed with her own feelings that she hadn't even considered his.

"About Jacob," she said. "I think it's important that he come here."

A huge smile spread across Sarah's face, and Amanda hurried on, anxious to get it all out before Sarah celebrated too much.

"I don't know if I'll ever be able to feel about Jacob as a daughter to a father. Maybe he should know that before he comes. I just…" She let the words trail away, unable to find the words to explain her feelings, especially to Sarah, who seemed to want so much.

But Sarah was nodding. "I understand. And Jacob will, too. He'll be satisfied just to see you and to know that you're all right. He won't ask for more than you can give, that I can promise you."

With that, Amanda had to be content.

WHEN THEY REACHED the barn, Isaac started to pick up the scattered hay bales.

"Wait just a minute on that, will you?" Trey said. "I'd like to take a look at the loft before anything is moved."

Isaac nodded, his eyes wide. "Are you thinking someone set out to harm Cousin Amanda?"

So the family was already claiming Amanda as kin. In a way, he understood why she was having difficulty accepting that, but at the same time, he didn't want to see Sarah and her family hurt.

"Whether or not, we ought to see what made the bales fall," Amos said. He nodded to Trey and motioned for him to go up the ladder first.

Trey climbed, wishing he were wearing something other than dress pants and a shirt and tie. But if they were snagged, it was in a good cause. He stepped into the loft and stopped there, not moving while he surveyed the floor.

Amos emerged behind him. "What are you thinking?"

"I hoped we might be able to find marks made by someone coming up who didn't belong here, but I suppose you're all up and down too often to tell."

"Yah, every day someone is up to throw the hay down to the stalls." Amos pointed. "There's where the bales fell."

They advanced cautiously, but there weren't any identifiable footprints in the loose sprinkling of hay and straw on the wide boards. "The boys say the bales were stacked two feet away from the edge, like they should be."

"It looks to me like they were here." Trey squatted next to the imprint of the bales. As Isaac and Thomas had claimed, it was at least two feet away, maybe closer to three.

"That's where we put them." Isaac stood on the ladder, his head and shoulders above the floor. He didn't make an attempt to come farther, probably having heard what Trey said. "If they were at the edge, someone else did it."

Trey nodded. "I believe you. Look, you can see where the bales were dragged over to the edge. Looks like they were set far enough to protrude over it. All it would take from that position was a shove to send the whole stack down."

"Who would do such a thing?" Amos demanded. "It's wicked."

"Yes, it is," he said soberly. "Somebody wanted to harm Amanda. If it's the same person who was throwing rocks against the cottage the other night, they've escalated their game."

He could see Amos struggling to believe it, but finally he nodded. "I can see no other answer."

"Whoever he was, he must have been watching Amanda so he knew that she went to the horse barn every morning to check on the foal. And that she didn't take Barney with her, so he didn't run any risk from the dog."

"He didn't count on the mare's sensing him," Isaac put in. "She knew something was wrong."

"And Amanda was quick enough to read her behavior and back away," Trey finished the thought. "If not, she could have been hurt much worse."

"But who?" Amos demanded. "Are you thinking it was one of the Winthrop family?"

"Maybe. Or maybe someone connected with one of them." He thought again of that boyfriend of Carlie's. Maybe it was time to have the police ask him some questions. He continued his train of thought. "So he pushed the bales, and then what? Climbed down the ladder and risked Amanda identifying him?"

Amos shook his head. "He didn't come out the front. We'd come back from working on the fence, going to put the tools away. We heard something fall in the horse barn and Amanda cry out. We'd have seen him if he came out that way, that's certain sure."

"Look," Isaac said, pointing toward the back of the barn. "The door at the back is standing open. We never left it like that. He must have gotten down that way."

The three of them worked their way back to the small door at the rear of the barn. The larger one in front provided access when they were putting hay in, and the back one allowed more ventilation when needed. Isaac was right, it swung wide at a touch.

"Have you had it open lately?"

They both shook their heads. "No need to in this weather," Amos said. "Everything's nice and dry, anyway. That's been shut up tight for a couple of months."

Trey leaned out, holding the edges of the frame. The ground sloped up toward the barn at the back, and the drop wasn't all that far. The landing would be cushioned by the soft grass beneath.

"He must have sneaked in after we'd finished morning chores," Isaac said. "For sure no one was in here when we turned the other horses out in the pasture."

"All he had to do was sneak in when no one was around. He probably opened this door then, to have it all ready for him."

Trey didn't like the image that was forming in his mind. An image of someone who'd go to any extreme to keep Amanda from…from what? From coming in for a share of the Winthrop estate? That seemed most likely, though he hadn't entirely dismissed the possible machinations of Juliet's brother, to say nothing of the agent who might have something to gain.

"Are you going to the police?" Amos asked. He didn't look unduly anxious, although Trey knew he'd hate being involved with the authorities.

"Not without talking it over with Amanda and seeing what she thinks. We're going to have to keep her safe, one way or another."

"I wish I'd gotten my hands on him," Isaac said. With his hands clenched into fists and the muscles standing out on his arms, he looked formidable.

"You would not strike the man," Amos said firmly. "No matter what he did."

"No," Isaac admitted. "But I could hold him until the police came, ain't so?"

Amos considered. "Yah, I think that would be acceptable."

Trey found his own fists tightening. If he encountered anyone who threatened Amanda, he'd know what to do. And he wasn't hampered by the Amish belief in nonviolence.

CHAPTER TWELVE

AMANDA STUDIED TREY'S face when the men came back into the kitchen. "Well, did you find anything?"

"Nothing that would tell us who was there, but enough to convince us someone did it deliberately. Right, Amos?"

Amos gave a reluctant nod. "Yah, that's so. Someone moved the bales and then most likely pushed them over."

Sarah was drying her hands over and over again on a tea towel. "It's hard to believe people can be so evil. Why would someone do such a wicked thing?"

Obviously this was very far outside Sarah's normal world, and Amanda couldn't help feeling guilty that she'd brought this trouble to their home.

"For gain, most likely," Amos said. "Some folks will do almost anything for money. We can't pretend there's not evil in the world."

"It seems to me that the best thing would be for me to find another place to stay." It was the least Amanda felt she could offer. "I'll…"

"No." Amos and Sarah spoke simultaneously and then looked at one another and smiled.

"You belong here," Sarah said firmly. "We are agreed. If there is trouble, we'll face it together. In fact, I think you should move into the farmhouse. The girls can move in together. They don't mind a bit."

"No." Now it was her turn to dismiss the idea. "Thank you. I appreciate the offer, but I love staying in the cottage. All my things are there, and I'm settled. Besides, I have Barney. He won't let anyone near me."

"Tonight you're going to have me, as well." Trey sounded determined. "I'll sleep on the sofa. You shouldn't be alone after the pummeling you took in any event."

"I can do it," Sarah offered.

Trey shook his head. "I'm doing it."

Somewhat to Amanda's surprise, Sarah didn't argue. Maybe she knew it would be useless.

"I'll take up a pillow and bedding later. And we'll bring supper for both of you."

"Sounds good," Trey said. "I'll have to go to the office for a bit and get a few things, but I'll be back by suppertime. You'll look after her until then?"

"Will you stop talking about me as if I'm not here?" Amanda said, her voice tart. "I'm capable of looking after myself."

"Not today." Sarah could be just as firm. "You might not realize it yet, but you had a shock. And probably plenty of bruising. You need to rest and let us baby you for now."

An argument would be futile, she realized. Maybe the best thing was to remove herself for the moment. "You might be right about the resting. I think I'll go back to the cottage and curl up with a book."

"I can carry you, Cousin Amanda," Isaac said, giving her a big grin.

"Thanks, Isaac, but I can walk." *Cousin.* The word

jolted her. It seemed the whole family was determined to adopt her, whether she wanted it or not.

She got up slowly, not giving herself a chance to wobble in front of them. "I'll take it slow."

Trey put a supportive arm around her. "I'll see you there and turn you over to Barney."

Once again, arguing would do no good. Besides, if she could get him alone, she could pump him about what exactly they found in the barn. So they went slowly up the lane, his arm around her, their hips touching as they moved.

She freed herself and turned to him when they got inside the cottage. "Thanks, and again, I'm sorry to drag you away from your office."

"Forget it." He took her arm and led her firmly to the sofa, with Barney whimpering a little at her heels. Obviously he sensed something was wrong. "Now, sit down and get comfortable. Can I get you something? Coffee?"

"I'm sloshing already," she protested. She'd like to say she didn't need to sit, but the softness of the sofa was too welcoming when she sank into it.

Trey took a quilted throw from the sofa back and tucked it around her as she leaned against the pillows. He was very close as he bent over her, and he brushed her cheek with his lips.

"Stay put. I'll be back later."

"You don't need…"

"I'll be back." His voice was firm, and he touched her lips lightly.

She probably should assert her independence, but she had to admit that it was comforting to be taken care of once in a while. She relaxed against the cushions, and Barney rested his head on the edge of the sofa, his eyes on her face. Patting him, she closed her eyes. She'd just rest for a few minutes.

A few minutes turned into much of the day, only interrupted by visits from Sarah and several of the children bringing food and checking on her. Trey arrived in the late afternoon and took Barney for a run. After supper, again provided by Sarah, Amanda was only too happy to return to the sofa.

She sank down with a sigh of relief, and Trey gave her a long look as he pulled a chair up next to her.

"Sure you don't want to have a doctor check you out?"

"I am a doctor," she said with a trace of tartness. "The human frame is much like an animal's. If anything were broken, I'd suspect it." Regretting her sharpness, she smiled. "Sorry. I appreciate the concern everyone is showing, but I'll heal. I'm developing some spectacular bruises."

"I'll bet." He seemed to make an effort to keep his tone easy, but she saw how his face darkened at the thought. "Amos and I were talking about whether or not to call the police. I guess I should have mentioned it to you earlier, but… Well, anyway, what do you think?"

She suspected he'd wanted to wait until she'd had a chance to recover her balance before presenting her with a decision. But she'd already been thinking about what action to take.

"I would, but will it really do any good? If I file a formal complaint, police will be swarming over the farm. I hate to do that to Amos and Sarah and the children. And I've got enough to deal with between the Winthrop family and my possible father's family as it is. What do you think?" She was actually asking his opinion.

"I know how you feel about the Burkhalters, but I don't like the idea of letting this character go wandering around looking for another chance at you."

"Neither do I." A shiver went through her.

"Look, how would it be if I talked with Chief Carmichaels in more general terms, saying you've been harassed but not filing a formal complaint? I think he'd be willing to check into Carlie's ex-boyfriend."

She nodded slowly. "I guess so. I just don't want to bring any more complications into Amos's and Sarah's lives." She gave him a questioning look. "Do you think I should go elsewhere to stay?"

Trey frowned, considering. "You wouldn't be as isolated at an inn, but you wouldn't be able to have Barney with you. All in all, this might be the safer choice, especially since everyone is on the alert. Amos and the boys insist they'll check things out periodically." His face lightened. "Unless, of course, you'd like to move in with me."

"And your parents?" she asked, knowing he wasn't serious.

"I'm one of the grown-ups now. I have my own house. And my own mortgage, for that matter," he added, in the tone of one reminded of a fact of life.

"I didn't realize you were a homeowner." Put that up alongside all the other things she didn't know about him. "In town?"

"It's not as impressive as it sounds...just a little two bedroom cottage that's a converted garage. Unfortunately, my guest room is taken up by exercise equipment and boxes of things I should get rid of."

"But you don't because you might need them someday," she said lightly. "Or are they mementos of past girlfriends?"

"I'm not one to hold on to reminders of failures," Trey said, just as lightly.

"All failures?" She was probably venturing too far into his private life, but he didn't have to answer if he didn't want to.

He considered for a moment. "Not exactly. I almost got engaged once, but we both woke up in time and realized we were drifting that way just because that was the path our friends were taking."

"What happened to her?"

"She has a successful career in Chicago, along with a nice husband and a baby on the way, according to the grapevine."

She couldn't detect any hint of regret in his voice. "Not sorry?"

"Not a bit. We weren't the real thing for each other." He leaned back in the chair, seeming ready to relax. "The trouble with living in a small town is that if you go out with someone more than twice, they have you engaged, and if you don't watch out, you'll be following the line of least resistance. So it's better not to move to the third date unless it's worth the risk."

"That's quite a philosophy. You wouldn't have to stay in a small town, of course."

He shrugged. "This is where I belong. The Alter family has invested three generations in the law firm. And having my own house gives me a little independence while keeping me close enough to look out for my parents. You never realize how suddenly that can become necessary." He stopped, seeming to wonder if he'd said too much. "I didn't mean…"

"I know what you meant." She thought of her mother with sorrow, but the shock of her death seemed to be fading. "I'm just glad, in retrospect, that I came home for that last year of her life."

Trey reached across to take her hand, holding it lightly. "I'm sure. But…" He hesitated, maybe wondering how much he should ask.

"But what?"

"You fit in so well here. I've watched you with the animals, remember? I have trouble picturing you tending to pampered pooches for a living."

"Not just pooches. There was the occasional cat or parakeet."

He didn't seem satisfied with the nonanswer. "You said you expected to go into large animal practice. In fact, you did. What sent you back to Boston?"

Her decision hung in the balance for a moment. She didn't have to tell him. But she found she wanted to be honest with him.

"There was a guy." She smiled. "My mother used to say that all my doubtful excuses started with those words when I was a teenager. Anyway, this guy was serious, or at least so I thought."

"Someone you were in vet school with?" He was leaning forward, intent.

"Yes. We decided we'd start a practice together. It made sense at the time—we were involved, we both wanted the same thing, maybe more to the point, my mother was willing to front the money to set up my practice."

She sensed, rather than saw, his reaction. He could probably guess what was coming.

"Maybe that's unfair to him. I don't know. Everything went well at first. There's plenty of work in Lancaster County for a large animal vet, and of course we each had barn calls that took us out at all hours." She stared down at their clasped hands. "So the predictable happened. I came back unexpectedly from a late call and caught him with another woman. Our receptionist, of all the trite things."

"He was a jerk."

"Not even a very original jerk." Funny, that she could talk about it now without the stab of pain and humiliation. Maybe experiencing real grief had wiped away the shadows. "Anyway, I sold the practice, repaid my mother and took myself back to Boston to lick my wounds."

"Understandable. But you're over it now, aren't you?"

"I am. Really. I think I knew even before what happened with my mother that it was time to make a fresh start. I just had to find the courage to do it." She leaned toward him, as serious as if she were making a solemn promise. "No matter how this situation turns out, I'll be starting over professionally. It's time I did what I was meant to do."

"Good." He was holding her hand with both of his, and he lifted it to his lips. "When I said he was a jerk, I understated the case. No one in his right mind would let you go."

His breath blew warmly across her skin, and then his lips pressed to her hand. Still holding it, he rose, stepped over Barney, and sat down next to her, drawing her against him.

She relaxed, her arms going around him, feeling the warmth of skin and muscle through the soft knit of his shirt. Their lips met, and what started as a gentle embrace turned abruptly into something far stronger, far more passionate.

Amanda didn't even think of her bruises as she returned kiss for kiss, embrace for embrace. She welcomed the weight of his body against her, emotions reeling along with her senses. It had been so long since she'd been held this way. She hadn't even known she'd longed for it until this moment. Trey...

Stop and think, a faint voice cried in her head. She didn't want to listen, didn't think she could listen to it, but then Trey drew back, just a little, so that he could see her face. He brushed her tangled hair back, his fingers lingering on her skin, sending a flare of heat through her.

"Much as I hate to say it, I think we'd better call a halt for a moment." His voice was husky, filled with a wealth of regret. "Quite aside from the question of professional ethics, there are Amos and Sarah to consider. If she thought..."

"I know." She took his hand and drew it away from her skin. After all, there was only so much a girl could take. "This...whatever it is between us...isn't appropriate right now for a lot of reasons."

He let her go slowly and sat back, looking at her with eyes that were still darkened with desire. "Somehow I think it might be better if there were a closed door between us." He managed a slight grin with the words.

"So do I." She couldn't pretend she didn't feel what he did. "I'd better say good-night."

Trey nodded. "Take Barney in with you, just to be safe. I'll sleep on the sofa, near the door."

"Right." The reminder that she might be in danger had a chilling effect. She clicked her fingers to Barney and headed for the bedroom.

Trey, moving beside her, stopped at the door. "Good night. Sleep well." He had himself well under control now, she thought. He touched her cheek, then kissed her again, soft and dreamy this time.

Then he clasped the doorknob, stepping back. "This situation won't go on forever. Once you're not my client, it will be different."

Amanda nodded, but her thoughts weren't the same as his, she knew. Once she wasn't his client, she wouldn't be here in Echo Falls. So whatever might happen between them was doomed even before it started.

Trey had slipped out of the cottage early the next morning, after quietly opening the bedroom door to check on Amanda. She'd been sleeping soundly, her hair on the pillow in wild disarray, her lips slightly parted. His reaction had been sufficient to send him straight back to his own house for a cooling down period.

Now, shaved and changed, he was heading for an early breakfast at Esther's café. He happened to know that Chief Carmichaels went there for breakfast most mornings since his wife passed away, and a casual talk over coffee would be a lot less formal than calling at the police station.

He understood why Amanda didn't want to file a complaint, but he hoped that a private chat with Carmichaels might bear fruit. Fortunately, the chief was a man of habit, and he was sitting at a corner table with bacon and eggs in front of him.

Carmichaels gave him an assessing look when he approached and gestured to a chair. "Trey, join me."

He'd no sooner sat than Esther was there with the coffeepot and a thick white mug. "What'll it be, Trey?"

"Just the coffee, thanks, Esther."

She nodded, moving away to check on another customer.

The chief raised his eyebrows. "And some conversation?"

"You read my mind." He'd always known the chief was shrewd.

Carmichaels took a gulp of coffee and put his mug down, his graying eyebrows drawing down. "You started something when you came to me with your questions about Melanie Winthrop's death, you and Ms. Curtiss."

Trey looked a question, and the chief shrugged in response.

"Thing is, I haven't been able to get it out of my mind. So I went back through what records there are again. Not much there, when all's said and done."

"No, I suppose not, if you felt it was clearly an accident."

"I wasn't the chief then, remember? It wasn't my business to be thinking anything. Just to follow orders. And Clifford Barnes…well, he never was one to rock the boat."

Trey vaguely remembered Barnes, who'd been chief before Carmichaels. "I don't suppose he thought there was reason to make things worse for the Winthrop family."

"That's about the size of it." Carmichaels stared at his congealing eggs as if seeing something else. "It had me wondering, though. Even at the time. And when you and Ms. Curtiss came in, that brought it all back."

His words came as a surprise. There hadn't been any hint before that he hadn't been satisfied with the investigation. "What bothered you?" he asked, trying not to sound too urgent.

"That whole business of how Melanie got here, for one thing. We didn't find an abandoned car any-place, so she didn't drive herself. And I'm the one who checked the buses. There was still regular bus service through town then, you know, but she didn't come in on the bus. The driver insisted, I checked a couple of days back, but no dice. And she sure couldn't have been hiding out in town for longer than that. Stands to reason someone would have known."

He and Amanda had gone over that very question without coming up with an answer. "So what's your gut reaction?"

"Somebody brought her, that's what I figure. But who? And why didn't they ever come forward?" He eyed Trey. "You or Ms. Curtiss have any ideas on that?"

He shook his head. "We did talk about it, but you probably know more than we do. If Melanie was Amanda's mother, then Amanda was a two-month-old baby then. Did she leave her with friends? I take it there was no sign of an infant at the scene of the ac-cident?"

"Nothing. Her handbag was there, but I never got

a look at the contents. And I checked the coroner's files as well as ours. There wasn't any record of the bag. My guess is that the chief just passed it on to her grandmother."

"Odd." Elizabeth apparently hadn't mentioned anything about that to Amanda when they'd talked, but then, why should she? "There might have been some indication in the bag as to where she'd been living and how she got there."

"There's too many loose ends to grab hold of anything." Carmichaels pushed his plate away in disgust. "Look at that, now. I've ruined Esther's three-egg breakfast with too much talking."

Trey couldn't help grinning. "Your arteries are probably thanking you."

"Yeah, well, that's about what my Jessie would have said. She's probably up there right now, thinking I'm going to pot without her." Carmichaels planted his elbows on the table. "So what's going on that you want to talk to me about so early in the day?"

Trey picked his words carefully. "Since Amanda's story got around town, she's been…well, harassed, for lack of a better word."

The chief's gaze sharpened. "Harassed how? Phone calls? Anonymous letters?"

"Nothing like that." In fact, that pointed to someone with a definite objective in mind that wouldn't be gained by letters or phone calls. "A few days ago when she was on her way back to the Burkhalter place, a guy on a motorcycle forced her off the road."

"Some of those guys think they own the road," Carmichaels muttered. "And they don't have the control they should over those machines."

"This was apparently deliberate. She ended up in the ditch, and her car had to go in for some bodywork. She just got it back. He had followed her for over a mile and then cut her off just when a tractor was coming, so she couldn't get out of the way. You can ask Phil Shuman. He saw the whole thing."

"Why didn't she call us?" Carmichaels demanded. "Or the township boys?"

Trey shrugged. That was a good question. "She figured she'd already caused quite a stir and didn't want to make it worse. Besides, she'd just had an unpleasant encounter with Carlie Shay."

"Carlie, huh? Well, she's been up to more than her folks know about, most likely. But I don't know that I see her driving a motorcycle."

"She had a boyfriend with one, didn't she?" *Careful*, he thought. *Don't accuse. Just comment.*

Carmichaels looked at him for a long moment. "Shawn Davis." He supplied the name. "I heard she broke it off because her grandmother put her foot down."

"That's what I heard, too. But I don't know that Carlie's the type to quietly knuckle under."

Carmichaels grunted but didn't directly respond. Maybe with the introduction of Carlie Shay's name, he'd gone too far. The chief wouldn't be eager to make enemies of a family like the Winthrops.

"Is that the only thing that happened to your client? Because if so…"

"No. Somebody came prowling around the cottage at the Burkhalter farm late one night…pounding on the side and chucking stones at it."

Carmichaels looked skeptical. "Could have been a

lot of things. Your city-girl client probably never stayed alone in a place like that."

"Not such a city girl. She was a large animal vet in farming country before she returned to Boston. She's not someone who scares easily. Besides, the dog was carrying on. He knew someone was out there. Amos heard him barking and came to check."

"So what did Amos think about it?"

"That it was an animal, most likely."

"You see? If Amos wasn't convinced..."

"He wasn't convinced until we found the rocks that had been chucked at the cottage. And the dog came back carrying something to show he'd caught up with the intruder. A piece of black denim."

"So someone was there," Carmichaels said slowly. "That still doesn't prove it's anything to do with what Ms. Curtiss claims. Anything else?"

If he told the chief about the incident at the barn, he'd be bound to investigate, and Amanda was emphatic about not bringing the police in on the Burkhalter family.

He shrugged. "I guess that's it."

Carmichaels studied his face for another moment, and then he pulled out his wallet and tossed money on the table. That *was* it, apparently.

Well, what else could he expect? He was walking a fine line as it was between what his client wanted and what he thought was wise.

Carmichaels rose, standing for a moment with his hand on the table. "Shawn Davis, huh? No reason that I can't lean on him a little."

Trey stood, too. "Thanks, Chief. I owe you."

"Just remember that when you decide to tell me the

things you left out this time around," Carmichaels said. "I'll be in touch."

So Carmichaels had known all along he was holding something back. He wasn't surprised. It was about what he'd expected of him.

At least he'd taken a step toward keeping Amanda safe. But was it enough?

CHAPTER THIRTEEN

WHEN SHE LEFT the cottage the next morning, Amanda intended to take her usual walk with Barney. By the time she'd reached the farm outbuildings, she realized that was going to be impossible.

Sarah, coming out of the chicken coop, waved to her. Amanda detoured toward her. She was probably walking like an old woman by this time, unlike Sarah, who came to her with a step as light as if she were a girl.

"Taking a walk?" Her face expressed concern. "Are you sure that's wise?"

"I've just decided it's not the smartest thing I might do," she admitted. "My bruises seem to have bruises."

Sarah linked arms with her. "I have just the thing for that—a liniment that's as gut for people as it is for horses. Komm to the house, and I'll give it to you."

She couldn't very well reject Sarah's good intentions, though she had her doubts about the efficacy of horse liniment on her bruises. Still, she could take it. She didn't have to use it.

They were nearing the house when Sarah landed a bombshell. "I heard from Jacob. He was able to get a driver quickly, so he left Ohio early this morning. He'll be here today in time for supper."

She couldn't catch her breath, just for a moment. It

reminded her of her first fall from a horse, when she'd had the wind knocked out of her.

"So soon," she managed to say.

"Yah, well, he wants to see his daughter." Sarah's smile was gentle and loving, and she patted Amanda's hand.

"It's not certain," Amanda said quickly. "You did tell him that, didn't you?"

"I told him." Sarah's steps slowed. "Isn't this what you want? You did say to tell him to come."

Saying she didn't know what she wanted didn't seem a viable option. "I think it's best if we hear his story for ourselves." Trey would surely want to be there…that should make it easier. "All of this is a little hard to handle. Six weeks ago I was living in Boston with my mother. I knew who I was and what my role in life was. Now…"

Sarah seemed to consider that carefully, her forehead wrinkled in thought. "I understand, I think. Would it help if you knew a bit more about Jacob?"

She hadn't even been curious enough to ask about Jacob's life. That must have hurt Sarah, and she'd been oblivious.

"Yes, it would. Did he marry?" Someone else. Someone who wasn't his first love. Natural enough, she supposed.

"He did." They'd reached the porch, and Sarah sat down on the padded swing, patting the place next to her. Amanda lowered herself cautiously, but it was more comfortable than it looked.

"Jacob married, and he and Katie have been happy, I think. They have five young ones—two boys and three girls."

So she had half siblings. Or at least, they might be that. Funny, she'd always wanted a sister or brother.

"I always wished…" she began, but the ringing of her cell phone cut off the confidence she was about to share.

It was Trey. "You won't believe this, but I found the place where Juliet stayed when she was in Echo Falls. It just fell into my lap. And the woman is willing to talk to us. Can you come to the office now?"

"I'll be there in fifteen minutes." She clicked off without waiting for more and sprang from the swing, nearly forgetting her bruises until a stab of pain forced her to remember. "I have to go. I'll talk to you when I get back."

She went back up the lane a bit faster than she'd come down, energy pumping through her, Barney trotting eagerly beside her. Progress, at last.

When she pulled up in front of the office, Trey was waiting for her. He climbed in beside her.

"I knew you'd be eager, right?"

"Right. Where to?" Apparently he was the unusual man who didn't feel the need to be in control of the vehicle.

"Just drive down to Maple Street and turn left. I'll tell you when."

She pulled back out onto Main. "How did you find out?"

"First things first," he said. He reached across to clasp her hand lightly for a moment before returning it to the steering wheel. "How are you?"

Amanda shrugged. "About as you'd expect after having a ton of hay fall on me."

"I don't think it was quite that much, but I get the message. Do you want to stop at the pharmacy?"

"Not necessary. Sarah has some horse liniment that she claims will do the trick."

She heard his soft chuckle. "Everyone in the area knows Sarah's horse liniment. Actually works pretty well, but it smells to high heaven."

"Guess I'd better be cautious about using it, then." She shared his smile, loving the ease between them.

"Left at the corner. The house is the second one on the right."

"You still didn't tell me..."

"Sorry. The woman's name is Arlene Lockhart. I stopped by to see my parents, and my mother mentioned Arlene had just come back from visiting her married daughter in Virginia. Then she went on to say it was a good thing Arlene had given up taking guests or she wouldn't be able to travel."

He glanced at her. "I know. I should have thought of that, but I never knew she'd run a guesthouse. I called this morning. She's happy to talk to us, and she remembers your mother, because Juliet was actually her last guest."

Amanda pulled to the curb. "This one?"

He nodded, and she parked. He came around to help her get out. She paused for a moment once she was standing to recuperate.

"Sorry. I'm not really as decrepit as I appear."

"Only approaching eighty, not ninety?" he teased gently.

They started up the walk, and he held her arm unobtrusively. The house was one of the Victorian homes that Echo Falls seemed to have in abundance, a solid-looking brick with glossy black shutters.

The woman opened the door before they reached it. She'd obviously been watching for them. Lean and angular, with tightly curling gray hair, she swept them inside with a glance.

"So this is what it takes to get you to stop and visit me, Trey Alter," she scolded, smiling. "And you're Amanda." She took Amanda's hand and held it for a moment. "I remember your mother speaking of you."

She led them into a living room furnished with an eclectic mixture of modern electronics and furniture from a variety of periods, all coexisting comfortably. Trey, after a quick glance around, chose an old-fashioned rocker rather than a chair of molded plastic with chrome legs.

"It's been a long time," he said, ever the cautious lawyer. "You still remember her?"

"There's nothing wrong with my memory." The woman's voice was tart, and she drew Amanda down on the sofa next to her. "Besides, she was my very last guest. I'd already made up my mind to close, but she seemed so nice when she came to the door, and besides, the room was ready." She shrugged. "Glad I did. Your mother was a fascinating woman. So intent on her painting, but interested in everything around her, too."

Amanda gave Trey a quick glance. Of course Juliet would have been interested in the town. She'd come here because of Melanie. A thought stabbed at her. Had she suspected that Melanie's death wasn't an accident?

"Did my mother say anything about why she'd come to Echo Falls?" she asked.

Mrs. Lockhart nodded. "Said she'd seen pictures

of the falls and wanted to paint them, and that's what she did. Up early every morning she was, off to the falls." She smiled. "I remember giving her the directions. When she heard she'd have to hike through the woods, she just went out to her car and got a backpack to put all her gear in."

Juliet hadn't been to the falls before, then. That disposed of the idea that she'd been the person with Melanie at the falls the day she died. Lost in her relief, she came back to the moment to hear Trey asking how long Juliet had stayed.

"Four days—no, no, five. She came on a Sunday late afternoon and left Friday. After you called, I went back and checked, and sure enough, I still had my guest book tucked away on a shelf. So I'm sure."

"Did she ever show you the painting?" Trey seemed to have taken over the questioning.

The woman nodded. "She was funny about it. Looked sad, I thought, so I made sure to say how good it was. Which it was," she added.

She turned to Amanda. "No use in pretending I haven't heard all the gossip, is there? But she never mentioned Melanie, so far as I can remember. And that's about all I can say, I guess." She looked regretful, as if she'd like to have more to contribute to the topic everyone was talking about.

Amanda collected herself. "Did she have any visitors while she was here? Or any calls?"

The woman frowned a little, obviously searching her memories. "It does seem to me that someone called for her that week. I just answered and passed the phone on to her."

"A man or a woman?" Amanda asked.

"I just don't remember." She shook her head. "Too bad. I just know it was for Juliet. Oh, and it was a local call." She reddened a little. "I suppose you think it was odd that I asked her that, but I'd had some trouble then with people making long-distance calls on my phone. So I mentioned that if she called them back long-distance, that would be added to her bill, and she said it was a local call, and she wouldn't be talking to them again, anyway."

Amanda exchanged glances with Trey and knew he was thinking just what she was. Who would Juliet have known locally that might have called her?

"You can't tell us anything else about the call?" Amanda waited, watching the woman's expression as she considered it. But finally she shook her head.

"Sorry. I wish I could help, but it was a long time ago. Like I told Trey, the only reason I remember as much as I do is because she was my last guest."

"Thanks, Arlene." Trey gave Amanda a questioning look, as if to ask if there were anything more. She shook her head.

"Yes, thank you," Amanda echoed, rising, wishing she could think of the question that would unlock all the things she wanted to know. "I do appreciate it."

"Anytime." Arlene pressed her hand again. "You think of anything else, you don't need to wait for Trey to bring you. Just you stop by."

Repeating her appreciation, Amanda let Trey usher her to the door. There didn't seem to be anything else to be learned here, and there was no reason to be disappointed. Still, she kept hoping for the one breakthrough, and it didn't come. Maybe it never would.

TREY PAUSED AS they neared Amanda's car. She seemed lost in thought, making him wonder if she'd heard more from Arlene than he had. "Mind if I drive?" he asked.

She blinked, as if waking. "That's fine." She smiled. "I wondered when your need to be in control would assert itself. So what did you think about that local call Juliet apparently got? I didn't think she knew anyone in Echo Falls, so who would be calling her?"

He frowned, trying to concentrate on the question while other concerns bounced around in his brain. He helped her in, slid behind the wheel, and pulled out. "It could be nothing. She might have asked someone from the tourist office to call her, or something like that."

"Maybe." She looked dissatisfied. "But it suggests to me she knew someone here. Or was in touch with someone. A friend of Melanie's, maybe?"

"It could be. If so, it's odd that person hasn't come forward now that they've heard about you. I don't relish the thought of trying to call everyone in town who's the right age." He turned at the corner and headed down toward the river.

"Where are we going?"

"I have something I want to discuss with you that needs both attention and privacy."

"Something's happened?" Her voice was sharp and alert.

"Not exactly." He pulled up near the park where there was a view of the river.

"Well?" The look she gave him had a trace of exasperation, but she leaned against the door so that she was facing him more directly.

"Sorry. I'm not trying to be mysterious. I just didn't want to break this to you while you were behind the wheel of a moving vehicle." He stretched, his fingers brushing her shoulder. "I had a call from my guy at the lab. The written report should reach the Winthrops in tomorrow's mail, but he wanted to give me a heads-up."

Her breath caught, and he thought she hadn't expected it so soon.

"Out with it. Am I Melanie's daughter, or has this all been a wild-goose chase?" There was nothing of the apprehension he'd expected—just an impatience to learn the truth.

"He says the comparison of your DNA with Elizabeth's was pretty definitive...something technical about the markers in the female line. You are definitely related closely to her, presumably through Melanie, since there's no other viable possibility."

"Viable...okay, I get it. If there'd been another granddaughter of hers floating around who'd been pregnant at the right time..."

"Yes. There wasn't. So I think it's safe to consider it a sure thing. You are Melanie Winthrop's daughter."

Amanda was silent for a moment, and he found he couldn't read her face. "So that means I'm Jacob Miller's daughter, too."

He nodded. "Unless you subscribe to some other far-fetched solution. I don't think Sarah has any doubts."

"No." She shook her head slightly. "I didn't tell you. Sarah says he's on his way. He'll be here by late afternoon."

So that accounted for her reaction. "You'll be meeting your father tonight. And tomorrow the Winthrop family will have to accept you as Melanie's child." He hesitated, thinking that prospect, at least, wouldn't fill him with glee. "How do you feel about it?"

Amanda's usual spirit seemed to bounce back. "I think I'll enjoy the Miller relatives better than the Winthrop ones, from what I've seen of them."

"Can't say I blame you. Elizabeth will probably try to bully you the way she does the rest of them."

"She'll find that harder than she thinks." Amanda's jaw set. "If she'd ever admit she handled the situation badly with Melanie... But she won't."

"It would be the first time," he said. "But to get back to practical matters, you may well find yourself in line for a share of the Winthrop property. I say *may*, because I can't predict which way Elizabeth will jump. But as Melanie's daughter, you ought to."

Amanda shook her head. "I don't want anything from them. I'm getting tired of saying it. I just want the truth, and I'm beginning to think it can't be had."

He clasped her shoulder. "You're not getting discouraged, are you? With Jacob coming today? He may spread some new light on Melanie's death."

"He may, but we've probably heard everything he has to say from Sarah." She paused. "Will you join us when I talk to him?"

"Nervous about meeting him?"

"No." She made a face. "Actually, yes. Did you know he has a family? I have five half siblings. I always wanted a brother or a sister."

"Your wish has come true, then." He sensed that she was still getting used to the idea.

"I guess." She shrugged. "We've talked about this before. I'm not sure how I'll feel when I see him."

"I thought you were more concerned with facts than feelings."

"I suppose I said that at some point, didn't I?"

She turned her face toward him, and they were close enough that he could see the flicker of laughter in the blue of her eyes. "I say a lot of things."

He smiled back. "We've had a lot to talk about. There's nothing like a crisis for forcing you to get to know someone quickly."

She nodded, but the smile faded from her eyes. "I don't want to hurt Jacob, but I can't manufacture feelings for him."

"He won't expect that." At least, he hoped not. Amanda had enough to deal with without coping with the feeling she'd disappointed this father she'd so suddenly acquired.

Amanda stirred, as if she'd like to be doing something, anything, so long as it was active. "The frustrating thing is that I still haven't found any proof as to my adoption. Without that…"

"Without that, I'd guess that the court would still take Juliet's obvious wishes into consideration. And Juliet's brother might not like the time and expense involved in a prolonged court case. He might be willing to settle."

Her hair brushed his fingers as she turned her head again. "He might," she admitted. "But knowing how my mother felt about him, it would go against the grain to let him pocket anything of hers." She hesitated, and it was clear she had something else she wanted to say. "I remembered something about Juliet's brother that probably explains his interest. I was very young, probably five or six, but I overheard them arguing. He referred to me as 'a stray kid' and basically said he knew I wasn't hers."

He gave in to the urge to run his fingers through

her hair. The strands clung to his hand, curling around it. "So he suspected all along. But he didn't have any proof, or he'd have brought it up by now. Still, where he's concerned, you might have to decide what you'll give up to be free to start that new life you spoke of."

A new life...maybe here? He didn't think that had even entered her reckoning at this point. After everything that had happened here, the idea would probably leave a bad taste in her mouth.

He had to accept it. Once she felt she'd learned all she could here, she'd leave. It would be for the best. Wouldn't it?

AMANDA TRIED TO maintain a pleasant, smiling facade as she waited with Sarah's family for the approaching car to pull up. Trey stood next to her, and she was grateful for his presence, little though she wanted to admit it. She could handle this meeting with her father alone, but it wasn't a sign of weakness to be glad he was there, was it?

The car stopped, and a man slid out of the passenger's side. The driver rolled down his window. "I'll be off now. Have a good visit."

Jacob was already being rushed by Sarah, closely followed by Amos. While Sarah hugged him, Amos pounded his shoulder in typical male fashion. A spate of Pennsylvania Dutch flowed out, and then stopped when Sarah raised her hand in warning.

"Ach, Englisch, everyone. Remember." She linked arms with Jacob. "You remember our kinder." She waved at her assembled children.

"Yah, but Isaac and Thomas have surely grown a foot." It was the first time Amanda had heard her father's voice—a soft baritone with the characteristic Pennsylvania Dutch rhythm.

"And here is Amanda." Sarah smiled, but her eyes were anxious.

Amanda had a spasm of panic. What would she do if he tried to embrace her? Or should she offer to shake hands?

But he made both unnecessary by stopping a couple of feet away, as if trying not to crowd her. "It is wonderful gut to see you at last, Amanda."

His voice was soft, his smile gentle. He was approaching her, Amanda realized, as she would approach a skittish animal. The thought gave her smile a little more warmth.

"It was good of you to come." She gestured to Trey. "This is a friend, Trey Alter."

Jacob nodded, shaking hands with Trey. "I've heard about you from my cousin Sarah. She tells me you're helping with—" a shadow darkened the clear blue of his eyes "—with all of this."

"I'm doing everything I can," Trey said, his tone easygoing, as if this sort of meeting happened every week. "Thanks for coming so quickly."

Jacob nodded. "Maybe I should have…"

"Business can wait until after supper," Sarah said. "It's ready, so all of you get to your seats. Girls, help me dish up."

Her daughters abandoned their curious staring and hurried ahead of the others toward the kitchen.

Amanda's tension eased. Sarah was giving her a chance to adjust before they got into what must be a painful conversation. And giving Jacob that opportunity, as well. She didn't know about Jacob, but she was glad of the respite.

Conversation bounced happily around the table, giving Amanda an opportunity to watch Jacob without, she hoped, anyone noticing. Oddly, she hadn't formed an image of him in her mind, but she wasn't surprised to note that his eyes were as blue as hers. His face was that of someone who worked outside in all weather, his hair and beard a light brown, touched with lighter strands.

It was a kind face, she realized as he listened intently to a story told by Sarah's youngest, Mary Elizabeth. When Melanie fell in love with him she'd probably seen the strength, along with the blue eyes and fair hair. She found she was hoping Melanie had recognized the kindness, as well.

He glanced up at her in that moment, smiling a little, and his look was touched with a love and longing that disconcerted her. Confused, she looked away.

When the last crumb of pie had been eaten, Sarah put the girls to work cleaning up, while Amos and the boys disappeared toward the barn. A setup job, she decided, especially when Sarah gave the three of them a conspiratorial smile.

"You three might go out on the front porch and sit awhile," she said. "It's a fine and private place for a talk."

Amanda felt herself guided to the front door by Trey's hand on her waist. Maybe he was trying to assure her that he'd be there. Either that or making sure she didn't bolt away.

Jacob waited while Amanda and Trey sat on the porch swing and then pulled a chair up facing them.

"We must talk," he said. "I know you have questions, but first I must say how happy it makes me to see my daughter at last and to know you've had a gut life."

"Yes, I have. My mother—Juliet Curtiss, my adopted mother—was a wonderful parent. She encouraged me to follow my own dreams. Did Sarah tell you I'm a veterinarian?"

"She did. It's a fine thing. She says you have as gut a hand with a hurting animal as I do."

"Sounds as if Amanda got that from you," Trey said, filling the gap while she struggled with the idea of having inherited her gift from this stranger.

"I wish..." He shook his head. "We can't change the past, and I am happy with my Katie and the kinder. But I would have wanted to know you all those years, even if Melanie and I weren't together."

That startled her—that calm acceptance that they wouldn't have married. "Didn't you love her?" The question came out sharper than intended.

"She was my first love." Again, his voice was gentle. "But in the years since, it has wondered me how it came to happen. Melanie wasn't happy at home. Her grandmother...you've met her grandmother?"

"Yes. She isn't a very—" she sought for the word "—understanding person."

His lips quirked. "No. Melanie rebelled against all her rules, and I think maybe I was the means to rebel. If we'd married...well, I don't think she could have settled down to be an Amish housewife."

Trey put a hand over Amanda's. "You knew she was pregnant?"

"She told me when she was sure. I wanted us to run away and get married, but she thought she should talk to her grandmother first." His eyes darkened. "I never saw her again until the day she died."

"Sarah said you used to meet at the falls." Trey must want to get to the crucial point. "How did you know to go there that day?"

"I had a note. It had been left on the back door." Jacob's face tightened as he remembered. "It was very short. Just said to meet her at the falls at ten o'clock that morning. I went and… Sarah told you what I found."

"She did, but it's important that we hear it from you. There might be some little detail that she missed or didn't know."

Amanda discovered she was content to let Trey take over this part. It gave her a chance to wrestle with her feelings. She imagined, if she'd thought about it, that Jacob would have been pining for his lost love all these years. His insight into the past required some getting used to.

"Yah, I see." Jacob looked down at his hands, clasped loosely in his lap. "Well, I went right away, but I had to walk, and that took time. I was afraid I wouldn't get there by ten, but I was a little bit early."

"Which way did you go?"

"I cut through the woods to the lane that comes in at the top of the falls. Then I went through the woods again over that little ridge because it was faster on foot."

Trey nodded as if he understood the route.

"I was still in the woods when I heard Melanie's voice. I thought she was calling me, so I answered. But then I realized she wasn't. Someone was with her, and she was talking to that person."

"Man or woman?"

"I don't know. I think Melanie must have been facing toward me, so I could hear her more clearly. She'd speak, and then there would be the sound of words I couldn't make out. It worried me. Why would she bring someone else when she came to meet me? I hesitated, thinking maybe it was somebody she wouldn't want to see me. And then I heard it—the scream." Jacob's voice broke. He stared down at his hands, clenched together now, the knuckles white. "I ran through the brush, breaking it down and calling her name."

He cleared his throat and began again. "When I got to the place, there was no one there. I went closer, out to the edge where I could see down. She was lying there at the bottom. Like a broken doll."

Amanda realized she was holding her breath and let it out. "How could you be sure she was dead?" The first question she asked, and it was a terrible one.

"She looked…" He stopped, shook his head. "I had to get to her. I climbed down, slipping on the wet stones. I put my arms around her and lifted her out of the water, but it was too late. She was dead." He looked directly at Amanda. "I checked her breath, felt for her pulse. Nothing. I just…just held her in my arms and cried."

"We know eventually you went for help. But in all that time, you never saw or heard the other person?" Trey was gently insistent.

"No. If I had, I would say. But I don't know, just that someone was with Melanie when she fell. I'm as sure of that as that we're sitting here together."

CHAPTER FOURTEEN

A SILENCE FELL when Jacob stopped speaking. Trey expected a comment…a word…something from Amanda, but she sat, eyes lowered, seeming to communicate only with her thoughts.

A spark of irritation flared. She might at least acknowledge how difficult telling that had been for Jacob.

Apparently it was up to him. "I'm sorry. It can't be easy for you to relive it, even after all this time."

Jacob's face was somber, his blue eyes, so like Amanda's, bleak. "Yah." The muscles in his neck stood out like cords. "But it is Amanda's right to know how her mamm died. I should have spoken out at the time. Now…well, now I will do whatever she thinks best."

Trey grasped Amanda's wrist, compelling her to emerge from her absorption. "It's up to you, Amanda. What do we do now?"

She looked from him to Jacob. "The police should hear this." She gave Trey a challenging look. "You think it's too late to do any good, don't you?"

Trey tried to sort out his feelings even as he shook his head. "Not necessarily. I suppose it's still possible that it can lead to something. I'm just not overly optimistic of knowing everything after all this time."

Jacob stirred. "But surely the person who was with

Melanie will come forward once it's known that I heard someone, ain't so?"

"If that person is innocent," Amanda said, her tone sharp.

For a moment Jacob looked confused. "But what else?"

Trey stepped in before Amanda could mention murder. "At the very least, the person was negligent. By your own account, the scream followed so close on the voices that whoever was there had to have known, if not seen, the fall. Why didn't they try to help? Or call for assistance?"

Jacob nodded slowly. "Yah, I see. It was someone who didn't want it known he was there that day."

"And maybe still doesn't," Trey added.

Amanda's hand jerked under his. "Or her fall could have been deliberate."

"You think she was pushed?" Disbelief laced Jacob's voice. "Why? Who would do such a thing?"

"There's a lot of money in the Winthrop family." Trey might not want to believe it was murder, but he knew it was a real possibility.

Jacob shook his head slowly. "I don't want to bring trouble to my family here, but I can't be silent. I'll talk to the police. Just tell me when."

"I'll set something up with Chief Carmichaels for tomorrow. About ten?" He glanced at Amanda. "I'll pick you both up."

He stood, feeling as if he were about to put a stick into a hornet's nest. "I'll leave you now. You'll be wanting some time to talk…"

"No." Amanda got up abruptly, setting the swing rocking. "I… I'm really wiped out. I have to call it a night." She stepped off the porch before either of them could speak, and she hurried toward the cottage without another word.

Trey hated seeing the naked sorrow on Jacob's face. "I'm sorry…" he began.

"She's upset. It's only natural." Jacob laid a hand on Trey's shoulder. "You'll walk up with her, yah? See her safely in."

There seemed nothing else to say. Trey sped after Amanda, his long strides eating up the distance. She'd wanted Jacob to come. The least she could do was spend some time with him.

He caught up with her at the turn in the lane, grasping her arm.

Before he could speak, she'd twisted free. "I don't want company."

"I can see that," he snapped. "Your father asked me to see you safely to the cottage. Oddly enough, he feels protective of you."

"I don't need…" she began.

"I know. You don't need anyone. What's wrong with you? Maybe what you found out about your parents didn't fit into your ideas of them, but at least try to be polite to the man."

He thought for a moment she'd strike out at him. Then she seemed to deflate, the anger swept away by pain that seemed an echo of Jacob's.

"I thought I was ready to see him. That all I wanted was the truth." She drew in a breath. "I wasn't prepared to feel anything."

"And you did." His own annoyance was washed away by concern for her. "Jacob is your father. You'll never have a chance to know your birth mother, but you can get to know him. Can't you give him a chance?"

"I don't know." She rubbed her forehead with a tired gesture, making him wonder how much sleep she'd gotten last night, between her bruises and wondering when Jacob would appear. "I'll try, but it's not easy. You can't say anything about this situation is normal."

"No, I guess not." He ran his hands along her arms. Now was clearly not the time to push anything. "Try to get some sleep tonight, will you? Do you want me to stay?"

She shook her head. "I'll take Barney and my cell phone to bed with me. I'll be fine."

He touched her cheek lightly. "Okay. Go on in and lock up. I'll watch until you're safely tucked into the cottage."

She nodded, turning away before he could venture to kiss her. She walked steadily into the cottage, and even from here he could hear the lock click.

He tried to put himself in her place. She'd had a lot thrown at her in recent weeks, with everything she'd thought she knew about her family turned upside down, following so closely on the tragic death of her mother. Not surprising that she was hesitant about building a relationship with her father.

And what about his father? He started back to the car, thinking he ought to let him know before unleashing this bombshell on Echo Falls.

AMANDA PULLED ON her hiking boots early the next morning, smiling when Barney danced around her in anticipation of a walk.

"Yes, just give me a minute," she told him.

Standing, she fastened her hair back with a scrunchie, hoping she looked a little better than she felt. Easy enough for Trey to tell her to get some sleep. Not so easy to do.

After a lot of fruitless wondering about the effect of the past on the present, she had managed to fall into an uneasy slumber. But even that had been punctuated with dreams—seeing Melanie fall to the rocks, over and over again. And then the dream had twisted, and she was scrambling up the rocky trail next to the falls, feeling something behind her, grabbing at her heels. And then falling, falling...

It had been a relief to get up, and some careful stretching had eased the tension from her muscles. The bruises looked worse but felt better.

Hopefully a brisk walk would clear her head and help her face the day. Clicking to Barney, she went out the door, walking down the lane toward the route she usually took. Barney ran in a few widening circles, apparently to be sure nothing had changed from previous walks.

It was chilly under the trees, and she was glad of the flannel shirt she'd pulled on. She'd reached the open space where the farm came in view when she saw someone coming toward her.

Jacob stopped a few feet away, bending over to greet Barney, who cautiously sniffed his extended hand and ended by licking it. Jacob laughed, ruffling his ears.

"Gut boy." He smiled at Amanda with something of the same cautiousness the dog had displayed. "So this is your guard dog. I hope he helped you sleep well."

She shrugged. "I wasn't afraid, not with him there. But..."

"But there's a lot to think of, ain't so?" He nodded. "I was the same. May I walk with you?"

She could hardly refuse. "Of course. Barney and I like at least one good long walk a day."

"Yah, I am the same." He fell into step with her. "Every day after the morning chores, I have to walk over the farm. My wife teases me, asking if I think it will have changed."

She realized she understood. "But it does change, doesn't it? There's always something fresh to be seen on a farm."

"Even if it's just how much the corn has grown or if the berries have ripened enough to pick." He nodded, accepting her understanding.

They'd reached the trail that led through the woods before she asked the question that was hovering on her tongue. "Did you think I needed protection on my walk?"

He shrugged. "I would want to walk with you, anyway. But Sarah told me about the hay bales falling on you." He was quiet for a moment, musing. "I thought all the bad things that happened were in the past. But it seems that isn't so."

"No. If I'd known before I came to Echo Falls what would happen…" She let that trail off, not sure how it would end.

"Would you rather never have known about your mamm and daad?" Jacob seemed unwilling to let it rest there.

She considered for a few strides, noticing that Jacob kept up with her easily. Finally she shook her head. "No, I guess not. My mother—my adopted mother—expected me to face troubles, not run from them."

"And yet she didn't tell you about your parentage." It wasn't said in a condemning way, but as a matter of fact.

"I've gone over and over that in my mind." She was surprised by her readiness to confide in him. "I wonder now if it was more than just making me feel secure. Maybe she thought there'd be trouble if it became known."

"She would have wanted to keep you safe. Any parent would. Have you found out how she came to have you?"

"Not yet, but my lawyer in Boston is looking into it." She frowned, thinking aloud. "In the early years, before she was successful, Juliet often worked as a waitress. I'm thinking she somehow met Melanie that way after Melanie ran away from the place they sent her to." She glanced at him. "You know about that?"

"That the Winthrop family wanted you given up for adoption? Yah, I heard. They didn't know who the father was, but if they had, they wouldn't think I needed to be told." There was a faint trace of bitterness in the words.

"Melanie didn't want to give me away. That much is clear. As to why she came back that day…" Amanda glanced at him. "You would know that better than I."

The lines in his face seemed accentuated. "She wanted to see me. I thought she wanted to get together. For us to get married and be a family."

Amanda tried to read his expression. "Was that what you wanted, too?"

His smile broke through. "Yah, for sure. We were deep in love. Now, well, like I said, it wonders me how it would have worked out."

"You think your love wouldn't have lasted?" She wanted to believe in a love that endured for a lifetime.

"We wouldn't have stopped loving. But it's not an easy thing, living Amish. Especially for someone raised the way Melanie was. I feared she would miss all the things she was used to."

The trees thinned out where the hillside sloped sharply downward. Jacob pointed. "That's the farm where I grew up. My younger brother has it now."

Standing beside him, Amanda saw a neat Amish homestead, looking like a toy farm from this distance. The barn, the stable, the twin silos, the neat patchwork of fields…they were all similar to Sarah and Amos' place.

"Do you regret going out to Ohio?" She leaned against a convenient tree trunk.

"No, not now. At first I was homesick, but after Melanie died, I couldn't settle. I had told my parents about the baby in my grief, and they tried to help me, but it was better to go away. Now I have my family, my farm, and I'm content. It's a gut life."

"You have children, Sarah says." She rose, turning back down the hill. She had to whistle for Barney, who'd gone off on a jaunt of his own.

"Katie and I have five, three girls and two boys. Gut helpers on the farm, all of them, and growing as fast as weeds."

"How old are they?" It wasn't just being polite. She found her curiosity growing about those unknown siblings.

"Our oldest boy is twelve, and turning into a man almost before our eyes. Then came the three girls, all looking alike, but so different in themselves. Our

Becky is only seven, but she is our little scholar, always with a book in her hands. And then comes Joshua, just turned four and the image of his mamm."

Given the ages of the children, he must have waited some time before marrying. Grieving for her mother?

Amanda could read the affection and pride in his expression when he spoke of his children, and for a split second wished it was for her. But that was foolish. She lived an entirely different life, and they had nothing in common but an accident of birth.

Jacob was watching her face—studying it, she thought, with a sort of wary hope.

"You would like to meet them someday?" he asked.

Amanda hesitated, not sure she wanted to commit herself that far. But the yearning to see those half sisters and brothers was strong. "I'd like that. Someday," she added, cautious.

He seemed satisfied, and they walked back down the hill companionably enough. He kept up a gentle flow of talk about his childhood, avoiding any of the potential hurtful times.

When they neared the stable, Jacob gestured toward it. "I hear from Amos you generally check on the foal you delivered. I'd like to see it."

"He's a good-looking colt. Fine stock, Amos says." She told Barney to stay, and he sat down obediently, giving her a reproachful look.

Jacob chuckled. "He wants to come, too. If he had been with you, he'd have sensed the stranger in the loft, ain't so?"

"Yes. That makes it seem the man had been keeping an eye on things here, to know that I went in every morning and didn't take the dog."

"Yah. Made Amos mad, that did. He says he and the boys have been walking the property a few times a day and in the night, just to be safe."

She opened the gate of the box stall and slipped inside, Jacob following her. "Amos and Sarah have been so kind. I hate thinking I'm causing them problems."

"They don't see it that way," he said. "You're family."

Maybe this was the opportunity to say what she'd been feeling. "All my life it was just my mother and me. Suddenly having a big family is a little disconcerting."

"Just take it slow."

They'd reached the stall, and he approached the mare in just that way, gaining her confidence before looking toward her baby.

Amanda knelt, running her hands along the baby's soft hair, feeling the long muscles that carried their promise of strength to come.

Jacob squatted on the other side of the colt, doing the same. "Yah, Amos made a fine choice of his Percherons. Not that I doubted it. Amos was always a gut judge of horses. And this youngster..." He broke off as the colt turned his head and slobbered generously on his cheek. His surprised laugh made Amanda laugh, as well. Their gazes met over the foal's back in a moment of perfect agreement.

Amanda rose, confused. She didn't believe in some sort of instinctive recognition. Did she?

TREY HAD PICKED up Jacob and Amanda in time to meet Chief Carmichaels. He'd been a little surprised when she'd waved Jacob into the front seat next to him, and even more so when she maintained a nearly complete silence during the drive. A look in the rearview mirror showed him her expression. She looked as if she were puzzling something out.

He'd hoped she'd have come to terms with the arrival of her father by this morning, but apparently not.

He pulled into a parking place in front of the police station. "Here we are," he said unnecessarily.

They got out, pausing for a moment on the sidewalk. Amanda had been so determined about talking to Carmichaels that he'd expected her to charge ahead. Instead she hung back. Then, to his surprise and also, he expected, to Jacob's, she took her father's arm.

Jacob looked as if she'd given him a present. Together they followed him into the station.

Carmichaels was waiting for them. He greeted Jacob with a handshake and led them into his office.

He settled himself behind his desk. A couple of folding chairs had been brought in to augment the office's sparse furnishings, so they took their places across from him.

"Now, then." He zeroed in on Jacob. "I understand from Trey Alter that you'd like to make a statement about what happened when Melanie Winthrop died."

"That's right." Jacob sounded calm, but his hands were clenched on his black broadfall trousers. "I should have told the whole thing that day. I want to make up for it now." He glanced at Amanda. "My daughter has a right to know the truth."

"Daughter?" Carmichaels looked from Amanda to Jacob. "I see. Guess that explains a lot."

Jacob nodded. "Here is what happened."

For the third time Trey listened to Jacob's account.

It was becoming familiar enough to him that it had lost its power to shock. But probably not for Amanda. Her face was tight, her eyes dark.

When she met his gaze, he gave her what he hoped was an encouraging look.

Carmichaels listened without comment, making an occasional note. When Jacob fell silent, he nodded. "That's very clear. Now for a few questions."

He led Jacob through virtually the entire story again, questioning each step. *Fair enough*, Trey thought. No one could expect him to accept the belated story without questions, especially after such a long time.

Jacob's answers remained calm. Under questioning, he remembered a detail here or there, but nothing that would lead them anywhere near the identity of the person who'd been with Melanie that day.

In the end, it was just as Trey had expected.

"You have to understand that we still have no proof that Melanie's death was anything other than an unfortunate accident." When Amanda looked like she was about to burst into speech, he held up his hand to stop her.

"I know. I agree it's suspicious that the person, whoever it was, never came forward. But there are a lot of possible reasons for that. Plenty of people don't want to be involved in that sort of thing."

Jacob nodded. "Yah. I should have told what I knew, but I didn't."

"You had good reasons for that," Amanda said with a surprising bit of loyalty.

"Others might have good reasons, too," Jacob said, his tone gentle.

"But not for failing to go to Melanie's aid when she fell," Amanda said.

Carmichaels cleared his throat with the air of one seizing control again. "The bottom line is that in my judgment, there's not enough to justify opening up a full-scale investigation again."

"But…" Amanda drew breath to argue.

"That doesn't mean I'm ignoring it," Carmichaels said firmly. "I'll have some quiet talks with all the people who might know something. But if nothing comes to light…well, I don't see that it ever will."

Before Amanda could start arguing, Trey grasped her arm.

"Leave it for now," he murmured. "It's not over."

To his surprise, she took his advice. But as they started out, Carmichaels called him back.

"A word, Trey."

He nodded and then turned to the other two. "I'll meet you at the car in a few minutes."

As the door closed behind them, Carmichaels came around the desk and perched on it, a sign that they were now off the record.

"About this Shawn Davis," he said. "I've had Sam do a little nosing around." Sam Jacobson was Echo Falls' youngest patrolman. "Supposedly he and Carlie had broken up on her grandmother's orders, but Sam says they've been seen around together. So I decided it was time to have a little talk with him." His face expressed distaste. "Smart-mouthed punk. Sat right there and sneered at me. Pretty much dared me to prove he'd done anything. Which you know I can't, not with nothing more than a scrap of fabric to go by."

"Sounds as if Carlie ought to watch what friends

she picks," he commented. He'd known they had no proof that Shawn was their joker, but he'd hoped he was the type to cave when leaned on. Apparently not.

"Yeah. Anyway, I wanted you to know. Maybe you'd better talk to your client. He might be warned off by my interest, but he struck me as the type who'd have another try just to prove how smart he is."

"I will. And I'll try to make sure she doesn't go taking any chances." He'd try. But Amanda had a mind of her own.

Amanda and Jacob both looked at him expectantly when he came out.

"Well?" Amanda said. "Did he want you to discourage me?"

"Nothing like that. He wanted to talk to me about that boyfriend of Carlie's."

Jacob looked lost, as well he might.

"What did he say?" Amanda jumped on it.

"We can't talk about it here." He nodded to the elderly couple who went slowly by, their eyes on Amanda. "Let's go over to Esther's place and have coffee."

Amanda bit off whatever she'd been about to say. She nodded, and they crossed the street toward the bakery.

Esther surged forward at the sight of them. "There you are. I was wondering when you'd stop by again." Her gaze stopped on Jacob's smiling face. "Ach, can I believe my eyes? If it's not Jacob Miller, come back to see us. Look at you. You haven't changed at all, except for the beard."

"And a few gray hairs," he said. "But you are the same as ever."

"Yah, except for a few extra pounds," she said, laughing. "Komm, sit. What will it be?"

It took a while to detach Esther, determined as she was to hear all about Jacob's family and what he was doing back when it wasn't either a wedding or a funeral. Trey decided coming here might not have been such a great idea. Esther was capable of putting two and two together. Still, was it realistic to think they could keep it secret?

Finally, seeming to realize that she was monopolizing Jacob, Esther left them alone to talk, but he could see her wondering as she walked away.

It didn't take Trey long to communicate what the chief had said about Shawn Davis, but of course they had to fill Jacob in on their suspicions that he'd been the muscle, if not the brains, behind the mishaps that targeted Amanda.

When they'd finished, Jacob frowned at Trey. "You should have called the police after the first accident."

"That was my call," Amanda said firmly. Obviously she didn't intend to let either Trey or her newfound father make decisions for her. "We didn't get the license number, and he was completely unidentifiable. Besides, then I assumed it was a genuine accident."

"The important thing now is to make sure he doesn't get any more shots at you. Carlie might call him off since it's been proved you're Melanie's daughter," Trey said. "But that kind of person is unpredictable. And I'm not even sure it's a safe assumption that Carlie gave him orders. She may have just complained about your arrival, and he decided on his own to chase you away."

Amanda didn't agree with that, he knew, but it was still a possibility.

"Anyway," he hurried on, "the important thing now is to keep you safe. Don't go anywhere unless Barney is with you or one of us, okay?"

She looked predictably rebellious.

"I know," Trey said before she could give voice to her thoughts. "You can take care of yourself. Just do this for our peace of mind."

"I would," she said, too sweetly to be believable. "But I'm going somewhere this evening where I can't take Barney. And neither of you would be welcome, I suspect."

He was instantly wary. "Where?"

"I've been invited to the Winthrop house for dinner. Apparently they received the DNA report this morning. Sounds as if they mean to welcome me into the family."

CHAPTER FIFTEEN

NOTHING MORE WAS discussed about it while they were in the café, but Amanda suspected Trey was only waiting until they had a bit more privacy to have his say.

Sure enough, once the three of them were in the car and on their way back to the farm, Trey turned a frowning glance on her. "I think your first meeting with the Winthrops as relatives should be in a neutral place. My office, for instance. Not on their home turf."

Amanda shook her head impatiently. "I should think you'd be happy. This must mean the Winthrop family is willing to accept me as Melanie's daughter. Just as Jacob's family has done." She met Jacob's gaze in the rearview mirror, seeing again that fleeting resemblance that Sarah had recognized immediately.

"I suppose so." Trey was still frowning, but at the road ahead now. "I just didn't expect it to be that easy. Not with them. And we can't ignore those accidents of yours."

"There's no proof that the family knew anything about them," she said.

"I don't believe in coincidences. And unless you think Juliet's brother has been lurking around Echo Falls incognito..."

"As you keep reminding me, strangers stand out here. And I don't think it's his style, anyway."

"Well, then…" he began, but she cut him short.

"I'm suspicious of the whole lot of them. And they'll be fortunate if I don't tell them exactly what I think of their treatment of Melanie."

"That's the other thing that worries me." He was silent for a time, probably waiting for her to argue. Then he flipped on the turn signal and slowed as he approached the lane. "A big blowup might relieve your feelings. But it wouldn't help anyone else."

"Worried about your reputation?" She couldn't help the edge in her tone.

"I have a practice here, remember? You may be able to walk away afterward. I have obligations." He stopped at the back door. "I'd rather not be the one who let the firm go down the drain."

Jacob was already getting out of the car. She sat for a moment, not sure what to say but not liking the abrupt chill between them. "Sorry," she said finally. "I wasn't thinking." She got out quickly.

Trey lifted his hand in a gesture that might have meant almost anything and drove off again.

Amanda stood where she was for a moment, wishing she knew what it was that made her so apt to say the wrong thing to Trey at least once a day.

She became aware of Jacob, still standing beside her. "Sorry," she said again. "I shouldn't have lost my temper with Trey."

He looked a little amused. "We are sometimes hardest on the people we care for most, ain't so?"

Amanda decided there was no way she could respond that wouldn't give away the confused state of her emotions, so she just shrugged.

Jacob seemed to accept that she wasn't going to talk about it. "I'll walk up to the cottage with you."

Sarah was looking out the kitchen window of the farmhouse, probably eager to hear all about their visit to the police. Well, she'd let Jacob handle that one. She nodded.

"One thing I didn't understand," Jacob said as they started up the lane. "Trey spoke of your mother's brother?"

"He meant my adoptive mother, Juliet." She frowned, trying to think how to explain the situation. "She had a brother, but they weren't at all close. Her will left everything to me, as her daughter, but apparently if I was never legally adopted, he might have a claim. That was why I started looking into who my parents are to begin with." The situation had quickly become so complicated that she could hardly believe it had once seemed that simple.

Jacob was studying her face. "Is it so important to you? The money?"

"I... I don't know." That was a lame answer. She'd have to do better. "Not the money as such. But there's the house I grew up in. And her paintings—I don't think I'd want someone who didn't care to have control of those."

He nodded, seeming to understand. "The work of her hands and her heart. Yah, I see." He hesitated. "But memories...memories live in the heart, not in a place."

Somehow the way he put it, so simply, resounded. With Juliet gone, the house in Boston was just a house, aside from the personal mementos she'd want to keep.

Jacob seemed content to remain silent as long as she wanted. She roused herself, reminded of something she ought to know before meeting again with the Winthrop family.

"Did they—Melanie's family, I mean—ever know that you were the father of her baby?"

"I don't think so, but I could never be sure." His blue eyes seemed to look into the past. "The last day we met, I thought that she planned to tell them and to say that we wished to marry. She said she would first talk to someone who would help her."

Someone who would help? Amanda puzzled over that for a moment. "Did she say who?"

"No, she never did. I didn't hear from her again until the day she passed." Even after all these years he seemed to have trouble saying it.

"How…how do you feel about them knowing it now? It doesn't seem as if we can keep it quiet, since you've spoken to the police."

His solemn expression slid away when he looked at her. "I am wonderful happy that people should know you are my daughter, even if Melanie never had a chance to tell them."

He must be thinking of Melanie's return. Of how that ended. Amanda's thoughts spun onward from that day. "You never heard anything from them afterward? They never tried to contact you?"

"No. And that is why I think they never knew. They would have wanted to make sure I'd be silent."

That one sentence seemed to encapsulate the gulf between the Amish farmer and the spoiled daughter of the wealthiest family in town. Romeo and Juliet, apparently—an old, sad story. If not for that, she wouldn't be the person she was.

"Whatever else happens, I'm glad I found you," she said at last, and knew she meant it.

AMANDA LET THE knocker fall on the massive front door of the Winthrop house, wondering why she felt even more nervous this time than she had previously. That didn't make any sense.

Before she had a chance to analyze it, Helen Lindstrom was swinging the door open. Some of the nervousness seeped away at the warmth of the woman's smile as she drew her in.

"You see," the woman whispered. "I thought all along you were our Melanie's daughter, even though I didn't dare say so." She clasped Amanda's hand for a quick squeeze.

Mrs. Lindstrom might be able to fill in some of the blanks about Melanie's life for her, if she could ever get her alone.

Amanda glanced toward the parlor where she'd been received before. "How are they taking it?" she murmured.

"Them." The woman's tone was tinged with contempt. "They'll do what Mrs. Winthrop wants. She calls the tune."

Maybe so, but not with her. Amanda couldn't help but wonder how long it would be before she and her great-grandmother clashed over that one.

Mrs. Lindstrom led her to the parlor, and once again, Donald Shay had his family assembled to meet her.

He came forward, outwardly jovial and with hands outstretched, smiling as if her arrival were the most delightful thing that had happened all day. "Amanda, welcome. Betty, dear, come and welcome our niece."

Great-niece, actually, not that it mattered. Clearly he'd decided to put the best face possible on the situation.

Betty came obediently to press her cheek against Amanda's for a brief second. "Welcome," she murmured. Again she looked at Donald as if for some indication she'd done it correctly, but he was busy directing his children to greet their new cousin.

They were both reluctant, she suspected, but they did as they were told, Carlie with a spark of rebellion in her flashing eyes and Ethan with a stammer that made him blush.

Amanda responded to Ethan more warmly than she'd expected to, moved by his obvious shyness. He seemed so much younger than his years, and was surely an unlikely person to be groomed to take over Winthrop Enterprises. Still, maybe he showed a different side of himself at work.

"Elizabeth will be down momentarily, and we'll go in to dinner." Donald moved to a mahogany sideboard bearing a tray with assorted bottles. "Meanwhile, may I fix you a cocktail?"

She didn't really want anything, but holding a glass would give her something to do with her hands. "A small glass of white wine, if you have it."

"Of course." He poured out a glass and handed it to her before serving his wife and children. When his daughter asked for a whiskey sour he allowed himself a slight grimace before making it.

Conversation lagged once the drinks were served, and Amanda caught several furtive glances toward the door, as if they were hopeful Elizabeth would relieve them of the responsibility of entertaining her.

Given a choice, Amanda decided she'd prefer to try to draw out Ethan than talk to the others, so she moved to his side.

"I understand you're learning the business. I'm afraid I don't know much about it."

Carlie, overhearing, snorted. "Neither does Ethan." She deliberately turned her back on them and began talking to her father about something to do with the mill.

Aware of Ethan's flush, Amanda sought for a more acceptable topic of conversation. To her surprise, Ethan saved her the trouble.

"Is it...is it true that your mother was Juliet Curtiss, the artist?" He sounded almost eager.

"That's right. Are you familiar with her work?"

"I'll say." Interest brightened his eyes. "I had hoped to catch one of her shows, but I never had the opportunity."

"You'll have to come to Boston to visit," she said lightly. "I'll give you a private view."

"You mean that? Her painting of a child with flowers...that was you, wasn't it?"

He really did know Juliet's work, then. That was a familiar point in an unknown environment. "It was, but I can't say I ever thought it was me when I was a child. Most eight-year-olds don't care for impressionism, I expect."

"I envy you, being brought up with an appreciation for art and—"

He was interrupted by his father before he could finish. "Ethan, don't be bothering your cousin with prattle about art."

"On the contrary," she said with deliberation. "Since my adoptive mother was an artist, I'm quite interested."

That left Donald a bit nonplussed, as she'd hoped it would. "Well, then…" he began, and then turned gratefully at the appearance of Elizabeth, leaning on her cane and with Mrs. Lindstrom in attendance.

"What are you all standing around for?" she demanded. "Let's go in to dinner before the food is ruined."

After that inauspicious beginning, Amanda foresaw an uncomfortable meal. But once they were seated, Elizabeth seemed determined to be a model of civilized dining. She directed the conversation into topics of general interest, ably assisted by Donald, firmly urbane, and a few timid ventures by Betty.

Elizabeth didn't seem to appreciate those contributions, and after a particularly pointed snub, Betty fell silent.

Amanda, trying to keep up her part of the talk, found herself contrasting this meal with the one in Sarah's kitchen. Sarah's table might not boast linen and fine china, but the talk had been lively and the laughter constant.

She smiled at the memory, only to find herself the target of Elizabeth's piercing glance. "Tell me, Amanda, where in Boston did you receive your education?" Her tone relegated Boston to the fringes of the educational world, which would be quite an affront to the good citizens of that city.

"I had a couple of years at a public school, but after we moved to our current house, my mother sent me to the Foster Academy."

Elizabeth gave a grudging nod, so apparently she'd heard of it. "Boarding student?"

"No, day student. My mother never considered anything else until I went off to college. Then I lived in a dorm."

"I should think, given her career, a boarding school would have been preferable."

Amanda wasn't sure whether that was a slam at artists and their supposed lifestyle or a commentary on working mothers. "My mother wanted to have me with her," she replied. "And that's what I wanted, as well."

In fact, the only time she could remember that Juliet had gone off on a trip without her had been that visit to Echo Falls. That, she decided, wasn't something she wanted to bring up here.

Donald steered the conversation to college education, seeming to make an effort to draw her out, and Elizabeth gradually thawed. She seemed relieved that Amanda's education had been conducted at exemplary schools. Amused, Amanda couldn't help wondering what she'd expected.

The meal finally came to an end, and they all moved back into the parlor for coffee. It was there that Elizabeth introduced the subject that was surely on all their minds.

Stirring her coffee with a firmness that must endanger the fragile china cup, Elizabeth focused on Amanda. "I suppose I should say that we are satisfied that you are Melanie's child. Obviously, if we had known of your existence, we'd have done something about your upbringing, but Melanie took that out of our hands."

Amanda couldn't help but feel relieved that her

mother had entrusted her to Juliet. "I understand your feelings. But Juliet was all the family that any child could have asked for."

That didn't seem to have quite the comforting effect she'd hoped for, since Elizabeth's eyes grew icy. "You were a Winthrop, whether you were an accident or not. I didn't see it at the time, but you should have been brought up as one, despite your questionable unknown parentage on the father's side." She looked as if the words left a bad taste in her mouth.

That was nothing compared to Amanda's reaction. Jacob and his family had been nothing but kind. Elizabeth had no right to look down—she clearly hadn't known who the father was.

But someone might have—that person Melanie had said she'd confide in. Amanda would give a lot to know who that was, and maybe there was a way to find out. Watching them, she spoke deliberately. "Didn't you know? I've met my father. He's Jacob Miller."

Her momentary satisfaction dissolved at the look on Elizabeth's face. She grew red, and the color deepened to almost purple. "Jacob Miller? That Amish boy? How dare he? My own granddaughter…"

She stopped, seeming to struggle for breath, and Mrs. Lindstrom instantly appeared, bending over her, murmuring softly.

Amanda collected herself. "I didn't mean to upset you." She considered saying what a good person Jacob was but decided that might only add fuel to the fire.

Her great-grandmother's color slowly faded under Mrs. Lindstrom's ministrations. "Not your fault," Elizabeth said finally.

Amanda guessed that was as close as Elizabeth would ever come to an apology.

She nodded, not speaking, and resolved not to explode any more bombshells if she could help it. She'd been too shaken by Elizabeth's reaction even to look at the others, so it hadn't gained her a thing.

"That's all in the past," Elizabeth said firmly. "The future is what's important. Naturally you'll want to get better acquainted with your family." She sent a cold stare around the room and everyone, even Carlie, nodded. "So you may as well move in here now and begin. I'm sure you can deal with any business revolving around your adoptive mother's estate from here."

The assumptions in that statement left Amanda speechless for a moment. Then she took a breath. If Elizabeth thought she wanted to give up her own life to move in and become as dependent on her as the rest of her family, she'd better think again.

She opened her lips to say just that and caught a warning glance from Mrs. Lindstrom, who gestured slightly with the vial in her hand. Nitroglycerin, probably, for her heart. No one had said anything about Elizabeth's health, but obviously there was a problem.

Seizing control during the silence that greeted Elizabeth's announcement, Amanda rose. "That's very generous of you, but I think that would be better discussed another time. I've tired you, and I didn't mean to. Thank you for the lovely dinner. I should be going."

Elizabeth looked as if she'd argue, but Mrs. Lindstrom bent over her, again saying something softly. Finally, she nodded.

"I am rather tired," she said regally. She rose with an effort and held out her hand to Amanda.

Amanda took it, then impulsively leaned forward and pressed her cheek against Elizabeth's. The elderly woman's skin was as soft and crinkled as a rose petal.

For an instant Elizabeth looked startled, and then she reached up and patted Amanda's cheek. Almost before the touch had registered, Elizabeth turned away. Taking Mrs. Lindstrom's arm, she moved out of the room, toward what Amanda now realized was an elevator in the hallway.

Sensing the constraint in the air, Amanda said her goodbyes to the others quickly. They were polite, probably afraid Elizabeth would get to hear of any deviation from her order to accept Amanda.

But certainly no one was eager to have her stay any longer. The door closed behind her, but not before she'd caught the unguarded malevolence in at least two of the faces turned toward her. Donald and his daughter were not reconciled to Amanda's intrusion into their lives.

Amanda felt a wave of relief as she made her way outside. Relatives or not, she wasn't going to allow herself to be maneuvered into that house.

TREY HAD BEEN sitting in his car outside the Winthrop property for what seemed an eternity. At last he spotted, through the screening of trees, the movement of the front door. Amanda emerged and walked to her car so quickly that it looked as if she were fleeing.

He'd parked a half block back, not wanting to be spotted. He started the engine but kept his headlights off until she'd driven through the gate and headed down the street. Then he turned them on and pulled out a circumspect block behind her. It wouldn't do to let her spot him. He could imagine, only too well, what she'd say if she knew he was trailing her around town.

Once she got to the farm, he felt confident she'd be safe. Jacob was acting like an overanxious parent, and he wouldn't sleep unless he knew Amanda was all right. With him, Amos, and the older boys on the alert, no one could get near her. To say nothing of the dog.

The danger zone was that stretch of lonely country road once she was clear of town. He'd have to close up there, whether she spotted him or not. All she'd be able to distinguish would be a pair of headlights, in any event.

Trey could only hope Carmichaels or one of his patrolmen was in place in the farm lane on the opposite side from the Burkhalter property. And that no one would jump the gun too soon, or worse, react too late.

Was he letting his emotions get the better of him? Maybe so, but if there was going to be another attempt to get rid of Amanda before Elizabeth did anything rash such as changing her will, it would have to be soon. This lonely drive home might be the best opportunity there would be.

They'd reached the last of the streetlamps, and Trey punched the chief's number, putting his phone on speaker.

"Carmichaels."

"We're just leaving town. I'll get as close as I dare behind her. Be ready."

Carmichaels muttered something he couldn't hear. Then he spoke more loudly. "We'll do our part. *If* anything happens."

The chief had been skeptical about this, but he wouldn't risk doing nothing when Trey had insisted.

"Right. I'll keep my phone on."

He neared Amanda's car, close enough to see the movement of her head when she checked her rearview mirror. Belatedly, he realized she might well think he was her assailant. He could call...but that would mean cutting his contact with Carmichaels. He didn't dare do that.

Better to apologize than explain. Trey didn't remember who had said that, but it seemed appropriate.

Forming an apology in his mind, he alternated between studying the movement of Amanda's car and scanning the road ahead. Nothing. Maybe he'd been wrong. If he cried wolf too often, Carmichaels might find it hard to believe Amanda was in danger.

Amanda's car was nearing the boundaries of the Burkhalter farm, and nothing had happened. Then a shaft of moonlight momentarily reflected from chrome in a lane to the left.

"He's there," he said quickly, fingers tightening on the steering wheel. "In the Shuman farm lane. We'll reach him in a moment."

The rev of the patrol car's engine reached him through the speaker. "Got it," Carmichaels snapped.

The motorcycle roared to life, swinging out into the road and fully into Amanda's lane. He obviously planned to come as close as he could, hoping to force her off the road. And then? If he intended to make certain Amanda wasn't around to inherit, his plans probably hadn't included another car coming so close behind. Just how reckless was he?

They'd find out. Trey accelerated, pulling out beside Amanda's car, giving the motorcyclist no room to run. He had a quick impression of Amanda's face, a white blur as she glanced toward him.

No time to consider her now. Trey focused on the advancing bike. Was he crazy enough to ram them head-on? He'd be the loser in that event.

The biker must have thought so, too. He swung in an abrupt turn, nearly wiping out, and started to accelerate away from them. At that moment the patrol car came toward him, siren blaring and lights flashing.

Confronted from both ahead and behind, the biker tried to turn again, seeking an escape, and he capsized.

Amanda slammed on her brakes to avoid hitting him, and Trey did the same. Jumping out, he shouted at her to stay in her car. The police car wailed to a stop, both doors opening as Carmichaels and his patrolman ran toward the fallen biker. They had him now.

But just before they could reach him, the motorcyclist jumped back up onto the bike. There was an instant when his escape hung in the balance. But the engine caught, and he roared away, past the two policemen.

Carmichaels swore and ran back toward the car. "Get after him."

The young patrolman beat him to the vehicle, and in a moment they set off in pursuit, siren screaming. Trey blew out an exasperated breath and went to Amanda.

"They'll be lucky to catch him with the start he had, but they'll have his plate number, and Carmichaels will put out an alert. He won't be free for long."

Amanda unclenched her hands from the steering wheel. He could see the movement, but he couldn't make out her expression. She'd be angry, of course. He didn't blame her.

"You're assuming it was this Shawn whoever—Carlie's boyfriend?"

He nodded. "No doubt in my mind. Besides, that was his bike. I wasn't too rattled to notice."

She eyed him. "You didn't look especially rattled to me."

"Believe me, I was." Since she hadn't exploded, he allowed his face to relax in a smile. "I didn't know whether to expect you to hit me or him."

"If I hit you, it would be deliberate." Her tone was tart. "I thought you were the guy who was after me."

"Sorry. That didn't occur to me until it was too late to do anything." He reached through the open window to touch her shoulder. "Forgive me?"

"On one condition."

"And that is?" he asked.

"The next time you intend to use me as bait, let me know first."

He grinned, fingers tightening. "Okay. I promise."

CHAPTER SIXTEEN

AMANDA REACHED THE FARMHOUSE, Trey following close behind her, to find that Sarah, Jacob and Amos were outside watching for them. Sarah rushed to her car as soon as it stopped.

"You're all right. Thank the Lord. We heard the sirens, saw the lights, and we were so worried."

Amanda slid from the car to discover that her legs had gone rubbery on her in the aftermath. At least, with Sarah's arms wrapped around her, it wasn't noticeable.

"Sorry." Trey joined them. "I'd have alerted you, but Chief Carmichaels thought the fewer people who knew about it, the better."

"That man you told me about—he tried again to harm Amanda?" Jacob contented himself with putting his hand on her shoulder, apparently reluctant to try a hug.

"We thought we were ready for him." Trey sounded rueful. "He managed to elude the police. But they'll get him. He can't go far without being spotted, and by now Carmichaels will have alerted the state police and the surrounding communities."

"What did he do?" Sarah said, not letting go of her. "You shouldn't have let Amanda risk being hurt or..."

"I'm fine," she said, suddenly realizing how comforting it was to have people worried about her. "Trey was right behind me, and the police were waiting."

"He tried to run her off the road again. But I think this time he probably wouldn't have just ridden away." Trey was blunt, and his voice sounded strained.

She hadn't considered that. If Trey hadn't been close at hand...

For a moment she was back in the car, seeing the headlights looming in her rearview mirror. She'd been as scared as she'd ever want to be in that moment, thinking he was the threat. It wasn't until he'd pulled up beside her that she'd recognized Trey. And by then, everything was happening too quickly for her to think about it.

"You'll come in the house, ain't so?" Sarah urged. "Have some dessert, at least."

She caught Trey's expression and knew he was thinking what she was—to Sarah, comforting someone was synonymous with feeding them.

"Thanks." She gave Sarah a quick hug. "But I don't feel hungry after all that's happened. I'd better go up and let Barney out, anyway."

Sarah nodded, giving her a little pat. "Someone must walk you up..."

"The danger is past now." Amanda said the words firmly, but a small, niggling doubt remained. "Good night, everyone." She smiled at Jacob, who still looked worried. "I'll be fine."

"I'm going with you." Trey captured her hand in his. "We still have a few things to talk over."

With quick good-nights to the others, they headed up the lane toward the cottage. Amanda waited until they were out of earshot before she spoke.

"I keep thinking this is over, and then something else happens. Too many questions are unanswered."

"Faced with arrest and time in prison, Davis will probably spill whatever he knows."

"If the police catch up with him," she said. "If not, we may never find out."

"We might not in any event," Trey pointed out. "He may refuse to talk. Or say he was acting on his own. And I doubt that anyone would have confided in him."

"You mean if this isn't just about the money. If the person who was with Melanie that day at the falls has anything to do with this…" She couldn't have imagined that it would mean as much to her as it did.

"I know. They're hardly likely to come forward now unless they're forced to. But that person, whoever it is, might have nothing to do with Davis's actions." Trey grabbed for his phone when it rang, glancing at the screen. "Carmichaels."

He raised it to his ear, and Amanda strained to hear the chief's voice.

"What happened?" Trey was terse, but she couldn't make out any words on the other end of the line.

"Yes, all right. Call me when you hear something."

He ended the call, sliding the phone back into his pocket with a frown.

"Let me guess," she said. "They didn't catch him."

"He apparently turned off on a logging road and cut through the woods where the police car couldn't follow. But he can't get far." He repeated the words he'd said earlier, as if by saying so, he could make it happen.

"If he's not caught, I'll have no chance of finding out if Carlie was in on it." She didn't like the thought of facing her cousin again while wondering if Carlie had actually plotted to get rid of her.

Trey was silent for a moment. "Maybe that would be better."

"How can you think that?" she demanded.

"I don't like the idea any more than you do. I'm a firm believer in the rule of law. But I can imagine the consequences, and they'd touch you." His fingers tightened on her hand. "Oddly enough, I was thinking of sparing you, not the Winthrop family. You'd never be free of the story, any more than they would."

"I suppose not." She shivered involuntarily, thinking of the headlines when Juliet was killed. "That would certainly end my relationship with Melanie's family, wouldn't it? Not that that is altogether a bad thing."

He shot her a sympathetic glance. "A difficult family dinner, was it?"

"That's putting it mildly. Nobody wanted me there, but with Elizabeth's eye on them, they had to pretend." She considered. "Well, your friend Mrs. Lindstrom was happy to see me. And Betty wasn't bad. But the rest of them—I'm not sure which was worse, Carlie's obvious antagonism or her father's pretense."

She thought he repressed a chuckle. "They're not your typical happy family, are they? Ethan's not too bad, I've always thought, but he'd be better off away from his father's and grandmother's expectations of him."

"Apparently Melanie was the only one brave enough to make the break." She knew she was getting worked up again, but she couldn't help it. "Can you believe it? Elizabeth actually expects me to give up my own life and move into that house."

"I have to admit, I wouldn't mind having you around all the time. But not living there."

"You should have seen her reaction when I told her Jacob is my father." Seeing his expression, she spoke quickly. "I know, I shouldn't have said anything without telling you, but Jacob was okay with it. I thought I might be able to tell from their expressions if one of them already knew."

"And?"

"Since Elizabeth looked as if she was about to have a heart attack, I was too distracted to look at them."

They'd reached the cottage, and Amanda used that as an excuse to put a pause on their conversation. She trotted up the steps and opened the door, letting Barney out. He danced around her with his usual joy at seeing her again, as if this time he'd thought she wasn't coming back.

She nearly hadn't. Maybe it was the effect of that close call that sent her back to Trey instead of keeping a safe distance between them. What had he meant by saying he'd like to have her around? Flirtation? Or something more, something real.

She kept her gaze on his face. "You keep saying things like about having me around, and I might just decide to take up practice in Echo Falls."

"You heard what Doc said." He was smiling as he slid his arms around her waist to draw her closer. "He'd be glad to have another vet in practice with him. You could stay."

"It would have its advantages." She rested her hands on his arms, sliding them slowly up toward his shoulders, feeling the solid bone and muscle under the softness of his sweater. "But then there are the Winthrops to contend with. It might have been easier when I didn't have a family."

"Hey, every family isn't like that one." His grasp tightened, pulling her closer. "Everybody needs someone."

She didn't speak—didn't want to spoil the moment with her doubts. And then his lips found hers, and everything else slipped away. The world came down to the close circle of his arms, the desire in his kiss, the crisp male scent of him. To forget every problem, to give in to the slow languor that crept over her...

She became aware of a cold, wet nose pressing against her knee as Barney insinuated himself between them. The kiss ended in her gurgle of laughter.

"I may be out of practice, but I don't think Barney is supposed to figure in this scene." The laughter was in Trey's voice, as well. "Or is he playing the part of prudence?"

"He might be," she admitted. "Maybe I should go in."

"And maybe I should go home. Not that I want to." He kissed her lightly. "But I will."

Amanda hurried to the cottage door, clicking to Barney as she did. Not too fast with this relationship. She'd made that mistake before. This time, she had to be sure.

THE NEXT MORNING, Trey walked up the familiar steps and in through the kitchen door of the house where he'd grown up. He hadn't stopped by for breakfast lately, and he resolved to do that more often. His father was usually at his best in the morning, more alert and eager for conversation.

"Trey!" His mother rose quickly from her seat at the breakfast table, hurrying to give him a quick kiss and then flitting back to the stove. "You should have called. I'd have had blueberry pancakes ready."

"That's why I didn't," he said, exchanging a grin with his father. "After a stack of your blueberry pancakes I want to take a nap, not go to work."

"Well, at least let me make some scrambled eggs." She was already taking the carton from the refrigerator. "It won't take a minute."

Dad waved him to his usual chair. "You may as well let her. She's only happy when she's feeding people. Although she insists on giving me fruit instead of bacon at breakfast." He frowned at the bowl of fresh peach slices in front of him.

"That's better than what I usually have."

Trey poured himself a mug of coffee, reminded of Sarah's efforts to feed everyone who came within her orbit. The maternal instinct, he supposed. And he would not let himself wonder what kind of a mother Amanda would be.

"Are the rumors true?" his father asked abruptly. "Has the Winthrop family actually accepted your client as Melanie's daughter?"

Trey took a gulp of coffee and put down the mug. He should have expected that the news would spread quickly. "The DNA tests came back positive. They didn't have much choice about accepting them, so apparently they decided to put a good face on it. At any rate, they invited Amanda for dinner last night. Amanda and Jacob don't care who knows. I'm not sure about the Winthrops, but they're not my clients."

His mother had turned away from the stove to listen but now spun back, exclaiming, "Gracious!"

"Don't spoil the boy's eggs in your excitement," his father said.

"I didn't," Mom said quickly. "But you can't deny it's fascinating. It's like a fairy tale."

Wicked stepsister and all, except in this case it might be wicked cousin. But he'd already decided not to say anything to his parents about the attempts against Amanda unless he had to.

"I don't imagine some of the Winthrop clan thinks that. If Elizabeth takes to her, it means they'll have to share." His father sent a questioning look at Trey. "I was afraid Elizabeth might hold it against the young woman because she's illegitimate."

"Apparently not even Elizabeth is that rigid these days." Trey slid his fork into the fluffy scrambled eggs his mother set in front of him. "It could have turned out very ugly for all of us if it came to a fight."

His father gave him a steady glance, seeming to read between the lines. "You have to do your duty to your client, no matter what the consequences. But yes, I'm glad they're being sensible. The young woman deserves some consideration. How is the family taking it?"

Trey shrugged. "I wasn't invited to the dinner, but from what Amanda said, they were at least on their best behavior. I imagine Elizabeth insisted on that, and they're too smart to go against her wishes."

"That's for the best in this case. But they might all be better off if they didn't knuckle under so readily to Elizabeth. She's too used to having her own way."

"She's not going to get it with Amanda, at least."

Trey had to smile, thinking of Amanda's instant reaction to Elizabeth's assumptions. "Elizabeth actually wanted her to give up her independent life and move into the Winthrop mansion."

"She won't do it?" his father questioned.

"Not a chance. She's one independent woman."

"Good for her," his mother said unexpectedly. "She wouldn't be able to call her soul her own with Elizabeth looking over her shoulder all the time. Although at Elizabeth's age, I don't suppose she'll be able to boss them all around for too much longer."

"I hope they're not counting on that." There was a sarcastic edge to Dad's tone. "Elizabeth is capable of living forever just to thwart them."

Trey grinned, glad to see his father's spirit hadn't dimmed. "I guess I'm glad you don't have millions to leave us, then."

"Consider yourself lucky on that score." His father's smile faded. "This young woman—is she after the Winthrop money?"

On that subject, Trey had no doubts. "Not at all. Like I said, she's an independent woman. She came here to find out the truth, not to cash in. As far as I can tell, she's more pleased at being a part of the Miller family than anything else."

"Miller? Jacob Miller?" Dad was sharp this morning. "So that's who it was. I knew there had to be some good reason why Melanie was so tight-lipped about the father of her baby. Elizabeth wouldn't have countenanced that marriage for an instant."

"More fool her, then. Jacob's a good man." He'd been favorably impressed with what he'd seen of Jacob thus far. Amanda was fortunate in having him for a father.

"I'm sure you're right. That's a fine family." Dad pushed the empty fruit bowl away.

"You must bring your Amanda over for supper some evening soon. We'd like to meet her." His mother was obviously trying to remain neutral, but she couldn't quite hide the rampant curiosity in her eyes. She probably suspected that her son had more than a professional interest in Amanda. "Maybe over the weekend? Why don't you ask her?"

"I'll see what she says, okay? As long as you promise you're not going to bring out my baby pictures."

Mom's cheeks flushed. "I only did that once."

"I know." He'd polished off the eggs and the toast that had come with them, so he stood, bending over to kiss her cheek. "I'll mention it."

His father seemed to be lost in a reverie. "Dad? I'm going to the office now."

He nodded, his gaze coming back to Trey. "I'm glad that Melanie's child found her way back after all this time. I was never happy about the part I played in that situation."

"I thought you split with the Winthrops over that."

"I did, but not soon enough." The lines in his father's face seemed to deepen. "When I saw how determined they were I knew none of the things I'd said had made a difference. So I found the place where they sent Melanie, and I made the arrangements."

He paused, shaking his head. "Maybe I should have told you, but Elizabeth was my client at the time."

"I understand," Trey said quickly. "It doesn't matter, because Elizabeth told Amanda where it was. She's already put the private investigators on it."

"Good. I'm glad. When Elizabeth wanted me to write a new will for her, cutting Melanie off, I'd had enough. It was no good telling myself she'd just get someone else to do it. I had to live with myself." His gaze sharpened on Trey. "I said earlier that your duty was to your client. But that's not always the case. Your first duty is always to your belief in justice. And to your own principles."

Trey nodded, reflecting that justice wasn't always quite so clear-cut. One thing was sure, though. It would be best if Amanda never knew the part his father had played in what happened to her mother.

THE CHANGING PALETTE of color on the ridge intrigued Amanda, and she lingered on the porch the next morning when she returned from her usual morning walk with Barney. The autumnal air was crisp, with just a hint of mist rising from the valley floor.

She'd miss this when she lived in Boston, she realized, after the taste she'd had in Lancaster County. The city had its charms, but the constant daily touch of nature seemed to draw her to this place. Maybe that indefinable longing to be close to the natural world came along with whatever she'd inherited of her father.

The sound of a car coming up the lane brought Amanda instantly alert. Barney, catching her emotion, rose to his feet and gave a single warning bark.

"It's all right." She pacified him with a pat, reminding herself that there was no need for alarm. Her assailant was far away by now if he hadn't been picked up by the police.

But she didn't recognize the car that nosed to a stop behind hers, and she fingered the cell phone in the pocket of her windbreaker. Even when the woman stepped out, she was blank for a moment before she realized it was the person who'd spoken to her in town one day about Carlie. Lisa Morgan, that was the name. She'd wondered afterward if the woman had been a friend of Melanie's. She looked about the right age.

Amanda's welcoming smile hid, she hoped, the questions that seethed in her mind. What was behind this unannounced visit?

She descended the steps, Barney at her heels. "Mrs. Morgan, isn't it? It's nice to see you again."

"Lisa, please." Well-dressed in a casual style suited to the surroundings, the woman was much like any of the well-to-do matrons who'd brought their pets to the practice in Boston.

Was this how Melanie would have turned out, had she made different choices? Maybe, but she'd think the teenage rebel might have been a little less conventional.

"I hope you don't mind my dropping by, but I didn't have your number, so I couldn't call."

"Not at all." Amanda gave the expected polite answer. "Won't you come in?"

Lisa glanced at the porch. "You were relaxing on the porch, weren't you? It looks like a delightful spot. Let's sit there. If you're sure you have time for a visit?" Her tone made it a question.

"Of course." She led the way to the comfortably curved rocking chairs. "I'm glad to have a chance to talk to you. Were you, by any chance, a friend of my mother's?"

Lisa's eyes sparkled with sudden amusement. "I

suppose it's pretty obvious, since I seem to be forcing my acquaintance on you. I wouldn't have intruded, but I imagine any version of Melanie you'd get from the Winthrop family would be a little…skewed, shall we say? Maybe you'd like to hear from a friend."

Warming, Amanda smiled back. "Elizabeth is a bit prejudiced. I take it you've heard that Mrs. Winthrop has accepted the results of the DNA tests."

"I hope you weren't trying to keep it a secret. Thanks to Carlie and her brother having a noisy quarrel about it outside the office at the plant, most people know." She leaned toward Amanda, reaching for her hand. "I can't tell you how happy I am that you've been found at last. All these years I've wondered…" Her voice faded, and she wiped away a tear that spilled unexpectedly onto her cheek.

Amanda was moved. "You knew about the pregnancy, then." Here, finally, was someone who might be able to fill in some of the blanks.

"Oh, yes. And I knew about Jacob, too. Probably I was the only one who did."

"Melanie must have confided in you." Her thoughts buzzed with questions, but she tried to rein them in. She didn't want to seem to be giving Lisa the third degree.

"Mel and I were best friends." Lisa had a reminiscent smile. "BFFs, as my daughter and her friends say. We told each other all the things we kept from our parents, I suppose. It's sometimes terrifying now to think about that from the parental point of view."

"I suppose so." Amanda thought of the secrets she'd tried to keep from Juliet. She hadn't been all that successful. "Did you hear from Melanie after she left here?" She held her breath for the answer.

"What an idiot I am—that's why I came." She shook her head. "It's just so disorienting, talking to you and seeing flashes of Melanie as I knew her. But yes, I did hear from her. She sent me letters from the facility, telling me not to let her family get hold of them. So it was all very secret—I was afraid of my parents finding out."

Amanda had a mental image of those two naive teenagers, still holding on to their secrets and not daring to ask for advice. "She didn't call?"

"That was pre–cell phone era, remember? If she had called, it would have come through on the family phone and been impossible to hide." Lisa shook her head. "When I think how immature we both were, trying to deal with something that was completely beyond our abilities…"

"I'm sure you did your best for her." She found herself in the role of comforter. "She must have appreciated your help."

"I'm not sure how much help I was," Lisa said ruefully. "But I'm dithering. The important thing is to tell you what Melanie was thinking and doing." She paused for breath, and Amanda decided she'd have to take control of the conversation if they were going to get anywhere.

"How did she react when she first told you she was pregnant?"

"Shocked," Lisa said promptly. "We thought we were so sophisticated, but I doubt she'd seriously considered the possibility. She said Jacob wanted to get married, but she was underage. She hoped her grandmother would consent." Lisa shrugged. "Obviously that didn't happen. I didn't hear from her again until she was in that place in Massachusetts."

Amanda tried unsuccessfully to put herself in Melanie's shoes. Too much of society had changed in the intervening years for her to manage it.

"So, anyway, Melanie complained about going there, but she seemed to settle down, and she said people were nice to her. I started to think she'd go through with it, give up the baby for adoption and come back afterward with some story about being away at boarding school. Nobody would have believed it, but it would have saved face for the family."

Yes, that would have been important to the Winthrops, secure in their mansion on the hill. The problems that beset normal people couldn't be allowed to touch them.

"Still, she can't have been that happy there, since she ran away," Amanda probed.

"I didn't hear from her for a time. Then she wrote, and she said everything had changed once she started feeling the baby kick and move. You," Lisa added, smiling. "You became so real to her then that she couldn't possibly consider giving you away to strangers. So she left."

"I can't imagine how she got along…alone in a strange city, pregnant, without resources…" She was beginning to manage putting herself in Melanie's place.

"She was determined. And she showed a lot more independence than I'd have believed. More than I could have," Lisa added. "She got a job as a waitress, and that's where she met Juliet."

Amanda let out a breath, something in her easing. Here was the link that had haunted her.

"Melanie said she couldn't believe her luck, to find a friend when she needed one so desperately. I admit I was a little jealous that Juliet was doing what I couldn't for Mel. They moved in together, and Melanie started sounding…well, hopeful. As if she could manage things."

Nodding, Amanda thought that it was probably Juliet who'd given her that confidence. Juliet was a strong woman, and she expected that of other women, too.

"We seemed to be growing apart about then. I guess it was natural. I was worried about a date for the homecoming dance, while Melanie was preparing for a baby. But I had a note from her when you were born." Lisa's smile was tender. "She was so happy—raving about her beautiful little daughter. I remember sneaking around to buy a gift for the baby, a little pink sweater set. I didn't want to have to answer any questions about why I was buying it."

Amanda was touched by the image, but even more by her birth mother's apparent love for her baby. "Did you hear anything more about how they were doing?"

"I received one more letter after that." Lisa hesitated, eyeing her warily. "Unfortunately, I didn't receive it until after her death."

"I see." She swallowed, wishing her throat didn't feel so tight. "What did she say? Did she mention coming back?"

"She enclosed a picture of you." She reached into her bag and pulled out an envelope. "I destroyed the letter, as we'd agreed, but I couldn't bring myself to get rid of the photo. After I heard about you, I went searching in the attic and found it packed away with a lot of high school mementos. You should have it."

For a moment Amanda could only stare at the envelope. Then she roused herself to take it, open it. The photo slid out—a fading picture done with an instant camera, by the looks of it. Still, it was sharp enough to show Melanie, sitting in a rocking chair, cradling a baby in a pink blanket. The baby slept, its small face relaxed, lips slightly parted. A fluff of fair hair was visible on its head.

But it was Melanie's face that drew her. Gone was the naive young schoolgirl of the photo her grandmother treasured, with her unformed, untried face. This was a woman, not a girl, a little too thin, maybe, with maturity in her face and fierce maternal love in her eyes.

"Thank you," she whispered at last, sliding the picture back into the envelope. "I'm more grateful than I can say." She cleared her throat, dragging her attention back to the important issue. "Do you remember what she said in the letter?"

"I couldn't forget it, coming when it did the day after she'd been found." Lisa's tone was somber. "She said she was very happy, but she'd been thinking a lot about little Amanda's future. She'd made up her mind to come back here and talk to the family, thinking if only they'd accept her and her baby, her daughter would have all she'd had."

"No mention of coming back to marry Jacob?"

Lisa shook her head. "But she may have had that in mind, of course. At the moment, she seemed concerned about how best to manage the family. She said she wasn't sure when it would be, but there was a trucker

who frequented the restaurant where she worked who'd
promised to drop her in Echo Falls the next time he had
a trip in that direction. And that Juliet would take care
of the baby while she was gone. Oh, and she said she'd
try to get in touch when she came. But she never did."

"I suppose they asked you—the police, I mean."

"The chief came by and talked to me. But my parents were there, so I didn't say anything. It wouldn't
have made a difference, and I was afraid of messing
up any arrangements she'd made for you."

Amanda nodded. She was still frustrated by how
the situation had all petered out at the time, but she
was glad nothing had happened to take her away from
Juliet. "That's all you remember?"

"Well, there was one thing I didn't understand. She
said something like she was thankful she had someone here in Echo Falls who would help her. I thought
she might have meant me, but then I wondered if there
could have been someone else."

A little silence fell between them. Maybe she should
say that Lisa was right, that she couldn't have done
anything, but how could they ever know?

Lisa seemed to rouse herself. "When I heard people whispering about suicide, it made me so furious.
That's one thing you can dismiss from your mind entirely. Melanie was happy. I know that. And she was
confident she could take care of herself even if her
family turned her down. She'd never have killed herself and left you alone."

CHAPTER SEVENTEEN

TREY HUNG UP the phone in his office and sat for a moment, staring at it. The call from Robert McKinley, Amanda's Boston attorney, had surprised him initially. He couldn't imagine why Robert was calling him instead of getting in touch with Amanda directly.

It had taken the man time to get to the point, leaving Trey with the sense he'd been uncomfortable with what he was about to ask. Finally, he reached the bottom line. An extensive search of court records had not turned up any trace of adoption proceedings. Unless Juliet Curtiss had traveled very far afield, it seemed unlikely that there had ever been a formal adoption.

Worse, Juliet's brother had hired an attorney, who was making noise about why Juliet's will had not been submitted for probate. McKinley felt sure that meant he intended to contest the will, and he hadn't, of course, been able to submit until all loose ends were tied up and any outstanding debts paid, as well as the complicated valuation of the artwork still in Juliet's possession at the time of her death.

Trey sympathized. The details involved in winding up an estate, especially when the death had been abrupt and unexpected, took time. But that hadn't been the man's point. McKinley had called because he wanted Trey to break the news to Amanda.

It was understandable, he supposed. From everything Amanda had said, he'd formed the impression that Robert had been much more of an uncle to her than an attorney. He'd been an important figure in her life from the time she was a child.

Now, faced with telling her something he thought would upset her, he'd like to justify handing it off to someone else. Trey was there on the spot, he'd been representing Amanda, he was the logical person to discuss it with her, or so McKinley reasoned.

Trey wasn't all that sure Amanda was going to be upset. In his opinion, she'd been expecting it all along.

Making a sudden decision, he picked up the phone again and called her. When just the sound of her voice saying hello caused his heart to jump, he knew he was in deep. And sinking faster all the time.

"Can we get together, maybe for lunch? Something's come up I want to talk with you about."

"What a coincidence. I was just going to call you and say the same thing." The hint of laughter in her voice assured him that whatever it was, it wasn't bad. "Do you want to go to Esther's again?"

"Let's try for a little more privacy this time." An idea struck him. "How do you feel about a picnic?"

"Picnic?" she echoed.

"You know. The kind of thing where you bring your food with you and have it outside. An alfresco meal, so to speak."

She laughed. "Idiot. I know what a picnic is. Are you expecting me to rush off and make potato salad?"

"Let's be unconventional. I'll get the food and pick you up. Barney can come, too. That should make him happy."

"I'm sure it will. We'll be ready. When?"

He glanced at his watch. "Say forty-five minutes?"

"Sounds good. That will give me time to change and dissuade Sarah from loading us down with a little of this and a little of that. See you soon."

"Don't discourage her if she mentions pie," he added, hanging up. He shoved a day's accumulation of work aside without regret. This was business, wasn't it? At least, to some extent.

An hour later Trey was setting a couple of bags on a picnic table at Green Lake. "What do you think?" He gestured toward the scene—the water glowing with color as it reflected the turning leaves on the trees surrounding the small lake.

"It's beautiful. I had no idea this was here. It can't be more than ten miles or so from Amos and Sarah's." She gestured to Barney, and he dashed off, nose to the ground, tail wagging furiously.

"Surprisingly, not that many people frequent the spot. The lake is too cold for swimming most of the year, and motorboats aren't allowed, so that cuts down on the traffic." He began setting food out on the table. "I took the easy way out and stopped at the deli counter. I hope there's something here you like."

She surveyed the spread. "Looks as if you got some of everything. I'm not that fussy, believe me. And as you supposed, Sarah sent pie, half an apple and half a cherry pie. Apparently she thought you'd be hungry."

"So I am." He sat down on the bench opposite her. "Let's help ourselves while we talk. Why don't you start with your news?"

She speared a dill pickle from the container. "I don't suppose it amounts to a great deal, but I had a visitor this morning. Lisa Morgan. Apparently she was Melanie's best friend in high school."

"I know Lisa and Bart. But I didn't know that. Well, no reason I should. They are older than I am, and I didn't really get to know them until we were all adults. Lisa and Melanie. I wonder why she didn't come forward before."

Amanda shrugged. "I suppose she didn't realize it was important. But she did introduce herself to me in town one day. Remember? I mentioned it. Apparently hearing that my parentage was confirmed made her decide to talk to me." She hesitated, looking down at the cabbage and beet slaw she'd just put on her paper plate. "It was rather touching, actually."

"I guess it would be. What did she have to say?"

Amanda's account of her conversation with her mother's friend was clear and concise. Right up until the moment when she pulled out the photograph of herself with Melanie. Then tears filled her eyes, and she blinked rapidly as if trying to force them away.

He took the photograph when she held it out to him, holding it carefully by the edges to avoid causing it any more damage. Trey actually found his own throat getting thick. Not so much at the sight of Amanda, beautiful baby as she was, but at Melanie's look of sheer joy.

"Cute baby," he said, handing it back. "I especially like the little wisp of hair standing up on top of your head."

She took the bait, her tears vanishing in a half smile. "Suppose I take a look at your baby pictures one day?"

"I've already told my mother she's not to show them under any circumstances." He grinned. "Amazing the ways your parents find to embarrass you, isn't it?"

For a moment he thought he'd been insensitive, but Amanda smiled back. "My mother once insisted on showing the current boyfriend a picture of me at seven with no front teeth. It's a wonder he didn't run at the sight." She sobered. "Seriously, though, I was moved by the image of Melanie. She's very different from the immature girl in the pictures I've seen."

"Responsibility made her grow up fast," he suggested.

"I suppose so. I'm sure she had regrets, but from what Lisa said, I wasn't one of them." She put the photograph away. "What did you think of Lisa's account of the way things went?"

"Pretty much the way we figured, but it was good to have it confirmed. And to have an inkling of how Melanie got back here. That's one thing that bothered Carmichaels. I don't suppose anyone even thought she'd hitch a ride with a trucker."

"It fills in some of the blanks, at least. And what Lisa said about the possibility of suicide—well, I never believed in that anyway, but it confirmed it for me. If she cared that much about what happened to me, she wouldn't have deliberately robbed me of a mother."

He studied Amanda's face, moved by what he saw there. "You're beginning to know Melanie, aren't you?"

"I guess I am." She sounded surprised. "Strange, that she could come to life for me when she's been gone all these years. I didn't expect to find that when I started looking for my parents."

Amanda seemed to notice that his plate was empty, and she slid the pie from its container and brandished a knife. "Apple or cherry?"

"A sliver of both, please."

She shook her head but did as he asked. Barney came bounding back then. He was too well trained to beg, but his nose told him there was food on the table, and he raised his head to sniff the air.

"No chance," Amanda told him. She reached into her bag and pulled out a plastic bag of dog treats. She tossed one, and he caught it deftly and wolfed it down.

"Well, you said you had something to tell me. Can you eat pie and talk at the same time?"

"I'll try, but Sarah's pie deserves my full attention." He put his fork down to judge her reaction. "Robert McKinley called the office this morning."

"Uncle Robert?" She sounded surprised. "Why? What's wrong? Why didn't he call me?"

"Reading between the lines, I'd say he's too fond of you to want to break what he thought was bad news. And he's probably feeling a little bad because Juliet didn't trust him to handle the situation for her."

"The adoption," she said quickly.

"There wasn't one. At least, the firm he hired did what sounds like a thorough search in and around Massachusetts, especially Worcester and Boston. Nothing turned up. It looks as if Juliet never went through the formality of adopting you. She just…kept you."

As he'd expected, she wasn't all that upset. "That's what I've been thinking for some time, especially the more I came to find out about the Winthrop family. She'd have known about them through Melanie, of course, and Melanie can't have painted a very flattering picture."

"No. Juliet probably feared that if she started legal action, there would be questions she couldn't answer about your parentage."

"She'd have thought the Winthrops would take me away from her. Which I suppose they could have done?" she asked.

"In a heartbeat, I imagine. Juliet didn't really have any claim on you that would stand up in court, other than her unsupported word that your mother wanted her to care for you. She was wise not to risk it."

"I got the best end of the deal." Amanda's tone was firm. "I'm a better person for Juliet's influence on me. If I'd grown up in that house, I'd probably have rebelled, like my mother. Or turned bitter, like Carlie."

She fell silent, musing on that possibility.

"There was more from Robert." He met her gaze when she looked up. "He says that Juliet's brother has hired an attorney. Robert's convinced he intends to contest the will."

"I'm not surprised. I didn't think he'd let it go, not if there was a chance of money in it for him. What does Robert want me to do?"

"He thinks you ought to try to settle it out of court."

"Is that what you advise, too?" She shot the question at him.

"It's what any attorney would advise under the circumstances," he said. "I'm sure you'd rather fight it out, but court battles are expensive in themselves, and it's risky. Juries can be unexpected, as can judges. You might end up with the lot, but more likely the court would recognize some claim on his part. You'd end up sharing, anyway."

He waited for an explosion, remembering her opinion of her mother's brother, but to his surprise, none came. She seemed to be considering it.

She glanced at him, smiling at his expression. "You

expected me to give you an earful about that idea, didn't you?"

"You did seem pretty adamant about it earlier."

"I've learned something since then. And I talked to Jacob about it. He gave me some food for thought."

He hoped he didn't look as startled as he felt. "What did Jacob have to say?"

Amanda shrugged. "He helped me think about what's really important to me. And what's worth a battle. Does Robert expect an answer right away?"

"I think he'll expect you to call him to discuss it in the next few days."

"Right." Her tone effectively ended the discussion. She began putting disposable trash into one of the bags. "Are you finished, or do you require more pie to keep you going?"

He grinned in response. "Maybe later." He put lids on containers, coming around the table to her side as he packed them away. "Have you heard anything more from the Winthrop family?"

"No." She frowned. "That's a little odd, now that I think about it. Elizabeth was so vehement about my moving in that I'd expected to be badgered."

"Maybe she realized she's met her match in you," he said lightly, brushing a strand of hair back from her face and letting his hand linger against her smooth skin.

She smiled. "I doubt that. Or at least, that she'd admit it."

"Why not?" he said. "I do."

He'd come dangerously close to saying he loved her, and he could see the startled withdrawal in her eyes

for an instant. Then she covered his hand with hers.
"A bit of a public place, isn't it?"

"Nobody comes here this time of year." He kissed
her, forcing himself to keep a tight rein on his emotions. "But I'll behave." He dropped another light kiss
on her lips. "We're making progress, I see."

"Progress?"

"Barney has stopped trying to come between us."
He glanced at the dog. "In fact, I think that might almost be a look of doggie approval."

She laughed, her warm breath caressing his cheek.
"The only thing he approves of right now is that bag
of leftovers you're holding." She drew back, letting her
hands trail down his arms. "We'd better go."

Trey nodded, finding he took pleasure in the thought
that she didn't want to stop any more than he did.

WHEN THEY WERE in the car heading back toward the
farm, Amanda sought a topic that would keep them
safely away from emotional matters. "Did you hear
anything from Chief Carmichaels today? Any news
on Shawn Davis?"

"Sorry, I forgot. I did talk to him. Robert's call sent
it right out of my mind. No news at all. They haven't
found any trace of him."

He was frowning, straight brows drawn down. In
profile, Amanda was very aware of his sharply cut
cheekbones and the strong lines of his face. It was
the kind of face that wouldn't change much with age.

"That worries you?" she asked.

"I'd expect someone in the surrounding area to have
spotted that bike of his, at least. It looks as if he's gone
to ground. Frankly, I'd rather he kept running."

She nodded. The farther away Davis was, the better, as far as she was concerned.

Trey muttered a startled exclamation and hit the brakes. She looked ahead of them and saw what he had—two police cars, lights flashing, pulled onto the side of the road.

"That's Carmichaels." Trey pulled in neatly behind the cars and got out. "Stay here."

Curiosity impelled her out of the car. Barney leaped out after her, pressing protectively against her side.

"What's going on?" Trey called.

A patrolman started to wave them on, but Carmichaels, seeing them, stopped him.

"Where the devil have you been?" he barked. "I called your office looking for you." Carmichaels looked from one to the other of them.

"We went out for lunch. Just heading back to the farm. Did you catch up with Davis?"

"Not exactly." Carmichaels gestured to what Amanda now realized was a gravel road, leading through the woods and up toward the ridge. "They're logging up on Joe Mills's land. One of the drivers called in. They spotted the motorcycle. See for yourself. Looks like he just shoved it in the undergrowth and left it there."

Moving forward in the direction he indicated, Amanda saw the glint of chrome through the thick growth of bushes on the edge of the woods. "Why would he do that? I'd think he'd want to get away."

"He probably does." Carmichaels grunted the words. "Young Sam had a look at the bike. Says it conked out on him."

"That explains what it's doing here, then," Trey said. "Do you think he hitched a ride?"

Carmichaels shrugged. "It's what he'd want to do, but there's precious little traffic along this road at night. No, I figure he'd try to make it on foot over to the interstate and get a ride there."

"Makes sense, I guess. But what was he doing here? He'd have been well past this spot before you lost him, wouldn't he?"

"Yeah." Carmichaels and Trey exchanged looks.

"So he was headed back. Toward the Burkhalter farm." Trey's face had tightened, as if the skin was drawn tightly against the bone.

"We don't know that." The chief glanced uneasily at her. "He might have been trying to get to one of his buddies. Someone who'd hide him and help him get away."

She was trying to decide whether that was reassuring or not when Barney set up a salvo of barking.

"Drat that dog. What's he doing?" Carmichaels took an angry step toward the sound.

Amanda hurried past him. "Sorry. I'll get him." Rounding the bike at a careful distance, she headed for the dog. "Barney, quiet. What's gotten into you?"

The barking turned into a whine that was nearly as bad. She broke through a cluster of berry brambles. She saw Barney—saw what he was standing over. Her stomach roiled, and she put out a groping hand to grasp the nearest tree.

Black leather jacket, black denims. Shawn wasn't wearing the motorcycle helmet now. The back of his head was a bloody mess.

She found enough breath to call out. "Trey! Chief Carmichaels!"

Sinking against the tree, she fought down the nausea that rose in her. She should say more, should tell them what she'd found…

Men crashed through the bushes, obviously drawn by the horror in her voice. Barney abandoned the motionless form to press himself against her. She buried her hand in his warm fur, holding on.

The next few moments passed in a blur. She was aware of Trey's arm around her, supporting her, of a steady stream of low-voiced profanity from the chief, of the other officers gathering, mute.

"Don't just stand there," Carmichaels ordered. "Get crime scene tape up around the area where the body is. Sam, get on to the state police. We'll need their crime scene team here ASAP. Then get the camera and start taking photos. Here and the bike. That better be roped off, too."

His arm around her, Trey eased her farther away from the body. "You want us to clear out?"

Carmichaels frowned at him. "Not yet. Wait till I have time to talk to you, but move back to the road."

Once they were out of range, Amanda found her rubbery legs could carry her. But she wasn't eager to give up the feel of Trey's arm around her.

"Better?" he asked, scanning her face.

"Much." She tried for a smile but didn't succeed. "Sorry. I've never seen…"

"Neither have I. Not like that, anyway."

They leaned against the car, prepared to wait. Amanda ruffled Barney's ears and tried to focus.

"What did the chief mean? About the state police, that is. Won't he be in charge of this?"

"They'll probably work together," Trey said absently, his gaze focused on the moving figures they could see in the woods. "Small towns don't have the facilities to process a complicated scene like this. It's not as simple as they make it sound on TV shows." He glanced around. "For all he knows, the cop cars may have already eliminated evidence just by parking here."

"Evidence?" She straightened, wondering if she should pick up her feet.

"Somebody did that to him. He didn't make that whacking great hole in the back of his head by himself. And that somebody must have gotten here somehow."

Chief Carmichaels emerged from the trees, walking toward them. "Guess I should thank the dog. Not that we wouldn't have found him anyway, making a routine search like we'd have done."

"Any idea how long he's been there?" Trey asked.

Carmichaels frowned. "Hard to say until the coroner's seen him. But the logging truck drivers saw the bike when they started up about sunrise, most likely a little before seven." He made a disgusted sound. "Course they didn't bother calling us until they'd taken the trucks in and out a couple of times, messing up any tracks there might have been."

"He was murdered." Amanda still had difficulty accepting that, even though some isolated part of her brain suggested she should be getting used to the results of violence after what happened to Juliet.

"Somebody picked up a chunk of stone and hit the back of his head with it. We found the stone. Probably too rough to give us much in the way of fingerprints, but the lab boys may bring up something." He pulled out a small notebook and thumbed through it. "Now, about you two. Where were you from the time you went back to the farm until, say, about seven this morning?"

A jolt of anger broke through Amanda's numbness. "Are you saying you suspect us?"

Carmichaels stared at her, startled by her tone. But it was Trey who intervened.

He clasped her hand. "Of course he doesn't. But this is routine for an investigation. If…when the case comes to trial, a defense attorney might try to pick holes in the police case by claiming they hadn't done a thorough investigation."

"Exactly right." Carmichaels's jovial tone didn't quite come off, but he was trying. "Just for the record."

"I saw Amanda back to the farm, talked to everyone for a few minutes and then headed for home. That was it. I didn't go out again until I left for work this morning."

Trey had taken the initiative. Mollified, Amanda followed his example. "More or less the same for me. The family was worried about me and wanted to hear about what had happened, but then I went to the cottage and turned in early. And I couldn't have taken my car out again without being seen or heard by someone."

The chief, jotting down notes, nodded in satisfaction.

"Okay, now that that's taken care of, let's get serious," Trey said. "This must be related to Davis's attempts to harm Amanda. So this proves that someone else was involved. Maybe that someone feared Davis would betray them if he were caught."

Carmichaels didn't look entirely convinced. "Could be, could be. But you're assuming Amanda's affairs are the only thing Davis was involved in. I told you he's been skirting the law for a couple years now. The state police drug team have had their eye on him, but no proof. Could be other people who had reason to want to get rid of him."

It sounded reasonable, but Amanda found she wasn't convinced. Neither, judging from his expression, was Trey.

"I think Amanda should have police protection." His jaw set. "We all know that Davis's murder is more likely to be connected to his actions against Amanda than anything else. There are four people in the Winthrop family who stand to lose if Elizabeth should change her will."

"I don't want—" she began, but Trey interrupted her.

"Whether you want the money or not doesn't enter into it. What matters is how they're thinking about it." He glared at Carmichaels. "Like I said, she needs police protection."

The chief looked harassed. "Come on, Trey. Be serious. You know I don't have that kind of manpower. Maybe there's something in what you say, but I can't seriously suspect any of the Winthrop family of sneaking around in the woods and cracking Davis over that head."

"Not even if he threatened to expose them? Blackmail is a powerful reason to get rid of the blackmailer."

"That's speculation." Carmichaels's tone was flat. He'd obviously decided. "And even if it weren't, I still wouldn't have the manpower. To say nothing of how

Amos would feel about having a cop planted on his farm."

"Amos would want Amanda to be safe." They glared at each other like two dogs about to snarl.

"This is pointless," Amanda said. "I don't want police protection, and I'm not asking for it. I feel perfectly safe where I'm staying. No one can get near me without Barney or the farm dogs giving the alert. I'm only a cell phone call away from help."

"Amanda..." Trey began, but she shook her head.

"You're being overprotective. And before you say that I should move into town where you can keep an eye on me, I'll tell you. I won't do that, either."

Carmichaels eyed them with what might have been amusement. "I don't think you're going to change her mind." He looked up at the sound of an approaching vehicle. "That'll be the boys from the state police lab now." He sounded official again. "You two can go. I'll keep you posted."

Trey looked as if he'd continue the argument. Amanda tugged at his arm.

"Let's get out of the way of the police. Come on. You can drive me the rest of the way home."

He nodded, and when they were both in the car, he glanced at her, a question in his eyes. "Home?" he asked. "When did the Burkhalter farm come to be home?"

Amanda had spoken without even thinking, but she realized now what his question implied. She really had begun to think of Sarah and Amos, to say nothing of Jacob, as her family.

CHAPTER EIGHTEEN

WHEN SHE ARRIVED at the Winthrop house early in the afternoon of the following day, Amanda slid the local newspaper she'd picked up in town under the seat. It hardly seemed tactful to have headlines reading Motorcyclist Killed left where anyone might see.

She wouldn't have come anywhere near the place today had it not been for a summons from her great-grandmother, delivered via a phone call from Mrs. Lindstrom. When she'd waffled a bit, Helen Lindstrom had lowered her voice.

"Please come. She's not doing very well today, and it might do her good to see you."

Amanda had had no choice but to agree, but she privately thought that an encounter with her today wouldn't add to anyone's peace of mind, let alone her great-grandmother's. And the last thing she wanted to do was to encounter Carlie while the vision of her late boyfriend's body was fresh in her mind.

Leaves had begun to fall from the mature trees in front of the house, she noticed as she walked to the door. She'd guess the Winthrops had a lawn service, since the days of having a personal gardener seemed long gone.

The door opened even before she reached it, and Helen Lindstrom welcomed her with a quick smile and a furtive glance behind her, as if to make sure no one else was around.

"Worried someone might see me?" she murmured.

The woman's pale face flushed slightly. "Sorry. It's just that Mrs. Winthrop said there was no need for anyone else to know she'd sent…asked you to come over, and wouldn't you know it, both Mr. Shay and Ethan came home for lunch today."

She may as well be amused as annoyed. "I'll try to avoid them. Do you want me to go straight up to my great-grandmother?"

"You can't. I mean, the doctor is with her now, so you'll have to wait. You will, won't you?"

Mrs. Lindstrom looked so anxious that she nodded quickly. "No problem. But is she ill? I didn't realize."

"Well, she's nearly ninety, you know, even though she doesn't like reminding of it. Dr. Milburn says she has angina and heart failure, but she doesn't accept that, either."

This was said with a little vicarious pride, as if refusing to admit to age and illness was a virtue.

"Since I'll be waiting anyway, maybe we could have a chat. I'm sure you could tell me some stories about my mother when she was young."

Helen's eyes filled with a kind of reminiscent warmth. "Best of the bunch, she was, and don't you let anyone tell you otherwise. She was the only one who would stand up to her grandmother, and they had some fine battles, that's for sure."

"She must have been a rebel, running off the way she did." *And trying to keep me.* It hadn't worked out that way, but she had to honor Melanie for trying.

The woman nodded, glancing around again. "I've

never seen Mrs. Winthrop so angry. But that's the way it was between them. They made each other furious, but they loved each other more than anyone, too."

"It's sad that they never had a chance to make it up." Such a waste, holding on to anger that way.

"If Melanie had come back, or even called her grandmother and told her about the baby—about you— she'd have welcomed her home in an instant, not that she'd admit it. And now it's too late."

Too late. Surely those were the saddest words in the language. She knew all about longing to have someone back, even just for an hour, to say all the things that had been left unsaid.

A step sounded somewhere in the house, and Helen jerked as if she'd been shocked. "Maybe it would be best if you waited in the garden until the doctor is finished. Would you mind? No one will be out there this time of day."

"That's fine." Clearly this wasn't the time to probe for memories of her mother. She'd have to get to Mrs. Lindstrom away from this house for that.

The woman showed her past the sunroom and on out into the garden behind the house. The trees here were mature as well, and the rather formal garden seemed to have settled into its current pattern over many years. She started down a flagstone path and quickly found that Mrs. Lindstrom had been wrong about one thing. The garden wasn't empty. Ethan Shay sat on a wrought-iron bench, his head bent over the sketchbook on his knee.

She didn't make any effort to quiet her footsteps, but Ethan was so engrossed he didn't detect her presence. Only when she stopped behind him did he look up, flinching. He made a quick motion as if to hide his drawing.

"Too late," she said. "I've already seen it. And why wouldn't you want to show that? It's lovely."

The delicate fronds of a small weeping willow, overhanging the stones of a low retaining wall, had been drawn with a grace and sparseness that startled her.

For an instant Ethan regarded her suspiciously. Then, seeming to accept that she wasn't attempting to flatter him, he let a tentative smile appear on his face.

"I don't know about that, but at least I got it down. The way it is in my mind, you know?"

"I think so. I was the despair of all my mother's colleagues, because I was hopeless from an artistic perspective. But I had to develop some appreciation—I couldn't spend years with my mother and not do that." She hesitated, knowing how sensitive people could be about showing their work. "May I see more?"

He held the sketchbook between both hands, hesitated and then thrust it toward her, turning away as if he couldn't bear to watch her look at his drawings.

Amanda took her time, sensing that Ethan's fragile confidence could be shattered at a word. She studied each drawing. Finally, she closed the book and turned to him.

"One question. Why are you doing work you obviously dislike instead of pursuing your gift?"

His face settled into a sulky frown, making him look like a discontented teenager. "Easy for you to say. Your mother might have appreciated what I can do. My family can't. Don't you get it? I'm the only male of my generation of Winthrops." The savage way in which he said the words made it clear he was quoting someone.

"I guess. My mother didn't understand my passion for veterinary medicine, but she still supported my dreams."

"You were lucky, then." He brooded for a moment, and then abruptly his mood seemed to change. "Is it true? That you had something to do with Shawn Davis's death?"

Well, it had been in the newspaper. She could hardly expect that he wouldn't have heard. "Not anything to do with it, except that my dog found him." She couldn't repress a shudder. "Is your sister very upset?"

He shrugged. "I can't tell. Nobody can. Shocked, maybe. But I never thought there was much of that on her side. She was just determined to jolt the parents." He gave a short laugh. "She sure did that. Dad was furious, and as for Grandmother—well, you don't ever want to see her that way."

Actually, she'd already seen the worse of Elizabeth, as far as she could tell, and was still standing. But there was little use saying that to Ethan, who obviously didn't consider rebelling.

"Ethan!"

The sound of his father's voice galvanized Ethan. He looked around wildly. Donald wasn't in sight, but his footsteps were coming in their direction around the curve of the flagstone path. Ethan cast an agonized look at the sketch pad.

Amanda promptly slid it under her on the bench, the flare of her skirt hiding it.

Just in time. Donald, looking thoroughly irritated, was almost on them. "If you intend to ride back to the mill with me…"

He stopped abruptly when he saw Amanda. It

clearly took him an effort to put on a smile. "Hello, Amanda. No one told me you were here." Maybe realizing that sounded as if he expected a report on what she was doing, he turned on his son. "I expected to find you at the car. It's time we were going back to work."

"I'm afraid I held him up," Amanda said. "He's been keeping me company while I wait to see my great-grandmother. She wanted me to stop by."

That was obviously unwelcome news. "I believe the doctor is leaving now," he said stiffly. "Come along, Ethan."

With a grateful glance at her, Ethan followed.

Amanda waited until they were out of sight before she rose and picked up the sketch pad. Maybe Mrs. Lindstrom could be counted on to return it to Ethan privately.

She approached the door with care, looking through the glass panels for any sign of movement. An encounter with Carlie was best avoided now. But no one was in sight except Mrs. Lindstrom, beckoning to her.

As she went to join the woman, Amanda had just enough time for a quick thought. How accurate was Ethan's assessment of his sister's feelings for Shawn? If she hadn't cared for him, did that make it more or less likely that she'd use him as a tool to get rid of Amanda?

Holding out the sketch pad to Mrs. Lindstrom, she spoke softly. "Can you get that back to Ethan without anyone knowing?"

The housekeeper didn't seem to need an explanation. "I'll slip it into his room." She tucked it under her arm and motioned toward the stairs.

"How is she?" Amanda followed her.

"She's weaker than the doctor likes," Mrs. Lind-

strom said. "She should rest, but she insists on seeing you."

Amanda wasn't all that eager for a confrontation,
either. "I'll try to cut it short if she'll let me."

They stopped at an upstairs door, and Mrs. Lindstrom tapped lightly before opening it. She gestured
Amanda in with a warning look.

Entering her great-grandmother's room, Amanda
shoved thoughts of Carlie from her mind. Was it too
much to hope someone had kept the newspaper from
Elizabeth, at least, this morning?

Elizabeth wasn't, as she'd half expected, in bed.
She sat in a Queen Anne armchair by the window, her
neatly shod feet on a cushioned ottoman. She was pal-
lid in the morning sunlight, but she gave Amanda one
of her usual glares.

"I expected you earlier." There was no trace of fee-
bleness in her voice.

Was the accusation a technique, designed to put the
other party in a defensive posture from the start of the
conversation? If so, she declined to play.

"I understood the doctor was with you, so I waited."
She took the chair opposite to her great-grandmother.
"I hope the doctor was able to help."

Elizabeth gave an unladylike snort. "He fusses too
much. Every time I get a little excited, the whole bunch
of them think I'm going to pop off." She paused, eyeing Amanda. "That would suit them, you know. If I
died without changing my will."

"I'm sure they're thinking no such thing." It was
the only possible response, but she did wonder. How
much did Donald count on maintaining control of the
mill? And what about Carlie and Ethan? If she'd left

them anything directly, they might see it as a pass to freedom.

"If you believe that, you're a fool. But I don't think you really do." Elizabeth leaned back, satisfied.

Did the old woman read minds? Or was she that transparent?

"You may as well know now as later." Elizabeth's mouth clamped shut for a moment. "I've spoken to my attorney about doing just that. You're Melanie's child, illegitimate or not, and it's only fair that you have her share of the property."

Amanda watched the elderly face just as intently as the woman had been studying her. "The rest of the family wouldn't believe this, but I think you might. I don't want anything from you."

"Why not? As I understand it, if you weren't legally adopted, your inheritance from your foster mother is in doubt."

Now how did she know about that? Or was it simply guesswork?

"Even if, as it appears, Juliet didn't legally adopt me, I still won't walk away with nothing." At least, that was Robert's expectation, and she agreed. Juliet's brother would prefer quick cash to a long-drawn-out court battle that would cost him. "Besides, I have my profession. I'm not going to starve. I'd rather not owe anyone anything."

"Your profession." Elizabeth dismissed it with a gesture. "You can move in here and never have to work again."

"I'm sorry, but that's not possible." She'd like to believe Elizabeth would accept that as final, but she couldn't bank on it.

"Why not? This was your mother's home. You belong here."

"Juliet Curtiss was just as much my mother, but I don't necessarily belong in her house, either. I'm a grown woman with a life of my own."

Elizabeth eyed her without, it seemed, much surprise. "In my day, young women of good family weren't expected to have professions."

"Times have changed. Haven't you noticed?" She softened the comment with a smile, inviting her great-grandmother to join her.

Elizabeth didn't quite smile, but there might have been amusement in her ice-blue eyes. "So they tell me. If you don't want my money, and you don't want to move in here, what do you want?"

The question startled her, and she thought it deserved as honest an answer as she could provide. "Initially, I just wanted to find out if I'd been legally adopted. But then I realized I needed to know who my parents were. Not to do anything about, but just to understand where I come from."

Watching the wrinkled face, she thought she detected signs of approval. "Well, think about it. This is always your home."

Too bad she hadn't said that to Melanie. But all of that was far too late, and she wouldn't gain anything from pointing that out to a woman who was old and sick. So she just nodded, not wanting to say anything that could be misinterpreted.

Elizabeth sank back in her chair, suddenly looking tired. "You're like her, you know." Her voice was becoming weak. "Like what she might have been."

"Thank you." Touched, she moved to Elizabeth's

chair and bent to kiss her cheek lightly, surprising herself as much as her great-grandmother. "You're getting tired. I'll leave you to rest."

Perhaps it was a measure of how exhausted she was that Elizabeth didn't protest.

Amanda slipped out into the hallway, hoping for a quick escape, only to find Betty lingering outside the door. Listening?

"I didn't know you were here until I heard your voice. I mean, I just happened to be passing and heard you." Betty twisted her hands together with an ineffectual motion. "I hope my mother's all right. She shouldn't be tired. I mean, I know you wouldn't mean to tire her, but..."

Amanda broke in before the woman could say everything all over again. How the decisive Elizabeth came to have a daughter as uncertain as Betty, she couldn't imagine. Or maybe she could. It might be the natural result of having a mother like that.

"She did seem to be tiring, so I came away." She started down the stairs, aware of Betty behind her.

"You shouldn't mind all the things she says, you know. Like that business of having you move in here. Not that you wouldn't be welcome, but you have a lovely home in Boston to return to. It's not as if you'd be settling down in Echo Falls, of all places." A nervous laugh punctuated the words.

When she reached the bottom, Amanda swung around to face her. "You don't need to worry. Even if I stayed in Echo Falls, I wouldn't move in." What was she saying? Was she really thinking of such a plan?

Betty flushed and stared at her for a moment.

Shocked by the possibility Amanda suggested? Then she found her tongue.

"Donald will talk to her, so don't worry. He always knows just what to say to help her understand. Donald takes care of everything."

Does he? Including getting rid of inconvenient heirs who might have a claim to his mother-in-law's estate?

She'd been focused on Carlie, but Donald might equally well have found Shawn a useful tool.

And she suspected he'd be far more dangerous than Carlie ever could be.

TREY HAD FINALLY succeeded in talking Amanda into going out to dinner, but it had taken some persuading. She probably didn't relish the idea of being stared at, but after all, no one could fault her because her dog happened to find a body.

He'd taken her to his favorite upscale restaurant in Echo Falls, which was also the only upscale restaurant in town. Bobby's was, despite its unpretentious name, a haven for local foodies and the only place that didn't equate good dinners with mountains of food.

Taking a last bite of her coq au vin, Amanda leaned back in her chair with a sigh. "I take back any disparaging thought I had about the quality of dining in Echo Falls. That was wonderful."

"Bobby Felder grew up in the area. Went off to culinary school when his friends were headed to trade school or college, and came back to start a restaurant. People looked askance at the menu at first, but once they'd given it a try, you can't keep them away."

"I can see why. And the atmosphere is great, as well as the food." She glanced around with satisfaction.

Their table was screened by a latticework partition that lent it an illusion of privacy, and candlelight gleamed on the white tablecloth and the gold-rimmed china.

"See? I told you no one would stare at you in here." He reached across the table to touch her fingers. "Nobody imagines it's our fault for stumbling across a body."

"I guess I was being hypersensitive," she admitted. "But you can't deny my presence has led to considerable talk. Do you suppose everyone here knows about my relationship to the Winthrop family?"

He grinned. "By this time they probably know everything down to your shoe size and your fourth grade teacher back in Boston." He hesitated. "Speaking of Boston, have you talked to McKinley yet about your mother's will?"

"I called him earlier." She was frowning, looking down at their entwined fingers. "I asked him to sound out Juliet's brother on a possible settlement. The one thing George is adamant about—he wants the house."

Trey tried unsuccessfully to guess her thoughts. Would she give up the place that had always meant home to her?

"I suppose he thinks he'll get a substantial sum if he sells. Property must have appreciated substantially in that area."

She nodded. "It makes sense to let it go, I guess. As Jacob said, memories live in the heart, not in a place."

She'd let her father come pretty far into her life if she was ready to take his advice about something so important to her.

"It makes sense," she repeated, as if arguing with herself. "My head knows that. But my heart is giving me grief. It seems so final—as if I'm cutting myself off completely from the life I led in Boston."

"You said yourself you were ready to move on," he reminded her.

"I know." She gave him the hint of a smile. "Silly, isn't it? Among other things, it's foolish to hang on to a place where I'll never live again. What would I do with it? I'd have to rent it just to pay the taxes, and there'd still be strangers living there, even though I'd own it."

"Sounds as if you've made up your mind," he pointed out. "You're just reluctant to cut the last cord."

"Wouldn't you be?" She flashed the words back at him. "If it was your family home?"

"Probably."

The admission seemed to defuse her, and her face relaxed. He didn't really have a right to give an opinion on what she did with her childhood home. But he found he was wishing she wanted his opinion, anyway.

He noticed the waiter heading their way with a dessert menu in hand.

"Dessert? They do a wonderful crème brûlée, I hear."

"I couldn't possibly. Just coffee."

Trey ordered the coffees. Amanda seemed content just to sit and relax, and he suspected it was a relief to get away from the pressures of her newly found families. He'd love to know what happened when Elizabeth Winthrop sent for her earlier, but she probably needed the respite more.

Movement flashed at the corner of his eye, and Trey turned to discover that Amanda's respite, such as it was, was over. Carlie Shay was bearing down on them, eyes flashing. Amanda noticed her, her face tightening, hands bracing against her chair as if she prepared for battle.

"Enjoying yourselves? Celebrating coming into money, maybe?"

He could only be thankful that Carlie, with some slight instinct for propriety, had kept her voice down. That restraint probably wouldn't last. He put a handful of bills on the check folder the server had left on the edge of the table.

"How are you, Carlie?" He spoke before Amanda could respond. "Having dinner?"

Deflected from Amanda, Carlie glared at him. "I heard you were here. Thought I'd take the chance to have a word or two with my *cousin*." She said the word as if it were poison.

"This isn't the time or place..." he began, but Amanda silenced him with a gesture.

"I'm sorry about your friend's death." She kept her voice even. "I don't think harassing me is going to do you any good."

"Not with my grandmother." She shot the words like arrows. "You saw to that, didn't you? Sweet-talking the old woman into writing you into the will."

"I've said it often enough. I don't care about her money. She believes me. It's too bad you find it impossible."

The Winthrop fortune clearly meant a great deal to Carlie. Independence, he supposed. She couldn't understand that Amanda didn't see it that way.

He rose. "We're just leaving. I'd suggest you discuss your problems in private with your grandmother, instead of in a public place."

Carlie turned on him, and the venom in her face

shocked him. "I saw the two of you holding hands. Looking to redeem your family firm by snuggling up to the new heiress, are you?"

"Trey is my attorney. That's all." Amanda picked up her bag, clearly ready to get out of this situation before it worsened.

Wasn't he more than just her attorney? He shoved that question away. Whatever Amanda felt for him, she'd hardly announce it to Carlie.

"Tell that to someone who might buy it. You trust him, don't you? Depend on him to advise you? But then, you don't know much about Trey Alter or his firm, do you?"

"This is useless." Amanda stood. "I'm not interested in what you have to say." She turned to push her chair in, moving toward him.

"No?" Again that venomous look speared him, but now it shouted a sense of triumph.

Trey knew, suddenly, what she was going to say. And he couldn't stop her.

"I don't suppose you know that Trey's father represented the family at the time of your mother's scandal. Or that he's the one who made the arrangements to have her sent away from her family. They'd do anything to protect the precious Winthrop name, and Trey's father helped them, didn't he?" She threw that at Trey, clearly enjoying herself.

Amanda stood still for a moment, face and body frozen. She turned, very slowly, to look at him. It was as if she didn't see anything else.

"Is it true?"

Cursing himself for not telling her the whole thing as soon as he learned it, he reached toward her.

"Amanda, listen to me. It's not the way she makes it sound."

"Is it true?" She wouldn't be deflected, looking at him as if she could see right through him.

"Yes. But..."

There wasn't time to say more. Amanda spun, walking quickly toward the door.

He should go after her. Try to explain. But he knew at this moment it wouldn't do any good. He'd kept something important from her, torn by his conflicting loyalties. And now it had come back to tear their relationship to bits.

CHAPTER NINETEEN

WHEN AMANDA DREW into the lane at the farm, Sarah popped out of the house. She didn't want to talk to anyone right now, not even Sarah, with her warmth and instant sympathy. She'd rather crawl into a hole and suffer in silence. Or rage in solitude, anyway.

She had to stop, with Sarah standing right by the lane. But she didn't have to get out. Amanda let down the driver's window.

"Did you have a nice dinner?" Sarah glanced back down the lane. "Didn't Trey follow you home?"

"A lovely dinner." She managed a smile. "Trey had other things to do. I think I'll go on up to the cottage." She reached for the window switch.

"But I have coffee and cherry pie all ready. Don't you want to come in?"

"I'm too full to eat anything else. And I really am tired." She pressed the switch and the window started up. "I'll see you in the morning. Good night."

The closing of the window cut off anything else Sarah might have said. Amanda pressed on the gas, hoping she hadn't been rude, but unable to face any questions at the moment. Maybe by morning she'd be over the worst of it.

But somehow she didn't think so. It was dark once she was under the trees, and she slowed, watching as a rabbit scuttled out of her headlight beams. The cottage looked lonely, despite the fact that she'd left the porch light on.

There was nothing to fear now, she reminded herself. Shawn had clearly been the person who'd prowled around the cottage. Witness the scrap of black denim Barney had snatched. And Shawn was beyond hurting anyone now. Besides, Barney would be raising a storm if there were anyone else around. Other than his single welcoming bark, he was quiet.

Still, she crossed the space between the car and the front door quickly, the key in her hand. Unlocking the door, she opened it to Barney's effusive welcome.

"Yes, I know, you're glad I'm back. And you want to go out. Go ahead." She gestured, and he darted off the porch and began nosing around the bushes.

Amanda went inside, closing the door and leaning against it. She felt as if she'd been beaten with sticks. Who would have guessed that betrayal could have such a physical, as well as emotional, shock?

How could he? She clenched her hands into fists. How could Trey let her down that way?

All right, rationally she could concede that he wasn't to blame for what his father had done all those years ago. But he hadn't told her. In all the times they'd talked about what happened to Melanie, he'd never mentioned his father's involvement.

She struggled to remember exactly what he had said. Something to the effect that his father's firm had once represented the Winthrop family, but that they'd come to a parting of the ways over Melanie. Maybe they had, but not before his father had been complicit in sending her off to that institution. And Trey hadn't told her.

He'd lied to her. She'd thought he was different—thought that what was beginning between them might be the real thing. She'd actually toyed with plans for moving here. And all the time he'd been lying to her.

She'd been lied to before. In fact, she must have a genius for picking men who deceived her.

Barney scratched at the door, and she opened it and let him in. Patting him, refilling his water dish, locking the cottage, all the mundane chores seemed to settle her. At least she no longer felt as if she'd bounce off the walls in her anger and frustration.

But the pain was still there—an actual heaviness in her heart. She rubbed her chest as if that would help, but of course it wouldn't. The only thing that would heal this wound was time, and a lot of it.

And space, she realized. How could she expect to dismiss Trey Alter from her thoughts when she was here, where everything reminded her of him? With an abrupt decision, she stalked into the bedroom, pulled out her suitcase and began throwing things into it.

Run away, Amanda. Run away like you did before. But the last time she'd had her mother to run home to. Now she didn't have anyone. The house in Boston was just a house, not home any longer.

The loneliness swept over her, even stronger than she'd felt it when she'd learned she wasn't Juliet's biological child. She sank down on the bed, dropping the tops she'd been about to put into the suitcase. What next?

A knock on the door sent Barney running, as if he'd answer it. His tail wagged, and he let out his single welcome bark. It was someone he knew, obviously. Trey. The name brought with it an instinctive shiver, before common sense asserted itself. It couldn't be Trey, because she'd have heard his car. Sarah must have come to see what was amiss. She wouldn't have been fooled by Amanda's manner.

But when she opened the door, already framing words of excuse in her mind, she saw it was Jacob. Impossible to shut the door in her father's face, she stepped back, motioning him in.

Once inside, he patted Barney, but his gaze never left her face. "Sarah told me something is wrong. She's worried about you."

Amanda turned away from that probing gaze. "I'm all right. She shouldn't worry about me."

"She can't help it. She loves you, ain't so?" His voice was gentle. "So do I."

Amanda blinked back the tears that welled in her eyes. Then she looked at him, seeing the warmth and concern in blue eyes that were very like her own. "I know. I appreciate everyone's concern, but I'm all right. I just don't want to talk about it right now."

He nodded, but he didn't make for the door. Instead he perched on the arm of the sofa. "I haven't known you as a daughter for long, but I know what I would say to any of the other kinder right now. Trouble shared is trouble halved. I'm here to listen, whatever you want to say."

The tears were persistent, and she had to wipe them away this time. "Thank you. Someone has…disappointed me. Someone I relied on."

"Trey, ain't so?" He hesitated. "He seems like a

good man, from what I've seen and what Amos and Sarah know. Is it maybe just a misunderstanding?"

She shook her head. "He kept something from me. Something important. He didn't deny it."

"So you're thinking you will leave?" He smiled when she glanced up, startled. "The bedroom door is open. I can see the suitcase you were packing."

Why should she feel guilty? She would have told him, given time. "There are a lot of things to be taken care of in Boston. My attorney there has been asking me to come back. I really should go and deal with the issues there."

Not that she'd even considered doing it until this moment. Her father's face was a study in disappointment. "Do you have to go right away? I had hoped we could spend some more time together."

The ache in her heart now was quite separate from the anguish Trey had caused her. It wasn't fair to punish others for what Trey had done, but how could she stay and risk seeing him again? It would be easier if she could convince herself to be angry, but she couldn't manage it. She could only try to control the pain and disappointment.

"If...if I decide to go soon, I won't do it without seeing everyone to say goodbye. And I'll plan a trip to Ohio, so I can meet your wife and my little brothers and sisters."

"That would be wonderful gut." Tentatively he reached out to clasp her hand. "I hope you will stay. But if not, I understand."

She nodded, unable to speak. Maybe Jacob sensed that, because he stood, pressed her hand again and left.

When the door closed behind him, she went automatically to snap the lock. Barney, walking beside her, looked at her with intelligent eyes. He whined softly, sensing her mood.

Going back to the sofa, Amanda sank down on it, trying to focus her thoughts on the future. Barney rested his head on her knees, looking up at her.

The future. How could she make plans for what happened next in her life, when everything seemed completely out of her control? She was sure of only one thing. Her plans, whatever they might be, wouldn't include Echo Falls.

AMANDA WALKED DOWN the elegant staircase at the Winthrop house the next afternoon, sliding her hand along the polished rail. She'd thought it right to stop and see her great-grandmother before leaving town, but she couldn't say it had been a successful visit. Elizabeth had been irritated—to say nothing of irritable. She didn't see any necessity for Amanda to rush off so quickly, and Amanda had been forced to invent reasons, citing the ongoing battle over Juliet's estate and the need to consult with her attorney there.

Only when she'd fudged the truth, implying she'd be back for a long visit soon, did Elizabeth calm down. With any luck, by the time Juliet's estate was settled, Trey would have receded to a distant memory.

She could tell herself that, but she couldn't manage to believe it. Amanda frowned, pausing for a moment on the steps.

"Amanda? Is anything wrong?" Mrs. Lindstrom had come into the hallway from the back of the house, and she stood drying her hands on her flowered apron.

"Nothing." She couldn't tell the woman what was

really on her mind, and she tried to focus on more immediate concerns. "I thought Mrs. Winthrop seemed even more breathless than she was on my last visit. Maybe you should check on her."

"Was she using her oxygen while you were there?" The housekeeper started up the stairs.

"No, no, she wasn't. I noticed the tank, but I thought it might just be for emergencies."

"She's supposed to be using it, but that's Mrs. Winthrop all over. Didn't want you to think she was unwell, most likely." Mrs. Lindstrom clucked her disapproval. "I'll deal with her, stubborn as she is."

Amanda nodded, smiling. They were a pair of stubborn women, but she didn't doubt Mrs. Lindstrom's ability to get her way when it came to something important.

The woman disappeared upstairs, and Amanda headed for the door. She seemed always to breathe a sigh of relief when it closed behind her. Unfortunately, this time she'd done it too soon, because she came face-to-face with Carlie, who had just parked her car behind Amanda's.

Carlie stopped, too close to her for comfort. "Sucking up again?"

She tried to maintain her composure, but meeting Carlie again was too much. "Come off it," she snapped. "If you don't get along with your grandmother, don't blame me for it."

"So you do have a temper. I suppose you unleased it on Trey last night."

"That's none of your business." She was suddenly exasperated, almost pitying this discontented cousin. "I get it that you don't like the way things are here.

I don't even blame you. But you're a grown woman. Why do you put up with it? Is your potential inheritance that important?"

"What do you know about it? If you've been raised all your life to expect something, then to have it snatched away—you don't know what that's like."

Actually, she did. She knew exactly what it was like, although it wouldn't do any good to tell Carlie that. She wouldn't believe it, anyway.

"Look, you're an educated person. You have talents. If the family won't let you use them here, why not go somewhere else? Don't you see how abnormal it is, all of you hanging on in this house, waiting for your grandmother to die?"

For a brief instant Carlie's brittle facade seemed to crack, as if the real person inside was struggling to be free. Then she spun away, ran to her car and jumped in. Yanking the wheel to pull out, she grazed Amanda's car and sped off down the drive toward the street.

Wincing at the scrape of metal, Amanda went to inspect the damage, running her finger over the scratches in the paint. Not bad, but annoying. Her poor vehicle was really taking a beating since she'd been here.

But the repair work could wait until she got back to the city. She slid in, started the car and took the driveway slowly. She was certainly getting an odd assortment of goodbyes, although Carlie, of course, didn't know she was leaving. She'd no doubt find that cause for rejoicing.

Her cell phone rang as she stopped at the end of the driveway, and she took a quick look. Trey, again. He was persistent, but she could be stubborn enough to match. She ignored the call and then turned the phone off for good measure. Explanations weren't going to help, and she didn't want to listen to them.

She'd go back to the farm, finish her packing and get ready to leave tomorrow. The goodbyes that waited for her there almost made her want to sneak out in the dead of night. But she'd go through with it. They'd all been too kind to her to walk away without regrets.

And then what? Go back to the city, talk to Robert, pick up the threads with her friends and notify the clinic she wouldn't be back. She didn't have the slightest idea what was next for her.

When she reached the farm, no one was in sight. Glad she wouldn't have to stop and chat at the moment, she drove on to the cottage.

To her surprise, she saw a note shoved into the door-frame. Pulling it free, she unlocked the door and went inside, letting Barney out as she did so.

Frowning, she unfolded the sheet of paper. If it was from Trey…

But it wasn't. Printed in pencil, it was from her father.

I feel I should make a last visit to where I found your mother that day. I hoped you might go with me. I am going now, but I hope you'll meet me there.

It was signed Jacob. Maybe he didn't feel comfortable enough yet to say anything else.

Amanda hesitated, glancing at her watch. He hadn't said when he was leaving, but it couldn't have been too long, surely. He'd been helping Amos with fence repairs when she'd driven out, and her visit to the Winthrop place hadn't been lengthy.

. He shouldn't be there alone. That thought came with a certainty she couldn't question. There wasn't any danger now, was there? She ought to be with him.

Quickly she changed pants and shoes, substituting her heavier walking shoes for the flats she'd worn to town. By the time she was ready to leave, Barney was waiting at the door.

There was no reason not to take him, and she'd feel better with him along. Clicking to him, she hurried back to the car, the dog at her heels.

TREY SNAPPED OFF the cell phone and glared at it. He'd probably called Amanda at least seven or eight times. Not only wasn't she going to answer, she'd apparently turned her phone off to avoid his calls.

He shoved himself to his feet. Fine. If she wouldn't respond to his calls, they'd just see what happened when he turned up in person. Although he might do better to lose the belligerent attitude before he saw her.

Leaving the office with a quick goodbye, he headed for the Burkhalter place. He might as well admit it to himself. He was annoyed with Amanda, when the person who was really in the wrong was himself.

No explanations, unless she asked for them. A plain and simple apology was called for here. He'd been wrong, and he had to admit it. He'd been trying to see both sides, trying to balance his loyalties, and it hadn't worked.

The ironic thing was that his father, whom he'd told himself he was protecting, would have been disappointed in him. He knew now what his father would have said if he'd put the matter to him. *You owe a duty to your client, to the law and to yourself.*

He'd taken the easy way out, thinking Amanda need never know that his father had taken part in the actions that sent Melanie away. Worse, he wouldn't have been able to tell them where she went because of client confidentiality. But the easy road had turned out to be a dead end.

Trey pulled into the farm lane to find himself directly behind a horse and buggy. Sarah was driving, and from the bags piled in the back, it looked as if she'd been grocery shopping.

She stopped by the back door, so he had to halt, as well. He pulled over and parked. It would be faster to walk to the cottage than to wait for groceries to be unloaded.

"Trey. I'm glad to see you. You want Amanda, ain't so?"

"Is she here?" He seized a couple of the grocery bags, but Sarah grasped them from him.

"The kinder will take those in." And they must have been watching for their mother, because three of the girls hurried out of the house to begin unloading. "I don't know if she's back yet or not. She left some time ago, I figured to see her great-grandmother."

"I'll go up and see…" Trey began, but again Sarah forestalled him.

"Ruthie will go." She caught one of the girls. "Run up and see if Cousin Amanda's car is there."

Nodding, the child spurted off, probably preferring that to grocery detail.

Sarah studied his face. "Is something wrong?"

"I just have to talk to her. To apologize," he added.

"Ach, if that's the case, you'd best find her." Her eyes were amused, probably thinking it was nothing worse than a lovers' spat.

Ruthie reappeared in the lane, shaking her head.

"Was ist letz?" Jacob came around the house, unbuckling a tool belt. "What's wrong?"

"Trey just wants to see Amanda, that's all," Sarah said. "But she must have gone someplace."

"I think I'll call the Winthrop place and see if she's there." Trey pulled out his cell phone, but after a brief few words with Mrs. Lindstrom, he clicked off, turning instinctively to Jacob. "Mrs. Lindstrom says she was there earlier but she left some time ago."

Ruthie, who'd been watching them with her blue eyes wide, tugged at her mother's apron. "I thought I heard Cousin Amanda's car come in, but then it went back out again in just a little bit."

"How long ago was this?" Trey asked. There was no reason for the alarm that touched him. No reason at all. That didn't seem to help.

Ruthie shrugged with a child's usual unconcern for time. "Not very long, I think." She darted a glance at her mother. "I was reading."

"If she was lost in a book, there's no telling how long ago that was," Sarah said, regarding her daughter fondly.

Frowning, Trey focused on Jacob as the one most likely to know. "Did Amanda say anything to you about leaving?"

"She was thinking on it," Jacob said. His steady regard told Trey that he knew at least something of what had passed between him and Amanda. "But she promised she would not leave without saying good-bye to everyone."

"Leaving?" Dismay showed on Sarah's face. "Why would she do that?"

"My fault," Trey said. "I don't like this. I know we thought the danger ended with Davis's death, but what if we were wrong?"

"Sarah, give us the key to the cottage." Jacob was decisive. "We'll see if there is anything to tell us where she went."

A few minutes later, he and Jacob were striding up the path, having dissuaded Sarah from accompanying them.

"You've tried to call her?" Jacob asked.

"She's not answering." He shot Jacob a look. "You know that I let her down."

"Just that she thinks so. Not what it was about."

"She was right," Trey said tersely. "I didn't tell her something she had a right to know. When she found out from someone else—well, once it was too late, I knew I'd been wrong."

Jacob didn't say anything comforting, probably because there wasn't anything to say. But he didn't condemn Trey, either.

They reached the cottage. When Jacob unlocked the door, they hurried in. "Wherever she went, Barney is with her," Jacob said.

Trey glanced around the neat room. Everything tidy, nothing out of place, except that a folded piece of paper lay on the floor where it might have fallen from the table.

He picked up it, unfolding it, and they read it at the same time.

Jacob stared at him. "But… I didn't write this."

"No." Trey's blood ran cold. "But Amanda probably never saw your writing. She'd have accepted it. And she's walking into a trap."

They raced out together, running down the hill to the car. Trey pulled out his cell phone as they jumped in. He hit Chief Carmichaels's number as he heard Jacob giving a brief explanation to Sarah and Amos.

He turned the car, tearing down the lane. After a glance at his face, Jacob fastened his seat belt.

"Please God, we'll be in time," he murmured.

"We have to be." Fear ripped at Trey's heart. "We have to be."

CHAPTER TWENTY

Fortunately, Amanda remembered the route to the falls that Trey had taken. She'd taken note of where they'd turned off, thinking she might want to go back alone another day.

As she remembered, once she was on the gravel lane that led upward toward the ridge, it was fairly simple. Just drive until she reached the area where they had parked and follow the path through the woods.

She bounced along, satisfied that she was on the right track. Sure enough, the land widened out where they'd parked. She pulled off to the side and parked at the…well, one could hardly call it a parking lot. It was more like a wide space where the road dwindled out. Getting out, she stowed her bag in the trunk, dropping her cell phone in her pocket. Barney, recognizing the spot, was already nosing around.

How had Jacob gotten here? She supposed some-one could have given him a ride, but it probably wasn't too far to walk. It might be shorter cutting through the woods rather than coming along the road.

In any event, he'd probably be here already. Finding the path easily, she hurried through the woods, Barney at her heels. Jacob shouldn't be alone to pay his last visit to the spot where his love had died. Amanda might not be as close to him as a daughter would normally be, but at least she could give him that—the gift of her presence at a difficult time.

Amanda could hear the sound of the falls now, and she walked faster, brushing past the wild berry brambles that overhung the path in places.

"Jacob!" She called his name as the path came to an end at the falls. But he wasn't there.

"Jacob!" she shouted again. She hadn't misunderstood his note, had she? She couldn't have been that far behind him, and she hadn't met him on the road.

Something that might have been a voice sounded. Not from the woods, but above her, at the top of the falls. Shielding her eyes from the slanting rays of the sun, she looked up. Something moved, a glimpse of color. Blue. Jacob often wore a blue shirt. He must have gone up to have a look at the place where he and Melanie had their stolen meetings.

A voice called, muffled by the falls into something almost unrecognizable. Almost, but not quite. "Come up."

Hadn't Trey mentioned a road that came in at the upper part of the falls? But she was here now, and she had no idea where that other road might be. She eyed the trail that ran up along the falls. Not too difficult, she'd think, other than some slippery spots where the spray reached. Trey had mentioned that it was dangerous in early spring, when it could be icy, but not now.

If Trey could do it when he'd been a kid, she could certainly do it now. But she didn't want Barney underfoot on the narrow trail. "Stay, boy." She pointed at a spot at the bottom of the trail. "Stay." He sat obediently, looking disappointed when she headed up the trail.

The first few yards were fairly simple, since the trail

led upward in a series of what were almost rough steps, winding around larger rocks and stepping over smaller ones. The noise of the falls seemed to fill her head.

Actually, the rough trail proved not to be as bad as she'd expected, at least for about the first half of it. Mindful of where she put her feet, she was still fascinated by the power of the water plunging down the cliff face just a few feet away. If she'd been simply a hiker, with no painful connections to the place, she'd have been creating an unforgettable experience.

But she wasn't in that position. And no matter what her reaction was to the place where her mother had died, Jacob's had to be so much worse. He had actually held her body in his arms, grieving over his love.

Amanda's foot slid on wet rock, and Barney gave a warning yelp from below. This was a particularly bad patch, nearly at the top, but running even closer to the rush of water. For an instant Esther's tale of something behind you, its breath ever nearer, closed in on her.

She shook it away, determined not to look back even as her nape tingled.

Now that she was this high, the roar of the water seemed to have lessened. Or maybe she was getting used to it. In any event, Jacob should be able to hear her now.

"Jacob?" Holding on to a convenient outcropping, she tilted her head back to look up, squinting against the sun.

Movement caught her eye. For an instant she thought it was Jacob. But Barney burst into a hysterical volley of barking, and the shape resolved itself into a large rock. It quivered on the edge for a second and then plunged right toward her.

Frantic, she shoved herself out of its path, thankful for Barney's warning, her hands scrabbling for something to hang on to, flattening herself against the cliff by instinct.

The rock hit bottom with a resounding crack and a splash, followed by a shower of smaller stones loosened by it. She ducked her head, compressing herself as if she could merge into the cliff while they bounced and rattled past her.

The echo of sound died away, and she could think again. Jacob—he must have heard the rocks fall if he was at the top. Why wasn't he calling to her? But Barney was barking furiously, and she could hear the scrabble of his feet as he tried to come to her.

"Barney, stay!"

Only the need to keep him safe let her raise her face from the shelter of her arms and assess her position. She was a good two feet from the trail, on the other side of the outcropping that had been her handhold. Now she gripped it with both hands, chest pressed to the surface, while her feet...

She managed to look down and was instantly sorry. She stood on a ledge of rock—solid enough, but barely deep enough to hold the balls of her feet. Her heels overhung a sheer drop to the rocks below.

Heart thudding, she pressed her face into the rock, struggling to get her breath back. How on earth had she gotten here? More to the point, how was she going to get out?

Slowly, very slowly, she tilted her face back. Jacob was here, somewhere. He'd help her. She scanned the top of the cliff rearing over her head, looking for his face.

But it wasn't Jacob who peered down at her. It was

Betty...passive, ineffectual Betty, who didn't look so ineffective at the moment.

Betty was looking at the base of the falls, no doubt expecting to see a body there, but finding only Barney straining up. For a moment she seemed puzzled, and then she spotted Amanda.

Betty shook her head, clucking as if she'd just discovered an outdated can of food in the kitchen.

"Why didn't you just let go?" Her voice was still querulous. "Now I'll have to shove even more rocks down."

"Betty, wait!" Frantic, she scanned the trail in either direction, but it was hopeless. She couldn't get to it, and even if she did she'd be a sitting duck whether she tried to go up or down.

"Well, what is it? I have to get back before anyone thinks I'm taking too long at the grocery store."

Was the woman mad? Or just so obsessed with her own agenda that she saw Amanda only as a pawn to be removed?

"You don't want to do this. You'll be caught. And it's not worth it. I've already told you I don't want anything from Elizabeth."

Betty's face contorted. "You think I believe that? That's what Melanie said, too. But she didn't mean it, and neither do you."

"Melanie..." Her brain started to work. "You were the person who was here with her that day, weren't you?"

"No one ever figured that out. No one even suspected. But then you had to come." Betty sounded vexed. "If only you'd gone away. I tried to show you that you weren't welcome here. Any more than your mother was."

Certainty settled deep. "You killed her, didn't you? You killed my mother."

"Poor Melanie. The golden girl, her grandmother's pet, child of the favorite son. Getting herself pregnant that way. I thought for sure she'd never come back. I'd finally get the attention I deserved."

Had Elizabeth ever noticed the seeds of division she was sowing in her own family with her favoritism? Had Melanie seen how much Betty resented her? Or had she innocently flaunted her status as the favorite?

This was no time to be thinking of family dynamics. She pressed herself against the rock, aware of how cold her fingers were, clutching their perilous hold. Her only chance was to keep Betty talking. At least while she was talking, she wasn't hurling rocks down.

If she sent Barney for help...but where? No one was near.

"How did you get rid of Melanie? Why didn't anyone else know she'd come back?"

"That was my cleverness." Betty actually preened herself. "I was always in touch with Melanie. She thought I was on her side. When she was determined to come back, I arranged to see her before anyone else did. I told her that her grandmother would never forgive her. That she should arrange to meet with Jacob so they could run away together. I even suggested the meeting place, and she went along with it."

"She trusted you." Well, why not? She must have thought her aunt Betty was sympathetic.

"She made it easy. I drove her here. And while she was leaning over, watching for the first glimpse of her lover, I just gave her a little push." She smiled. "No one survives a fall from the cliff. You won't, either."

With that, she shoved another rock over. Shaking, Amanda thrust herself against the rock face, holding on by sheer force of will. A rock hit her shoulder, sending pain radiating through her. Worse, numbing her arm so that she could barely feel her fingers.

Her cell phone was in her pocket, but it may as well be back in Boston for all the good it was doing. She didn't dare let go even with one hand to reach for it.

Below her Barney was barking again, shrill and furious, but he couldn't help her. She was alone.

How much longer could she hang on? Until someone came? But who would come? Obviously the note supposedly from Jacob hadn't been genuine. And after what had happened between them, Trey wouldn't be looking for her. She was alone. But Betty didn't know that. Maybe she could use that to her advantage.

"It's no good, Betty. Sarah knows I was coming up here, and she insisted on calling Trey. He'll be here soon." If only that were true.

"Not soon enough," she said. "You can't hold on much longer. You should have let go. This accident is going to be fatal. Maybe he'll arrive in time to pull your body from the creek."

"You arranged the other things that happened to me." Who would have suspected Betty?

"Not really arranged. All I had to do was tell that useless boyfriend of Carlie's how dangerous your claim was. I think he liked the idea. But he was inept. I could have done a better job myself. And when the police found him out, he actually tried to blackmail me. Me! I couldn't allow that."

Amanda's shoulder hurt abominably, and she couldn't feel her fingers. How could she hold on through another deluge? Her only chance was to keep Betty talking and hope for a miracle.

"Is he the one who broke into my house in Boston? No, that was you, wasn't it?" She remembered, now that it was too late, something Betty had said about her lovely home, implying she'd seen it.

"I was worried about the painting, you see. I kept track of you. I even knew when Juliet Curtiss came here to paint the falls. I thought it best if the painting vanished before it gave you ideas. All the time my mother was hiring private investigators to find you, I knew where you were. After all, Melanie confided in me. I just didn't know about that dog." She sounded aggrieved. "The painting led you here. Too bad."

Amanda heard her scuffling around at the top, probably lining up more rocks for another assault. It was no use. She couldn't hold on any longer. If she let go...

She yanked her mind back from that deadly place. Her mother would be ashamed of her. Did she mean Juliet? Or Melanie? She fought to clear her head. Did it matter? They had both been strong women in their own way, willing to fight for what they believed. Strength seeped back into her. Betty was pushing another rock to the edge. She could hear her ragged breathing and the scrape of the rock.

Be ready. Hold on. Don't let them down.

A scrape of rock, and she braced herself. It was coming—

But it didn't. There was a confused babble of sound. Voices. A volley of barks from Barney.

And then an arm coming around her, supporting

her. Jacob. Her father. And from above, Trey's voice, anxious.

"Hold on. They're bringing the rope. Can you manage until then?"

"Yah, for sure." Jacob sounded strong, and his arm was steady. "My girl isn't going to fall."

She wouldn't let go, not now. Now with Trey there, and her father's arm around her. Somehow the name that came to her lips was the Pennsylvania Dutch term the children used. "Daadi."

"That's right." Relief filled his voice. "You hold on until I get the rope around you. Listen for Trey. He'll tell us when they're ready to pull you up."

More voices up on top. And then Trey, seeming very close. "We're ready."

She looked up, to find him just above her on the trail. He reached out, tantalizingly close but not able to touch her.

"Amanda, listen. The rope will keep you safe. But there will be a moment when you have to let go. Just a moment, and then you'll be close enough that we can grab you. Do you understand?"

"Yes."

He looked reassured by the single word. "Okay." He glanced up, as if signaling someone above him. "Now."

She peeled her fingers off the rock, forcing herself to focus on each one. For an agonizing moment she hung free, suspended. Then her father's hands were grasping her legs, swinging her feet over to a secure foothold while Trey wrapped his arms around her, holding her close.

Safe. She was safe.

CHAPTER TWENTY-ONE

IT SEEMED TO Amanda that it took only seconds until they'd reached the top. Or had she blanked out for a moment? She sank down on the ground a safe distance from the edge, nursing her injured shoulder.

"You're hurt." Trey squatted beside her. "How bad?"

She managed a faint smile. "You always seem to be picking me up after a mishap." She glanced at Jacob, kneeling on the other side. "You and my father."

Chief Carmichaels bent over her, his ruddy face concerned. "Paramedics are on their way. We'd already called them for her." He jerked his head toward the huddled, weeping figure that was Betty.

Amanda looked once and then averted her gaze. It was somehow indecent to see her that way.

She closed her eyes and found herself leaning against Trey's shoulder. "I think I'll just rest until they get here."

"Good idea." He brushed a kiss lightly against her forehead, and she sensed him exchange a look with Jacob. "We won't leave you. Not ever."

AN HOUR LATER, after a visit to the emergency room for Amanda, Trey drove her and Jacob back to the farm. Chief Carmichaels, after one look at Trey's determined face, dropped his insistence that Amanda give a statement, muttering that tomorrow would be soon enough. Relieved that he didn't have to engage in battle on the subject, Trey had agreed.

Now they sat at the welcoming table in Sarah's kitchen, with the older of the kids grouped behind them. Amos seemed to give up any thought he might have had of excluding them. Not only were they deeply concerned for their cousin, but they'd inevitably hear a garbled tale from someone else. Best to be armed with the truth.

Trey and Jacob sat on either side of Amanda. Trey studied her face, still pale and drawn in profile. She probably ought to be in bed, but she'd insisted she couldn't relax just yet. She rubbed her left arm, enclosed in a sling to give her badly bruised shoulder extra support.

"Hurting?" he murmured, leaning close. "Those capsules the doctor gave you…"

A faint smile flickered across her face. "I'm not ready to be woozy just yet. I'll take one when I decide to lie down. Besides, Sarah's herbal tea is what I need right now." She extended the smile to Sarah, who lifted the fat brown teapot, ready to freshen the cup.

"Just a little," Amanda said, watching the amber brew refill the cup. She darted a look at Trey. "Did Chief Carmichaels say anything about what…about Betty…"

He clasped her left hand. "They took her straight to the hospital for evaluation. He said she was in no state to be kept in the local jail."

"No, she wasn't." He felt the shudder that went through her. Amanda would probably be a long time forgetting that experience.

And it would take some doing for him to erase the memory of looking down and seeing her clinging so precariously to what seemed like sheer rock. No pleasant picnics at the falls for him, not anytime soon. It was just as well that he and Jacob had decided to split up, with Jacob going to the base of the falls and him to the top. When they'd heard the dog, they'd known they were right.

Amanda tightened her grasp on his fingers. "I don't know what a psychiatrist would think about it, but a lot of what she said in the intervals of trying to knock me off the cliff pointed to a lifelong grievance against her mother for favoring first her older brother and then his child. When she saw a chance to claim everything for her children, she grabbed it."

"Wicked, that's what I'd call it," Sarah said. "Downright wicked. But we have to forgive, or we'll be forever tied to the woman."

Was that directed toward Jacob or toward Amanda? Whichever, it was good advice. Sarah had a gift for putting spiritual truths into language a child could understand.

Trey rested his arm across the back of Amanda's chair, letting his fingers touch her uninjured shoulder. Could she forgive? He wasn't too concerned about Elizabeth or Betty, but for Amanda's own sake, it would be for the best.

But the expression she turned toward him was free of anger and resentment. "I'm just relieved I'm still in one piece. And that all the questions have been answered."

"Yah," Jacob said. "We all needed that, ain't so?"

Into the brief silence that followed his comment

came the sound of a car outside. Barney stirred from his position at Amanda's feet, wedging himself protectively against her chair. Poor Barney. They'd finally had to tie him to a tree to keep him from launching himself into space to get to Amanda. Trey knew how he'd felt.

He rose, touching her shoulder lightly before moving toward the window. "If that's Chief Carmichaels with more questions…"

But it wasn't a police car. Mrs. Lindstrom got out of the stately black sedan and went around to assist Mrs. Winthrop from the passenger seat.

He turned to meet Amanda's inquiring gaze. "It's your great-grandmother."

She looked shocked, but no more so than he felt. "I thought she didn't go out." She started to get up.

He and Jacob simultaneously reached out to stop her. "You stay put. I'll help her come in, if that's what you want. Whatever she has to say, she'll have to say it in front of your family."

To his surprise, she didn't argue. Reflecting that she'd have something to say about his making decisions when she felt better, he went out in time to give Helen a hand in getting Mrs. Winthrop up the steps to the porch.

"Should you be out? I'm sure Amanda would have come to you, maybe tomorrow."

"I'm not helpless yet," she snapped. Shrugging off his hand, she forged into the house, with Helen rolling her eyes as she followed.

"Sorry," she muttered. "When she had the whole story from Chief Carmichaels, nothing would do but that she come. I couldn't stop her."

In the kitchen, Amos moved quickly to hold a chair for her, motioning to the boys to bring another for Helen Lindstrom. "Please, sit here."

She sat, propping her cane against the table next to her. Her hooded eyes seemed to scan every face until they came to Amanda. "You're hurt."

"It's not bad," Amanda said quickly. "Just a bruised shoulder from a rock."

Elizabeth's face grew bleak. "I can't believe I didn't see. Betty. All this time, right under my nose."

He held his breath, waiting for Amanda to say that it was partially her own fault, but she didn't. Her face was filled with pity.

"I'm sorry," she said, her voice soft.

What else could anyone say? Whatever her sins, Elizabeth was already paying the penalty.

"Yes, well, that's not what I came here to say." She glanced around the table, her gaze lingering on Jacob's face. "Small wonder if you prefer your father's side of the family to the other. But you're always welcome in my house. I hope you won't feel you have to stay away from us because of Betty."

He could almost feel the generous response welling in Amanda. "Of course not. You are my great-grand-mother. I hope we can get to know one another better."

"That's more generous than I expected. Or deserve." Trey had never seen Elizabeth Winthrop being humble before, and it unnerved him.

"I think it's time to let go of the past." Amanda looked from her father to him. "We'll make a fresh start."

"Good." She thumped her cane once and then rose, so quickly that Amos and Helen both had to jump to their feet to assist her. "That's all I came to say. Except…" Her voice softened. "If Melanie had come to me that day, I'd have welcomed her back. And you."

Tears glinted in her eyes, and she turned and stumped her way out of the kitchen.

ONCE HER GREAT-GRANDMOTHER had gone, Amanda was swept with a wave of exhaustion. She suddenly found herself too tired to keep her eyes open. She stifled a yawn.

"I think I'm not going to make sense if we talk any longer. Bed is sounding very good to me. That injection they gave me at the hospital must have been stronger than I thought."

"You should be in bed, resting," Sarah said.

Trey rose, helping Amanda up and clasping her arm. "I'll take you up to the cottage."

Somewhat to her surprise, no one jumped up with offers to help. Then she realized they were all being tactful, supposing she wanted time alone with Trey. Which she did.

Sarah smiled at her. "You'll send word by Trey when you need my help, yah?"

She nodded and then bent to put her cheek against Jacob's for a moment. "Good night. And thank you."

She carried the warmth of his smile with her as she and Trey went outside. He helped her into the car to drive the short distance up to the cottage. He was clearly concentrating on avoiding any ruts, so she didn't speak until he was helping her out.

"You know, I think I'm going to like having a father." She leaned on his arm, reliving the moment when he'd drawn her against him on the cliff, a secure anchor to keep her safe.

"They are important," he said. He hesitated a moment. "About my father…"

"It's all right," she said quickly.

"No, it's not. I should have told you. He was honestly trying to do what was best for Melanie, probably afraid of what Elizabeth might do if he didn't take a hand. But the more important point is that I'm sorry I didn't tell you. I should have."

"You should have trusted me enough to tell me." That still rankled, but it no longer felt like betrayal.

"I guess I was afraid you'd think ill of him. And me." His lips quirked. "I admit to considerable self-interest. I didn't want to risk losing you. I was wrong."

"It might have led to some strong words," she admitted, thinking of how near she'd been to a flash point then. "But I don't think you could lose me if you tried."

"I'm not going to try." He opened the door and helped her inside. "Where do you want to be?"

She gestured. "The sofa for now. Sarah will help me to bed later. That's what all that tactfulness was about."

"I know." He sat down next to her, and Barney settled on the floor by her feet, as if afraid to let her out of his sight. "What are you going to do?"

She knew he didn't mean about the immediate future. "Finish things up in Boston. I'm telling Robert to settle with my mother's brother. I know he'll make the best deal he can. I just want it taken care of. Then…"

Then was the tough part.

"Then what?" He was very close, his breath touching her face. Maybe it wasn't so tough after all.

"Well, I should walk away with enough to buy a

partnership in a veterinary practice I'll be happy with. Say in a nice rural area, where I can work with large animals. Can you think of any place that fits the bill?"

He smiled, and a steady flame seemed to burn in the depths of his eyes. "I know just the place. It's a charming town, once you get past some of the crazy things that have happened there. And I know a good attorney to handle the practice agreement for you."

"So do I." She reached up with her free hand to caress his cheek.

He planted a warm kiss on her palm, then bent his head a little to claim her lips. She nestled against him, feeling the restraint it took him to handle her gently.

But he did. He always would put her first, just as she would put him first. They'd both have other duties and responsibilities, but this was what was important. Home wasn't the house in Boston or the mansion on the hill. This was home—the two of them, together.

* * * * *

*Turn the page for a look at the story of
Jase Glassman, Trey's law partner,
in ECHO OF DANGER, available now
from Marta Perry and HQN Books,
and don't miss SHATTERED SILENCE,
the exciting conclusion to the ECHO FALLS series!*

CHAPTER ONE

HER FATHER-IN-LAW SET down the coffee she'd poured for him and glanced around Deidre Morris's sunny, country-style kitchen. "I've found a buyer for your house."

The seemingly casual words, dropped into what had supposedly been an impromptu visit to see his grandson, sent ripples of alarm through Deidre. Her own cup clattered, nearly missing the saucer. "I... What did you say?"

Judge Franklin Morris gave her the look he'd give an unprepared attorney in his courtroom. "I said I've found a buyer for you. He's offering the best price you can expect for a place like this. And you'll be able to move into Ferncliff by the end of the month."

Deidre pressed suddenly cold hands against the top of the pine table that had belonged to her grandparents. She should have guessed that there was something behind this visit. Judge Morris was far too busy to drop in on anyone. And nothing he said was ever casual.

She was going to have to take a firm line, clearly, and that wasn't easy with a man who was accustomed to speaking with the force of law. *Stupid*, she lectured herself. *He can't force you to do anything you don't want to do, even if he is Kevin's grandfather.*

"I'm afraid there's some misunderstanding. I have

no intention of selling this house." And certainly not of moving into the chilly mansion where every moment of the day was governed by her formidable father-in-law's wishes.

"I realize you have a sentimental attachment to your family home." He seemed to make an effort to sound patient. "But since you won't have any need of the house once you and Kevin move in with us, selling seems the sensible solution. You can invest the money for the future. However, if you prefer to rent, I suppose that can be arranged." He'd begun to use his courtroom voice by the end of his little speech.

But she was neither a plaintiff nor a defendant. And this house had been home to her family for three generations, now four. "I don't want to rent or sell. This is my home, mine and Kevin's. This is where I plan to live." Surely that was clear enough.

The judge's face stiffened, making it look very much like the portrait of him that hung in the county courthouse, marking his twenty years on the bench. The firm planes of his face, the small graying mustache, the piercing gray eyes all seemed granted by providence to make Franklin Morris look like what he was—a county court judge.

The chink of a glass reminded her that they were not alone. Kevin sat across from her, his blue eyes huge and round above the chocolate milk that rimmed his mouth. Deidre's heart clenched. A five-year-old shouldn't be hearing this conversation.

"Kevin, why don't you run upstairs and finish the get-well card you're making for your grandmother. That way Grandfather can take it with him when he

goes." She gave him a reassuring smile, wishing someone would send reassurance her way about now.

"Yes, that's right." The judge's face softened into a
smile when he regarded his grandson in a way it sel-
dom seemed to do otherwise. Maybe he felt he had
little else to smile about, with his only child dead at
thirty-two and his wife constantly medicating herself
with alcohol. "She'll love to have a card from you."

Kevin nodded, his chair scraping back. Without a
word, he scuttled from the kitchen like a mouse es-
caping the cat.

Her son's expression reminded Deidre of the most
important reason why they'd never be moving into
Ferncliff. She wouldn't allow Kevin to grow up the
way his father had, doubting himself at every turn,
convinced he could never measure up to what was expected of him. She turned back to the table to be met
by a stare that chilled her.

"Deidre, what is this nonsense? I could understand
your reluctance to make a move in the immediate aftermath of Frank's death. But you've had nearly a year.
It was always understood that you and Kevin would
move in with us. We have plenty of room, and it's the
sensible thing to do. With Frank gone, I'm the only
father figure the boy will have."

And that was exactly what Deidre feared most.
This was her own fault, she supposed. She should
have stood firm when the subject had first come up,
but she'd still been dazed at the suddenness of Frank's
death, unable to come to terms with the thought of the
screaming, shrieking crash of his treasured sports car
against the bridge abutment.

She hadn't been in any condition then to mount a

major battle with the judge, so she'd taken the easy way out, claiming she couldn't possibly make any more abrupt changes in their lives until they'd become accustomed to the tragedy. When both the family doctor and her minister had chimed in with their support, the judge had graciously backed down.

But now it was the day of reckoning. Taking the easy way out had only postponed the inevitable.

"I realize that you hoped to have us close, especially after Frank's death." Deidre chose her words carefully. No matter what damage she considered he'd done to Frank by the way he'd raised him, the judge had lost his only child. "But Frank and I chose to live here, and all of our plans for the future included this house as our home."

"All that has changed now." The judge brushed away the years of her marriage with a sweeping gesture of his hand. "Without my son…" He paused, and she feared his iron control was going to snap.

He'd never forgive himself or her if he showed what he'd consider weakness in front of her, and a spasm of pity caught at her throat. His only child gone, his wife an alcoholic…small wonder he had all his hopes centered on his grandson.

The judge cleared his throat, vanquishing whatever emotion had threatened to erupt. "I'm only thinking of what's best for Kevin. We can offer him so much more than you can alone. Surely you realize that. An appropriate school, the right background…these things count for something in the world beyond Echo Falls."

Ambition, in other words. That was what he'd wanted for Frank, and he'd never let Frank forget what he'd supposedly given up by coming back to Echo Falls and marrying her instead of going out into the glittering future his father had wanted for him.

But she could hardly use that as an argument with her father-in-law. "Kevin's only five. There's plenty of time to be thinking about the right school for him. At the moment, he needs security, warmth and familiarity in his life, and that's what he has." She saw the argument shaping in his eyes and hurried on. "Please don't think I don't appreciate all that you and Sylvia do for Kevin. You're a very important part of his life and nothing can change that." She managed a smile. "After all, we're less than a mile away as it is."

Less than a mile, yes, but to her mind there was a huge difference between the comfortable family house on the edge of town, surrounded by fields, woods and Amish farms, and the cool, elegant mansion on the hill.

Her father-in-law's chair scraped back as he rose, standing rigid to look down at her for a long moment. "I'm sorry you can't see the sense of my offer, Deidre. It would be easier all around if you did."

He turned, stalking without haste from the room, down the hall and toward the front door. Deidre, hurrying after him, reached the door in time to have it close sharply in her face.

Well. Her hands were cold and trembling, and she clasped them together, needing something to hold on to. Surely she must be imagining what seemed to be a threat in the judge's final words. Hadn't she?

"Mommy?" Kevin scurried down the stairs, waving a sheet of construction paper. "Grandfather left without the card I made."

"I'm sorry, sweetheart. I guess he forgot."

Deidre put her arm around her son to draw him

close, taking comfort from his sturdy little body. She held the picture he was waving so she could see it. Kevin had drawn himself, holding a handful of flowers in all sorts of unlikely shades of crayon. He'd printed his name at the top in uncertain letters.

"But my picture…" He clouded up. "I made it especially for Grandma."

"We'll put it in an envelope and mail it to her right now, okay?"

That restored his sunny smile, and Kevin ran to the drop-front desk in the corner of the living room. "I'll get an envelope."

"Good job, Kev. I know this will make Grandma feel better."

She hoped. A report that Sylvia was ill usually meant that she'd gotten hold of something to drink. Once started, she couldn't seem to stop. Much as Deidre grieved for Sylvia, she didn't mean to expose Kevin to the difficulties inherent in living with her.

That was one more reason why the judge's plan was impossible. She just wished she could get rid of the sinking feeling that Judge Franklin Morris didn't give up on anything until he had what he wanted.

JASON GLASSMAN HAD been in Echo Falls, Pennsylvania, for less than twenty-four hours, and already he was wondering what he was doing here. He'd elected to walk the few blocks from his new apartment to the offices of Morris, Morris and Alter, Attorneys-at-Law, so he could get a close-up look at the town that was supposed to be home from now on.

Small, that was one word. He'd imagined, given that Echo Falls was the county seat, that there'd be a bit more to it. It was attractive enough, he supposed. Tree-shaded streets, buildings that had stood where they were for over a hundred years and would look good for a hundred more, a central square whose fountain was surrounded with red tulips on this May day.

He passed a bookshop and spotted the law practice sign ahead of him. Morris, Morris and Alter would, if all went as planned, be changing its name to Morris, Alter and Glassman before long. He should be grateful. He *was* grateful, given that the alternative would have been practicing storefront law in a city where everyone knew he'd escaped disbarment by the skin of his teeth and where disgrace dogged him closer than his shadow.

He didn't often let the memories flood back, keeping them away by sheer force of will. Now he let them come—a reminder of all he had left behind in Philadelphia.

He'd gone to the office unsuspecting that morning, kissing Leslie goodbye in the apartment building lobby as they headed toward their separate jobs—he at the prosecutor's office, she at a small, struggling law firm.

And he'd walked into a firestorm. The materials that had been so painfully collected as a major part of the prosecution of George W. Whitney for insider trading and racketeering had unaccountably been compromised. Someone had given away their source, who was now swearing himself blue in the face that he'd never been in touch with Jason Glassman, that the records had been altered, presumably by Glassman, and that the whole case was a put-up job designed to vilify a valuable and civic-minded citizen.

The case lay in shreds at their feet. All the hours of

tedious work, all the manpower that had been poured into it, were wasted. The district attorney had needed to find someone to blame, and he hadn't gone far. Jason had found himself out of a job and lucky to escape arrest.

Disappear, the district attorney had said. *Don't give statements to the press, don't try to defend yourself, and we won't pursue criminal charges or disbarment.*

A devil's agreement, he'd thought it, but he hadn't had a choice. He'd left the office, driven around in a daze, had a few drinks, which hadn't helped, and finally headed for home, trying to think how to explain all this to Leslie.

But Leslie hadn't been there. All of her belongings had vanished, and she hadn't bothered leaving a note. Clearly she'd heard and decided it was too dangerous to her career to continue an association with him.

He'd thought that was all it was, and that disappointment had been bad enough. It was three days before he learned that Leslie was now an associate at Bronson and Bronson, the very firm defending George W. Whitney.

So all those nights when he was working at home, when she'd leaned over his shoulder looking at his progress, offering suggestions and support, had just been so much camouflage for an elaborate betrayal.

He'd been incensed. But when his first attempt to confront her had resulted in a protection-from-abuse order being filed against him, he'd had just enough sense left to cut his losses. The last he'd seen of her had been an elegant, expensively dressed back disappearing into the recesses of Bronson and Bronson while he was dragged away by security guards.

And here he was in Echo Falls, Pennsylvania.

Jase paused, hand on the door of the firm's office. Franklin Morris had made a generous offer to his son's law school classmate, especially since Jason and Frank had never been close. But Jase knew perfectly well that Judge Morris wanted something in return.

The receptionist seated behind the desk in the spotless, expensively furnished outer office was fiftyish, plumpish and looked as if she'd be more at home baking cookies than juggling the needs of a busy law practice. She greeted him with a smile and a nod of recognition. Word of his arrival had obviously preceded him.

"Mr. Glassman, of course. I'm Evelyn Lincoln. Welcome to Echo Falls. The judge is waiting for you." Not pausing for a reply, she led the way to a paneled oak door bearing Franklin Morris's name in gilt letters, tapped lightly and opened it. "Mr. Glassman is here, Your Honor."

He followed her in, not sure what welcome to expect.

"Jason, I'm pleased to see you again." Morris's smile was polite but restrained, suggesting that it was up to Jase to be sure this was indeed a pleasure. "Come in." Without rising from behind the massive cherrywood desk, he nodded to the leather client's seat.

"Thanks. And thank you as well, for lining up the apartment for me."

Judge Morris waved the gratitude away. "Evelyn took care of all that. You've met her already. Trey Alter, my associate, is out of the office today, dealing with another matter for one of our clients."

"I look forward to meeting him." He'd been wondering how Alter would react to the judge's hire.

"You'll want to take some time to move into your office and get up-to-date on the cases we have in hand," he continued briskly. "Trey will be relieved to have someone to share the load, since my judicial responsibilities keep me from taking a more active role."

Jase nodded. Judge Morris couldn't be involved in anything that might conceivably appear before his court, but that still left plenty of work. It had been assumed that the judge's son would take over, but his death had changed things. There was obviously a need here.

He just wasn't convinced that he was the right man to deal with it. He suppressed a grimace, thinking that old sayings became clichés because they were true most of the time. *Beggars can't be choosers.*

"I've gone over the case material Alter sent me, and I'm ready to dive in right away." He hesitated, but it had to be said. "As for the other matter we discussed, it's not going to be easy to investigate your daughter-in-law in a town this size, not without making people suspicious."

Morris's jaw tightened. "I don't expect you to mount a stakeout. Something a little subtler is required."

"I see that, but I'm not sure what you think I can do." Jason tried to keep his distaste for the strings that had been attached to the job offer from showing in his voice.

Swinging his chair around, the judge reached out to grasp a framed photo from the shelf behind him. He thrust it across the desk so that Jase could see it clearly. "My son. And my grandson." The boy was hardly more than a toddler in the picture, face still round with babyhood curves. Frank hadn't changed much from law school, still a good-looking guy, attractive to women, but with an ominous weakness about his mouth and chin.

Judge Morris paused, emotion working behind the facade of his judicial face. "Deidre was never good for Frank, never. He had a brilliant future here, could have become the youngest county court judge we've ever had. But she didn't encourage him. From the day they married, she tried to separate Frank from his family."

Not that unusual a story, was it? In-law relationships were notoriously dicey. Jase sought for a way to deliver an unpalatable truth. "Even so, I'm afraid that's not a basis to file for custody of your grandson…"

"I do know something about the law." Morris's tone was icy. Maybe he realized it, because he shook his head quickly. "Of course not. My goal isn't to take Kevin away from Deidre. She *is* his mother, after all. But she's always been rather unstable, subject to irrational likes and dislikes, making quick decisions that end up hurting someone. If Frank were alive, he could serve as a balance to that…but he's not, and I'm determined to do what I can to protect his son."

This was becoming more unpalatable every minute. But how did he say no to someone who'd just given him his future back? "If you don't intend to sue for custody, then what?"

"Leverage." Judge Morris pronounced the word heavily. "I need leverage to convince Deidre that she and Kevin should move in with us. Once that happens, we'll be able to provide the stability and the good life the boy needs. Without a father, subject to his mother's whims… Well, I'm concerned about what will become of him."

It sounded like the kind of messy, emotional case that had sent him into specializing in financial fraud, where the only emotion involved was greed. "Naturally you're worried about your grandson. But I'm not sure what I can do."

"Deidre is having an affair with a married man." His expression was harsh with condemnation. "At least, that's what my son thought. For all I know, that might have been what sent him speeding into a concrete wall. Find me proof, and I'll know what to do with it."

"If you're sure of your facts…" he began.

Judge Morris stood abruptly, the framed photo in his hands. He stood at the window, staring down at the photo and then setting it back on its shelf, centering it carefully.

"In my position, I have to be careful. It wouldn't do for a county court judge to be seen as collecting evidence against his own daughter-in-law. I don't expect you to shadow her or sneak around taking photographs. You're close to Deidre in age, living right next door. It shouldn't be hard to gain her confidence and keep an eye on the situation."

He caught Jase's expression and gave a thin smile. "It wasn't a coincidence that Evelyn rented the apartment in the old Moyer house for you. Deidre's family home is the white colonial to the left as you face the house."

"The place with the swing set in the backyard." He could hardly help noticing it. His bedroom windows overlooked the property. Obviously the judge's staff work was excellent. "There's no guarantee that I can find anything to help you," he warned.

Judge Morris gave a curt nod. "I accept that. Don't imagine that your position here is conditional on success." A muscle in his jaw worked. "Deidre is a manipulative woman who betrayed my son. I have to keep her from damaging my grandson."

Manipulative. Betrayed. Did Judge Morris know that those words would strike fire in him? Maybe, maybe not, but it didn't really matter. He already knew what his answer had to be.

"All right. I'll do my best." Now his jaw clenched. He didn't have a very good track record when it came to outwitting a manipulative woman. But this time, at least, he was forewarned.

DRESSED FOR HER evening meeting, Deidre peeked into Kevin's room. He'd been determined to stay awake until the arrival of Dixie, her neighbor, who'd offered to babysit tonight. But he was already sound asleep. She tiptoed to the sleigh bed that had been hers as a little girl and bent to kiss his smooth, rounded forehead. Kev slept with abandon, as always, one arm thrown over his head and his expression concentrated.

"Sweet dreams," she whispered.

She'd told him that the bed, with its curved headboard and footboard like an old-fashioned sleigh, had always brought her good dreams. Maybe it worked for Kevin, too. Although he woke easily at any noise, he never seemed frightened, going back to sleep as quickly as he'd wakened.

Leaving the door ajar so Dixie would hear him if he called out, Deidre hurried downstairs, glancing at her watch. This first meeting of the Echo Falls Bicentennial Committee would probably be a fractious one, with representatives of every segment of town life in attendance. She'd promised to arrive early at the library and start the coffee—one of the inevitable chores falling to the only person on the library board who was under seventy.

A tap on the front door heralded Dixie's arrival, and she came in without waiting for Deidre to answer. "Am I late?"

She slung her jean jacket over the nearest chair and pushed her black hair over her shoulders with a characteristic gesture. She eyed Deidre's tan slacks, blue shirt and camel sweater with disappointment. "You look as if you expect this meeting to be boring. Why don't you spice things up a little?"

Dixie herself wore a scarlet tank top that clung to every curve of her body. Her voluptuous body, Deidre amended. When they'd been kids together, and every other twelve-year-old girl had been straight as a board, Dixie had seemed to mature overnight into someone who'd befuddled the boys in their class and even drawn covert looks from a few male teachers.

Even though Dixie had returned after years away, divorced and apparently ready to start over, some things hadn't changed. She still attracted males like a magnet. After all, single women their age were a rarity in Echo Falls.

"I'm representing the library board, remember? Besides, I don't have the figure to wear something like that outfit." She nodded to Dixie's bright top and form-fitting jeans.

Dixie tossed her hair back, laughing. "Sure you do.

And I'd like to see the expressions on the old girls' faces if you turned up in this."

One thing about Dixie—she never apologized for anything she wore, said or did. It must be nice to feel that confident. Deidre never had, and she'd settled for an updated version of her mother's style, typically small town, middle-class and designed not to raise a single eyebrow.

"I'm almost ready, and Kev is sleeping. I promised him you'd come in and kiss him good-night, but I didn't promise you'd wake him up." She retrieved her cell phone and tucked it into her bag.

"Okay, will do." Dixie picked up the television remote but didn't switch the set on, a sign she had something to say. "Did you see the new tenant next door yet?"

"Someone moved into the second-floor flat at last?" The old Moyer place had been converted into three apartments, with Dixie renting the top floor. "I hope they're not going to be noisy."

"Not they, he. Thirtyish, single and sexy. Just what we need in the neighborhood."

Deidre gave her a look. "Had a long chat with him, did you?"

Dixie grinned. "We barely exchanged two words. But believe me, I didn't need conversation to make up my mind about him. Lean, dark and tough-looking. He's the brooding, dangerous type, and that suits me fine."

She could only hope Dixie didn't intend to launch herself headlong into a new romance. Her past was strewn with the guys she'd been convinced were the real thing. Needless to say, they hadn't been.

"Who is this paragon? And what brings him to Echo Falls? Maybe you'd better be sure he's going to hang around before you make a dead set at him."

"That's the thing." For a moment Dixie looked uncertain, an unusual expression for her. "I hear he's actually the new lawyer in your sainted father-in-law's firm." Dixie gave her a sidelong look. "You hadn't heard?"

No, she hadn't heard. Silly, to be bothered by the news that someone was taking Frank's place. After all, it had been almost a year, and the firm was constantly busy.

"I knew they needed someone, but didn't know they'd made a decision. Funny that the judge didn't mention it when he was here today."

She didn't think her expression had changed at the mention of that visit, but Dixie knew her well.

"What's he up to now?" She held up a hand to stop Deidre's protest. "Don't bother denying it. The judge is always up to something, isn't he?"

Deidre shrugged. It would be a relief to vent to someone, and she and Dixie had been friends long enough for her to know Dixie was safe. "The same conversation we had before. I thought it was settled, but apparently not. He wants us to move in with him and Sylvia." A chill slid down her spine at the thought.

Dixie abandoned her lounging posture on the sofa to sit bolt upright, anger flashing in her dark eyes. "You can't be considering it. Move into that mausoleum? I'd rather be dead."

"No, of course I'm not considering it. If I wouldn't move in there when Frank was alive, I'm certainly not going to do it now. I couldn't raise Kevin in that…"

She couldn't find a suitable word that was compatible with her sense of politeness.

"Mausoleum," Dixie repeated. "Good. Don't you even think of giving in to him."

"I'm not," she protested. "But you know what the judge is like."

"He's a boa constrictor." Dixie spat out the words with more than her usual emphasis. "Get caught in his coils, and the next thing you know you'll be digested, just like that poor wife of his."

"Sylvia has other problems. I'm not sure her husband can do much for her."

"He's probably the one who drove her to alcohol to begin with," Dixie muttered. "And you know how he treated Frank when he was growing up. You can't let him get his hands on Kev."

"I'm not going to." She didn't know when she'd seen Dixie so passionate. "All I have to do is keep saying no. He can't force me. Honestly, Dixie, there's no need to get so upset about it."

"You're too trusting, you know that? You think everyone's as nice as you are. They're not."

Dixie's reaction was fueling her own, and she had to look at this sensibly. "I've got to get going. Again, thanks so much for staying with Kev. And don't worry about the judge. I'm not. Really."

Deidre reminded herself of those brave words as she drove to the public library, just off the square in Echo Falls, and pulled into the parking lot behind the building. No worrying. Obsessing about Judge Morris's plans wouldn't do any good.

She shifted her focus firmly to the upcoming meeting. At least she wasn't the first arrival. The lights

were already on, a welcome given the fine mist that
was forming.

She picked up the tote bag with the coffee and
doughnuts and ducked through the mist to the back
door, hurrying inside. In the flurry of greeting people
and getting the refreshments ready, she managed to
shove Judge Morris firmly to the back of her mind.
Like Scarlett, she'd worry about that tomorrow.

The meeting was being held in what was normally
a quiet reading area in front of the fireplace. Folding chairs had appeared to supplement the sofa and
love seat donated by some library patron who'd probably been redecorating. Concentrating on refilling the
doughnut tray, Deidre didn't notice that someone was
coming toward her until he spoke.

"Hard at work as always, I see." Adam Bennett,
the pastor of Grace Church, was mature enough to
be aware of the status his collar gave him and young
enough to be made a bit uncomfortable by it. He
flushed now, as he often seemed to when he spoke
to her.

"Not very," she said, smiling. "Will you have a
doughnut?"

"No, no, thank you." He shied away as if his wife
had lectured him about the dangers of fatty foods. "I
wanted to introduce someone to you. Deidre, this is
Jason Glassman, the new associate in Judge Morris's
office."

For an instant Deidre could only stare at the
man who'd come up behind Adam. Brooding and
dangerous-looking indeed, as Dixie had said. His tai-
lored suit and tie would be more at home in a big-city
office, and his lean face gave one the impression of

a man stripped down to the essentials and ready for action. There was nothing casual about the assessing look he turned on her, and she was suddenly aware of the sticky icing on her fingers.

When in doubt, take refuge in good manners, her mother always advised. Deidre wiped her hand on a napkin before extending it.

"Mr. Glassman, it's a pleasure to meet you. I'm sure my father-in-law is relieved to have someone to..." She'd started to say *assist*, but this man didn't look as if he'd ever been an assistant to anyone. "To take over the extra caseload. I know the office has been very busy."

"Please, call me Jason." His deep voice held nothing more than conventional courtesy, but the clasp of his hand lingered a bit too long, and his dark eyes studied and probed, as if to warn he'd know everything about her before he was finished. "I'm just getting settled in. I understand we're neighbors, as well."

"We're all neighbors here in Echo Falls." Adam glanced from one to the other as Deidre pulled her hand away, his voice uncertain. "I was just telling Jason how happy we'll be to have his help with planning the celebration."

"Not planning, just listening. I understand no one else was available tonight, and the judge thought the office should be represented. I'm just holding a watching brief." The way his eyes held hers made it sound as if she were the one he was watching.

Deidre gave herself a mental shake and took a step back behind the protection of the coffee urn. Jason Glassman would have better luck turning his measuring look on Dixie. She'd know just how to respond.

"I see the chairwoman is ready to begin." She nodded toward the fireplace, where Enid Longenberger was shuffling through her notes. "Maybe we'd better take our seats." Busying herself with the arrangement of trays, Deidre gave the two men plenty of time to find chairs before she slipped into one as far away from Glassman's disturbing presence as possible.

What had the judge been thinking? Surely he couldn't picture this man settling into a quiet career in Echo Falls. He looked as if he'd be bored to death in a week. Certainly he did nothing to dismiss that opinion as he sat, eyes half-closed, through the inevitable suggestions, ranging from the mundane to pie-in-the-sky ideas that would only happen if a benevolent billionaire decided to lend a hand.

The meeting dragged on even longer than she'd expected, with Enid obviously determined to give everyone a chance to offer an opinion. Deidre found herself taking surreptitious glances at her watch. Dixie claimed to enjoy staying with Kevin, and she'd never let Deidre pay her, so she made a special effort not to keep Dixie out too late.

Finally, the subcommittees had been assigned, a general outline of ideas approved and the last grumbler had been satisfied. Enid banged down her gavel with an air of decision, and people started filing out the doors, some lingering to rehash the meeting with their friends, as they often did. Deidre kept herself busy clearing up the coffee service as the room slowly emptied. She didn't think Jason Glassman would approach her again, and she didn't want to give him any excuse to do so. Something about the man set her nerves on edge, and she didn't think it was the attractiveness and underlying masculine sexuality that Dixie had obviously noted.

When she went outside, locking the back door behind her, Deidre realized she had dallied almost too long. The lot behind the library was empty, except for her sedan, and darker than it usually seemed—or maybe that was just her mood.

The streetlamp in front of the building was blocked by the roof of the library, and the closest one in the other direction didn't extend its light this far. The massive brick block of the bank building on the other side of the lot effectively hid it from view of anyone passing on Main Street, giving it an isolated feeling.

Deidre walked quickly to the car, heels echoing on the concrete, fingers clasped around her keys. She'd never felt unsafe in Echo Falls after dark, and she wasn't going to let an odd case of nerves make her start now. Unlocking the car, she slid in and slammed the door, feeling like a rabbit darting into its hole.

She turned the key in the ignition, listening for the comforting purr of the engine. It gave a sputter, a grinding sound and then stopped. Nothing. She tried again. She couldn't have stalled it. But there was still nothing. The engine was dead.

It was pointless to keep turning the key. Fumbling for her cell phone, she tried to come up with the most sensible course of action. If she called the auto club, they'd undoubtedly send someone out from Williamsport, a good thirty miles away, and she'd be stuck here an hour. She could try one of the people who'd been at the meeting, but they wouldn't be home yet, and she suspected none of them were entered on her cell phone. If Dixie weren't babysitting—

A sharp rap on the window next to her sent her heart jolting into overdrive. She turned to see Jason Glassman peering in at her, his strong-featured face an ominous mask in the dim light.

"Trouble?" He raised an eyebrow, giving his face a hint of caricature, and she was swept with a feeling that trouble was exactly what the man represented.

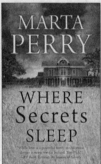
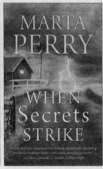
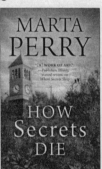

Get 2 Free Books,
Plus 2 Free Gifts—
just for trying the Reader Service!

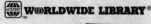

Get 2 Free Books,
Plus 2 Free Gifts—
just for trying the Reader Service!

Get 2 Free Books,
Plus 2 Free Gifts—
just for trying the Reader Service!

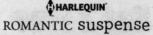

HARLEQUIN
ROMANTIC suspense

Get 2 Free Books,
Plus 2 Free Gifts—
just for trying the Reader Service!

✦ HARLEQUIN®
Paranormal Romance

Get 2 Free Books,
Plus 2 Free Gifts—
just for trying the Reader Service!